BY KIM HARRISON

BOOKS OF THE HOLLOWS

DEAD WITCH WALKING

THE GOOD, THE BAD, AND THE UNDEAD

EVERY WHICH WAY BUT DEAD

A FISTFUL OF CHARMS

FOR A FEW DEMONS MORE

THE OUTLAW DEMON WAILS

WHITE WITCH, BLACK CURSE

BLACK MAGIC SANCTION

PALE DEMON

A PERFECT BLOOD

EVER AFTER

THE UNDEAD POOL

THE WITCH WITH NO NAME

THE TURN

AMERICAN DEMON

MILLION DOLLAR DEMON

MILLION DOLLAR DEMON

KIM HARRISON

ACE
New York

ACE
Published by Berkley
An imprint of Penguin Random House LLC
penguinrandomhouse.com

Copyright © 2021 by Kim Harrison
Penguin Random House supports copyright. Copyright fuels creativity, encourages
diverse voices, promotes free speech, and creates a vibrant culture. Thank you for buying
an authorized edition of this book and for complying with copyright laws by not
reproducing, scanning, or distributing any part of it in any form without permission.
You are supporting writers and allowing Penguin Random House to continue to
publish books for every reader.

ACE is a registered trademark and the A colophon is a trademark of
Penguin Random House LLC.

ISBN: 9780593101452

Ace hardcover edition / June 2021
Ace mass-market edition / April 2022

Printed in the United States of America
1 3 5 7 9 10 8 6 4 2

Book design by Kristin del Rosario

For Tim

CHAPTER

1

CINCINNATI'S AIRPORT WAS PREDICTABLY NOISY WITH THE Friday crush, the press of people and chatter giving rise to an unexpected unease. Sitting straighter in the row of uncomfortable chairs, I scanned the throng of constant movement for a furtive shadow, someone making an effort to blend in, someone not moving. But there was only the lone TSA agent leaning up against the wall, his arms crossed over his chest as he stared at me as if I might start throwing spells. Seeing my attention on him, he made the "I've got my eyes on you" gesture, and, frowning, I ran my middle finger under an eye to give him the one-fingered kiss-kiss back.

Immediately he pushed off from the wall to blend in with the domestic travelers, but I knew there was probably a camera or six trained on me, and as I tucked a stray curl that had escaped my braid back behind an ear, I watched the oblivious mob to see if anyone had noticed. Quen, standing at a nearby table with Ellasbeth and the girls, gave me a knowing half smile and I warmed.

"Crap on toast, I'm not banned from air travel anymore."

Am I? I wondered as I tucked the curl back again, stretching to look over and around the milling people until I found Trent returning from the coffee counter with three coffees and two cups of juice. The cardboard tray and primary-colored kids' cups would have looked odd against his business suit and tie any other place, but here, at the Hollows International Airport, it all seemed to work.

My breath caught as he jerked to a halt, eyes going from the sloshing coffee to the tall, blond, beautiful living vampire who had cut him off. Oblivious, the man ghosted past with an eerie quickness, clearly late for his gate. Trent's gaze rose to find mine, a slight lift of his chin telling me he'd be right back. Lucy was shouting to hear her voice come back from the high ceiling, and Ellasbeth was becoming increasingly tight-lipped and frustrated.

I slouched, smile threatening as Trent distracted the girls into better behavior. Lucy downed her juice immediately, but her quieter, more reserved sister ignored the cup, focused on the three dogs trotting through the terminal before their abundantly tattooed and therefore clearly Were owners. They were the size of small ponies, and probably ran with the pack.

Ellasbeth looked frazzled in her professional, cream-colored suit, her thousand-dollar purse at her feet. My jeans, dark green leather jacket, and low-heeled, butt-kicking boots were out of place beside her boardroom polish, but that wasn't unusual. The six-hour flight and four-hour time shift were going to leave their mark. Fortunately, flying first class turned cranky little girls from annoying to adorable. That she'd dressed them alike in blue and white jumpers and matching hats stuck in my craw, but it *would* make keeping track of them easier.

If I was honest, I was glad I didn't have any luggage tagged for Seattle in the pile beside them. I was sitting this one out, but I still kept my gaze on the passing people with more than a mild scrutiny as they moved around the small family like water about a stone, leaving no mark in memory or deed. Oh, Trent was still recognized every time he stuck his beautiful blond head outside of his estate's gates, but lately, people were more inclined to whisper and snap furtive pictures than rush over to shake his hand and ask for a selfie.

A quiver of something spilled through me as Trent finished with the girls and came over, two cups of coffee in his grip. Smiling, I took the one he offered, shifting in the seat to make the row of chairs seem more private.

"They didn't have skim," he said, his expressive green eyes pinched in a charming, faint worry. "Two-percent okay?"

Nodding, I sipped it, appreciating the unusual richness. "Thanks. Yes." It was almost time. I could tell Trent was anxious as he glanced at his watch and settled in to wait. His familiar sigh went right to my core, and the touch of his knee against mine made me reconsider. But no. I had too much to do, and me leaving to tag along like so much baggage was not a good idea.

I'd miss him, but even if there was no trouble brewing in the Hollows, I wouldn't willingly spend seven days with Ellasbeth's family, pretending everything was peachy keen while Trent sparred with the elven mucky-mucks, demanding they recognize his Sa'han status.

Warm and nutty, the coffee slipped down my throat as I watched Ellasbeth over my cup. Her lips fell into a thin line when she noticed my knee touching Trent's, but her smile became real as she cajoled Ray into trying her juice. Still, that tiny line in her forehead never went away.

"I'm going to miss you and the girls," I said, and Trent took my hand, giving it a squeeze as he settled it on my leg.

"I'd love to have you with me for the week, but Quen knows their security and you have your playdate with Dali tomorrow."

Playdate? That was hardly the word, and I frowned, not looking forward to accompanying the self-proclaimed leader of the demons to meet and possibly mentor one of the surviving Rosewood babies. Dali wanted to teach him. For free. After three months of putting Dali off, I'd finally agreed to introduce him to the kid's understandably reluctant parents. "I could be on the moon and Dali would pick me up and drop me off for that," I said, and Trent chuckled, his grip on my hand becoming more sure.

"I think," he said, leaning to whisper in my ear, "that

what you are doing is admirable. This will help all your kin find their place in the world again. Give them something to be proud of after having put themselves above the law for so long."

A quiver of worry spiked through me. "And when Dali screws it up and Keric's parents come to me with a legitimate complaint, will you help me pound him for said law?"

Trent's smile widened. "He won't. He needs this. They all do. It's a connection to society, a reason to exist."

"More like a second chance to get the demon's rebirth going with innocent minds rather than with a witch who doesn't listen to them. Though I'll admit I'm glad I'm not the only female demon anymore," I said, and Trent hid a chuckle behind a sip of coffee. "Dali is going to screw it up," I predicted. "Sooner or later, he's going to manipulate Keric's morals, or teach the kid something his parents specifically said not to, or just outright lie to them."

Trent chuckled. "If you change your mind, I bought an extra seat to insulate everyone from the girls. They *do* sell toothbrushes in Seattle."

I winced. *Six hours on a plane?* "Me being there won't help your case."

Trent's good humor vanished. "It would if they weren't such—"

"Careful . . ." I warned, a tiny smile threatening. "You never know who's listening."

"Tradition-entrenched, frightened old farts blind to reality," he finished.

Loving him, I leaned to flatten his floating hair as he scowled at the way things were. The tingle of magic pricked my fingertips, and he made a visible effort to calm himself. "No, thanks," I said as the girls ran to the big plate-glass windows, excited as a jet pulled into the terminal. "I'm surprised they even let me through TSA to see you off at the gate. Trying to get *on* the plane is another story."

But I hesitated as the thought occurred to me that two years ago, he would have flown out on his private jet. He said he was being environmentally conscious, but I wondered if it was more than that. "Hey, tell Ellasbeth's mom happy birthday for me."

"I will." He sipped his coffee, focus vacant as he put his elbows on his knees and stared at the future. "It's only for a week," he whispered, then pushed back and up, forcing a smile. "Is David going with you today to look at more property?"

There was jealousy in his voice. I could hear it. "Yep," I said brightly, feeling loved, but also a little annoyed. If Trent came property hunting with me, the seller would jack up the price, thinking he was helping me pay for it. David was a quiet presence no one knew, and his insight into insurance was a big plus. "It hasn't come up on the market yet, but it looks good, and if I'm lucky, I'll have a new place by the time you get back."

"If not, you can always move in with me," he said softly. "The spelling lab is sitting there empty. I'm not using it."

I turned my hand palm up under his and gave it a squeeze. "It's too far out, Trent," I said plaintively, though I'd used his mother's refurbished spelling lab on the odd weekend. "No one will trek out there looking for help."

"They used to," he muttered as he shifted to put his ankle on a knee.

But they don't anymore, I finished silently. No one wanted Trent's help now that his Sa'han status was in question, and because of that, he was running out of favors owed to him, favors that he had once used to get things done. The above-the-law power had made him the elven Sa'han—but no more.

My chest hurt, and I held my breath to quash the pain as I looked at Ellasbeth doing mom-things with the girls, elegant and competent both. She could give that back to him, but only if I was out of the picture, or more realistically, out of Trent's bed. Sure, he could make a few more babies with Ellasbeth out of wedlock and satisfy the letter of the elven law, but that wouldn't rub out that he was in love with me, and my being a demon, even a witch-born demon, meant that was unacceptable.

Ellasbeth looked up as if feeling my gaze on her, giving me a somewhat smug smirk. Maybe her hearing was better than I thought.

I didn't want to move in with Trent. Oh, I loved him and the girls, but it was more than needing to be close to the city center for work. Everything was easy for him. He wanted to make it easy for me. It sounded great, except I'd never know if my success was thanks to me or him, and I wanted it to be me.

Unfortunately, moving in with Trent was looking more and more probable, even if only temporary. I had a bare two weeks before Constance Corson, Cincinnati's incoming master vampire, kicked me out of Piscary's old digs and took possession of it and Cincy both. Her people had been filtering in all month, causing trouble as they massed in the bars and hot spots to push out the old order with threat and fang. There'd been a surprising resistance, and as expected, the I.S. was ignoring it all, seeing as Constance was simply exerting her rightful power as the incoming master vampire: their new boss, basically. The human-run FIB couldn't do anything—obviously. So far, Constance's people were keeping the threats vamp on vamp. But that might change after she took control, and everyone was worried. Reason three for not leaving Cincy at the moment.

"I want you to be careful while I'm gone," Trent said, and I turned, surprised at not only his words but the real concern in the pinch of his green eyes.

"I'm always careful," I said, but just that he'd brought it up meant something was wrong. "What is it?" I said, voice low as I leaned closer.

He took a breath, then pretended to take a sip of coffee to hide his moving lips. "It may be nothing, but we might have had an attempted break-in at the estate last night."

Might have? My expression fell. I could feel it. "I'm coming with you," I said, reaching for my phone to call Jenks.

"No." He touched my hand, stopping me. "It was probably a nuisance attempt."

But his smile wasn't quite right. I would've believed him

six months ago, but now? I could spot his tells better than Quen almost.

And he knew it. Seeing my disbelief, Trent eased back into the chair to watch the passing world. "I wouldn't have mentioned it except the three vamps Quen scared over the wall weren't in Cincy's facial-recognition database."

I slowly nodded. "Out-of-town vamps causing trouble. I'm coming with you."

His gaze flicked to me, worry gripping my core when he smiled lovingly. "Rachel, I'd like nothing more than you coming with me, but not because three inept members of Constance's camarilla scaled the wall to mutter threats at me through my security system."

"Threats? What did they say?"

His hand in mine was warm, and he lifted it to give my knuckle a kiss. "Demanded that I acknowledge that Constance is the law in Cincinnati and the Hollows."

"Trent—"

"Relax, it's not anything that was unexpected," he said. "And as you said, I'm too far out to be a direct influence on anything that happens in Cincinnati." His lips pressed in thought and his focus blurred.

I gave his hand a squeeze, and his attention returned. "Promise you'll call if anything else happens. The second it does," I prompted.

"I will." His gaze went to his two girls. "Promise."

He would. That I believed. If there *was* trouble, I could be there in the time it took for me to shake a demon from his "poor me" sulk and buy a line jump. My credit was good.

"Here," he said, twisting where he sat, and my eyes widened when he took a ring box from his suit pocket. "This is for you. It has nothing to do with Constance's threats, but I know I'll sleep better at night."

"Uhh . . ." I stammered. Trent was not the kind of guy to give jewelry. A gun, a spell, or a charm, yes, but not jewelry unless it *was* a gun, a spell, or a charm, and I took the small gray box, glad he hadn't dropped down on one knee right there in the airport terminal. Yes, Ellasbeth was the mother of his child and he was devoted to another little girl who called Quen dad, but he was still single.

"It's a spell," he said, pressing close with the scent of cinnamon and wine. "Took me an entire month to research."

Shoulders relaxing, I opened the box to find a delicate pinky ring, the interwoven bands of silver holding a pearl. "Oh, Trent, it's beautiful," I said as I pulled it from the box—hesitating at the faint tingle of a charm. "What does it do?"

"It's so you don't forget me."

My eyebrows rose as he took the ring from me and put it on my pinky. "In a week?" I said dryly, and he chuckled as it fitted cool and perfect about my finger.

"Look. I've got one, too," he said, showing me his hand and a ring twin to mine apart from his being made of bands of gold, not silver, the setting decidedly more masculine. "If anything bad happens to either of us, both pearls turn black."

"Oh!" He took my hand, and I gazed at our fingers twined together, the rings catching the artificial light to almost glow. It was sort of a help-I've-fallen-and-can't-get-up charm. "Thanks. I love it." Then I hesitated. "When you say, if anything happens to either of us . . ."

Not looking at me, he shrugged. "It works by way of your aura."

My lips pressed, and I looked down at our interlaced fingers. So it was jewelry, but it was bling with a bang. "Thanks, Trent," I said, ignoring that it was a way to know if one of us was assassinated. "I love it." And I did. It was delicate enough to look good on my slim fingers, so small that most people wouldn't even notice it. Jenks would, though. The pixy saw everything.

Trent seemed to brighten, but that worry line still crinkled the edges of his eyes. "It only took me a day to make once I found the pearls. *That* took a good month." His gaze went to the girls, his focus distant. "They're from the same oyster. And as unique as you." Attention returning, he lifted our joined hands and kissed my fingertips. A shiver raced through me, and I felt myself warm. The public show of affection was unusual, but maybe he was making some sort of statement to Ellasbeth, who was clearly not happy.

For a moment, it was just us, surrounded by the bustle of hundreds, but then his hand in mine tightened as their flight was announced over the loudspeaker. Pulling upright, he sent his gaze to Quen. Immediately the older, dark elf began to effortlessly prep the girls, wiping hands and faces, tidying shoelaces, and directing their attention without looking as if he was manipulating them. *Crap on toast, he's good.*

"I have to go," Trent said as he stood.

I rose as well, gut tightening. "It's only a week," I said, the sensation of his loss already hard on me as his family bustled to get organized. I felt left out, especially when the girls ran back to the window to look at the plane, their Aunt Rachel forgotten.

Trent set his coffee on the chair's arm and pulled me close, his hand warm at the small of my back. "I've seen what can happen in a week," he said with a smile, his lips inches from mine and the scent of wine and cinnamon a heady wave. "Call me?"

"You call me," I said instead, and Trent took my cup and balanced it on the arm of the nearby chair as well before pulling me into a passionate hug that lit through me like fire. It was followed by a restrained but tender kiss that left me aching for more.

"Yes, Madam Demon," he said playfully as his arms lowered. And then he was gone and I was watching him walk away. Ray held his one hand, Lucy the other. Quen followed behind with Ellasbeth, the woman's head down as she fumbled in her purse for their tickets. They were the perfect family, and seeing them leave for a week to be surrounded by the over-the-top West Coast elves, I began to worry.

Leaving Cincy to Constance in order to follow Trent and keep Ellasbeth at bay might have been the better choice.

CHAPTER

2

"THE WIRING IS UP TO CODE, RACHE," JENKS SAID AS HE hovered before me, a faint rasp coming from his dragonfly-like wings. The sun shining in the big, street-grimed front window glowed in his short blond hair and the silver dust spilling from him, making him look *far* more innocent than he was. Spiderweb coated the garden sword at his hip, and dust dulled his red bandana, worn to convince any pixy whose territory he might stumble into that he wasn't there poaching. Considering that such an intrusion was grounds for death, it was an appropriate precaution. "Give me a sec, and I'll check the plumbing."

"Great," I said, thinking that with their insatiable curiosity and ability to wiggle through walls, pixies could make a fortune in home inspections—if anyone cared to ask. "See if you can track down the source of that smell while you're at it."

"And if it can be removed," David added, his hands on his hips and duster brushing the floor as he stood with his back to us to watch the light traffic passing outside. His shadow was short on the old oak flooring, but that the sun even made it into the downtown Hollows two-story was somewhat of a miracle.

Beside him, Sharron clasped her notebook like a fig leaf and smiled. "Remember that everything can be fixed except location. And, Rachel, this property has that in spades."

I nodded as Jenks hummed down the short hall to do a more thorough inspection of the tiny ground-floor restroom. Sharron was the epitome of professionalism in her bright yellow suit dress and her Cincy Realty pin, standing in the middle of the empty thirty-by-forty front room. The real estate agent had been working with us for three months. Anyone else would've given up by now, but she was just as perky, just as upbeat as the day I'd called her about a flat on the riverfront. It had rented out before I could get down to see it, but Jenks had a good feeling about the big-haired brunette who'd treated him like a person from the instant she beamed that wide-toothed smile and asked what *he* was looking for in a new property.

David was actually the one who had tipped us off about the old shopfront. It wasn't slated to be on the market for a few weeks, but that was exactly why Jenks and I had jumped on it. Everything was selling out from under us as Constance's people came in.

The narrow, two-story building faced a moderately busy downtown Hollows street. Even better, the downstairs was already zoned for business with living quarters for one upstairs—two if one of them was a pixy. Cars drove slowly past the big plate-glass window, and metered parking kept things moving. The building had old floors and painted metal tile on the ceiling, but I liked how the thick walls cut the noise, and the ornate, heavily carved moldings gave Jenks lots of places to perch. I'd done a quick look at the residual magic of the place the instant we'd crossed the threshold, and it was surprisingly clean, with only a rudimentary circle etched into the kitchen counter. A ley line wasn't too far away, either.

It was a "charmer," in Sharron's Realtor-ese, meaning small. It had "lots of character," which meant the floor plan made little sense and the fixtures were old. It was also in an "up-and-coming" neighborhood, which Jenks said meant we'd be paying top dollar even though the shops to either side were kind of . . . well . . . dumpy.

"Sharron! Will you turn this on for me? I want to check

the water pressure," Jenks shouted from the second floor, and the woman immediately headed for the stairs. He hadn't come out of the downstairs bathroom, meaning he'd followed the piping up through the walls.

"What do you think?" David drew back from the window as two I.S. vehicles tore by, sirens off but lights flashing. "You can't beat the location," he added, but I said nothing as I moved behind the oak display case and began opening drawers so old they had to be original. "Price is right for what you're getting."

I struggled with the bottom drawer, finally giving up when I heard him cross the room, boots lightly scraping. "Street seems a little busy," I said, rising up to see him moving with the confident grace of an alpha Were. Behind him, a FIB cruiser raced past, the human-run police force forever outclassed by their Inderland counterparts. *Late to the party again.*

"Busy street, busy business," he prompted as he leaned one elbow on the counter, his dark eyes on the street as the traffic resumed. There was a hint of gray around his temples, but it only made him look better, in my opinion. Pack life agreed with him. He was his best when taking care of someone, and his pack was growing. Fast. Sometimes I wondered what might have happened if I hadn't abdicated my female alpha position.

"You'd have a clear definition of public space and private with the living quarters upstairs," David continued. "A door that locks between them. The church never did, and it always bothered me."

"Who is going to mess with the last living Tamwood heir?" I countered, tucking a stray curl of red hair behind an ear in a show of unease. But Ivy was still in DC trying to convince the long undead that it was a much better thing for her to hold the soul of her undead lover instead of letting it slip away, in essence allowing Nina to sip her own soul along with Ivy's blood. It gave Ivy a smidgen of control in the traditionally one-sided scion/gnomon pair, and the old undead didn't like it. At all. Even if Ivy had been in

Cincy, she wouldn't be living with me anymore. All good things, even if they hurt.

But even I had to admit that this was a great space. I could maybe turn the display counter into a coffee bar, put my desk behind it, make a good first impression. The downstairs storage room would make a serviceable small spelling lab. I could work and man the door at the same time, freeing Jenks to do what he needed to do. Add two chairs and a low table in front of the window for interviewing clients, and a rack of service brochures—maybe lawyers specializing in Inderland issues, morgues, state-licensed day quarters for the poor undead, that kind of thing.

Leaving the church for good would be hard, though. It had been standing fallow for the last three months, repairs having abruptly halted when the construction crew saw the pentagrams etched on Kisten's pool table. Apparently word had gotten around, and I couldn't get a construction company to even take my calls anymore, much less set foot in the church.

Jenks was ready to sell, which had surprised me until I put it all together: he'd lost his wife there, and with his kids scattered, there was nothing left for him but reasons to leave.

My shoulders were almost to my ears and, not wanting David to know it bothered me to just . . . abandon the church, I forced them down, took a breath, and tugged my short leather jacket square as I came out from behind the counter. Yes, a locking door would be nice, but I'd have to pay someone to reroute the gas line under the floor to make an area where I could set an unbreakable circle. Not to mention that after the expanse of the church, and then having Piscary's old restaurant/lair all to myself for the winter, the two tiny rooms, half kitchen, and upstairs cubby bath felt confining. Tight. There was no outside space at all, and trying to do my calisthenics anywhere within the walls was impossible. I'd have to go to the gym.

Welcome to the real world, I thought as I leaned back against the counter beside David and watched the traffic as we waited for Jenks. But then I frowned, recognizing that same beat-up brown Volvo that I'd seen in the morning at the airport parking. I remembered it because I'd thought it odd that someone would be sitting in their car at the curb, risking the airport police yelling at them, instead of parking it where they were supposed to. A dark-haired living vamp was behind the wheel this time, his black glasses and scruff giving him a rough look. Two blonds dressed like him sat in the back, and a bad feeling crept out from between my soul and reason. I didn't like it when vamps dressed the same, even if the leather was classy. Unified looks meant unified purpose, and that could be deadly when it came to vamps.

"That's the third time around for them," David said softly.

"Maybe they're looking for an open meter." My eyes went to the three substantial locks on the door. Only one was mundane, the others were spells. They had expired, but I could fix that, and as I gazed out at the world, I decided I could handle downtown Hollows just fine—even if I'd miss the church like the undead miss the sun.

I forced a smile when Jenks's wings rasped on the narrow stairs. Sharron was following, going almost sideways in her tall heels. "Roof looks okay," he said as he alighted on the counter to brush the dust from his head-to-toe black silk. "It's old and flat, so snow might be an issue. But it's not leaking, and it gets sun for a good part of the day. We could put some boxes up there. Get something green growing."

Which would help take care of Jenks's needs. It wouldn't be a garden, but as a widower, he didn't need much. He was right about the sun. It would be on the face of the building most of the afternoon, making it bright and pleasant.

"It's a good neighborhood," David said, wincing when a fire truck roared past, honking to clear the nearby intersection. "I've got a few pack members a block down. They could hear you if you shouted."

Hence him knowing about this place, I thought, wondering how I'd become the deciding voice here.

"Lots of restaurants, shops," Jenks said, now on David's shoulder to look right as rain among the man's long, wavy hair. Distracted, Sharron gazed out the window, eyes following the emergency vehicles. "We'd have living quarters upstairs, and a public area downstairs." His wings hummed. "New furniture that doesn't smell like Ivy. With a few pictures on the wall and a rug, this could be a nice place. You could spell in that back room and still hear the door." He hesitated, and then, as if he was only now checking, he added, "Ley line is pretty near."

Again I reached out a thought and found it, agreeing as a soft, welcoming warmth and tingle spread through me and a stray strand of red hair began to float. It was close. Not as close as the one we used to have in the church's backyard, but not bad.

But even as I considered it, a feeling of loss took me. Flowerpots and raised beds were not a garden. I'd have to buy everything I used to get for free. There was no view, no space, and the off-street parking that came with the place would hardly hold my tiny MINI. Being right in downtown Hollows might sound good on paper, but maybe I'd be *too* accessible, spending all my time tracking down straying familiars and telling people I didn't make love charms instead of finding murder suspects and kicking ass.

What concerned me most, though, was that my line of work wasn't always conducive to being a good neighbor. The church was unlivable because of a misunderstanding with Cincy's resident vamps, made worse when the elven goddess threw a tantrum in my front room. Not both at the same time, fortunately, but imagining that in downtown Hollows? The potential collateral damage was enough to give even Trent pause.

Jenks's hopeful expression, though, ate at my resistance. Constance would be in Cincy in two weeks and our rent-free situation in Piscary's old digs would be over. We had to live somewhere, and the church needed a new kitchen before it could get an occupation permit. Without that, no one would even consider buying it.

"Could you excuse us for a moment?" I said to Sharron, and Jenks rattled his wings in anticipation as Sharron beamed.

"I'll be outside," she said, heels clicking as she headed for the sidewalk where her bright yellow, big-ass, four-door Cadillac waited at the curb. "This is a good one, Rachel. You could look for a year and not find anything better in your price range. It makes me glad all those others fell through. What did I tell you? Things happen for a reason."

David eased himself up to sit on the counter, knees wide in a classic manspread as the dusty door chime clunked and Sharron went outside. His scruff, so different from Trent's always-smooth cheeks, held my eye. Must be a Were thing.

"Well?" Jenks prompted as the street noise cut off. His expression was hopeful, and I quashed a rising worry. Jenks would have the funds from the church to cover his side of things, but my share would take everything I'd managed to scrape together. I had to trust myself that the money for the mortgage would come, but even more important, I *could* trust myself.

Again I looked out the wide window. *Is this the place?* I wondered. I'd have a nice view of the river if I put a larger window in upstairs. Maybe the roof was better than I thought, and Jenks and I could make a potted paradise up there. "I like having off-street parking," I said slowly, and Jenks rasped his wings in agreement.

"The building is sound," David encouraged, reaching for his phone when it dinged for his attention. "If you like it, you should take it. You can always sell it later if you change your mind. Downtown property moves pretty fast."

I took a breath. Held it. Exhaled. Jenks was right. It was time to let go. I needed a more professional image, and I hadn't picked out the church in the first place. Ivy had, and the reason for having it—sanctified ground where the un-dead and demons couldn't tread—was no longer an issue.

"I like it," I said, and Jenks inked a bright silver. "We should put in an offer."

"Great!" Jenks darted to hover by the door, waiting for one of us to open it. "I'll tell Sharron. How much you want to start with?"

My shoulders slumped as if having decided made everything easier. *Gold lettering on the door. Maybe a light over the window. Nice rug . . .* "Anything less than the last place sounds good to me. Go for it, Jenks. You've got a good feel for our finances."

Smiling, David slipped from the counter and went to open the door a crack.

"Good-bye, stinky pizza place, hello, downtown living. I'm a city pixy!" Jenks exclaimed, and then he was on the sidewalk, making circles around Sharron until she clapped her hands and gave me an enthusiastic smile.

David lingered by the door as I took one last look to imagine the space with me and Jenks and all our stuff. "Thanks for bringing this to our attention," I said as I found my phone and took a picture of the old counter, then another of the big front window to show Trent. "I can't believe how fast property is going right now. This is, like, the seventh place we've almost bought."

"It's a great building," David said, louder since I'd gone to take a picture of the back room. "Nothing weird in the history apart from a lizard issue in the eighties. Still don't know what that was about." He chuckled. "I'm surprised you didn't ask Trent to look at it."

"Trent?" I clicked off the light and came out. "And have the owner jack up the price?"

"I suppose."

"Besides"—I stared at the ceiling, wondering if it was higher out here than in the back—"he and the girls left today for the West Coast with Ellasbeth to visit her mom. It's her birthday, and apparently elves make a big deal about it when it's got a zero attached to it." Nose wrinkling, I waved at Jenks that I'd be right there. He'd plastered himself against the window like a highway casualty. Translation: I was killing him. "I would have gone, but I've got an appointment with Dali tomorrow." Annoyed, I ushered Jenks off the window, and he darted back to Sharron.

"Still, an all-expenses-paid vacation to the West Coast?" David said, and then his expression blanked. "You didn't get banned from Seattle, too, did you?"

"No, but being surrounded by Ellasbeth's family for a week doesn't sound like a vacation. He's going to be busy with the enclave elders cementing his Sa'han status. My presence would *not* help."

David put an arm over my shoulders in consolation. The eon-long war between the demons and elves had crusted over, but the scab was new and they both seemed to be looking for a reason to scratch it. "I'd think having a demon on your payroll would be a positive thing," David said as he opened the door and the sounds of the city at noon rose to soothe me.

"Sure, if I wasn't also in his bed," I muttered, and David laughed.

Jenks looked up from his hover over Sharron's shoulder as she gave me a thumbs-up that could mean anything from "I'm on the phone with my mom" to "we cinched the deal."

"I'm sure it will work out." David's arm fell away as he came to a rocking halt in the sun, his dark eyes scanning the street. "You've got a solid in with the elven dewar for saving Landon from the baku. Zack doesn't have a problem with a demon shacking up with the prince of the elves and, come his eighteenth birthday, he'll be the head of the dewar."

"Trent is not the prince of the elves," I said, my gaze dropping to my new pinky ring, glinting in the sun.

"Tink's tampons, he isn't," Jenks said as he abandoned Sharron. "The guy is pure Rachel candy. Vast power and clout—"

"—on the skids," David finished, to make Jenks laugh and bob his head, golden hair shining. "Face it, Rachel. You're kryptonite to the high-powered elites."

"Am not." I fumbled to put my phone in my bag, head rising to follow the sounds of sirens two blocks over.

Jenks gave David a sidelong look before landing on his shoulder. "You bankrupted Al in three years flat," the pixy said, raising one finger. "Did the same for Trent in, what? Six months?"

"Al was trying to *own* me," I said in my own defense as David checked his phone and frowned. "And Trent still has money," I added, but him flying out first class instead of in his jet left me wondering. "Why does everyone think he's broke?"

"Maybe it's the lawsuits," Jenks smart-mouthed. "Ivy is still trying to recoup her losses after hitching her wagon to you. Paycheck to paycheck doesn't look good when you're slated to be Cincy's master vampire after death. Poor girl."

"I didn't ask her to leave the I.S. with me," I said, but Jenks was on a roll.

"I'm the only person who has come out of this better than they went in," he said proudly.

"I'm better off," David said, his head down over his phone. "Ivy is better off by far. Al is, too, for all his complaints. And Trent?" David grinned, showing his teeth. "I didn't have to kill Trent to prevent another Kalamack from taking over the world."

Because of me, I thought, but I was too embarrassed to say it. Because of me, Trent had grown into who he wanted to be, not what his father had made him: frighteningly resolute in his pursuit of a goal and blind to another's pain.

"It's harder to scare people into doing what you want when you don't have any money," David said, ruining it.

Jenks laughed as I put a hand on a hip. "Why do I even listen to you?" I said.

"Because I look good in leather and scruff," David replied. "And what would the papers print if Rachel Morgan went out without a boy toy?"

They were both laughing, but Sharron had finally gotten off the phone, and I pushed past David, willing to ignore it.

"Good news!" Sharron said brightly. "They like the terms that Jenks offered, and with your preapproval, we're all set. The place is yours."

My God, we are going to do this, I thought, breathless as Sharron locked the front door, beaming as she turned to face us. "I'll jump back to my office," she said, eyes bright, "print out the contract, and move this forward before the weekend and everything slows down. Congratulations! If everything looks okay in the inspection, you can be in by the end of the month. I've got your good-faith check from the last place that fell through. All you have to do is pick out your furniture."

"Month?" I turned to Jenks, wincing. I could probably couch surf for a while, but it wasn't the image of self-reliance I was trying for, and interviewing clients at a coffee shop would get old really fast.

"Can we move this any faster?" Jenks asked for both of us.

Sharron turned, the big key in her hand. "It's empty," she said, her eyes distant on the future. "So maybe a few days to line up the inspection." Her focus cleared on David. "I'm sure you can get proof of insurance expedited, and your mortgage is sitting there from the last time we thought we had something. I'll keep an eye open for a closing cancellation. They don't like it when we push for speed, but things have been easier since the Turn." She hesitated in thought. "Maybe two weeks if nothing goes wrong?"

I exhaled, and beside me, David seemed to relax. "Two weeks is better," I said, wondering whether, if I was really nice to Constance, she might let me and Jenks hang out on the boat tied to Piscary's quay a couple of extra days. *Probably not,* I thought sourly. I'd downed Pike, her scion, after catching him poking around the boat, and pride meant everything to the undead.

"Great!" Jenks took flight. "I can still get a late spring garden in if I hustle."

Sharron extended her hand first to me, then David, the woman clearly pleased. "This feels good, Rachel," she said as she backed to her car, her phone still in hand. "I told you we'd find something before you lost your place."

"Nothing like waiting to the last moment," I muttered, and Jenks bobbed his head. Constance was coming. I could see it in the new graffiti and the uncomfortable headlines. Not to mention my new escorts driving around Cincy in a beat-up brown Volvo. "Thanks, Sharron!" I called out as the woman crossed in front of her car and waited for traffic to clear. "I can't believe it took this long."

"Everyone finds their place eventually!" she said happily as she got into her car and slammed the door shut. I could tell she was relieved we'd pulled the trigger on this one so fast. We'd been looking for ages, and her time-invested/commission ratio was probably nearing the break-even point. Not that she would ever complain. She was too professional for that.

Jenks landed on my shoulder, the barest hint of a sour green dust spilling from him. "It wasn't as if we weren't trying," he muttered, and I nodded. We'd lost the last two places due to miscommunications and a buyer's market.

Sharron's passenger-side window went down with a whine. "I'll text you when I've got the paperwork in hand," she said as she stretched across her front seat. "Where are you going to be the next couple of hours?"

Hours? I thought, thinking she must be tired of properties being jerked out from under us, too. "Ah, Junior's?" I suggested. "It's close to your office. I could use a coffee."

David leaned closer. "She has no idea what you are talking about."

I stifled a wince. No, she wouldn't. Only a handful of people called it that. The why was a long story. "Coffee shop a few blocks from your office," I added. "The one with the circles on the floor."

"You got it. See you in a few." Sharron's car window went up, and, after looking behind her, she pulled out and was gone.

"Congratulations, Rachel," David said, and I waved for Jenks to go hover by the door so I could get a picture to send to Trent and Ivy. "I'm glad you're moving out of Piscary's and a door that half of Cincy has a key to."

I looked up from my phone and met his eyes. "Seriously?"

Jenks zipped closer, and I tilted it so he could see the picture. "Who's going to bother Cincy's resident demon?" he said, and I blew his dust away before it blanked the screen.

"We do okay," I added, but he was right, and I quashed my nervousness as I pocketed my phone and we started down the sidewalk to where I'd left my car.

"I know you do." David took a long step to catch up. "It's just . . ."

My unease deepened. His hands hung free and his eyes were on the rooflines. "What?"

He scrubbed a hand over his bristles sheepishly. "Three idiots tried to jump me this morning on my run. They fled in a brown Volvo."

My eyes widened and Jenks's dust shifted to a surprised red. "Seriously? Are you okay?" I blurted, and David looked at his fist. It was skinned. I hadn't noticed until now.

"Me? Fine," he said, flashing me a thin smile. "They weren't much of a threat. Besides, I needed the workout. All this domestic bliss is making me flabby."

Flabby? I eyed his flat stomach.

"They told me," he said, his expression becoming angry for the first time, "to look to Constance instead of you. That she's the law in Cincinnati, and that if I knew what was good for me, I'd put a leash on my people and give her the room she needs."

"David . . ." This wasn't good. First Trent, and now David? It was almost the same threat. Look to her, or else.

But he was grinning, his eyes on his knuckles again. "I told them where they could lick themselves. Rachel, relax, it will take more than three living vampires to scare me. I handled it. They won't be back. Vampires are homebody cowards. Once they find out they can't bully you, they leave you alone."

Maybe, but in two weeks, Constance would have more

than a handful of vampires at her beck and call, she'd have her entire camarilla.

"I wouldn't have even told you, except that a little warning goes a long way. If you have a new lock instead of being six feet under the ground or on a boat where you can't reach a ley line, I'll feel better."

I smiled, finding a compliment in there. "You're right, but as you say, it's a mistake they'd only make once."

"True, but why bust heads when you don't have to?"

Because a little tussle now prevents a big misunderstanding later, I thought, but he'd scuffed to a slow halt, and I stopped. His car was one way, mine the other. If he offered to walk me to mine, I was going to punch him. Escorting people through the bad guys was my *job.*

"This is a nice neighborhood," he said, but the way he was scanning the rooftops was disconcerting. "I'm glad you got it. Let me know when you're moving and I'll bring the pack."

"Deal," I said. Exchanging pizza and beer for an afternoon of companionship and a fast move was a win-win. "Thanks again, David." I reached out, tugging him closer for a quick hug to say thanks for more than the tip on the property, but also for letting me be me. Jenks flung himself back off my shoulder, swearing as I breathed in the delicious scent of Were: woodsy, spicy, and earthy. "Tell me if Constance's chipped-fang thugs bother you again."

"Will do." His eyes were crinkled in worry when he dropped back, but his smile was warm. "Always a pleasure," he said as his phone rang. He reached for it, and my eyes went to the ambulance coming up the street, hitting its siren for a quick *brupp* to clear the intersection. Something was going on. I could hear angry shouting a few blocks away.

"You need to take that?" I said as David frowned first at the number, then the ambulance as it slowly wove through the stopped traffic.

"Excuse me," he said, shoulders hunched as he hit the connect key and turned away.

"Jenks," I called so the curious pixy wouldn't eavesdrop, and he jerked to a short stop, dust spilling gold in annoyance. "This is okay, right?" I said as he came back and we looked at the store front. Most of the closing costs were coming from him and the probable sale of the church—if we ever got it into saleable condition.

"Absolutely," he said, but a hint of depressed blue showed in the dust spilling from him. "I never liked living where dead humans were rotting in the ground."

I'd heard his complaint before, but I wasn't sure I believed him.

"And I can always gather stuff from the garden before we sell it," he added, making me doubly unsure. It would be great having a downtown office, but I couldn't help but wonder if I would miss the church more: the solitude, the cool quiet of the street, the solstice bonfires in the back, the noise of the kids riding their bikes on the walk in the dark, the garden I never seemed to have enough time to work in but which somehow gave me everything I needed.

The belfry where Bis had lived, I thought, head dropping to the new ring Trent had given me. Jenks had raised his kids there, lost his wife among the tombstones. Maybe . . . maybe it was better this way. Time to let my baggage sit on the curb for the trashman.

"Be right there," David said as he ended his call. His face was creased in concern as he turned to us. "You can get to your car from here okay, right?"

I followed his gaze to the ambulance vanishing around the corner. "Want some help?" I asked, and David fidgeted, clearly eager to be gone.

"If you say no, she's going to sulk for the rest of the afternoon." Jenks rose up, hands on his hips in his best Peter Pan pose. "Don't do that to me, Mr. Peabody."

But David was inching away, the mildly irksome nickname not even noticed. "It really is a nice street, Rachel. I gotta go." Turning, he ran off after the ambulance, duster furling and hat falling off his head.

He didn't stop to pick it up.

I frowned, and from beside me, Jenks said, "I don't know if I should say something about him being an ambulance chaser, or just cars in general."

"He forgot his hat," I said, striding forward to scoop it up.

Jenks took off his bandana and stuffed it in a back pocket, telling me he was working. "Maybe you should take it to him."

Nodding, I started off in a slow jog, then jerked into a faster pace when someone screamed and the small pop of a handgun echoed against the stone buildings.

Nice neighborhood? I thought as I began to run in earnest.

CHAPTER

3

I SKIDDED TO A FALTERING HALT IN THE STREET, LIPS PART-
ing as I gazed up at the low-slung, two-story apartment
building. All the windows were open with their screens
pushed out, and shadows of people were chucking clothes,
tables, books, anything that would fit and a few things that
wouldn't down to hit the patchy front lawn. I stood at the
back of a small crowd, jostling shoulders until someone
either recognized me or felt the tingle of our internal ley
line energy levels trying to balance and pushed back to give
me room. Yep, I had *that* kind of a rep.

I moved forward, arms over my middle as I stopped at
the "do not cross" tape stretched between the gangly street
trees. Three people, Weres by the look of the tattoos and
general hippie/free-spirit clothes, were facedown on the
front lawn, spread-eagled with their hands clasped behind
their heads. Two I.S. agents stood over them, yelling their
rights at them. A third held a rifle, presumably the one that
had gone off and was now confiscated. No one was at the
ambulance, so the situation looked contained.

In addition to the EMS, there was a total of six I.S. cars,
one FIB cruiser, the fire truck, and a news crew training
their cameras on the distressed people gathering their stuff
off the lawn. A second line of I.S. officers milled about, to
keep the crowd from testing the line.

"That doesn't look legal," Jenks said from the safety of my shoulder, and the crowd *ooh*ed when an entire bookcase came tumbling out, hitting the ground to break into three pieces and scatter paperbacks everywhere.

It might be understandable if the building was on fire, but despite the fire truck at the curb, it wasn't. This had all the earmarks of a mass eviction, one done without the usual painstaking legalities and paperwork, and my face burned. The I.S. wasn't doing anything about it except crowd control.

"You want me to tell David we're here?" Jenks said, and I scanned the crowd until I found the man standing beside one of the cruisers.

"That's bull!" I heard him say faintly as he gestured to the building. "You can't evict someone because you want the property. They're paid up. The property is in repair."

"Sir, if you don't get behind the tape, I'll detain you for obstruction," the officer said, one hand on his cuffs, the other reaching to push David back.

My breath caught as David shifted, the motion so fast the I.S. officer hesitated in surprise.

"I wouldn't." David almost growled the words, and the displaced Weres within earshot hesitated, turning from their growing piles. They were looking to him for direction, and a chill dropped down my spine. "I really wouldn't."

This was bad, but it could clearly get a whole lot worse. "Tell him I don't have bail money for this," I whispered, and Jenks darted away, ignored as he broke the "do not cross" line.

I lost his sparkle of dust in the sun, but I knew the instant he reached David, as the Were suddenly backed off, his posture shifting from aggression to worry. He turned right to me, frowning when I gave him a little wave. If they took him down, I'd get involved, and apparently he didn't want that.

"I won't tell you again," the officer said, bold now that David had retreated. "Behind the line!"

David raised a hand in acquiescence, but his anger hung

with him as he went to help one of the former residents carry a chair to the moving van that had pulled up to the curb.

My shoulders slumped, stiffening back up when I spotted that same brown Volvo cruising the outskirts. My eyes met the driver's, my lip twitching when he smiled mockingly at me and drove on.

Which made me wonder if this had been a ploy to lure David away and get me alone, or just general harassment. The people collecting their things were frustrated and angry, prevented from going upstairs to get their belongings by three I.S. officers standing at the door. They were protecting Constance's vampires, and my fists clenched.

Eminent domain? I thought, eyes narrowing. This was unicorn crap. City master vampires sucked. But without them, everyone would be prey, not simply one small group of vampires who thought it was a privilege to be the undead's next fix. In return, Constance was taking what she wanted. And the I.S. was going to help because as the city's master vampire, she was basically their boss.

"She's not going to be here for another two weeks," I muttered to myself. "What kind of legal loophole did they find to justify this?"

"One they made up this morning," a familiar voice said at my elbow, and I jerked, my anger shifting a little closer to home as I saw it was Captain Edden of the FIB looking both confident and apologetic in a light gray shirt, his black pants hoisted high above his slightly spreading middle. No tie.

Grimacing, I turned away, but not before I caught a hint of pleading in his eye. Too bad I was still mad at the balding, stubborn-as-nails, honest-to-a-fault, loyal, trustworthy, middle-aged former military man who only wanted to make the world a better place.

"The eviction date was moved up due to the courts going on vacation next week," he added, shifting closer. The "do not cross" tape was between us, which I thought was fitting.

"My backlog is already killing me. We don't have the jail space for what this is going to cause."

Ticked, I looked at him, words failing me. I had trusted him, and he had bitch-slapped me without even knowing it.

"Rachel," he said with a pained, forced joviality. "I never expected to see you here. Come on in. I could use your help. None of the former residents are human, and the I.S. is ready to kick me out."

He lifted the tape for me to pass under. Arms over my chest, I stared at him.

"If you're with me, they won't make me leave, and I'm trying to help someone," he added. Forehead wrinkling, he dropped the tape. "Rachel?"

I didn't move. My breath was shallow and my gut hurt. Behind him, a potted plant hit the ground and shattered.

"Okay, I'm an ass," he said, and I exhaled, almost tearing up in the relief that he wasn't going to pretend nothing was wrong. "You have every right to be mad at me. But this is an Inderland matter, and if you don't vouch for me, I'm going to get kicked out. What's going on isn't fair. Someone needs to hold them accountable, and the I.S. won't do it."

"That you admit to being an ass isn't admitting you were wrong," I said, voice low so it wouldn't shake. The hurt had been that deep.

Edden slumped. Pulling himself straight, he faced me directly, with more than tape hanging between us. "I was wrong to assume it was a demon causing the baku murders," he said. "And even more wrong to not stop that kind of prejudicial thinking right at my desk. Thank you for pointing out that my attitude was that of a xenophobic pig. I'm trying to fix that. Please tell me if I'm ever dumb enough to do it again."

Jenks hovered behind him, and I hesitated as he shrugged. The pixy would know if Edden was lying by way of his aura. I didn't need to see Edden's aura to know he was sincere. The older man was one of my favorite people, which was why it had hurt so much. But I could forgive

him. We all made mistakes, and our upbringing was sometimes hell to overcome. "What can you tell me?" I said,
almost breathing the words.

Edden exhaled, knowing what I was really saying was
that I forgave him. Motions fast, he lifted the tape again. I
slipped under it, feeling everything change as I accepted
his apology. He had acknowledged my feelings were legitimate, taken ownership of his actions, apologized, and
promised to be aware of it. If I was going to live in this
world, I had to let go of the hurt and move on.

"They're being forcibly evicted," he said as we turned to
look at the building, our shoulders almost touching. "They
were given four weeks' notice, but something shifted and
everything was moved up."

Jenks hovered between us, clearly glad things were getting back to normal, and the two men gave each other a
head nod. "What do you mean, everything?" Jenks said,
and Edden's worry turned to a frown.

"Constance Corson is taking possession this week," he
said, and I started.

"Crap on toast, this week?" I said, squinting at him. But
that explained the new, excessive vamp graffiti blotting out
the traditional Were territory signs.

"Are you sure?" Jenks asked, his wing pitch lowering in
worry.

Edden gestured to the building. "So far she's been smart
and is harassing only Inderlanders."

"So why are you down here slumming in the Hollows?"
Jenks asked for both of us, and Edden inclined his head, a
new smile on his face. He had made it his goal to make a
path for Inderlanders to come to the human-run FIB for
help, but tradition was hard to break. Clearly someone finally had.

"Could you . . . She's over here," Edden said in answer.
Hands in my jacket pockets, I followed him across the lawn
to where a woman in hospital scrubs was trying to organize
her things into a sad pile. My interest piqued at the candles

and chalk. She was probably a witch since an elf wouldn't be living in a middle-class neighborhood.

"Stephanie came to me about a week ago," he said as we walked, and I hustled to catch up with his long strides. "The entire building filed a complaint at the I.S., but when their paperwork landed on a carousel of death, she got desperate enough to try the FIB." He frowned at the open windows, his mustache bunching up. "This might be my fault. I was close to having the eviction notice declared illegal, so they moved it up."

I glanced at Edden, wondering how a witch coming to him for help had gone down with his superiors, but there was a good chance that no one in the system had known she was there until it was almost done—the I.S. handled Inderland matters, the FIB everything else.

Jenks landed on my shoulder as Edden stopped beside the woman, now staring up at the top floor as a slew of books began shooting out like cannon fodder.

"Would you just let me come up there and get my stuff?" she shouted, then snatched up one of the thick medical textbooks and brushed the grass clippings off it. "This cost me eight hundred bucks, you pathetic, cowardly, chip-fanged excuse of a bloodsucking mosquito!"

Jenks made an impressed sound, adding, "I think I like her."

Edden cleared his throat. "Stephanie? I want you to meet Rachel Morgan," he said, and the woman looked up, clearly not seeing me.

"Nice to meet you," she said by rote, then turned to drop the book on the others already assembled. Her straight auburn hair was darker than mine, framing her long face in a professional cut. She stood about my height. Her curves were ample and she was an attractive early-thirty-something. Her nose wasn't small, but it wasn't big, either, and she wore no makeup and a pair of wire-rimmed glasses that probably saw through spells. A veritable plethora of tiny ring piercings down the arch of her left ear gave her a witchy vibe, the black ringlets looking like a charm of some sort. There was a smallish, silvery black stone embedded in her earlobe as well. Metal was the go-to for ley line amulets, but stone could be used if it had a high enough metal content, and something about it said magic. *Where did she get a stone amulet?* I wondered.

A hospital badge hung around her neck and a radiation card was clipped to her lapel. I guessed nurse or tech by her angry, no-nonsense look combined with the obvious strength in her arms and a little extra weight from sitting in a chair too many hours in the day. And she was a witch. The slight scent of redwood lifting from her confirmed it if her piercings and that stone in her earlobe weren't enough. It wasn't much, though, so maybe she was just a warlock, able to invoke a charm or spell, but lacking the know-how to make one.

Feeling for her, I scooped up one of her books, brushing it off before handing it to her. She blinked, the small show of kindness hitting her hard as she held it close, clearly struggling to keep it together. "Ah, everyone calls me Stef," she said, eyes going to Jenks on my shoulder. "Edden," she complained as she set the book—on skin fungi and charms to eliminate them—on the pile. "Can't you do something? I've got two more weeks. We all do."

But Edden shook his head. "I'm sorry. It's been signed by a judge. By the time we get it revoked, they will have taken possession."

"One on Constance's payroll, I bet," Stef muttered, then jumped when her TV came crashing down. "What the hell is wrong with you! Let me up there so I can get my stuff!"

"I wouldn't advise it," I said before Edden could do more than take a reluctant breath.

"Why not?" she blurted aggressively, and I pointed to the three big I.S. agents at the complex's door.

"The entire building is full of vampires hyped up on themselves and the joy of I.S.-sanctioned illegalities," I said. "Even if you could get past them, you'd be hard-pressed to get back out without a bite, much less with your stuff. You can buy more stuff. It takes years to get over a bite. If ever."

"Which is why," Edden interrupted, clearly uncomfortable, "I'm glad you are here." He hesitated. "Why are you down here, anyway?"

"Looking at property," I said, unwilling to open up that far to him just yet. "Stef, I'm sorry this is happening to you, but my advice is to pack up what they chuck out and find a new place."

The woman's lips pressed together. "Do you know how hard it is to find anything in Cincinnati or the Hollows right now? The nearest place I could find is out at Hamilton, which would give me an hour commute instead of a ten-minute trip by bike or bus."

"I do, actually," I said, letting some of my own frustration show. "I've had eight properties jerked out from under me in the last three weeks. I've got my own eviction notice pinned to my chest like a big, red *A*."

Stef's eyes met mine, her entire attitude shifting as she saw us for the first time. *Hazel,* I thought, then I jumped when an end table hit the ground with a loud crack. Jenks darted from me in surprise, hands on his hips as he stared at the destruction. "Petty," he said.

"My cat is up there," she said, her fear hitting me like a slap in the face.

Damn it all to the Turn and back. . . . Jaw clenched, I looked at Jenks. I didn't have to say a word.

Spilling a bright silver dust, Jenks hovered closer. "I'll find it. What's its name?"

"His name is Boots," Stef quavered, blinking fast as she tried not to cry.

Of course it is, I thought, and after giving Edden a dark look to stay put, I headed for the door, arms swaying. "Anything else you want?" I called over my shoulder.

"That vampire bitch's head on a platter," she said, and Jenks laughed.

"I knew I was going to like her," he said as he came even with me.

But I wasn't anywhere near amused. I hadn't been embellishing the situation when I told Stef getting in and out without a bite was chancy. Peeved, I looked over the taped-off lawn to find David talking with a group of five Weres in cuffs. "Jenks, how long would it take for you to get David if I need him?"

The pixy flew beside me, fiddling with his bandana as he considered it. "Right now? About thirty seconds. If he gets himself cuffed?" Jenks hesitated. "Three to five minutes."

I didn't think David was going to get himself in trouble. Still . . . "Tell him I'm going in for a cat. I'll be nice about it, but if it gets sticky, I might need backup. Then meet me at the front door."

"You got it."

The three I.S. officers had noticed me coming, and as Jenks swooped over to David, they pulled themselves together into a unified front. I gave the guys, two skinny and one muscle-bound, a fake smile, artfully pulled a strand of hair from my braid, and went over what I had. Splat gun. Fists. My feet. *Attitude,* I thought as I slowed to a halt, staying one step down to give them a brain-dead smile.

"I'm going in to get a cat," I said pleasantly, immediately pegging the skinny guy with the bad shave as the ranking officer. He was a living vamp, obviously, because they wouldn't send a witch or Were I.S. agent to sanction Constance's will. "Are you going to give me a problem, or will we all go home tonight the way we came in?"

"You've been evicted, witch," the heavier guy said. Doyle, according to his badge. "You had your chance."

I put a hand on my hip, head cocked. "Seriously, I just want the cat. Five minutes. In, out, gone," I said, a hint of redhead attitude showing.

"And that was your warning," Doyle said, reaching.

It was a stretch because I was a step down, but I blocked him. Impact sang through my arm, and I used the pain to jab at his throat. He choked, predictably bending to put his ears in my reach. I gave them a good box as I brought my knee up, barely tapping his groin.

Doyle's breath exploded from him. His eyes widened, and I grabbed his shoulders, taking his weight and easing him off the step and to the ground. Sure, I felt for the guy, but what I really wanted was my hands on him in case his friends decided to do something and I needed him to take it instead.

But they didn't, both watching with wide eyes and a new reluctance to get involved.

Jenks dropped to the panting man. "Bad life choice. Breathe shallow. It will get better."

Not before I get that cat, I hoped as I rose, hands in the air in a show of innocence. "He touched me first," I said loudly. "Everyone see that?"

No one said anything. Smile back in place, I stepped over him and took my splat gun out of my bag. "Five minutes," I promised as I inched past the remaining officers, stifling a shudder as I went into the narrow foyer and the vamp pheromones hit me.

Damn, it was Mardi Gras and trick or treat all in one, the pheromones so thick I felt as if I had to brush them out of my way. Stuff lined the hallways, skinny vampires in jeans and tees perusing the piles as if shopping. Calls and shouts rang out as others claimed apartments, rooms, or floors. It was pathetic. And illegal. And it pissed me off that no one would do anything about it because the incoming city master vamp needed space for her camarilla. The people she was stealing from could do nothing, and the rest wouldn't say anything lest they find their home next on the list.

Breath shallow, I headed for the stairs. No telling what I might find in the elevator, and it was only two stories.

"Doyle is up," Jenks said as he flew backward ahead of me, his eyes on the bright patch of light through the open door at the bottom of the stairs.

"Is he following, or just bitching?"

Jenks sighed, his dust thinning. "Following. Sorry."

I grimaced and walked faster. "See if you can find Boots," I directed. "Check under the bed, the closet. You know where cats hide."

"You want me to put a bow on him and carry him out for you, too?" Jenks said sarcastically. Behind me, Doyle was yelling at everyone to leave me alone. I was his. Right. Slow learner.

Three steps from the landing, I stopped. "You look like a cat toy," I said, seeing Stef's open door amid the clutter. "Entice him out."

"Cat toy?" Jenks said indignantly. "That's exactly what *he* thinks you are," he added, chin lifting to indicate the angry vamp standing at the bottom of the stairway, glaring at me with narrowed eyes. "The thing is, I'm faster than any old cat. How fast are you?"

I went up another step, not so sure anymore. "I guess we'll find out," I said, and Jenks hummed off, just below the ceiling, to vanish inside Stef's apartment.

"You!" Doyle bellowed, and I turned, glad I had the high ground this time. "You have been evicted," he snarled as he came up, halting a good six feet away, wary now. "And I have every right to throw your ass in jail for assault and trespassing."

I shook my head, drawing this out to give Jenks time to work. "You reached for me. I'm within my rights. And you want to talk about illegal? Fine. Constance pushing up the eviction date isn't legal even if the I.S. is sanctioning it. And besides, I don't live here. I'm visiting. Anything in that eviction notice against visiting?" I shifted my foot side to side, balancing it on a toe. If I flung it out, either it would hit his jaw and knock him backward or he'd catch it and jerk me right into his arms.

"Visit," Doyle said, the first inklings of thought spilling through him as he looked behind him to where Edden stood on the stoop, chatting with the two I.S. agents as he kept my escape open. "You're Edden's witch," he added derisively, and my face burned.

"She's nobody's demon, fang boy," Jenks said as he re-joined me. "Get it right."

If Jenks was back, he'd found the cat. Thinking that I might pull this off, I found a pretend confidence. "You really want to do this?" I said, hoping to talk my way out rather than fight and risk the lawsuits that would soak up my time and bank account. "Just let me get the cat, okay? I'll be out of your hair, your life, and your report if you're smart. Deal?"

The thick-chested vampire backed down a step, clearly thinking about it. His ears were red where I'd hit him, and he had his weight on one foot. Yes, I had scored on him, but he wouldn't be so slow the next time.

"While you're thinking that over, I'll get Stef's cat," I said, and, breath held, I turned my back on him and took the last two steps, ready to react. "Is he following?" I whispered.

Jenks shook his head. "Not yet."

"Where's the cat?" My tension spiked as I picked my way through the clutter.

"Under the bed like you said."

"Swell." I could feel Doyle watching from the stairs as I checked my splat gun. I stocked it with sleepy-time charms so it would do no real damage, but it was embarrassing to have to be doused with salt water to wake up, and vampires hated to be embarrassed.

"There's two guys in there," Jenks said. "How do you want to play it?"

I hesitated at the doorway when I saw two raggedly dressed vamps at the window, enthusiastically throwing Stef's heavy-duty mixer out onto the lawn. The place already smelled like a bordello, and a tingle went all the way to my groin before rising back to where my vamp scar lingered under pristine, unmarked skin. *Damn vamp pheromones.*

"Ah, let's go with plan B," I said, and one of the vamps turned at my voice.

"Grab the cat and run like hell," Jenks said, head bobbing. "Keep them busy. I'll see if I can get Boots to come out so you aren't on the floor with your ass in the air, dragging him out."

"Thank you so much for that," I muttered sarcastically as he darted away, and the second vamp turned, beaming to show his small but sharp canines. "Good afternoon, gentlemen," I said, making sure they saw my splat gun and attitude. "I'm here for the cat."

"Who the hell are you, beautiful?" the first one said, and I inched deeper inside as I heard Doyle in the hall. "Not that it matters," he added, eyes flicking behind me as Doyle filled the doorway. He wasn't coming in, though, and I took the center of the room, ready to move.

"Right here, baby," the other said, gesturing. "Let me show you what teeth are good for."

I stifled another shudder, shoving the compulsion he'd put in his voice down deep. "Just don't," I said, and Doyle grunted in surprise. I had practice saying no to vampires. I had practice saying yes, too, and my entire side was tingling because of it. Crap on toast, it had been a long time since I'd put myself in such a chancy position, noon or not, and my stance grew provocative, daring them to try.

They hesitated, glancing back at Doyle as if for instruction, but he was content to watch, and somehow, that made me more nervous.

"Come on, you stupid cat," I heard Jenks say, and then the tinkle of wind chimes as he rubbed his wings together. "O-okay . . ." he added, and then a startled "Hey!" before he shot out the door, a gray tabby in fast pursuit.

Jenks darted for the ceiling, inches ahead of the jumping feline. I sprang forward, snagging the cat and thanking all that was holy that the killing machine was partially declawed as he struggled. I gripped him tighter, clamping him to my body and refusing to let go. I'd never had much luck with cats though I liked them well enough. Al said they sensed the demon in me.

"Hey, Boots," I said as I fought for control, my gaze go-

ing from vampire to vampire as I held the struggling cat.
"Let's go see your mom."

But Doyle wasn't moving from the threshold.

"You're Rachel Morgan, right?" he said, still hunched
and hurting.

I turned my back on the other two, confident that Jenks
would tell me if they moved. I didn't think they would. Doyle
was interested in me, which meant hands-off to subordinate
vamps. Clearly I'd misread who was in charge downstairs.
"Yep," I said, forcibly petting the big-eyed, frantic cat.
"Sorry about the throat. It was either that or your nose, and I
figured you didn't want to bleed in front of everyone."

He nodded a slow thanks, but he didn't move, either toward me or away, and Jenks hovered closer, the snick of
him easing his sword from his scabbard dropping a chill
through me. "I'm trying to leave," I said, using my court-
useful words. "Are you preventing me from leaving? Hey,
you all see that he's barring my egress, right?"

Doyle glanced at Jenks, and then, with a smile that
wasn't nice at all, he shifted into the room so I could pass.
"You may leave," he said, and my gut tightened.

"Thank you." Back stiff, I walked past, breathing in
both his anger and his interest. Vampires were weird like
that, attracted to anyone who said no, especially when they
had the strength to back it up.

Jenks hummed a warning, and I jerked when Doyle
grabbed my biceps. I was in the hall, and I tensed, eyes
darting to his, hating that he saw my flash of fear. His smile
grew even more nasty, and he almost whispered, "You
should leave the city."

"Because I hit you?" I said, holding the cat between us
like a shield, almost.

"No." He looked me up and down, smile widening. "Because Constance likes to play with her food."

I stumbled back, almost falling, when he let go.

"That's your real warning," Doyle said, chin flicking to
tell me to leave.

"Great. Thanks." I backed to the stairway. Wary gazes tracked me silently from around doorjambs. I shifted my grip on the cat, hardly breathing as I found the stairs. "Is he following?" I asked, and the pixy landed on my shoulder despite the cat's face being five inches away.

"No. He's throwing Stef's couch out the window."

I glanced over my shoulder at the sound of a hefty groan. "It fits?" I asked, then jumped at the sound of splintering wood and grunt of anger.

"It does now," Jenks said sourly.

My eyes went to the bright spot of light at the end of the stair, drawn by the crack of the couch hitting the lawn and the rising awe of appreciation from the rubberneckers. Edden was still on the stoop. His mood was casual as he talked to his I.S. counterparts, but his relief was obvious as he saw me heading down.

"Nice talking to you," he said to them as he took control of the threshold, halfway in as he held a hand out to me. "Hey, if you want tickets to the FIB fundraiser for Bikes for Kids, let me know. I've got a pair for both of you. Lots of food, fun, novelty bike races."

"Uh, hey!" I exclaimed when Edden grabbed my elbow and yanked me out the door and down the three steps and back into the mid-March sun.

"Sweet Jesus," Edden muttered, grip hard on my elbow as Jenks grinned and flew circles around us. "I don't think I've ever been more scared for a person. I can't believe you went in."

"Someone had to get her cat," I said. "And if you didn't want me going in, why did you introduce me to her, knowing I'd do it?"

"I didn't know about the cat," he said, finally slowing as Stef rushed forward. Behind me, her dresser came crashing down. They were emptying out her apartment in an ugly show of privilege and bad manners, but she didn't seem to care as she reached for Boots and cuddled him close.

"Boots, oh, baby! Did they scare you?" she crooned, and

the cat settled into the woman's arms, his eyes wide and black.

Crap on toast, I thought as I brushed the cat hair from me. *I'm rescuing familiars.*

"Thank you so much," Stef gushed as she caressed the unhappy cat. "Thank you, Edden," she added, eyes bright, though he'd done nothing but keep open my way out. Which actually was a tremendous help. "I'm not much of a witch, but he means the world to me."

Stef's clothes came down next in an eerie flutter, her shoes hitting the grass in ominous thumps.

"I'm glad it worked out," Edden said. Then he turned to me and my smile faded. "Can I have a word with you?"

He hadn't wanted to introduce us so I'd get her cat. That left one thing.

"Oh, no!" Jenks said, figuring it out when I did. "Rachel, say no," he insisted. "We can't take in two strays. We already have a cat. Rex and Boots won't get along."

But Edden was tugging me away, turning me so I was sure to see Stef, poor, homeless Stef and her cat with nowhere to go. "What he said," I told Edden. "This is your problem, not mine. She came to you, not me. You take her in."

"I can't take her in, Rachel," he coaxed, hunched and plaintive. "Think how that would look. And I can't put her in any of the FIB's safe houses."

"I'm facing eviction in two weeks, too," I said, and he leaned closer, agitated.

"She'll have found something by then," he said with a forced brightness. "Maybe you could room together. Eh? I'd feel better if it was more than you and Jenks. You need people, Rachel, and she's good people. Give her a break."

"Stay *out* of my *life,* Edden," I said, then lowered my voice. "I can make my own friends, find my own roommates. Besides, being my roommate isn't good for anyone's health."

But I could see her behind Edden, trying to hold her cat and get her shoes at the same time. Her forehead was creased, and I could tell she was thinking about where she was going to sleep tonight. If I didn't take her in, she'd be living at the hospital, trying to hide her cat. "I suppose she and Boots could stay in the boat for a couple of weeks," I said, and Jenks smacked his forehead to make sparkles fall from him like rain.

"Great!" Edden beamed. "That's just great." Arms swinging, he strode to Stef. "Stephanie!" he called jovially. "Good news. I've got a place for you to stay. Short term," he added when Jenks faced him, dusting an ominous black. "Down by the waterfront. You like boats, right? Nice place in the Hollows."

I frowned. David had just said the same thing about the street our new place was on. Unfortunately I was still wearing the frown when Stef looked up, and I quickly forced a smile.

"Ah, thanks," she said, eyes darting. "I can't impose. Boots and I will find something."

But I remembered what it was like being kicked out, all your stuff ruined by the I.S. and on the curb. "Sure you can," I said, coming to take the cat so she could handle everything else. He settled into my arms with a token growl, and I beamed at her, tightening my grip so he wouldn't jump away. "Jenks and I could use the company. I'll introduce you to my real estate agent. If she found us something, she can find you something. I guarantee it."

"Sure," Jenks said, wings a low hum. "Rachel can tell you all about how the I.S. screwed her over. Cursed all her stuff. She had to live in a church with a vampire for three years, but look at her now!"

I stifled a wince, sending a pleasant surge of ley line warmth through Boots when Stef's plates and flatware came falling down like silver rain.

"Thanks." Stef's expression became tired as she cataloged the mess. "I really appreciate it. Word is, even the hotels are full."

"Damn junior baseball tournament," Jenks said, but it was too early for that. It was Constance. How many people was she bringing, anyway?

Boots finally stopped jamming his back claws into my gut, and I looked across the parking lot to see David standing guard over a group of Weres, overseeing them as their handcuffs were removed and they began carrying things from the lawn to the three small moving vans at the curb. He turned as if feeling my eyes on him, and I gave him a wave, getting one in return. We were good.

Apart from Doyle still chucking Stef's things out the window, it seemed to be over. "Let's get Boots settled. Edden can get your stuff in a van." I turned, smirking at his sudden alarm. "Right, Edden?" I said pointedly, and he nodded, knowing he owed me. Owed me big. "My car is three blocks down," I continued as I began to lead her away. "Edden will bring your stuff by the boat when they get done throwing it out the window. You've got your phone, right?" I said as I ducked under the tape.

She nodded, a numb look on her as reality set in. People parted before us, wary after seeing what I'd done to Doyle, and I gave her the cat, as she seemed to need something. The crowd thinned fast until it was just us and normal foot traffic, and I valiantly tried to keep the conversation going about her job (she was a nurse), Boots (a rescue from a few years back), anything to distract her, but finally I let her subside into a miserable quiet. Jenks was silent as well, his dust all but nonexistent as he sat on my big hoop earring and sulked. But I couldn't walk away. The I.S. was abusing their power and acting like a bully. Ignoring that wasn't who I was.

And as I spotted the three vamps in that brown Volvo following us a block behind, I hoped it wasn't going to get me killed.

CHAPTER

4

JENKS'S CONTINUED MOOD HAD ME WORRIED AS WE LEFT the busy street and turned to the waterfront and Piscary's old restaurant. He was sitting in his usual spot on the rearview mirror, his feet thumping the long glass as he kept an eye out my back window. Boots was watching him with black eyes. Stef's grip was tight on the cat, but it was in distress, not to protect Jenks.

Meeting my gaze, Jenks shrugged at my unspoken question of how much of a problem I had taken on. Stef seemed nice. She clearly had a good job and was reasonably even-tempered if this afternoon was any indication. But what if she liked listening to seventies music? There was only so much "Muskrat Love" I could handle.

But anthropomorphic rodents in lust vanished from my thoughts as my phone rang and Jenks dropped down, his cheerful wing chirp telling me he recognized the caller.

"Hey, blood bag!" the pixy shouted, having stomped on the accept icon. "How's it dripping?"

"God, Jenks. Give me that," I said, jerking my phone out from under him and giving Stef an apologetic smile. "Hi, Ivy. Everything okay?"

"We're great," Ivy said, her low, smooth voice filling the car with the memory of midnight and dust. "I saw the picture. Looks nice. Where is it?"

"It's a shopfront in downtown Hollows," Jenks said as he hovered in front of the phone, his dust making wild patterns on the screen. "I'll give you the tour if you two ever get your lily-white asses back here."

"That's actually why I'm calling. We hit a snag," she said, and I felt my smile fade.

Her voice had been light, but something in her tone pinged my intuition. *First Trent, then David. Now Ivy?* "How many were there?" I said, my grip tightening on the wheel. "And did they drive a brown Volvo?"

"Uh, yes," Ivy said, and Jenks's dust went thin. "There were four. All living vamps, though I doubt the one will make it out of the hospital alive. Nina didn't like his attitude."

She said it with pride, but my eyes pinched in worry.

"I would've called you sooner, but I didn't know there was a problem until I tried to come home for the first Howlers game." She hesitated. "How did you know they were in a brown Volvo?"

"Because they're in Cincy now." I turned my signal on with an aggressive flick, maintaining a smooth, unhurried pace around the corner to Piscary's. "Telling all my friends to back off from me and toe Constance's line."

"Huh." Ivy's voice went faint. "That's pretty much what they told Nina and me."

"And you're okay?" I said, wondering if Stef was reconsidering my offer for a park bench.

"Us? Oh, sure. We're fine," Ivy said. "But I doubt we'll be allowed to leave until you kick Constance to the curb. She's not well liked here and rumor has it she was sent to Cincinnati with the expectation that one of you would kill the other. Either result will please them. They don't care. Apparently her appetites are . . . disruptive, but she's too well connected for them to attempt any sort of correction."

I took a breath to protest, then let it out. "Constance is the city's master vampire," I said, and Stef's jaw clenched.

"And you're a demon," Ivy said. "Stop letting her walk all over you."

She made it sound so easy, and my shoulders slumped as I turned onto the weed-choked, cracked street to Piscary's. "At least I've got two weeks," I muttered.

"Ah, that's really why I'm calling," Ivy said, but I'd slowed, breath escaping me in a heavy sigh as I saw the onetime restaurant turned vampire lair. It was surrounded by the river on one side, space and abandoned warehouses everywhere else. Today, there were three moving vans parked in the expansive lot with lots of back-and-forth activity. Two of the vans were small local jobs, but one had to be at least forty-five feet long. *Constance . . . Son of a bastard.*

"I don't have two weeks, do I," I said flatly, and Ivy made a soft sound of negation.

"Jenks?" I said, lifting my chin for him to follow my gaze, and the pixy's dust vanished.

"Mother pus bucket," Jenks said, and Stef sighed. "What the troll turds on a stick is she doing here? We had two more weeks!"

My breath didn't seem to want to come back in, and I forced myself to breathe. *This is so not what I need right now.* "Okay. Ivy, I've got to go. You're sure you're okay?"

"From them? We're fine," she said as I crept up the seldom-used street. "Face it, Rachel," she added cheerfully. "All your friends are capable of handling ugly vampires. Nip this fast, will you? I've got Howler box seats this year."

"Why does everyone think Constance is my problem?" I muttered.

"Son of a fairy-farting whore." Jenks hovered before the window, the high pitch to his wings hurting my ears. "Edden did say they moved everything up."

But I didn't think Edden had known about this.

"Jenks, is she okay, or is she lying to herself?" Ivy said, and the pixy dropped to the phone, hands on his hips.

"Hang up, blood bag. I got this."

"I love you, too, sunflower sniffer," she shot back, and then the call ended.

"She sounds happy," Jenks said, and I absently nodded,

more concerned about where my stuff was. Muscular men were moving mostly light-colored, Scandinavian-style furniture in, and Ivy's and Nina's new, mostly dark-colored, comfortable, carefully selected furniture out.

"Well, thanks for the offer," Stef said, her voice surprisingly even as she held her cat closer. "Maybe I should have gotten myself arrested. I'd have somewhere to stay then."

Pulse fast, I looked for a place to park that was not too close, not too far. A few boxes sat beside the boat in the sun, and I stopped the car right in the middle of the lot, throwing it into park, grabbing my bag, and getting out. I didn't see any I.S. agents or rubberneckers, and the thought to call Trent flashed through me, making me angry. This was my problem.

"Give me a second to sort this out," I said as I looked back into my MINI at Stef.

"I'm good here," she said, and I carefully shut the door. I didn't blame her. The vampires milling about all looked cheerful and happy to be moving in, but the thick scars and thin bodies said there was a price to pay when your gnomon, or vampire master, was a long undead.

Jenks joined me, his dust an angry red. "At least they aren't chucking everything into the river," he said, and I flicked my attention to the pile by the boat, then back to the mass of beautiful people moving about with an air of excitement and promise.

Okay, they were treating everything with respect, but they were still forcibly moving me. Ivy's and Nina's things were slowly filling the two moving vans, furniture in one, boxes in the other. Some of my kitchen things were in there, too. *Bis,* I thought, stifling a moment of panic. They wouldn't know he was alive. They would have *packed* him like a knickknack.

"Pike," Jenks said, distracting me, and I followed his glare past the shifting people until I spotted him at the open loading dock. He had a clipboard in his hand and was clearly directing the inflow of Constance's stuff. Sensation rippled through me. Anger mostly, but damn . . . he looked good for a beaten-up, scarred, once-beautiful vampire. His black hair glistened in the sun, cut short to show the scars etched into his neck. Not quite tan, he nevertheless gave the impression of loving the sun as he stood on the loading dock in his short-sleeved black shirt and lightweight black slacks.

The woman with him jostled his elbow and he looked up. My slow pace bobbled as he found me, and I frowned, forcing myself to go a few more steps while he gave the woman his clipboard and a few instructions. He jumped to the pavement, taking the four-foot drop in stride. Hands in his pockets, he started over, wind deliciously ruffling his hair. Behind him, the woman whistled and pointed, and two movers resting in the shade of one of the small trucks pushed off and headed to the boat.

Pike *looked* meek as he took off his dark glasses and tucked them in a front shirt pocket, smiling at me with his lips closed as he approached, but I knew he was anything but. Not if he was Constance's scion, and it was obvious that he was the undead vampire's number one, responsible for seeing that her bidding was done when the sun was up.

Pike might have been beautiful once, but it was gone now, lost under the scars. They were at his wrists, his neck, and undoubtedly under his expensive, black, silver-threaded shirt. His confidence was absolute, and it pulled at me even as I refused to let it take hold and sway me.

"You okay, Rache?" Jenks said.

"Fine."

"Your pulse just shot up, and your temperature—"

"You want to make sure they don't throw out your food stocks? Ask them where they put Bis, while you're at it," I interrupted, and Jenks hovered backward, eyeing me.

"Sure." Hesitating, he rose up. "Tink-blasted Rachel candy," he muttered as he gave me a last, wary look and flew to the two movers standing over the boxes by the boat.

Pike's smile widened to show his sharp but small canines. The sun was in his face, and I could tell it bothered him as he squinted. He'd been sipping too much undead blood to feel comfortable under the noon sun, but he tried. I could see it in the way he moved, silky smooth and without a wasted motion. He drifted to a halt before me, a suggestive question in the back of his eyes as he looked me up and down.

Sensation plinked through me, breathless like silver fire. I hadn't allowed myself to enjoy that mix of allure and danger since Kisten, and I quashed it, blaming it on wading through the pheromones at Stef's apartment.

"Rachel," he said, and I locked my knees, shocked. Damn. He'd been doing more than sipping. "I tried to get ahold of you this morning," he said, his lips quirking into a knowing smile as he saw what he'd done to me with just his voice. "Maybe I have a bad number."

Stupid-ass vamp pheromones, I thought, hating that I looked like a pushover. "I don't answer my phone unless I know who it is," I said, then cleared my throat. The two movers with Jenks had their arms full of boxes and were heading to the car. "I've got two more weeks according to my eviction notice. What gives?"

Pike shifted to get his face out of the sun. "Constance moved up her plans. The prep is done. No need to wait."

"I've seen your prep," I said, remembering that I was angry, not infatuated. "It's sitting in my back seat, homeless."

Pike's lip twitched. Clearly he didn't care. "I took the liberty of clearing out the boat. We're taking possession of that today as well. It's better for everyone that way." His gaze went from my car to the moving vans. He had shifted closer, and the scent of dusky incense plucked a long-fallow chord. "Ivy and Nina asked me to move their things to storage as well."

A flash of fear lit through me, and his eyes darkened as he sensed it. I wasn't afraid for me, but he didn't know that. "I swear—"

"Yes, I've noticed that about you," he interrupted. "Vocabulary can make or break you, don't you think? That and what we choose to wear."

"Really? That's where you want to start?" I said as he looked me up and down again. I'd had just about enough of his slick-vampire attitude. He was getting away with breaking the law, sending a poker-hot jab into my sense of fair play. Breath held, I took a step forward to give him a piece of my mind, only to drop back when Jenks darted up between us.

"The boat is cleared out, Rache," the pixy said, angry enough for both of us. "Where's my food stores, fang boy?"

"Fang boy?" Pike's amusement faded when Jenks touched his sword hilt, wings rasping in threat. "Everything in the fridge was packed in a temperature-controlled box," he said, voice edged in warning. "First van."

Jenks flew off in search, his dust lingering to look like a touchable sunbeam. The movers with my stuff had dropped their load and were going back for more. "Pike, this isn't right, and you know it," I said, trying to be pleasant, but he was taller than me, and it ticked me off that I had to look up at him. "I need the boat for a few more weeks. I'll stay out of your hair. No wild parties. Promise," I finished, but it sounded sarcastic to even me.

"No," he said flatly. "You've had three months to find new lodgings. Not my problem."

Stymied, I took a breath and he turned his big, pupil-black, fully dilated eyes on me, stifling my protest.

"And if you make it my problem, you will find my fee too large to pay," he added.

My car door slammed and I jumped. Stef had gotten out. She was still holding her cat, and she watched the movers set two more boxes down by the car and go back for the rest.

Face warm, I backed up, not caring if he knew I was cowed. There'd been real threat in those words, the ability to enforce it coming not from Constance's borrowed power but his own, hard-won and eager to be exerted. "You might be surprised at how big my bank of clout is," I said, chin raised.

"Would I?" he mocked, and then his eyes shifted to the street, his expression blanking.

I turned as well, wondering what Pike was uptight about. It was only a man dressed in a suit standing beside a black car, almost hidden beside one of the abandoned warehouses. I'd say he was from the paper even if his car was too sleek for your average reporter. It made sense. Who wouldn't go out on a limb to get an interview with the new master vamp?

"You should close your mouth and say thank you that your knickknacks and witchy charms aren't being left on the curb," Pike said, and my frown deepened at the faint, sour scent of angry vamp now rising from him. "Ivy paid for this with her blood. Be grateful."

"If you hurt her . . ." I threatened, weight on my toes, and he laughed, the bitter sound bringing everyone to a standstill for one eerie moment.

"Me?" His hands went into his pockets. "Not me."

I could do nothing, and frustration bubbled up. "This is harassment."

"No, it's reality," Pike said, his mood bad, clearly done with me as he flicked another glance at the watching man. "The entire city is being reorganized. Rather egotistical of you to assume it's to put a chip in your fang." He turned away, then immediately spun back. "You, Rachel, have been living in city-deeded property for six months, rent free. Piscary's belongs to Cincinnati's master vampire. Get out."

I blinked, shocked at the softly erotic sensation as he said my name. "I don't like you," I said, and he shrugged and turned from me. "I'm not leaving Cincinnati!" I called after him.

"You may not have a choice!" he shot back over his shoulder, and I took three steps after him before I jerked to a halt. He was walking away. I should let him go. Following an angry vampire was saying, "Bite me, I'm yours."

"Is that a threat?" I said loudly, my feet planted solidly on the pavement.

No surprise, he stopped and turned. "God no," he said, smiling again, though it hid his anger now whereas before it had only been fake. "It's only . . ." He glanced to where the watching man had been, the space now empty, then back to me. "You won't find any room in Cincinnati for a witch-born demon to rest her head." He looked at my car and Stef standing beside it. "Anywhere, and especially not in the Hollows."

I closed the gap between us, stifling my anger so I wouldn't set him off. The thought flicked through me that perhaps Constance was actively behind the trouble I'd had closing a deal, not just passively by way of her peeps needing space. If so, she had failed. "Is that so?"

Pike put a hand on his waist. He leaned in, head tilted, and I held my breath so I wouldn't breathe in the delicious scent of frustrated vampire. "Here's my advice, though I know you won't take it," he said, eyes black as my anger and confidence hit him hard and he struggled with his instincts. "Constance is coming in tonight. You have this one instant in time to graciously back down. Save yourself a lot of money and maybe your life. Leave. Get out of town." He straightened, eyes fixed on mine. "Go live with your rich boyfriend and make spells."

"Wow, condescending much?" I said, and his eyes narrowed.

He tossed the keys of the van to me, and I fumbled, almost dropping them. "Put Ivy's stuff in storage, will you?"

"I'm not your lackey. Do it yourself," I said, flinging them right back at him.

He caught them in one raised hand, and I turned away before my anger and frustration tipped him over the edge. There was an art to arguing with a vampire, and I'd had enough practice with Ivy to know when to walk away. I'd pushed Pike further than I'd feel comfortable going with Ivy, but Pike wasn't a slave to his bloodlust as Ivy was. Had been. She was better now.

Playing with Pike would be . . . amazing, I thought, immediately dismissing it.

Lips pressed, I stomped past a wide-eyed Stef to the back of my car. "Go live with my rich boyfriend," I muttered as I opened the rear door and put the boxes inside. Waving for Stef to wait, I went to the van. "Make spells," I added as I levered myself inside to find Jenks darting over the clutter, clearly looking for something. "This is hot, pink fairy crap," I griped as I opened a box marked *Kitchen* and took out my spelling bowl, salt, and ceramic spoons. The splat balls I left, not knowing if they had been tampered with.

"Did you find Bis?" I all but snarled, and Jenks's expression shifted from worry to anger.

"They put him in a box," Jenks said bitterly. "The moss wipes."

Moss wipes was rather benign, with the way I was feeling, and I ripped the tape off the box he was hovering over.

My shoulders slumped and the anger washed away as I found the kid nestled among the packing peanuts, the bottle that held his soul right beside him. His skin was a dull white, and his eyes were closed, wings clamped tight about his body curved into a fetal position. I'd say he was dead, but his skin was warm and his tail curled around my wrist as I lifted him free.

Heartache slammed into me, and my gut clenched. *Son of a bastard,* I thought as I held the cat-sized gargoyle close and tucked the bottle in a pocket. This wasn't going to bring me down, but it hurt. It hurt bad.

Bis in my arms, I looked out the open van to see Pike vanishing into the dark confines of the back loading dock. His voice was raised in anger, shouting for someone to bring up the cat before I left.

"They caught Rex!" Jenks exclaimed, but his excitement faltered and he looked at Stef and Boots. Jenks's cat had been lurking in the lower levels of Piscary's for months. I hadn't been about to go down looking for him. I figured if his food was vanishing and the litter box needed to be cleaned, he was doing fine.

"Let's hope they put him in a box, too," I said as I held Bis in one arm and gathered my spelling bowl with the other.

Jenks landed on my shoulder as I made the jump to the ground and back into the sun. "Where are we going, Rache? David? He likes cats."

My thoughts went to Trent. He wouldn't care if I camped out at his place for a few days even if I brought a guest with me, but Pike's crack about going to live with my rich boyfriend and make spells pissed me off.

"The church," I said, and Jenks's wing hum faltered for a second. "For now," I added as we went to my car and I dropped my spelling bowl, salt, and spoons in with the rest.

I felt as if I'd lost more than a place to live as I got in the car, slammed my door, put on my belt, and sat there, hands on the wheel and Bis on my lap as I waited for them to "bring up the cat." Jenks darted about, nervously checking on everything as Stef slowly got in, somehow managing the increasingly annoyed Boots and her seat belt both. "I'm sorry," she said, and I unclenched my jaw. "I guess we're both screwed."

I started my car and smiled at her, but it was forced. "Not yet," I said, smile faltering as I saw the vampires toting in an elaborately carved headboard that had to be Constance's. The scratches and iron rings kind of gave it away. "I'm sure my Realtor can arrange for us to stay at the space Jenks and I just put money down on. Most sellers will let you pay rent until you take possession. Until then, we can camp out at the church."

"Church?" Stef's hand soothing Boots halted. "The one that blew up last summer?"

"That's the one."

"It's got a new roof," Jenks added as I tracked a woman in a flowing white dress coming across the parking lot. She had a cat carrier, which would make things easier, and Jenks flew out of the car to make sure Rex got in the rear seat okay.

"It was only the back half that blew up," I said. "We'd be in it now, but it's been a devil of a time finding a contractor to put in . . . a . . . kitchen." My thoughts swirled as the woman opened the back door and slid Rex in, Jenks all the while crooning at the irate cat through the little holes. Constance wanted me out of Cincy. Was she why we couldn't find a contractor? *Son of a fairy-farting whore . . .*

"Ah, can you get along without a kitchen for a few days?" I asked Stef as the door to the back shut. Jenks hovered outside, talking with the woman about where Rex's food was, and I started the car. *We can stop on the way home and get more, Jenks. Let's go. . . .*

"As long as I get coffee in the morning," Stef said. "It's only for a few days, right? I can do anything for a few days."

Nodding, I put the car in drive and headed for the street, my anger dulling to a hard certainty that this wasn't over. I wasn't sure where the money would come from to rent out the shopfront until we closed, but Jenks and I would find it. Damn it all to hell. I'd had this until someone started taking things they had no right to take.

Only a few days, I silently agreed as I drove to the church. But "a few days" was exactly what I'd thought four years ago.

CHAPTER

5

THANK THE EVER-LOVING LEY LINES THAT I'VE GOT MY CAR, I thought. The dappled shade was pleasant as I drove down the quiet, residential Hollows street with the back full of my stuff and an unhappy cat. Up front, Stef stared out the window, silent in thought. A to-go bag of sub sandwiches and a tray with two cooling coffees sat between us. The car was full, warm, and smelling of coffee, and I didn't know how I would have coped without it. The car, that is, though going without coffee would have put me on the nonstop, fun-sponge train to Pissy Town.

Jenks spilled a contented gold dust as he dozed on the rearview mirror, having missed his usual four-hour nap around noon. Which sent my thoughts to Trent and the girls sleeping their way to Seattle. He hadn't been gone even a day yet, and I already missed his calm, certain presence—though if he'd been around, I'd probably still be at Piscary's with Trent's lawyer, arguing about legal loopholes rather than on the way to the church to regroup and have some lunch. Arguing wasn't going to change the situation. Not when Constance owned the I.S.

The memory of Pike's black-eyed, tantalizing anger as he walked away sent a stab of desire-tainted guilt through me, and my grip tightened on the wheel. It felt as if I'd cheated on Trent somehow, though it had been one hundred percent vampire pheromones that had lit me up. Maybe it was because I kind of enjoyed the erotic danger he was in a backassward sort of way. It had been a long time since I'd teased a living vampire, and Pike was skilled at holding his instincts in check, making him an easy target and fun to play with.

A smile quirked my lips, and I shushed Rex growling at Boots. I was still wearing it when I turned down my old street and my shoulders slumped. It felt like coming home, but the new place would, too, eventually. I'd moved before.

But never from somewhere where I've changed so much, become someone whom I really like, I thought as I slowed to take in the changes on the street.

"I'm sorry about this," Stef said, clearly misreading my soft sigh.

"Hey, I should be apologizing to you," I said, and Jenks stirred, stretching to make his wings shudder and sift dust. "I offer you a place to stay that dries up, and then you buy me lunch?"

"It's the least I could do," she said as she struggled with Boots. "This is a nice street."

I nodded, remembering being dragged down it in the ice and snow, terrified when Al had tried to abduct me. The danger had been real, which made the demon being my admittedly on-the-outs friend now even better.

My smile became fond as I looked up at the steeple and recalled ringing the bell for the kids every Halloween. I was going to miss seeing them on our front steps begging for candy and tomatoes. But then my smile faded. I'd found Ivy blood-raped on those very same steps.

My hand dropped to cup around Bis in my lap. *What the hell am I doing back here?*

One-handed, I pulled into the carport and hit the brake inches from ramming the end of it. *Practice . . . thou art my shield and sword.* "Here we are," I said, and Stef unclicked her seat belt. "The front door is probably open. Jenks, you want me to take in your food stocks? The contractors' dorm fridge was still there the last I checked." The work crew had left their paint-spotted, dust-caked boom box, too, and a cassette of Johnny Cash's greatest hits. *Weres . . .*

"Thanks, sure," Jenks said, surprising me, but an odd realization made my stomach hurt. Constance blacklisting me explained why even David hadn't been able to convince them to come back. It hadn't been the six pentagrams on the pool table that had chased them away. It had been Constance.

"Hey, Stef. You think Boots and Rex might use the same box?" Jenks asked as he rose up. "Or we could put a cat door out to the backyard. Rex is an outside cat," he added proudly.

A cat door sounded rather permanent for two weeks, but I wasn't four inches tall and had trouble with knobs.

"Boots is an inside cat," Stef said as she got out, then hesitated, leaning to look back at me—seeing as I hadn't made a single motion to get out yet.

"I'll be right there," I said as I waved them on. "I want to let Rex out. And I should probably text Edden to bring your stuff here and not Piscary's. Jenks can show you the place." *Or what's left of it,* I thought sourly. "I'll bring the sandwiches. Your hands are full."

Stef's expression shifted to relief. "Thanks." Baby-talking to Boots, she headed with Jenks for the front steps, her soft-soled hospital shoes silent on the shady, cracked sidewalk. I watched them, glad that the offerings of food and flowers that had once adorned our door had slacked off. There was just a handful of wilted, handpicked daisies, and I hadn't been out here for a week. Boots's tail was switching. He was clearly done with being held. Stef had been holding him the better part of an hour. She was a good cat-mom.

"Speaking of which," I said as I gently shifted Bis to the now-vacant front seat. His tail had curled around my wrist again, and my breath caught in heartache as I disentangled it. "Hey, Rex," I said, forcing my voice light and airy as I got out to open the back door and pull the cat closer.

The orange tabby leapt out as soon as I opened the carrier, his ears alert as he sniffed my fingertips and got his bearings. Tail high, the young tom sauntered to the backyard, easily making the jump to the top of the fence, where he stared at me and cleaned his ears.

"That's my good boy," I said, resigned to the little love I ever got from the cat. Leaning against the car, I breathed in the cool damp and closed my eyes, letting the peace soak in. They flashed open at an almost ultrasonic complaint. Rex was gone, probably terrorizing whatever pixy had taken up residence in Jenks's garden.

I reached for my phone and large shoulder purse, dropping Jenks's stuff and the bag of takeout into it. One-handed, I quickly texted Edden to bring Stef's stuff to the church.

"Why?" he immediately texted back.

The pleasure that I was again on speaking terms with Edden vanished. I frowned, started a message, then erased it. I'd tell him when he got here.

"Coming back to the church is not a failure. It's temporary," I said as I jammed the phone in a back pocket and carefully lifted Bis into my arms. The tray with the coffee went in my other hand, and with my heavy shoulder bag making me walk funny, I headed up the front path.

I couldn't help but compare the church to the other properties we'd been looking at. It had great overnight street parking along with the covered carport. The lot ran deep to give tons of room, stretching all the way to the next street over. Mature trees made lots of shade, and the bus ran right past the far end of the graveyard.

"Yard is a lot of work," I whispered, eyeing last year's leaves still in the fallow flower beds. Not to mention that the front door only locked from the inside. But after seeing the expired charms on the storefront, putting in a few of my own here was an option.

I struggled to not spill the coffee as I bent to get the wilted daisies. The sign over the door with all our names on it was bittersweet. I'd paid a guy three hundred bucks one winter solstice to put it and the light over the door so everyone could see we were here, day or night.

I nudged the door open with my foot, closing it with a backward kick before Boots, hiding under the pool table, could even think to run out. Jenks and Stef were in one of the bedrooms, their voices too soft to hear words. "Hi, sweetie," I crooned to the cat. "We'll get your box up soon." But all I got was the cat-stare.

The sanctuary was dim with all but one of the stained-glass windows broken and boarded up. Ivy's baby grand piano was shoved in a corner, forgotten, and I set the daisies on Kisten's de-felted and de-bumpered pool table. It wasn't much more than an enormous single piece of slate with holes now, still sporting the chalk lines of the last curses I'd twisted on it. Hodin hadn't put the table back the way he'd found it, and now I was too angry with him to insist.

Somehow, I felt as if Kisten's table was indicative of my life and the damage I wrought on everyone around me. Because of me, a perfectly good table wasn't usable for its intended purpose. Likewise, because of me, Kisten had died because he had stood up to Piscary, becoming the man I knew he was—and then dying for it.

Head down, I went to the low stage that had once held the altar. The hole was still in the middle of the floor, covered by a sheet of plywood. Even so, there was tons of room to practice my martial arts. The ceiling was tall, beautiful with exposed rafters dark against the ceiling. I could almost hear pixy kids singing up there in my memory. Ivy's abandoned furniture was covered in sawdust, and I set my bag on the long, low coffee table. It was made of slate, too, thanks to Hodin magicking the glass to stone. Sharron would call this a "unique" property with "renovation challenges." Meaning it was a church you couldn't occupy without a massive rebuild.

But even with the kitchen gone, the sanctuary had been a pleasant place to both interview clients and spell in.

There'd been no need to reroute the gas or electric lines to make a secure circle. *So why did I feel so unprofessional in it?* I wondered as I ran a finger across the chalk lines still lingering on the coffee table.

I was talking myself from a bad mood to downright depressed, and I set Bis on one of the chairs. Jenks's and Stef's words were a soft murmur as I put Jenks's food into the tiny fridge and turned it from half-frozen beer to root-cellar cool. I took the bag of sandwiches out of my bag, hesitating before setting it on the dusty table. I didn't want to eat in the dark when there was a perfectly good picnic table only half burned in the garden.

But even as I thought it, I remembered how the sun used to spill into the sanctuary all day. If you could look past the construction filth, there were a lot of pluses to living here. *Minuses, too,* I thought. Even the graveyard wasn't looking quite so bad anymore.

"It's Ivy's old room," I heard Jenks say clearly, and I picked the coffee tray back up. "There's a cot in the belfry you and Rache can bring down. I know it's not much, but it's better than sleeping under a cabbage leaf."

"What about Rachel?" Stef asked as I strode past the his-and-her bathrooms long since converted into a bath/laundry and a more traditional full bath.

"It's his church," I said as I eased to a halt and looked in on the tiny, empty ten-by-ten. "So whatever he says is good with me. My room is across the hall." I eased out of the threshold, remembering my mom's phobia about liminal spaces. "There's two bathrooms, so take your pick. I'd show you the rest, but the kitchen and living room are gone, and the belfry is being used for storage. This is kind of it. Except for the graveyard."

Stef began to blink fast, her eyes reddening from more than the cat hair coating her. "Thank you so much," she choked out, and then, dropping her head into her hand, she began to quietly cry. "I don't even have a toothbrush, and I'm so grateful that Boots and I aren't on the street. You guys are being so nice, and you don't have any reason to be."

Jenks flew up, clearly embarrassed. Coming closer, I gave him a dark look. "What?" he complained. "I told her she could set up a cot."

But I remembered what it was like to have the world take everything, leaving you with ugly, empty spaces where comfort had once been. Ivy had made a place for me to gather myself and make a new beginning. Okay, Ivy had had ulterior motives, but that hadn't lessened what it had meant to me. Stef needed the same. She looked like a giver, not a taker. She wouldn't overstay her welcome.

"Hey, it's okay," I said as I came close and gave her an awkward, supportive hug, the bag of subs crackling as it hit her back. "If you don't mind the dust, we've got the room. The bus runs past the east side of the graveyard into Cincy if Edden doesn't have your toothbrush."

"Yeah." Jenks hovered close. "Rache knows the schedule. She went an entire year without a car. And then months without a license until the DMV put demon as an option on the application."

Stef stiffened and I let go, dropping back as she sniffed, looking at the ceiling as if embarrassed. "Look at me," she said with a rueful laugh. "I'm a mess. I should call work and let them know I'm okay. The last they knew, I was flying out the door."

"Okay, sure." I edged away until I hit the doorframe. "The room is yours for as long as you need it or the city kicks us out for not having a dwelling permit. Whatever happens first."

"Thanks again." Stef looked over the tiny room still smelling faintly of vampire as she took her phone from her pocket. "I'll probably head into Cincinnati later. Find out when the bus hits the hospital from here."

"Sounds good." I retreated into the hallway to give her some privacy. "Sandwiches will be in the backyard when you're ready. Jenks, you may want to check out the garden," I added when he showed no signs of leaving. "I heard Rex scare up some pixies."

"Yeah, I saw them," he muttered, his dust shifting a

middling gray and red of indecision and anger. "They know better than to be here."

"Well, be nice, okay?" I said, knowing it would be hard as they were trespassing and he was very garden-proud. Stef was already on her phone, giving me a distracted wave as Jenks and I headed down the hall to the temporary back door.

He probably had a pixy-hole somewhere he could use to get outside, but he waited, humming at head height as I juggled the coffee and sandwiches and worked the make-shift latch. Finally the door swung out and the sun and cool breeze flowed in, shifting my hair and going all the way to the belfry to stir the dust. It was as if the church had taken a cleansing breath, and I stood where I was, gazing out past the drop and into the early spring garden and long-grassed graveyard.

Jenks rasped his wings, darting to the group of pixies who had circled Rex.

"Be careful!" I called, and his dust flickered red.

"I'm not going to be eaten by my own cat, woman!"

I hadn't been talking about the cat. Jenks was one sword to their many, and though pixies generally didn't fight other pixies for land, it *was* a large, productive garden. *Remind me again why we're trading it for a few roof boxes?*

Someone, a construction worker, presumably, had put a fifty-five-gallon drum on end as a step. That got me part-way down, and from there, a couple of stones taken from the busted-up foundation got me to the damp earth.

My expression eased as I picked my way through the remaining foundation to the cement pad that once held our back steps. There were tiny leaves opening up on the oak tree that shaded the picnic table, and a smile flickered over me. It had survived. I hadn't been sure. It might be worth breaking my silence with Al to ask him if there was a curse to mend it.

A blessed contentment rose through me as I set the coffee and sandwiches on the burned table and eased my back-side onto the slightly damp bench. "Coffee and BLT," I whispered as I unwrapped the crackling paper, happy with this one moment in time. My eyes closed as I took my first bite, the tart tomato going perfectly with the extra bacon the guy had put on for me.

Until my phone rang, ruining it.

Sighing, I wrangled my phone from my pocket. If it was Edden, I was going to let it go to voice mail. But it was Sharron, and, quickly swallowing, I hit the accept icon and put her on speaker. "Sharron!" I exclaimed, and from across the garden, Jenks turned from his on-the-wing parley. "I'm glad you called." I shifted down the bench until I found the drier boards in the sun. "What are the chances that we can rent out our new space until the closing date?"

I heard Sharron take a breath, then nothing.

"Sharron?" I said hesitantly.

"I'm here," she finally said, but her tone made me more worried, not less. "I'm a little embarrassed. And a lot mad, actually. We had a verbal agreement, and when I took it over for signature, they backed out. You just don't *do* that."

My lips parted, and my eyes went across the garden to Jenks. "They backed out?" I said loudly, and the pixy darted to me. I could not believe this. We'd lost another place.

Or had we? I thought, my anger sharpening as I remembered Pike's words. This wasn't happenchance. This was Constance.

"I'm so mad I could chew nails and spit rust," Sharron was saying, and I mouthed to Jenks, "We lost the storefront."

"That's a fairy-farting troll's turd bucket," Jenks swore, his dust shifting to an angry red.

"Sharron," I interrupted, but she was on a roll.

". . . so unprofessional," she was saying. "I can't believe Bob did this to me. To you."

"Sharron," I tried again. "It's not his fault. It's Constance, the incoming city master vampire." The woman's tirade cut off comically fast, and I added, "She doesn't want me in the Hollows or Cincinnati, and I think she's buying up or threatening everyone to not sell or rent to me." *Or come out and fix the church,* I thought sourly.

"Oh, no," she moaned in sudden understanding. "Maybe I shouldn't have reamed Bob out. We'll find something before you get evicted. Even if it's someone's basement."

Which, as I sat in the sun and felt the earth come awake around me, sounded as appealing as, well, living in a basement. "Actually, it's kind of a moot point at the moment," I said, gaze flicking to Jenks. "Jenks and I were forcibly evicted from Piscary's. We're camped out at the church. It's okay, actually," I said when she made an unhappy noise, surprised to find "okay" wasn't a wish, but true. "As long as the city doesn't come down on us for the lack of a dwelling permit. Do you know of any contractors who aren't in the area that might come out here? I think I've been blackballed there, too. I'm hoping that the city can't force me out if I'm showing that I'm trying to get a kitchen put in. We've got zero chance of selling it without one, too."

"I'll give Finley a call," Sharron said. "She's pricey, but worth it. She's been on the West Coast the last few years doing renovations on TV, but she's back and is looking for something real to sink her teeth into. I'll shoot you her number if she's interested."

Something real? With our itty-bitty budget? I thought, wincing at the missing back end of the church. All I wanted was to make it easier to sell. "Ah, Sharron?"

"This is wrong," she was saying, not listening. "We have laws against this."

"That depends who you ask," I said bitterly. Then I brightened in a wicked thought. "Hey, could you do something for me?"

"If I can."

I glanced at Jenks, torn between me and those pixies, his hands on his hips. "You know the old biolabs on the west side of Cincinnati?"

"By the abandoned hospital? Sure," she said. "But you don't want anything over there. The cleanup cost to remove the contamination from the Turn puts it way out of your reach. The buyer is responsible for paying for it."

Hence no one doing anything with it for forty-plus years. "That's them. Could you check into it anyway? Lot sizes, available utilities. Don't make a lot of noise about it."

"I can;" she said, sounding unsure. "But why? What she's doing isn't legal. If you can prove it, it will stop."

"Just looking into all my options," I said, then stuck a pinky into my coffee and warmed it with a stray thought.

"Okay, but even a small lot at the edge is cost prohibitive."

"I might ask Trent to help with the finances," I lied. "Isn't there a creek that runs through there? That would be nice." *And really, really expensive to clean up . . .*

"I'll see what I can do," she said distantly, and then the screen blanked.

I wasn't going to live or work at the outskirts of a plague-created dead zone, but if Constance was going to buy up the property I was interested in, I may as well make her do a few city improvements. Costly improvements. "You mess with the witch, you get the broomstick," I said, my gaze rising to Jenks and the eight raggedy pixies facing him.

Seeing him still there, I wondered if he was considering letting them stay in return for upkeep. It would be both amazing and unheard-of in pixy culture, but Jenks was used to breaking tradition, having survived past Matalina's death. Not to mention the garden really needed it.

I truly owed Jenks a huge debt. Ivy had installed the garden years ago in the hopes of luring me to live here, which it had, but Jenks and his family had been the ones keeping it up. Whoever Ivy had contracted to put it in had done it right, and the city garden space had everything from the staples of willow and fern, yarrow and yew, to the more exotic and esoteric plants like moonflower and wolfsbane. The graveyard had the messy, wild plants like Queen Anne's lace, chicory, plantain, and even poison ivy. I actually had a lakeside daisy growing on a limestone grave marker where no one could see it, and rue outside the gate for easy pilfering—because to be effective, rue had to be stolen. I got mine from the Cincy Botanical Garden. They kept it by the curb. Otherwise, witches might be tempted to take more than the rue.

My gaze rose to the back door as Stef came out, blinking at the bright light. "I've got the week off to find a place," she said, head down and straight auburn hair swinging as she managed the chancy steps. "It might be easier to deal with this if I had work as a distraction. Otherwise it's going to bug the hell out of me."

Jenks rejoined me as Stef settled herself across and down a little, her eyes on the graveyard. "Rache, you mind?" the pixy said, indicating the coffee, and I opened the lid for him.

"So what's with the pixy clan?" I said as he dipped some out into his pixy-size cup.

Jenks turned red. Stef hesitated as she noticed, the paper crackling as she opened her sandwich. "I'm letting them stay if they keep up the graveyard," he muttered, now sitting on the edge of my cup to enjoy the warm steam. "I'm taking their patriarch, Baribas, on a tour in about an hour to tell him what plants you need in good repair. The backyard garden and the oak tree are mine, though," he said, and I smiled at his territorial tone. Understandable when your life depended on what a small scrap of ground could produce and there was seldom enough for everyone. Evolution had made him what he was: a savage warrior poet who I trusted with my life.

"I'm proud of you, Jenks," I said, and his wings flashed red.

"I could use the help and they don't have anywhere to go. The entire family was turned out. You know that park over on Edison?"

"The one they bulldozed for the theater parking?" Stef said, then made a face at her cold coffee. "How come yours is still warm?" she said, and I touched the cup to make the brew steam. "Oh, wow. I don't know anyone who can do that."

"I can show you if you're any good with ley lines," I offered, and her eyes widened.

"I'm letting them stay until they find something," Jenks grumped, clearly embarrassed.

Which might not happen, I thought. But maybe Jenks could make the situation permanent when we moved out of the church. God! Constance was screwing everything up. The Weres were unhappy as their traditional borders were squeezed. What was left of Piscary's vampires were really unhappy as they were poised to lose whatever clout they had under Ivy and Nina. And the witches were unhappy, being the easiest group to displace as Constance's people moved in, soaking up or taking all the good housing.

I picked at my sandwich, eating the bacon first. "I'm failing to see how Constance moving in is helping anyone," I said. Between the pixies and Stef, the church was making good on its all-but-forgotten status as a paranormal shelter—which I thought funny since it wasn't livable.

"Yeah." Jenks's dust had shifted to an almost blinding white under the caffeine. "We were handling everything fine without a city master vampire. Who needs a master vampire when you've got a resident demon?"

"Dali?" I said in confusion, and Stef's eyes flicked to mine, telling me she'd heard of him. "What does he care?"

Jenks laughed himself off the rim of my cup. "I'm talking about you, witch." He dropped down and sliced a corner of tomato off my sandwich for himself. "Cincy's vamps heard what you did to San Francisco. They're toeing the Tink-blasted line, baby!"

"What did you do to San Francisco?" Stef asked, her forehead pinched in worry.

Jenks opened his mouth, and I knocked the underside of the table with my knee to get him to shut up. He flew up, laughing. "Tell you later," he said. "You. Me. Some hot chocolate."

"Deal," Stef said, but I didn't like Jenks thinking that it had been me, not Ivy and Nina, keeping them in line. It had been Ivy. She knew what to do, who to talk to, what nose to break to make things right. Everything. She'd been strong-arming Cincinnati under Piscary for the last ten years or so. It had probably been easier without him mucking it up with his needs and demands. That things were copacetic while she was in DC only meant they knew she'd bust heads if they made trouble when she was gone.

But even so, it bugged the heck out of me that Constance thought she could force me out. This was my home, damn it. And as I eyed the weed-choked garden, I had an idea.

"Jenks?" I said, and he pulled his gaze back from the pixies following Rex through the graveyard at a careful four feet. "Did any of those Easter lilies under Ivy's window survive her last 'cleansing'?"

He snickered. "There might be a few bulblets she missed. Why?"

I took a sip of coffee, feeling it bringing me alive, back to the witch I used to be. "She tore them out because she couldn't stand the smell, right?"

Nodding, Jenks watched the pixies. "I have yet to meet the vampire who likes lilies." His gaze returned to me. "It reminds them of funerals."

My head bobbed, and I wrapped up the remainder of my sandwich. "Can you show me where they are? I want to make Constance a welcome-to-Cincinnati housewarming gift."

Stef snorted, almost choking on her coffee. "You want to give her flowers?" she said in disbelief, but Jenks was laughing.

"Tink's contractual hell, yes!" he exclaimed. "It's about time. Edden and I had a bet going as to how much you were going to take before you smeared her nose in a little Rachel Morgan justice." His wing hum quickened. "I won."

Justice. That was a good name for it. Rachel Morgan justice. Filling Constance's quarters with the smell of lilies couldn't be traced back to me—if I did it right—but she'd know. And maybe she'd back off a little. It was perfect. Annoyance without any actual threat. Jenks said that was one of my best skill sets.

"You're making a spell?" Stef said, her hazel eyes wide. "Can I help? I owe her."

I froze. She was a warlock. It would be like a five-year-old helping mommy in the kitchen, slowing things down and increasing the cleanup. But seeing her eager, not-nice smile, I changed my mind.

"Sure," I said, and she beamed. "If you're going to be here for a while, you should know a little magic."

"Yeah. A little magic will increase your life span around Rache," Jenks said, and I flicked a drop of coffee at him. Laughing, he rose up and buzzed off to find the new resident pixies to help him dig up the bulbs.

But he was right. A little magic would help keep Stef alive.

CHAPTER

6

THE BELFRY WAS IN BETTER SHAPE THAN I REMEMBERED, stuffy now that the original open-air vents had been replaced with double-paned windows. The eight walls, once clapboard and studs, had been insulated and painted a neutral off-white, but the floor was the original wide, underfloor plank. Wayde had made the improvements over a year ago, creating a snug place to be where he could stay out of my hair and do his bodyguard thing both. It was his cot that was down in Stef's room. Even without it, the space was cramped, boxes from my room and the boat stacked on all sides. Books, mostly.

It was Wayde who'd fastened the big shelf under the bell for Bis, too. Guilt for not having thought of it myself layered over the deeper guilt of him being comatose as I stood on a box and carefully set the somnolent gargoyle in the cat bed that he had insisted wasn't needed. For a species that spent their entire lives out on church parapets, it was probably overkill. A picture of us in the garden sat propped up against the angled wall, and my gut hurt.

"I'm sorry, Bis," I whispered, wishing he was simply sleeping, not comatose with his soul in a bottle. Depressed, I draped the *Gargoyles* T-shirt he'd gotten at Disneyland over him. "We will fix this," I promised, but I didn't know how. Al wouldn't help as any success would increase my tie to Hodin, and the two demons hated each other. It was more than sibling rivalry, and I still didn't know how to get them to kiss and make up.

I took a long step backward off the box, the thump of my heels hitting the dusty floorboards going all the way up my spine. It had taken some effort and time, but I'd finally found a few spells and curses that I thought would work in tandem to perfume Piscary's. Jenks and Stef had gathered what I needed from the garden, then gone on to start a nice little fire in the graveyard when I'd mentioned doing the spell out there. It was a plant. Being outside would be advantageous.

Jenks had the tiny bulblets from the lily. Fern was no problem. The rosemary had been in the kitchen garden. The plantain grew in the weedy graveyard, and the black cohosh in the cooler, shady, more formal garden under the oak tree. The rest of the spell was tapping into the demon collective for the curse I needed. And of course using a ley line for the energy to do it.

The tricky, three-stage magic wasn't as straightforward as my usual spells, and I wasn't sure it would work. The first step was a demon curse to force the bulb to grow and mature. A mundane agriculture charm attached to it would make the lily more potent and long-lived than usual, and then finally, I'd use a ley line spell to link it to Piscary's, where the lily's scent would appear as if from nowhere. None of it was elven magic.

Which would please Al, I thought sourly as I moved boxes to get to a garden-facing window. All I needed now was a stylus made of apple or linden.

Tired, I wedged the window without a screen open and leaned out. Sunset-cooled air spilled in around me, and my shoulders slumped in the cool evening. I could see everything from up here. No wonder Wayde had liked it. The waxing moon had not yet set. It was a perfect time to craft a spell of growth.

Down below amid the rasping clatter and bright dust of pixy wings, Stef fiddled with the fire. Though technically a warlock, she had a good handle on spell implementation, just not how to make them from scratch. That she knew how to set a circle didn't surprise me. I'd found out early—and the hard way—that most nurses could.

I picked Jenks out from the cloud of wings and dust by his attitude, hovering beside Stef as if she needed protection. Seeing them together, a smile found me. If Jenks was one thing, it was a protector. And a warrior, a gardener, a dad, husband. Friend.

I tapped the siding under the window for his attention, and he immediately rose up, coming to a happy, gold-dusted halt before me. "The fire is nice," I said, glad to get rid of the waste wood the contractors had left behind. "All I need is a stirring rod."

"Yew?" he guessed, and I shook my head. Maybe if I was contacting the dead, but I was trying to confer a temporary state of immortality to lengthen the flower's life, and apple was good for that. Or linden.

"Apple or linden would work better."

"Crab apple okay?" he asked, and when I nodded, he saluted me and dropped back down, only the diminishing sound of his wings and fading dust saying he'd ever been there.

Immediately I pulled myself in and shut the window. I'd like to say it was luck that the garden held everything I needed, but I knew better. Whipping up a complicated, three-tiered, three-disciplined spell would be nearly impossible if I had to get everything at a charm shop. Especially when Patricia wouldn't sell to me anymore. *Demons crash your shopping spree one time, and no one ever forgets.*

"Bye, Bis," I whispered as I grabbed two spell books and started for the door. But then I jerked to a halt and returned, climbing back on the box to take the bottle from my pocket and nestle it beside him. It held his soul, along with the baku, and I was lucky that the vampires hadn't known what it was and had assumed it was a knickknack.

"We will find a way, Bis. I promise," I said as I touched

my forehead to his before backing down from the box and going downstairs. He had saved my life without thought. It had cost him everything.

But my depression shifted to surprise when I got to the sanctuary and found that while I'd been searching my library, Stef had cleaned. The lights were up to show that the furniture had been thoroughly dusted and vacuumed. The floors were swept, and all the bits and pieces of wood, nails, and even that frayed extension cord were gone.

It looked great, but now I felt guilty on top of everything, and I quickly made my way down the hall to the garden. The fifty-five-gallon drum was still the top step, but there was now a more stable layer of rocks leading to the slightly damp, dark earth. *Damn, she's been busy.*

Jenks's dust brightened at the door squeak. He rose up, waiting for me as I stepped over the low wall and into the graveyard. A cheerful fire burned a few steps in at a firepit made out of some of the smaller foundation stones. Three more were arranged like seats. It was a sweet setup, and I wondered why Ivy and I hadn't done anything like this. But then again, we hadn't had several tons of rock lying around in the backyard at the time.

"This is nice," I said, and Stef smiled and tossed another broken two-by-four on the bright flames. "But wow, I don't want you to think you're the maid."

"I don't like dirt." Stef grimaced. "And I didn't touch your room or that second bath."

"Good. Ah, we haven't been in the church all winter. I don't normally live like this," I said, even more embarrassed. "Very clever," I added, gesturing at the fire. "Foundation stone?"

Stef's head bobbed. "Yes. I haven't had the chance to have a fire since I started my internship. And then I got a real job and apartment, and . . . well, they won't let you have a fire in the parking lot. Even on Halloween," she finished somewhat sourly.

True. Jenks hummed closer to land on my shoulder. "She's got the knack to start one," he said. "Better than

Matalina ever did. That woman couldn't start a fire if I left her instructions."

He said it with love, and I felt good that he could again think of her and smile. Content, I sat on one of the rocks and put the books and ingredients on the stone between Stef and me. *Magnetic chalk, spelling salt, mortar and pestle, fern sap, cohosh flowers . . . and dew from a lady's mantle. All set.*

"I can't believe you're going to use *that* to make a spell," Stef said, her disbelief obvious.

Taking a short one-by-one, I poked at the fire. "Some of it's a spell. Some is a curse." Worried, I looked up. Stef had gone still, her eyes wide in the fading light.

"Stef, don't freak," Jenks pleaded. "It's a curse because of how far she's stretching the natural order of things. Not because it's bad. I've known her for almost four years, and she's never done anything bad."

Which was also a stretch, but Jenks had a flexible view of good and bad.

"San Francisco . . ." Stef said, eyes darting. "And Margaretville. I went online. They had to flash-point the building."

I grimaced, my attention on the flames as they warmed my shins. "I was fighting a psychotic demon." Either Stef would accept that I was a good person and stay, or she'd freak and leave. Showing her the process might help, and I flipped the first book to where I'd earmarked it. It didn't have a title and the curse had been handwritten. It also made my fingertips tingle, and when the ring Trent had given me began to glow, I spun it to hide the pearl in my fist. *Demon magic.*

"It's not illegal to practice curses anymore," Jenks said, his dust dimming in worry.

"Just hurt someone with them," I added with a forced cheerfulness. "Curses are governed by the same laws that address magic done with the ley lines or earth magic." I hesitated, and Jenks gestured for me to keep going. "You want to see it?" I added as I extended the book, hoping she'd look only at the page it was open to. If she saw the rest, it wouldn't matter what the law or Jenks or I said.

Stef leaned tentatively closer, the firelight catching the shine on her ear piercings. She didn't touch it, though. Jenks hovered right over the old tome as if to prove he wasn't afraid, a studious expression on his tiny face as he pretended to read it. His dust made the handwriting glow, and I blew it off before she noticed.

"Looks good, Rache. It passes the pixy test," he said and I put the book on my lap. It immediately began to make my knees tingle.

"I think it's the curse Newt used to make a surface demon live its entire two thousand years backward, then forward." *Like some perverted carousel,* I thought as I looked at the incantations. "Bringing a plant to maturity is well within the realms of a white curse. But first," I blurted when Stef's lips parted, "I'm going to make and attach a standard grow charm to it to extend the life and maintain the potency of the flowers. We want this to be more than a passing irritant."

Either she would stay or she wouldn't. This was who I was.

Settling myself, I tucked a strand of escaped hair back and looked at the budding branches. The sun had finally set, and the waxing moon had yet to vanish, sliding the ambient power to growth. It felt good here, but when I heard the kids in the street, I was glad the walls surrounding the place were over six feet tall and the firepit couldn't be seen through the rusted car gate.

"I use medicinal amulets every day," Stef said as she held up her left hand and rubbed her pinky with her thumb. It was thick from years of pinpricks of blood to invoke them.

"Well, this first part is going to be just like an amulet, but I'll be making it from scratch, not simply invoking it," I said as I set down the curse book and took the spell book instead.

"Can I help? I've never made a charm, but I had a couple of semesters of spell prep."

Jenks's wings rasped in surprise, and I hesitated. "Um, sure," I said. "Could you grind up the rosemary? I don't need a lot. A few leaves."

Stef reached for the mortar and pestle, looking professional in her scrubs as she plucked a few leaves and began to mash them. Jenks watched for a moment, then shrugged.

"I need a small amount of paste," I added, a little uneasy despite her confidence. "Our limiting factor is the fern sap, and I'm going to have to downsize everything to match it."

"Yeah." Jenks rose up. "You ever try to get fern sap? It's like squeezing stones."

Not sure what to make of the help, I studied the mundane spell text book. Trent had given it to me from his mother's library, and I knew he'd be tickled that I'd used it. The charm was a standard, industrial, plant nursery spell. "It's usually done on a much larger scale," I said, finger running down the print. "But we don't have any cacti. Fern sap will work if I supplement it with the dew from a lady's mantle."

"You're miniaturizing it with alternate ingredients?" Stef asked. "Isn't that risky?"

"It can be," I said. "But lots of plants can be used interchangeably, especially in earth magic. You just have to make sure you balance everything. Which is why," I added as I took up the drying plantain root, "I'm using this to make a bowl instead of a potato. Some things, though, you can't substitute. If we didn't have the black cohosh flower, I'd try a different spell."

"That stuff is like gold," Jenks said. "You're using what's left of Matalina's stores," he added, wing pitch lowering.

"That was lucky," Stef said, her head down and her ear piercings chiming faintly as she worked.

It wasn't luck, it was planning, and as I used my ceremonial knife to carve a pixy-size bowl from the thick, white root, I wondered why I was so intent on leaving. Jenks, though, had experienced too much grief here, and that was more important.

Slowly the companionable silence grew, and Jenks flew up on silent wings to check something out. If there was a problem, he'd tell me. The fire crackled, warming me as the spring damp rose. Stef didn't seem to have a problem with silence, and I appreciated that she didn't feel the need to fill every second with chatter.

"Good?" she said as she held out the rosemary for my inspection.

"Hang on." I wrangled my phone out and used the light to see. "Perfect," I added, and she eased back on her foundation-stone seat, clearly pleased.

The bowl was prepped, the rosemary pulped. Jenks had the fern sap and water from the lady's mantle in two tiny ampoules I'd given him to fill. The mix of new and old was comfortable, and as a kid in the street shrieked "You aren't being *nice*!" I cleared the rock between us to make a spelling area.

"Okay, moon is perfect. Time to spell," I said, and Stef gave me a firelit smile. Exhaling, I reached out a stray thought and touched a ley line with my mind. Energy flowed in, making me part of the circuit that ran from our reality to the ever-after to keep the artificial reality intact. It eased my slight headache and tingled to my toes. It also made my hair staticky, and after I tucked a strand behind an ear again, I used my magnetic chalk to draw a spiral on the bumpy stone.

I went from the outside in, feeling the energy spill from me into the ancient glyph as I went. This one called for three turns, one for each property I was trying to instill into the artificial seed: youth from the rosemary and fern, strength from the plantain, and potency from the black cohosh flowers. The energy slowly built until I reached the end and it flowed unhindered into the earth. I had my reasons for not liking spiral magic. But it had its uses.

Sparks flew when Stef tossed a few more pieces of my

broken past on the fire to light my present. I set the tiny plantain bowl at the center of the spiral, then emptied the ampoule of fern juice into it. The cohosh flowers I soaked with the dew from the lady's mantle, then added them. All that was left was a drop of blood, but I paused when I realized I'd forgotten to bring out a finger stick.

Grimacing, I reached for my ceremonial knife, but Stef had seen me look at my finger, and she fumbled in her pocket.

"Finger stick?" she offered, and I smiled my thanks as I took the plastic-and-metal spike she was holding out. Many were the witches who had faked a case of diabetes before the Turn to get these babies through insurance, and where I normally wouldn't dream of using a finger stick I hadn't bought myself, it still had the hospital's purity seal intact.

"Thanks," I said as I snapped it open and pricked my Jupiter finger.

A single drop was all that I needed, and I felt a smile find me when the dusky scent of redwood rose and the witchy enzymes my blood carried kindled the charm. It was working.

"You're, ah, going to put a Band-Aid on that, right?" she said when I wiped my finger on my jeans. "Antiseptic, now and then, keeps your fingers counting ten," she sang to the tune of "Twinkle, Twinkle, Little Star," and I stared. Maybe she'd worked in the kids' wing.

"Sure," I said, though I'd never used one since seventh grade. I hadn't gotten sick much after being kicked out of Kalamack's Make-A-Wish camp for dying children—unless you count the times it was from too much or too little magic.

"And a little rosemary to seal it," I said as I used the crab-apple-wood stylus to move a blob of pulped rosemary to cap the bowl and make sort of a seed. Again I drew heavily on the ley line, feeling the energy flow through the spiral to collect in the "seed" before the excess spilled out and away. It simmered at the center of the spiral, and I held my breath, knowing this was different from anything I'd ever

done before. The energy was there, and thanks to the fer
water and black cohosh flowers, it would stay even after
was removed from the spiral and ley line.

Earth magic at its finest, I thought as I snapped the apple
wood stylus in two.

"That's it?" Stef said, clearly not impressed.

"I haven't said the magic words yet," I said, and Jenk
dropped from the darkening branches, his wings cherry re
from the rising heat.

"It's a seed," he said as he hovered over it. "It won't d
anything until it's quickened."

"Isn't that what she just did?" Stef asked, and I shook my
head.

"Not exactly." Using the broken stylus like chopsticks,
lifted the "seed" free from the spiral, my breath catching a
the ley line lost its hold with a *twang* of sensation. Th
energy was still in there. I could feel it. "Jenks, I need
hole where you want this growing."

"I'll do it." Stef sprang up as if to prove she wasn't afrai
to spell with demon Rachel Mariana Morgan.

Jenks's wings clattered in annoyance, but he flew to th
spot he'd probably picked out that afternoon. "Here," h
demanded, and the watching pixies chattered at his audac-
ity in giving orders to a lunker. "Dig six to eight inche
down."

Stef used a busted one-by-one to dig a hole, and afte
Jenks inspected it and found it suitable, I set the "seed" in
it. The tiny lily bulb went in atop it, and then Jenks shooe
me away so he could cover it up.

"I don't know, Rache," he said as he worked. "That tiny
thing needs at least one summer before it will bloom."

"Then that's what we'll shoot for," I said, thinking *we*
was a word I hadn't been expecting to use tonight. *God,*
please don't let this go wrong. I'd die of embarrassment i
this flopped. Nervous, I strengthened my hold on the ley
line. Magnetic chalk didn't work in the dirt, so I used sal
to draw a small circle around the planted seed. "All circle
are really spheres," I said, not knowing how much lore Ste

had. "But most times the bottom half is under the floor, unseen. This way, all the magic will be contained, roots and all."

"'Cause if this works," Jenks added, "it's going to be really stinky."

"Got it." Stef's eyes flicked from the salt circle to the fire and back again.

I stooped to get the demon tome. *Rhombus,* I thought, to set my circle, and the ring of salt shifted to the ever-after, thereby creating a barrier that light, air, and not much else could get through. Circles carried a reflection of the maker's aura, and I wasn't surprised when Stef gave mine a hard scrutiny, visibly relaxing when she saw very little demon smut marring the clear gold. The slashes of red didn't faze her at all, evidence of a medically troubled past. The accumulated smut, though, was gone, added to the smut from all the other demons to give the new ever-after mass.

And now the tricky part, I thought as I angled the book to the firelight to read the cramped demon script. The words would tap into the demon collective, where I would "buy" a curse already prepped. The demon who'd crafted it might not even still be alive, but his magic was, and I'd pay for it by accepting the smut, or "nature imbalance," it caused. This one was going to be kind of hefty, seeing as I was trying to move the entire circle into the future and back, giving the grow/potency charm the chance to work its force over the span of a condensed year.

My eyes half lidded as I immersed my conscious into the demon collective and I was suddenly both here and there, existing in a space between space. Whispers of conversation rose up through my mind, echoes of half-heard deals and gossip. Overlying it were the usual feelings of mistrust, anger, and bad temper that the demons wore about themselves like a cloak to hide their deeper self-pity. The demon collective was a lot like a restaurant where you could chat quietly among yourselves if you didn't mind the ever-present threat of being overheard.

"Ab aeterno," I said boldly, finger just under the swirly

handwriting. It translated roughly as "from outside time itself," and it would move the circle outside of reality so I could manipulate it. A smile took me as, with a little hiccup of sensation, the circle and everything inside it became hazy and indistinct.

But the collective, I abruptly realized, had gone utterly silent. Thoughts were focusing on me, little trills of outrage and surprise marking their presence. *Someone get Dali,* I caught clearly from one of the demons, and my satisfaction took on a hint of worry.

It wasn't as if I could stop, though. *"Tria juncta in uno,"* I said quickly to bind the three intensifiers to the little bulb, and the stirring of complaint in my thoughts grew stronger, more alarmed.

"Festina lente!" I exclaimed to finish it. It was the part of the curse that would keep the plant alive under its accelerated growth, and with a little jump of line energy, the earth inside the circle gave a little burp . . . and a green sprout burst forth.

"Sparkling fairy farts, you did it, Rache!" Jenks crowed.

Then get Al! I caught in my thoughts, and I jerked from the collective.

I was still holding the ley line, and the curse unrolled before me, manifesting itself as the plant continued to grow. A sudden thirst slammed into me, and hunger.

"Stef, could you get me some water?" I stammered as I lurched and sat down fast. My eyes fixed on the plant stretching for the top of the circle. My tongue rasped like sandpaper, and worry hit me when the plant began to wilt. My head hurt, and when I put a hand to my stomach, Stef looked at me in alarm.

"You're dehydrating," she said, then ran for the back door.

"Jenks, show her where the hose is!" I exclaimed, then slumped, exhausted. This was going to need more than a glass of water. Struggling, I pulled my head up, my attention shifting between the growing lily stalk and Stef dragging the hose from the church. Okay, it was taking a lot out of me, but it was working. Obviously the collective wasn't happy about me using it, but I had it.

"Damn, girl," Jenks said as he came back, dust an excited silver. "I didn't know you could do that."

"Oh, God. Thanks." I reached for the hose and angled it so I could drink from it. My hands shook as the first of the water hit me, and I slammed it down, not caring if it tasted like old plastic. I was going to put not-getting-sick to the test, and as I finally felt my thirst begin to slack off, the single lily stalk withered and died.

"Oh, no!" Stef cried out. "I went as fast as I could."

"No, you're fine," I said as I came up for air and wiped my chin. "It's the end of the growing season." Because that's exactly what it felt like as I sensed the plant gathering what it could from the yellowing stalk, finally falling to the earth and collapsing. I thought it interesting that the weeds and grass hadn't grown at all, unchanged as the lily died back to bare earth. The "grow seed" focused and directed.

"See?" Jenks said, as proud as if he had breathed life into it himself. "It's coming back."

Two stalks pushed the earth aside this time. Again the thirst hit me, but I was beginning to figure this out, and instead of letting the energy pour through me unchecked, I narrowed my concentration down, easing the incoming ley line energy. Sure enough, the plant's breakneck growth slowed until it was only mildly disturbing watching the leaves widen and unfurl. Flower buds formed, and I kept drinking, feeling ill and sick. Clearly the plant was taking more than water from me, and hunger pinched my gut.

"You don't look so good," Jenks said. "And that plant doesn't, either. Be right back."

"Jenks?" I called after him. The plant seemed fine to me, but I eased off on the growth even more as the buds lengthened and grew . . . and began to lose their green tint.

"That is ever-loving amazing." Stef's eyes were fixed to the plant quivering in the firelight. "And you did it without killing anything."

I frowned, wondering if that was what everyone thought

I did to do demon magic. No wonder UPS wouldn't deliver to me anymore.

"Here, Rache. Eat this."

Jenks was hovering an annoying two inches in front of me, and I took the small, pixy-size wad of I-don't-want-to-know. "It's your pollen," I guessed. "You need this."

"Buy me a jar of peanut butter," he said, brow furrowed. "Eat it. Your eyes are going funny."

My stomach hurt, my head ached, and it didn't matter how much water I sucked down from that hose, I still felt ill. So I ate it, mashing the dry pollen ball up and swallowing it whole.

"That's better," he said, clearly pleased as he hovered back.

Behind him, the lily burst into bloom.

"Ohhhh!" Stef exclaimed, eyes wide in the firelight.

Thank God, I thought. *"Stet,"* I croaked to end the curse, and with a little hiccup of energy, the plant was again in our reality. Oh, I was still connected to it, but it wasn't racing forward in time anymore, and I heaved a shaky sigh and downed another gulp of water before tossing the hose aside to thump heavily into the tall grass.

My shoes were wet and one part of the fire had gone out and was smoking, but I didn't care as I sat heavily on the stone seat and looked at the two blossoming flowers amid a plethora of buds. They were enormous, but their beauty, longevity, and potency had been bought. By me. Maybe there was a reason the demons had gotten upset. Newt hadn't seemed to have any problem with it, but she'd been moving a soul through time, not a living thing.

"Rachel, that is amazing." Stef reached to touch it, pulling her hand back when Jenks cleared his throat.

Slowly I began to smile. I could smell it even through the confining circle. It was going to be as obnoxious as hell on your birthday.

"Not bad." Hands on his hips, Jenks tossed his short, wavy blond hair. "You did in five minutes what the sun and rain do in two years."

"So now what?" Stef asked. "Dig it up and drop it on her doorstep?"

"Something like that." I suppose I could have gone out and bought a lily, but they weren't blooming this time of year, and even if they were, they wouldn't have been grown with the added longevity and intensifiers that I'd bound to this one. "Let's see how that intensifier worked," I said, then dropped the circle.

"Oh!" Stef jerked away with her hand over her face, and Jenks shot backward, inking a sour green dust. The scent of lily hit me, thick and cloying, and from the shadowed garden, pixy complaints rose up.

"Damn, that's strong." Jenks landed on my shoulder and hid himself in my hair. He'd put his red bandana over his nose, and his eyes were tearing. "Circle it, Rache. That's awful."

But I wasn't done yet, and I dug the key to Piscary's out from a front pocket. "You think it's enough?"

"I think it could push the dead into the sun," he smart-mouthed, and from across the fire, Stef bobbed her head.

"Add a little ley line magic to send it to Piscary's," I said as I opened the small fold of cloth that I'd had with the key. Inside it was a thin red root looking like a twining tendril. It had taken me the better part of an hour to find it, and Jenks wasn't going to be happy.

"What is that?" he shrilled, clearly recognizing the parasitic weed. "Where did you get that? Throw it in the fire, Rachel. Now!"

"Relax, Jenks. I won't let it out of the circle," I said, and he flew up trailing a red dust as I used the length of flexible root to fasten the key to one of the lily stalks. My God, it was worse up close, and I held my breath as I tied a Gordian knot.

"That's devil's guts!" Jenks shouted. "Get it *out* of my garden."

"I prefer dodder, myself," I said, eyes watering as I backed up. Immediately I reinstated the salt circle, but the smell seemed to linger. "And it's useful."

"It's a noxious weed!" Jenks faced me, wings humming. "If it gets a foothold, you never get rid of it!"

My lips pressed. "Which is why it took me so long to find it!" I shouted. "And don't ask me where I got it from. I'm not telling."

Jenks's eyes narrowed. "Don't come crying to me when it covers your precious plants, witch," he muttered. "That stuff kills everything stuck in the ground."

"Good thing you kill everything else," I shot back, then softened. "Come on, Jenks. You should be thanking me. I found the one plant you missed and rooted it out. It's gone."

"What's devil's guts?" Stef asked hesitantly, and Jenks glared at me before going to sit on a tombstone on the far side of the fire.

"It's a particularly nasty parasitic plant that will link the plant to the key to Piscary's. And with that, the smell will go there, not here."

"Oh!" she said, glancing between us. "Sympathetic magic."

"Black magic," Jenks muttered, but he was just being pissy.

"White," I said. "I'm simply sending a nice smell into Piscary's to welcome the incoming master vampire." It was the perfect revenge. Annoyance at its best and not likely to get me in front of a judge even if it was linked to me. But as I prepared to magically join the plant and the key, the silhouette of a crow landing on the graveyard wall drew my eye.

My smile faded and, seeing it, the crow shifted from foot to foot. Crows were wily birds, but they generally didn't hang around watching backyard fires at night. That left only one option.

"Damn it, Hodin, if that's you, I'm going to pluck every last feather you have and jam them where feathers shouldn't go."

Jenks rose up, startled. His gaze followed my now-pointing finger, and his eyes widened. Wings angling, he made two piercing whistles, and every last pixy in the garden vanished.

Eyes narrowed, I tapped a line. The crow must have felt it and, cawing, he dropped to the ground just inside the garden . . . and dissolved into a puddle of feathers.

"Holy mother of God," Stef whispered as she fumbled for my spelling salt, spilling it into a hasty circle and invoking it. She watched from behind a green-tinted barrier as the feathers erupted into a fountain, making a mound that grew taller and taller. In a wave, the feathers soaked in and became a tall, annoyed, leather- and black-jeans-clad demon. His red, goat-slitted eyes fixed on me as he brushed the last of the gray down from his softly curling, very long dark hair. A patch of moon shone on him, and he somehow seemed to fit.

"It's a graveyard. Public space," he said, his voice as dark as the rest of himself. "I can be here if I want."

"I got a deed that says otherwise, demon snot," Jenks said. "How long have you been here spying on Rachel?"

I eyed the rings on his fingers. There seemed to be more of them. He'd found somewhere to spell, apparently. "Have you made up with Al?" I asked, and when he hesitated, I added, louder, "Have you figured out how to separate Bis's soul from the baku?"

This time, he winced, and my anger spiked.

"Then I don't want to talk to you," I said. "Go away. Make an appointment. I'm busy."

Stef gasped. Yep. I was making demands. But he'd been locked up somewhere for the last two thousand years for practicing elven magic and was now horribly out of date. They wouldn't even let him in the collective, meaning he had to rely on his own curses. He could, however, shape-shift like a mad dog. I wasn't saying he was harmless, far from it, but our encounters so far had been mostly . . . studious, not stressful. And I didn't like him showing up unexpectedly.

Hodin's chin lifted. "I doubt very much that you could enforce that demand."

"Yeah?" I pulled heavier on the line, and from behind the circle, the plant pushed out two more flowers.

"Whoa, whoa, whoa!" Jenks exclaimed, and I backed

off before I ruined my entire night's work. "Before you two start throwing stuff, Hodin, what do you want?"

I may have eased up on the ley line, but I hadn't let it go, and I began to slowly gather a ball of unfocused magic, hidden in my closed fist. My eyebrows rose when I realized it was making Trent's ring glow, and, not wanting Hodin to see it, I shrugged the energy through my shoulders and down to my left hand instead.

"What he wants doesn't matter if he and Al are still waging their little war," I said, and Hodin muttered "Little war?" under his breath, clearly insulted. Fisted magic on my hip, I said, "What is it with you two, anyway?"

"Same as you." He glanced at Stef cowering behind the stone and lifted his chin, clearly proud. "I freely mix elf and demon magic. The Goddess is a bitch, but a powerful one, and they're spelling themselves into a corner by ignoring elven magic."

"It's more than that, or I'd be shunned right with you," I said. "What did you do?" My eyebrows rose at the anger that flashed over him. "Or is it what you *didn't* do?"

Hodin's lip twitched. "There's not enough Brimstone in the world to get me fuddled enough to tell you," he said haughtily. "You promised to stand up for me. I'm here checking to see that my *investment* isn't killing herself with an old, antiquated, outdated curse she found at the back of the cupboard."

My annoyance fizzled as I recalled the stir in the collective. Nervous, I glanced at the flowering lily before letting the magic gathered in my fist flicker and go out. "Are they giving you trouble?"

"No," he said shortly, seeming to relax as well. "But that might be because I've been hiding in your graveyard the last three months. Just over four hundred of us left, and they are all cowards. Give them an excuse to ignore a problem, and they will."

I wasn't sure if he meant he hid here under my protection because they wouldn't risk ticking me off by routing him out, or that they were too lazy to do anything if he

didn't make himself a nuisance. Either way it wasn't a compliment.

The pixies were slipping from their hiding spots one by
one, and Jenks went to talk to them in hushed words too
fast to understand. Seeing my questioning look, he nodded,
confirming that the pixies had noticed *something*, even if it
wasn't a six-foot-eight, red-eyed demon in leather.

Relenting, I eased my grip on the line, startled when I
felt the small sensation of pain Hodin had put in me slowly
withdraw. It was an agony he hadn't inflicted, but could
have if I had thrown my magic at him. It was a knife at my
gut as I held a blade to his throat. *Not so much of a pushover as Al wants me to believe,* I thought grimly.

"It's a good garden." Hodin's head cocked as he looked
around with a forced casualness. "I might be persuaded to
take it off your hands when you're ready to let it go."

"I'll be sure to give you a call," I said, and Jenks rasped
his wings, seeming to be unsure who to go to: me or Stef,
still cowering behind that stone.

"What are you trying to do?" he said, and I followed his
gaze to the lily.

"It's a joke curse," I said, softening even more. He'd
once spent an afternoon helping me develop a new curse. It
was registered in the collective under my name, and the
spell I'd just used had probably been paid for by the royal-
ies from it, seeing as I hadn't noticed any new smut layer-
ing over my aura. *Nice.* "But it's stronger than I thought it
would be. I need a way to contain it, or I'm going to stink
myself out of the church."

Why am I even talking to him? I asked myself, then
aloud added, "I can't hold a circle indefinitely." Not to mention all Constance's people would have to do is drive around
town to find the source of the smell. Lilies don't naturally
bloom in March.

Hodin took a step forward, looking both charming and
mundane as he added a piece of plywood to the fire, and
awkwardly stood at the edge of the light. "Is this for your
war with Constance? You could always—"

"I'm not at war with her," I interrupted, and he inclined his head.

Jenks darted up from the watching pixies, facing Hodin until the demon frowned. "You been living here for three months? You owe me rent. What you got to contain that stink?"

Hodin eyed him, his gaze sliding to me, where it stayed until I shrugged for him to get on with it. Smirking, Hodin began gesturing with his hands, a soft mumble rising from him. Stef made a tiny noise, but I didn't see anything happening. The woman looked ready to pass out, and I casually inched closer to her.

"I-Is that . . ." she stammered.

"A demon?" I finished. "Yes, but he's rather harmless having spent the elven war as a sex slave."

Hodin's mumbling cut off, and the rising thread of magic flowing through the garden hesitated.

"But even a demon well-versed in the pleasures of the flesh can kill you," I added, attention going to the pixie now shrilling about something. Jenks rose, and my lip parted when shards of glass from the broken windows began lifting from the grass around the church, all of them headed our way, glittering in the moon- and firelight.

"Oh, wow, that's beautiful," Stef whispered, and Hodin pulled himself straighter, clearly pleased.

"It is," I agreed when the shifting, jagged pieces began to assemble themselves over the lily. Slowly a large cloche began to take shape and the smell began to lessen.

"Do you accept my payment, pixy?" Hodin said smugly as the last piece fused into place, and Jenks bobbed up and down.

"Sure. Great. We're good."

"Thank you," I said, appreciating what he'd done more than he'd ever know. "But I'm still not happy with you," I added, and Hodin's smile vanished.

"You say that as if you think I care," he drawled, and leaned forward over the fire.

"You should," I said, shoulders shifting when I dropped the circle, and the line surged before I let it go completely. "Hanging out here when I'm gone is bad enough, but we're back, and you need to find somewhere else to squat—or make up with Al."

Hodin opened his mouth to protest, but then he changed his mind and vanished into a puff of black feathers and flew away as a crow.

I stifled a shudder. Crows flying at night were really creepy. Stef rose, hands gripping the stone tight. "That was . . ."

"A demon," Jenks finished.

White-faced, she looked at me through the green shimmer of her circle. "He could've . . ."

"Turned us all into frogs?" Jenks said, smirking. "Forced us into a lifetime of servitude? They don't do that anymore, but yeah. I suppose."

She turned to me as I nudged a stick back into the fire. "You . . ."

"Stood up to him?" Jenks said proudly. "Yep. Rachel can hold her own with the demons. Probably the only one in Cincy."

"Oh." Stef sat down, inadvertently breaking her circle as she touched it. Still white, she stared at the fire. I didn't blame her. She'd had quite a day. "I'm okay," she said, waving off Jenks's concern. "I need a moment." Panic lurked in the back of her eyes as she turned to me. "You really are a demon. Your aura is clear, but you're a demon."

Embarrassed, I began gathering my stuff, jamming it into a basket and setting the books carefully on top. "Yep."

Stef made a little noise, eyes wide. "I'm rooming with a demon," she whispered.

"Pretty cool, huh?" Jenks said, then rose straight up at a distant wing chirp. Immediately he dropped back down. "Your stuff is here," he said, and Stef blinked at him as if he'd told her the sun was green. "Edden? Your stuff?" he added, and her confusion cleared.

I looked at the lily under the cobbled stained-glass

cloche. Hodin hadn't put the pieces together with regard to the original pattern, and it looked absolutely stunning in the firelight. *Maybe I shouldn't have been so harsh. . . .*

Stef got to her feet, wobbling as she looked at the wall between us and the street.

"You going to be okay, sunshine?" Jenks asked.

"Ask me tomorrow," she whispered, then turned to me. "Excuse me," she said, even softer, and staggered toward the gate and the sound of a car door slamming.

"I'll go with her," Jenks said, but he halted his mad dash when I cleared my throat.

"Hey, will you ask Edden if he's had any complaints about three living vamps in a brown Volvo?"

Jenks's impatience faltered, and he hovered closer. "The ones at the storefront?" he asked, and I nodded. "Sure. They were at Stef's apartment, too. Haven't seen them here, though."

And then he was gone, startling Stef as he hovered over her shoulder to light her way as he had for me so many times before. Slowly my smile faded, and alone—as a demon often is—I spoke the words to finish the curse.

CHAPTER

7

"SO HOW'S THEIR SECURITY?" I SAID, ALMOST SHOUTING since my phone was on speaker, way across the belfry on one of the sunlit window ledges. "Any more issues?"

"No. Flight was good." Trent's tone was light, the musical lilt that had first attracted me obvious even through the tiny speaker. "Quen has been out here before with the girls, so their security only needed a few tweaks to satisfy him. He's *finally* sleeping," he added with a small chuckle.

My head bobbed as I continued to search the cardboard box on the floor, fingers tracing the spines of my mundane spelling books sandwiched between my, ah, curse tomes. "He's careful," I said, then smiled as I found the one I'd been looking for and took it with me to sit on a box in the sun. The bright octagon room was nice with the windows open, the sound of distant traffic reminiscent of a waterfall.

"Where are you?" Trent asked suddenly. "Outside? I can hear birds."

"Belfry." Head down, I thumbed through the book's index. "Looking for a spell. One of your mom's," I added, grimacing as I remembered Hodin's visit. But what Dali didn't know about me talking to Hodin wouldn't get me in trouble. He was like the bad boyfriend your parents forbid you to date—not simply because he practiced elven magic, but for something else I hadn't parsed out quite yet.

"Really? Which one?" Trent asked, his pleasure obvious.

"Ah . . ." I flipped back a page. "Auditory Announcement of Demonic Presence," I said. "I'm going to put it on the steeple bell so I can hear it even if I'm in the garden."

"I thought you were selling the church," Trent said, and my breath caught. Damn it, I hadn't wanted him to know I'd been kicked out of Piscary's, and now I had to explain.

"We are." I rose, open book tucked under my arm as I dragged a closed box directly under the steeple. "But Jenks and I will be here a couple of weeks." I hesitated. "Constance moved up everyone's eviction notice. We've got a faire of pixies in the garden and a nurse from the hospital bunking in Ivy's old room."

I bit my lower lip, unable to bring myself to tell him that Jenks and I had lost another property. I didn't care if it was Constance's fault. He'd only ask why I didn't move in with him.

"Oh," he said, his unspoken question obvious. "How did the property hunt go yesterday? I saw the pictures. It looks great."

I stood on the box, stretching to reach the bell. My fingers grazed the old iron, and a shiver ran through me. "It looked good at first, but I'm not sure downtown is the right place," I said evasively. "Too much collateral damage if something untoward happens."

He was silent. My hand slipped from the bell. *Don't ask. Please don't.* "Ah, Hodin showed up last night," I blurted to change the subject. "He's been at the church for months. Jenks kicked him out, but I want to know if he comes back."

"Gotcha."

His words were soft, and I quashed a flicker of guilt. He wanted to help, but his estate was too far away to be anything but a gilded prison. His mom had found that out, but back in the sixties, a wealthy woman did not publicly work unless it was for a charity. Trent was still trying to get her first name added to the spells she'd developed. Most were registered only as Kalamack, and everyone believed them to be his father's.

"Am I hearing water?" I asked as Lucy's shrill cries and splashing became obvious.

"Beach," Trent said simply, and I could hear his contentment. "I'd forgotten how nice it is out here before it gets busy."

"Sounds idyllic."

"Hey, I offered you a seat," he said, and I chuckled, my envy vanishing as I imagined that Ellasbeth had taken the opportunity to put on a bikini, but maybe not. It was, like, eight in the morning out there.

"Do you need to go?" I asked as I stood on the box and read over the simple phrase to invoke the charm.

"No. Ellasbeth and her mom are with the girls. They aren't far. Is Jenks with you?"

I smiled at the concern in his voice. "Not far," I echoed, then tapped a ley line, eyes closing as it spilled into me like the summer sun. "It's an elven charm, but I don't need to call on the Goddess directly, so there shouldn't be a problem." I hesitated. "You want to listen in?"

"Yes," he said, so fast that I had to smile.

"Okay, tell me if I get the pronunciation wrong," I said as I touched the bell, the book splayed open on my other hand. *"Ta na shay, evoulumn,"* I said boldly as I imagined a circle large enough to encompass the church and most of the grounds.

With a delicious whoosh of power, I felt the large circle form, rising up from the earth where I had paced out a Jenks-assisted, perfect circle earlier that morning. Ten pounds of salt marked our path, and the molecule-thin barrier sprang up, arching high above the church, enclosing it in a force that would keep out all but the most determined unless they used the sewer, gas, or cable line to break it. I smiled, pleased with myself. The directions said this needed a group of elves to work, but I could hold a circle large enough by myself.

From outside came a shrill piping of alarm. *Sorry,* I thought, but the circle wouldn't be there long. And besides, Jenks knew. He'd calm them down.

My hand pressed the bell more firmly, filling me with the chill of cold iron never having seen the sun. The warmth of the ley line raced over my skin, and the two sensations mixed in an unreal, uncomfortable feeling. *"Rona beal, rona beal, da so demona bea. Ta na shay,"* I said, my hand cramping when the bell silently resonated. Three distinctive pulses radiated out from the bell, pushing my hair back with the force of the charm. It echoed out from me, racing to find the interior of my circle, where it soaked in, carrying the spell with it.

Until finally, it died away with the feeling of cold metal and warm sun.

I pulled my aching hand from the bell and dropped the ley line. Elven magic was stronger than demon, much as the demons hated to admit it. It would remain so until demons got over their eon-long sulk and once again called on the Goddess to supplement their power as did the elves. I was starting to doubt that it would ever happen outside of Hodin and myself. The two magics were really one and the same. But whereas elven magic was stronger, demon magic was more reliable. If you call on a deity to strengthen your spell, you might not like how she accomplishes it. It made elven magic unsettlingly unpredictable in the more complicated charms. This one, though, was really basic.

"Well?" Trent said, clearly anxious.

I stepped down from the box and squinted up at the bell. It was as if I could still feel it resonating, which was impossible. If there was no ley line connection, there was no energy. "The bell resonated," I said, glancing out the window to see that my circle was indeed down. "I felt it soak into the perimeter. I think it worked."

And then the softly vibrating bell seemed to shake itself awake and a distinctive *bong* rang out. I ducked, hands over my ears. The clapper hadn't moved. It had been a tiny burst of magic, like a ripple in reverse, echoing in from the outer edge, gaining strength as it neared the bell until it hit it with a hundred times the original strength.

"Maybe not," I said as the last of the vibrations faded.

"Maybe it's responding to you," Trent said.

The Turn take it! I hate it when I do stuff wrong, I thought, head down over the book. "The ones in your mom's hut and spelling area never responded to me," I muttered. "Did I mispronounce anything?"

"No, it sounded perfect."

"It calls for multiple spell casters. Maybe that's it," I said, then turned to the open stairway as Stef's voice echoed up.

"Rachel? There's someone to see you?" she called. "Mr. Dali?"

"Dali?" I looked at my phone for the time. I was meeting him at Junior's today to take him out to meet Keric. But that wasn't for an hour.

"It worked," I said, pleased as I dropped the book onto a box and picked up my phone. "I have to go. Dali's here."

Trent chuckled. "Tell him I said I hope he's well. And I love you. And be safe."

"You too," I said, then added, "I mean, I love you, too." I hesitated for a moment, reluctant to end the call. Trent, too, lingered, and in the silence, I knew he really did love me. More than was probably safe. "Bye," I whispered, then hit the end icon.

Why is Dali here? I thought as I stuffed my phone in a back pocket and thumped down the narrow, dark stairs to the foyer. My steps were light, but worry dogged me, worry about how the collective had reacted when I'd pulled that time-shift curse from storage. *Get Dali,* echoed in my thoughts. *Then get Al!* Crap on toast. If there was magic that I shouldn't be using, it needed to go in the vault with the rest of the war curses.

The foyer was bright with the light from the open door, and Stef smiled, clearly relieved as I came down the last stair and shut the door behind me. Dali stood on the stoop, looking decidedly odd and a bit peeved in a suit that was more gray than white. It was hard to tell. The color kept shifting.

He held a takeout cup, and he raised it when he saw me.

"I brought you a skinny demon," he said, his thick build and somewhat short stature making his voice deep and resonant. His red, goat-slitted eyes were hidden behind dark glasses, and with the suit, dull dress shoes, and jaded demeanor, he looked for all the world like a desk-heavy, middle-aged public servant. All of which was weird, but perhaps having a few wrinkles and graying hair gave him some cred in a society where you could be anything you wished. I knew for a fact it wasn't because he wanted to "blend in" with society.

"Thank you," I said, more than a little uncomfortable as I took it. "I thought we weren't meeting until noon." *And at Junior's, not my broken, unlivable church.* "Give me a sec, and I'll get my bag and we can head out," I added, knowing he was anxious to meet the toddler. Keric was a demon born to witch parents as I had been, surviving thanks to Trent's illegal genetic tinkering. Trent's dad had ironed out the methodology when he'd fixed me.

"Rachel, I'm heading into town." Stef picked her purse up from the side table and edged around Dali and out into the cool morning air. "I need a couple of things they didn't chuck out my window. Do you want me to pick up anything for you?"

"No, I'm good. Thanks," I said, and she smiled cheerfully, already on the walk. She looked good in her jeans and light top, hair sparkling when one of the new resident pixies dropped down to talk to her.

I turned to Dali, wondering how he got that purple tie to work with the rest. He was squinting despite the sunglasses, and a classy-looking, brimmed hat materialized atop his head, shading his face. "Gray is a new look for you," I said as I dropped back and gestured for him to come in. "Give me a sec. I need to get my bag."

"Do you know how hard it is to find something that says ultimate power without looking like a dime-store comic-book villain?" he muttered.

"Only every day of my life," I said as I tugged the door

shut behind him and lowered the locking bar. "But seeing as you're visiting a toddler, you might want to tone it down."

He sniffed, and the faint scent of burnt amber tickled my nose in the close quarters. He hadn't moved, and I finally inched past him to go into the dark sanctuary. "I am not wearing jeans," he said in disdain, and I stifled a shiver at the *scuff-click, scuff-click* of his shiny shoes.

"You've . . . taken a familiar?" he said, and I turned to see he'd removed his glasses and was squinting at the ceiling, a lordly look on his face.

"I have not," I said, insulted. "Constance kicked her out of her apartment. Stef is staying here until she finds a new place by the hospital." Ice dropped down my spine when his eyes found mine, almost glowing in the chancy light of the boarded-up windows. "That's where she works," I added, and he stopped at the hole in the floor, toes edging the plywood cover.

"Mmmm." He rocked from his toes to his heels and back again, and I wondered if he was contemplating fixing the hole rather than making the effort to walk around it. "It looks better in here. Better, but not good," he added, deciding to walk around it. "If you apologize to Al, you could make a tulpa of the ruined parts and be done with it."

Eyebrows high, I watched him heel-toe a slow arc, skirting the plywood cover. "Tulpas give me headaches," I said, though the reality was that making a solid object or place from nothing left me comatose from anywhere from an hour to three days. That was bad enough, but the real issue was that it required another demon to pull the thought construct from my mind and memory to give it a lasting substance. I only trusted Al to do it. Unfortunately, in the mood he was in, Al would likely rip through me like a fox in a henhouse—and Dali knew it. It was a suggestion that was designed to hurt, not help.

Whatever. I grabbed my bag, checked for my keys, and took a sip of the coffee. It was cold, but was I a demon or was I a demon? "You should rethink that suit," I said as I warmed the drink with a stray thought. "Keric is a toddler, and you want to convey the impression that you will play with him, not sit him in a high chair with a handful of Cheerios while you watch the news. If you were twenty pounds lighter, I'd say jeans and a tweed jacket. No?" I said when he glared at me. "Look, you've got, like, a zillion outfits to match the tulpas in that restaurant jukebox of yours. There's got to be a classy, casual something that says money and demon both. Maybe something like Newt used to wear. She could do money-casual like no one else."

Dali thought for a moment, then reappeared in a vivid purple, gold, and red robe, complete with a flat, cylinder-like hat. It was Newt from top to bottom, and I nodded my approval. The fabric was overwhelmingly exquisite, but the cut of the robe and pantaloons brought it back down to casual, and the hat softened the look even more. It was cut roomy for his bulk, and gave him a decided air of individuality and wealth.

"That's perfect," I said, and he grimaced as if not happy he had wanted my opinion at all. "Ready to go?" But he didn't move when I took several steps, and I scuffed to a halt, unsure.

"I'm early because I saw the need to talk to you," Dali said. "I assumed an hour would be enough time to access and fix whatever you might have done to yourself. Providing you survived." He looked me up and down. "It seems you have."

Mmmm. Uneased, I sipped the coffee he'd brought me, hip cocked as I stood before the ruined pool table and tried to hide my worry. I mean, it was Dali. "I can handle a parking lot of vampires at noon," I said, eyes widening as he moved to sit in the one chair that found the little bit of sun that made it in here. *He's sitting down?* Concerned, I edged closer. I didn't think he was here about the vampires. "Ah . . . do you want a coffee or something?"

"God no," he blurted, then resettled himself to stare at me. "You were in the collective yesterday," he intoned, red eyes glinting in the sun, and a chill dropped down my spine.

"Yeah?" I said, my tone anything but certain. My thoughts went to Hodin in my backyard, and I steeled my expression. *Damn it back to the Turn. How had he found out?*

Dali leaned forward over his knees, his eyes never leaving mine. "You accessed a very old charm. One Newt made. We don't use the curses Newt made. Ever."

"No one told me that," I said. "Is that why there wasn't any smut payment?"

His lips parted. My question hung in the air, the silence growing as if I'd completely derailed his train of thought. Then his focus cleared. "What did you shift forward in time? And how is it you are still . . . alive?"

Oh . . . boy . . .

"Alive!" Jenks shrilled, and I jumped when he dropped down, his silver dust making a living, temporary sunbeam over me. "Rache, you didn't say anything about it being dangerous."

"Because it wasn't," I cajoled, and Jenks spun in the air to Dali. The demon was shaking his head, and Jenks became more distressed.

"Al's pride will be your death," Dali said, and my anger flickered.

"I'm not talking to him," I snapped. "Not until he and Hodin can be in the same room without either of them trying to kill the other."

Dali made a harsh guffaw. "Then you need a new mentor. Preferably before you kill yourself with antiquated, unsafe curses. I say again, what did you try to move through time? Someday it may be possible to use Newt's curse successfully. But not in a half-conceived, ill-defended . . . back lot of a spelling lab."

"Hey!" I exclaimed, and Jenks rose higher, his wings a harsh hum and his hands on his hips.

"Try, hell. She did it," he said, and Dali's goat-slitted eyes darted to my smug shrug.

"You want to see it?" I said, and Dali blinked once. Slowly.

"It's alive?"

I stood, feeling sassy. *Knock it down a peg, Rachel. This is when things get jerked out from under you.* "It's outside," I said as I set my coffee down and slung my bag over my shoulder. I'd have to go out the back if I wanted to leave the front door locked. "It's in my sorry-assed, ill-defensed back lot of a spelling lab. We have time for a quick look before we go."

"It was *half-conceived*," Jenks whispered as he hovered by my ear, and I flushed.

"Show me." Dali pushed too close behind me in the narrow hall, and I backed up fast.

"Watch your step," I said as I opened the door, my embarrassment growing as I lurched down the fifty-five-gallon drum and then the makeshift stairs. *God help me, he's right,* I thought as my shoes squished in the muddy earth that had once been under my kitchen. My backyard was so far from the perfection that Dali probably had. Maybe I should give it up and move in with Trent. He at least had a decent spelling area and garden paths that didn't ruin your shoes.

Arms over my middle, I doggedly paced through the backyard, stepped over the low wall and into the graveyard.

"Ah, Rachel?" Jenks prompted, and I turned.

Dali had stopped. Expression blank, he was spinning in a slow circle, taking in my garden in all its broken, half-burned, dilapidated glory. I warmed, suddenly feeling like a kindergartner showing my rich uncle my big-girl desk and handprint turkey. "Your flora conservatory is considerable," Dali said, and I hesitated, seeing his silence in a new way.

"Ah, thanks." I waited as he made his careful way through the damp garden. The plants were bending away from him, and the faint, almost ultrasonic chatter of the pixies rose high. "It's over here," I said, needing two hands to lift the heavy glass cloche off the lily.

"Oh, Tink's contractual hell!" Jenks exclaimed, fumbling for his bandana as he darted away. "It's worse than last night. Cover it up, Rache. He can see it through the glass."

But Dali had bent close, and, unlike the weeds and

grasses that bowed away from his passage, the lily . . . leaned toward him. "A plant," he said, his red eyes watering at the smell. "You moved a plant forward in time?"

"Two seasons," I said, and Dali retreated, staring at it as he wiped his tearing eyes.

"It's extremely fragrant," he said instead of the obvious question as to why I'd done it. "Most living things die under the stress of shifting even a week."

I inched closer, more nervous, not less. "Making the scent obnoxious was the point. I used a supplemental nursery growth charm to boost the smell and make the plant stronger. Maybe that's why it survived."

"Perhaps." Dali leaned closer again, his breath held. "What part does the key play?"

Explaining things to the ever-after's most powerful demon was a new sensation, and I set the cloche down before I dropped it. "It sends the spell-enhanced scent into Piscary's."

"Ah." Dali lifted the glass cloche and covered the lily. "Sympathetic magic. How quaint. It has nothing to do with the time shift."

"Dali, no one told me not to access that curse," I began, but he raised a hand, cutting me off.

"This glass covering is beyond you," he accused, and I flicked a glance at Jenks.

"We should get going. Don't want to be late!" I said with a forced cheerfulness as I started for the back gate.

My back was stiff, and I could hear the grass whispering as Dali used his magic to push it from his path and keep his clothes pristine. "I don't know how you survive your ignorance," he muttered. "I've warned you once. Now I'm telling you. If you don't want to talk to Al, fine. I don't want to talk to him most days. But you will not take Hodin as your mentor. He is dangerous."

This coming from a demon? "The flower was my spell, not Hodin's. And I'm not all that keen on him, either," I said, trying to skirt the entire issue. My feet found the slate path to the gate, and I moved faster.

"Rachel."

His tone held warning, and I turned, stifling a shiver at him standing there in the weeds, looking as slick and evil and powerful as Death himself with the fallow graveyard behind him.

"You stink of elven magic," Dali said, lip curling and anger in his brow. "You reek of it, and that fool of a . . . I can't even call him a demon," he said, voice suddenly holding a mocking laughter. "That shape-shifting, treasonous bastard is the only one who would dare touch it."

Dali stepped closer, his eyes never leaving mine.

"I—I didn't use elven magic for the lily," I stammered, gaze going behind him to where the pixies now sat on the glass, coating it with their shifting dust. "I told you. I used a standard grow charm linked to the lily bulb, then the curse to move it all through time. It was pure ley line magic to send the smell to Piscary's."

"I'm not talking about your joke curse," he said, his eyes rising to the steeple.

I slumped, not believing this. "Oh, come on!" I cajoled. He was fussing over the spell I'd put on the belfry bell? "It was a *tiny charm*. Like you said, my house is a half-conceived, ill-defended . . ."

"Hey!" Jenks shouted from the overhanging branches.

". . . back lot of a spelling lab," I finished. "I did it so I'd know if Hodin was spying on me so I could kick him out. It's not like *you* have any spells to warn me that demons are about."

I'd said the last bitterly, and Dali seemed to hesitate, relaxing as he looked up into the branches for Jenks. "Is that true?" he said, and Jenks bobbed his head.

"I helped her walk the perimeter circle this morning," he said, but Dali only seemed to slump deeper into his bad mood as he followed me to the street gate.

"And this?" Dali said as we reached it, and I gasped, jerking as my wrist was suddenly in his grip. Ley line energy sang in me, and I choked, yanking the cresting wave back before it could touch him. I'd have to really try to hurt Dali with ley line energy. I mean, I could, but I'd probably fry my own synapses doing it.

Jenks's wings clattered, but he hung back, sword pulled, as I stood with my arm outstretched, stumbling when Dali yanked me a step closer.

"You expect me to believe that Hodin didn't give you that ring?" he said, and my eyes dropped to the pearl, now faintly glowing under the unharnessed energy arcing between us. "It's elven magic," he sneered. "I can smell the Goddess from here."

"Let go," I demanded, pulling away to no effect. "It's for knowing if someone attacks me, and it smells like the Goddess because Trent made it." Again I twisted my wrist, but he held on. "Let go of me, Dali, or I swear I will meet your new student with a synaptic burn."

"Kalamack made it?" His grip shifted, and I stumbled to find my balance. "I had no idea that he was so skilled."

"Surprise!" I said sourly as I rubbed my wrist. "God, Dali. I hope you aren't like this at Keric's house. Get off my case, will you? I'm not working with Hodin." My shoulders slumped. "Though I could really use the help. Constance is really cramping my day. Did you know she's blackballed me? I can't rent, I can't buy, and she's even chased off my work crew."

Dali's gaze lifted from my red wrist, and then, chin high, he pushed past me in a wash of burnt amber. "Don't expect help in dealing with Constance," he said. "And don't ask for it from Hodin."

"Why?" Jenks said belligerently. "Because her boyfriend gave her a ring and she used an elven charm to make a doorbell?"

"No, because if she can't control a master vampire on her own, she doesn't have the magical chops to be Cincinnati's subrosa," Dali answered back.

My steps following him to the gate faltered. "Whoa. Wait up. Cincinnati's what?"

Dali stopped, his slight bulk moving gracefully as he turned before the closed gate. "Subrosa?" he said, his goat-slitted, red eyes wide in question.

Jenks was a tight hum by my ear. "What's a subrosa?" he asked, and Dali grimaced.

"Not a what, a who. The one who rules the rulers," he said as if I was being stupid. "Al didn't mention this? Odd. Your actions over the last six months all point in that direction. It would explain your fascination with, and Al's acceptance of, a . . . *Kalamack elf.*"

He said the last with a grimace, and I followed as the gate creaked open. Al hadn't accepted Trent. He had simply stopped trying to kill him. "Hold up. I'm no one's ruler."

Three steps out of my garden, Dali turned, his fingers rubbing the faint damp from himself. "Obviously," he said, eyes narrowed in distaste as his gaze went past me to the covered lily. "A joke spell? That is your best idea to control a master of the undead?" he mocked, and Jenks bristled from my shoulder.

Lips pressed together, I stood in the threshold and stared at him. "What do you want me to do? Turn her into a kitten and get her declawed?"

Dali eyed the branches, a weird smile quirking his lips. "What a wonderful idea. You should do that. Then kill her and be done with it."

"Killing the undead is against the law, Dali," I said flatly. "One the I.S. is really particular about."

"That's why you turn her into a cat first," the demon answered, his faint smile rubbing me the wrong way. "Perhaps you aren't up to it," he added lightly. "Seeing as you enjoy living among the lesser. In a broken church. Looking for work."

"Says the demon slinging coffee," I shot back, but the reality was the unassuming job probably gave him an unparalleled opportunity to sell the occasional curse. "And I don't remember asking for anyone's help," I added, uncomfortable now because unless I moved, I was kind of stuck, not in the garden, not outside of it—right in between where anything could happen. "Besides, you were all ugly and demanding for eons, and look where it got you. Hiding in the ever-after. Afraid—"

My words choked off as Dali looked up, anger in his goat-slitted, red eyes.

"Okay, not afraid," I hastily added. "But I'm not going to kill Constance. The city needs someone to keep the vampires in line. I don't want to do it. And do you realize the garbage I'd have to put up with if I used magic to force my will on someone? Anyone? Cincy doesn't want to be ruled. They want to be left alone, like me."

"So don't use magic to enforce your will." Dali checked his wrist and a delicate watch misted into existence. "Though the subrosa is traditionally an accomplished spell slinger, his true power is found in silence. What is said under the rose is not spoken of. It is hidden. But it gets things done."

I did *not* like his smile. And then he abruptly turned, and I scrambled to follow.

"He's talking about a mob boss," Jenks said, but that was pretty much what a city master vampire was.

I had to stretch my legs to keep up as he headed for the street and my car. "You think I should pound Constance into submission," I said, pulse quickening. "Take control of the city. Protect it from itself? I'd be fighting every day of my life to stay out of jail. Every last day, Dali, forced to use stronger and more dangerous magic until I was just like you. An overbearing, paranoid, friendless, frightened demon. Circle complete!"

Again Dali jerked to a halt. I skidded to a stop. Jenks took to the air with a muffled curse, and I wondered if I'd gone too far. Dali looked ticked, eyes narrowed and hands clenched.

"Lookee there, Rache," Jenks said to pull Dali's attention from me. "The truth hurts."

My chin lifted, but I didn't dare tap a ley line. Dali would just smack me with it. He was stronger than me in every way you could count. *Except for one. No, two.* He couldn't make a tulpa or hold another soul next to his without destroying it. No male demon could.

But the anger left him as his eyes lifted to the sky, seeing the sun in the new leaves, hearing the wind make them whisper. "Believe it or not, Rachel," he said softly, "we had honor once. Long ago. When we were at our lowest. When we had nothing to put in our bellies but acorns and only rags between us and the cold. We had drive then. We had purpose. We were more than we are now when we had less. I find it odd—the things we lost when we gained supremacy over those who subjugated us. Power corrupts all it touches."

I felt odd, as if something had changed without me realizing it. Behind him, a car passed, slow and uncaring. "Power doesn't corrupt. Power brings what we are to the top, is all," I said, thinking of all the ugly I had fought against. "Be it good or bad."

"Just so," Dali said softly, sounding like Al. "Either you take control of your city or she will drive you from it. And Rachel? A demon with nothing is nothing."

I shook my head, arms over my middle. "The city has a master vampire," I said. "Constance will keep everyone safe."

"Perhaps." Dali sent his gaze higher to the distant skyscrapers of Cincinnati. "But ask yourself. Who fares better under her rule?"

Herself, I thought. *A handful of corrupt I.S. undead.* Certainly not the Weres, witches, or even most of the vampires. Not me.

"Letting someone provide for your security is expensive," he said, voice light. "I don't think your ego will allow it. Are you prepared to kneel before that weak-willed shadow of nothing and mouth platitudes? Let her eat away at your soul as she does what you could do for yourself? Look the other way when she threatens that elven bastard's out-of-wedlock children?"

"Hey!" I blurted, and Jenks's wings hummed in anger. "You need to think about what's coming out of your mouth," I said, the tingle of ley line energy rising in me. I let it flow until my hair began to float, and he shook his head as if disappointed.

"You are an embarrassment," he said abruptly. Again he looked at his wrist. "Look at what this ignored advice has cost," he muttered. "I do not want to be late. I shall pop us there."

"Oh, are we done with this now?" I said sarcastically.

"You. Here," Dali said, finger pointing as he gestured for me to step closer so he could fling us through a ley line and across town.

"No." I shook my head, and he stiffened in annoyance as Jenks snickered. "You're not jumping me. I'm not traveling by line until Bis can teach me, and I will not be stranded, forced to take the bus, when you screw up and they tell you to leave." Head down, I dug in my bag for my keys. "We have time to take my car," I said, and he sighed dramatically. "Jenks, you've got the con," I added, keys jingling as I found them.

"Aww, Rache," he complained, and I shook my head.

"If you're there, Dali will never hold the kid's attention." I turned to Dali. "Well, are we going or not?"

Dali looked at Jenks, and Jenks looked at Dali. "I'm not the Tink-blasted librarian," Jenks grumped, then darted back to the church, his dust an annoyed yellow.

Thoughts full, I pushed past Dali, warming when we went by the trash and recycle bins. He was right about me not accepting protection from Constance, but I'd never said I wanted it. I only wanted her to leave me alone.

"I honestly don't know how he fails to strangle her," I heard him mutter, his steps whispering on the cool slate.

My arms swung confidently, but inside, my thoughts churned. There was no way I could be Cincinnati's subrosa. It hadn't been that long ago that I'd been standing at Fountain Square with half the city screaming for my head. I was struggling to keep off the street, and he thought I could take control of the city? Keep the peace? God! What a nightmare. The only reason the vampires could do it was because they had the backing of the I.S.

"It will take forever to get there in afternoon traffic," Dali said when we found the cool shade of the carport. "I'm driving."

"No, you aren't." I fitted my key in the lock and opened my door, thinking that the forty minutes it was going to take to get across town was going to be agony in my tiny car.

Dali stared, clearly put out. "You let Al drive your car."

"You aren't Al," I said, then got in and yanked my door shut, waiting for him to go around and get in the other side. No. He wasn't Al, and anger began seeping into me, rising from an old hurt as he huffed and half hopped his bulk in, promptly shorting out the MINI's cheerfully dinging seat belt alarm with a quick puff of energy before adjusting his hat and robes.

Al should be the one helping me make stinky joke curses, not Hodin. Al should be the one checking on me to make sure I was alive after using Newt's curse. Al should be berating my life choice of wearing an elf-charmed ring tied to the Goddess. And Al should be the one trying to convince me to magic up and be Cincy's demon subrosa when I knew it was a really bad idea. Not Dali.

And as I backed up onto the street and headed across town, I began to regret my casual ultimatum that Al and his brother make peace or stay out of my life.

CHAPTER

8

ALL THE WAY DOWN TO THE WHITE-PICKET FENCE, I thought as I made my way along the uneven pavers from Keric's house to the shady curb where my red MINI waited. It was an old neighborhood on the outskirts of Cincy, meaning you couldn't easily tell who was Inderland and who was human—which was how some Inderlanders liked it. There were bikes abandoned on the front lawns and chalk runes on the sidewalk. Old trees were beginning to come down, but there were new ones replacing them, and the bright spots of light were filled with sun-loving plants and swaths of even green. *A good place to raise a demon,* I thought, smiling when I heard the little boy laugh through the window.

But my smile faded when Dali's low voice rose up to join it, pulling into memory our conversation about master vampires and demon subrosas. He was a conniving bastard. Maybe I should come back after Dali left and make them a demon bell. They were nice people, too nice to be taken advantage of. Average everything. He worked in retail; she, as a computer programmer. Neither were especially talented in earth or ley line magic, but I was betting they were going to learn if only to keep up with their kid. A bell might keep Dali out while they were sleeping if nothing else.

Americana suburbia. Not where you'd expect a demon

to spring from, I mused as I went through the low gate,
needing to wiggle it to make it latch. That is, unless you
were among the very few who knew that witches got their
start as genetically stunted demons, the result of a magical
assault inflicted by the elves thousands of years ago in an
attempt to slowly wipe them out. Occasionally the damaged
genetics lined up to produce a true demon from their
stunted children. Trouble was, it was linked to a lethal suite
of genes that caused the Rosewood syndrome. One hundred
percent lethal.

It had only recently been circumvented by Trent's dad,
and now, Trent himself. It still remained a question if
Trent's dad, Kal, had broken the elven genetic curse intentionally as a way to end the war, or accidentally in his efforts to help a friend. I was betting on the latter. Trent's dad
was said to have been a major phallus, and anything he did
would have been to further his interests, not for the greater
good, and certainly not to help the demons.

I was unlocking my car when I heard steps on the walk
and turned. It was Dali, and I waited, his knowing smile
widening when Keric's loud complaint at his absence
spilled out into the lengthening afternoon.

"You need a ride?" I said as he closed the distance between us. He couldn't be leaving now, not when it was going
so well, and he shook his head.

"I wanted to thank you," he said, an unusual gruff reluctance pinching his brow.

Oh. I leaned back against my car, arms over my middle
so Trent's ring caught the light. "You're welcome. I have to
admit you're more proficient at this than I thought you'd be."

He glanced back at the house, looking marvelously elegant in his demon robes and hat. A car drove past, slowing
down to look at him in the sun, then speeding up. "You don't
forget how to hold a child no matter how long you live."

My next words caught in my throat. Seeing the demons
now, it was hard to remember that they all had lives we
didn't know about, lives with chains and stolen children, of
hunger and madness, of defiance, of success, and bitter, bit-

ter payback that had brought both the demons and the elves to the edge of extinction.

"Dali, can I ask you to do something for me?"

Annoyance flickered over him. Posture stiff, he again became the hard-ass, why-should-I-care politician/public servant. "I'm not helping you with Constance. Get control of her yourself."

I pushed up off my car, startling him as I was suddenly inches from his face. "I want you to remember that Keric is going to live forever and his parents are not," I said softly. "They have eighty, maybe a hundred more years with him, and only twenty of them will be as his parents. I'm *asking* you to think past your singular desires and pride to respect their wishes about what to and what not to teach him as long as he's under their roof."

With one thick finger, Dali pushed me back until my butt hit my car. "I don't care—"

Anger bubbled up that he was going to blow this chance for them to find societal acceptance because of his pride. *"You can wait twenty years!"* I shouted, leaning back into his space. "You will *let* him have twenty years as his parents' child before you warp him with your twisted version of what's morally ethical or not." My pulse was hammering, but it was in anger, not fear. "Got it?"

Dali was silent. We both knew I had little to back up my words, except that I was the one who had shamed them into making the effort to survive when everyone else wanted them dead. There was a place for them, and I wanted them to live, not just exist.

The scent of burnt amber tickled my nose, and, not knowing if it was from him or me, I dropped back, tired of fighting for the demons when they wouldn't fight for themselves. "Fine," I said. "Okay. Do what you want. I have to go home and clean my room. It looks filthy now that Stef has cleaned everything else."

"You will kill yourself trying to be something you are not," he mocked as I walked away, making me more angry yet.

Frustrated, I yanked my door open, hesitating to look back as I got in. He was already heading up the walk and to the house, his head down in thought. Frankly, I was surprised he'd come out at all. "He's going to blow us all back to the Turn," I muttered, angry at his inability to let anyone have a contrary opinion.

Motions rough, I took my phone off airplane mode and plugged it in to charge. My phone dinged, then dinged again. Frowning, I risked a glance at it as it dinged a third time. *Voice mails.* "Can't the world spin for an hour without me?" I said, then put my car back into park and picked up my phone. I'd only had it off for an hour.

Lips pressed together, I stared at the screen. N. Lendorski. I didn't know an N. Lendorski. But then my frown deepened. It was local. From the monastery. Whoever it was, was calling from the dewar.

Nash? I wondered, a cold feeling slipping through me. Big, hulking, blond elf serving as Zack's bodyguard, Nash?

Again the phone dinged. Jenks had left me a message, too, but I hit Nash's first.

"Rachel, they took him," a tension-filled, masculine voice said, and my grip on my phone tightened. It was Nash. I'd recognize his musical baritone anywhere. "He's gone. I need your help. It was vampires. I can smell them, everywhere. They were here, and Zack is gone. It was Landon. He knocked me out." There was a pause. "Oh, God. The kitchen is destroyed," he said, voice cracking. "He put up a fight, and I wasn't here. I left word at the front desk to let you in. I'm at the monastery. Call me."

Fingers shaking, I hit the next message and put the car in drive, tires popping on the loose gravel as I headed for downtown Cincinnati.

"Rachel, it's Nash." His voice was more even, and a hard anger had replaced his fear. "I'm at the I.S. They aren't going to do anything. They say he ran away again and they can't do anything for three days. I'm going back to the monastery to get something of his so you can make a finding charm."

Horn beeping, I ran a yellow, my head almost hitting the low roof when I took a bump hard. My phone lurched, and I scrambled to catch it, managing to start the next message.

"It's Nash," Nash said, his voice soft but bitter with anger. "Where are you, Rachel? I just saw Landon. The smug bastard *gave* Zack to the vampires. He as much as admitted it. They won't let Zack go until he makes a public statement acknowledging that he looks to Constance for direction. He won't do it, Rachel. I know he won't do it. He wants the dewar to stay independent as it's always been. If they bind him by blood, he can't lead the dewar, and the dewar will put Landon back in control. The I.S. is giving me the runaround, and I can't get anywhere." His voice broke, and I could hear him trying to compose himself.

"Damn it back to the Turn!" I exclaimed as I flicked on my flashers and began weaving through traffic. "I should have let the bastard die on my church floor."

First Ivy, then Trent, then David. I should have seen this coming. All of them were unofficial city leaders that the average Joe depended on to keep them safe: Ivy with the Cincy vampires, Trent with the elves, David with the Weres. All of them had fended off Constance, laughing at her threats and demands, secure in their own strength, hard-won as they survived being my friend.

The only one she managed to take was the one I'd never thought to be worried about. Zack: head of the dewar in waiting, and vulnerable. So vulnerable.

"This was my fault," Nash said, voice cracking. "I turned my back on Landon for one second, and they took him. I know he's here somewhere. I'll call you if I find anything out."

He didn't say good-bye. The call simply ended.

"Get out of the way!" I shouted, smacking the side of my car just under the window, and, recognizing me, the driver sent his wolf-and-moon-painted van skidding to the shoulder to let me pass, gravel popping and tattooed arm waving me on.

Fear soaked in as I glanced down at my phone. Jenks had left me a message, too. If he wasn't okay . . .

"Rache?" His voice came out strong when I hit the icon, and relief filled me. "I'm on my way to the I.S. That slug snot Landon helped Constance abduct Zack. If Zack is there, I can sniff him out. See ya after your date with Dali."

The phone blanked off by itself, and I drove faster.

CHAPTER

9

THE MAN IN FRONT OF ME WAS FRUSTRATINGLY SLOW AS HE set his phone on the belt to go through the metal/spell detector. The I.S. lobby was noisy with the sound of bureaucracy even on a Saturday, the high ceilings sending the soft conversations bouncing against the cold marble walls and tiled floors until they blended into a background haze of nothing. Eavesdrop charms wouldn't work well, and the magic spelled into the huge I.S. emblem mosaic in the center of the large space would block all but the most powerful ley line charms.

"Come on. Sometime before the sun goes nova?" I moaned softly as I checked my phone. Nash hadn't gotten back to me, and I had no idea where he or Jenks was.

Finally the guy went through, the detector glowing a faint orange. Maintenance charms, most likely.

"Anything to declare?" the bored-to-near-death living vampire behind the belt said, and I smiled to try to hide my impatience.

I set my bag on the conveyer, then my keys, and finally, reluctantly, my phone. "Spell pistol, extra shot," I said, and the guy's eyes flicked up in interest. "There's some lethal-magic detecting charms on the key ring. I think that's it." Head high, I walked through the arch, stopping when it began to faintly bong.

I was pinging orange, just like the last guy, and I shrugged. "Oh, and I've got an I'm-dead-and-can't-get-up ring."

I held out my hand for him to wand, but a second vampire had joined him, and my arm dropped when neither of them moved to check it out.

"Could you please step over here?" the second vamp said, small teeth showing in a fake smile. "In the white box, Ms. Morgan?"

Crap on toast, they know who I am. "Seriously?" I looked at my bag being dumped out on a nearby table. I hadn't shown them any ID yet, and my face burned. "If you know who I am, you know why I'm here," I said loudly.

But the click of a finger stick snapping spun me around, hands in the air.

"Okay, okay," I said to the bulky witch in his too-tight uniform. "White box. Got it."

The two vamps behind the belt seemed disappointed, and the witch tossed the unused finger stick in the trash. I could feel his eyes on me as I went to stand in the white box taped on the floor. I was inside the I.S., but trapped in limbo as people in suits, jeans, and pretty, flower-print dresses flowed past. My arms were over my middle, and I wanted my phone.

The rasp of pixy wings brought my head up, and I gave Jenks a sour smile when he dropped to hover beside me. "Hi, Rache. Making friends?"

"Make sure they don't take or add anything, will you?" I said, chin rising to indicate the two vamps pawing through my stuff, and he flew over, startling them.

Three more people went through the detector, every single one of them pinging orange and even red. No one cared. This was harassment, a feeling that strengthened when I noticed Doyle grinning at me from the second-story balcony.

My breath slipped from me in a sigh and I slumped. Sure, I could start some trouble, try to break the no-magic seal on the floor and bust their heads against the wall of underestimating Rachel Morgan. But no. I wanted to live here, and unless I wanted to become the demon subrosa and kick some major ass, over and over and over, that meant playing by the rules.

Which got me in the white box.

I glanced up to find Doyle gone. "Hey, can I have my phone?" I said, but the two stooges weren't listening, both of them now on their radios. One looked confident and in control, but the other was scared as something came in. Something that probably had to do with me if Jenks's worried expression meant anything. My things were still on the table. Maybe they were waiting for someone to bring up a twenty-spot bag of Brimstone to plant on me. That would get me in lockup for at least three days.

Distressed, I scanned the busy floor: people coming in, going out, some in cuffs. The back must be busy.

I reached a thought out to find a ley line, and the humming in my head grew worse. It would take a lot to break the no-magic zone in the lobby. I'd seen it done, but the resurrected ghost who'd managed it had probably used a black spell. Not going to go there.

But my worried frown shifted to relief when a familiar, somewhat squat form paced through the busy lobby, heading for the big revolving door and the street. It was Edden, his arms swinging with purpose and his eyes fixed. He had on a visitor ID, and I waved for his attention.

"Edden!" I shouted, and he spun, his few wrinkles easing into a welcoming smile as he seamlessly shifted direction. Jenks rose up from the table on a column of cheerful gold dust.

"Rachel," Edden said as he wove through the increasing chaos. "What are you doing in the white box?"

"Being harassed," I said, so pleased to see him that I gave him a quick, professional hug. He smelled like bitter coffee and popcorn, and I wondered if he was trying to lose weight. Not that he needed to. Ex-military looked good on him. "How did you get a visitor badge?"

"City business," he said smugly. "The FIB was invited

in to meet Constance, and I was the only one with the balls to show. I, ah, got *lost* on the way to the auditorium." Eyebrows high in worry, he leaned in. "Got a call from a really big, really upset elf about Zack," he added softly as he took my arm and pulled me from the box. "Okay, you've had your fun," he said loudly when the two vamps at the table took notice.

"You have no authority here—Captain," the one said, and Edden beamed, unafraid but keeping his distance.

"Hey, we're on the same team, right?" he said, shifting his shoulder to show his building badge. "Making the world a safer place? They want Rachel downstairs. I'll escort her."

"She stays here," the same vamp said, and my expression emptied when the other reached for Edden's visitor badge. Edden rocked back, and Jenks touched his hilt, his dust shifting to an angry red.

"What's your name?" Eyes narrowed, Edden pushed foolishly into the vamp's space. "You want to be working the street rescuing familiars for the next three years? Back off. I'm the FIB's delegation here to meet Constance." He hesitated, mustache twitching when both vamps went ashen. "You, ah, want to tell me where she is?" Edden added. His bluster hadn't shaken them; it was Constance. I thought the distinction important.

Who is this woman? I thought as I exchanged a look with Jenks. She had their gonads in a rattle, and she'd only been here a day.

"Ah, the white box," one said doggedly. "Both of you," he added, the scent of stressed vampire rising thick and cloying. "Martin, call downstairs," he whispered. "Now!"

"Edden . . ." I muttered uneasily. Heads were rising all over the lobby as the smell of his fear thickened, setting them all on edge. I suddenly realized not getting in to find Zack was the least of my worries. I'd be the one blamed if the front security couldn't hold it together and something bad happened. Constance was creating havoc with her own people.

"They're better than this," I muttered, stepping to get

between Edden and the I.S. security as more faces turned our way, pulled by the scent of fear like flowers to the sun.

But one, I realized, was grinning at me in deviltry, stumbling as he was dragged across the lobby. It was a Were, scruffy and bedraggled, his jeans torn and his sneakers mismatched. His arm was in the grip of a uniformed vamp, and for him to be coming in the front door, he would've had to be tagged with a very minor offense. I didn't know him. His pack affiliation tattoo was new to me, and I paused as something passed between us.

"What's his deal?" Jenks said, hands on his hips as the Were actually winked at me.

"Jus-s-s-stice!" the Were suddenly shouted, jerking from the vamp's grip. "Hands off, you bloodsucking termite!"

His shrill cry turned everyone to him, the room taking a collective breath as he made a break for the doors. Someone snagged him, and he howled, fighting as he went down. "I.S. brutality!" he shouted as three more fell on him in a weird, unsettling display of overreacting. "Help! Help! He's breaking my arm!"

But the more he fought, the more vampires came until there was a ring of them watching, hoping he'd get free so they could bring him down again. It was like cats around a mouse, and seeing it happen in the I.S. lobby sent a chill through me. These were all professionals. They shouldn't have lost it like this. Something was very wrong downstairs.

"Let's go!" Edden pulled me forward and I stumbled, doing a double take as I realized the two security vamps dealing with me were gone. "Why didn't you come in the back door?" Edden grumped as he pushed all my stuff into my bag and shoved it at me.

"Because I found a parking spot right out front." I looked back as Edden tugged me to the elevators. The Were had been dragged to his feet and, seeing me, he gave me a thumbs-up before howling and trying to make a break for it again.

"Tink's little pink dildo," Jenks said, clearly impressed. "He's tougher than Matalina's June bug soup."

"Who was that?" Edden said as he drew me into the elevator, and I shook my head.

"No idea." The door shut. The last thing I saw was the Were, his face bloodied and his hands cuffed, kneeling before three shouting vamps. He was grinning despite the coming bruises, as if it had been an honor to have been beaten up for me. I wasn't sure I wanted, much less deserved, that kind of help.

"Sorry for not taking your call, Jenks," I said as we descended. There was a brief snap of connection to the ley lines as we went beyond the lobby's seal, and then it was gone again when we went below the fourth floor. We were too deep to reach a line, and I felt a headache start.

"Don't worry about it," the pixy said as he sat crosslegged on Edden's shoulder and ate a wad of pollen. "I didn't know where Zack was until twenty minutes ago."

"Is he okay?" I asked, and he shrugged.

"He's stashed in one of the lower offices." Jenks licked his fingers clean. "Strapped so he can't tap a ley line and more pissed than a troll on her wedding night." Grinning, Jenks rose into the air, his energy replenished.

"Thank God he's too young to appeal to the old undead," I said, but the worry line in Edden's forehead didn't ease. Constance might bite him anyway. An angry anything was of interest to the undead. "I should have been expecting this."

"You think?" The doors opened, and Edden put up a hand and went first. "Constance is *trying* to take control of Cincinnati and the Hollows, something that should be hers without saying." After looking up and down the empty hall, he beckoned me forward. "Half the city is happily oblivious, half is trying to adjust, and half is digging their heels in and snapping."

"That's three halves," Jenks said, and Edden gestured for him to take point.

"It's your fault," Edden said as we followed Jenks down the wide, empty hall. "You should do something about it."

"How is this my fault?" I took my splat pistol from my bag and tucked it in my boot top where everyone could see it. You get pinned by a vamp once, and you never put it at the small of your back again.

Edden smiled, his obvious pride surprising me. "Those in the know like things the way they are, I suppose," he said. "Some of the vampires are following Constance. The ones who were loyal to Piscary, and then Ivy and you in turn, aren't. It's making my day unreasonably hard. After I get done here, I've got Were and vamp graffiti dueling it out on Twin Lakes Bridge. Someone chained a Volvo full of live rats to a pole in a mixed-species subdivision. A gas station was vandalized and set on fire last night." He shook his head, glancing warily at the empty offices we were passing. "It was blue fire. I can't put out blue fire, and the I.S. won't even try. From what I can tell, it's mostly Weres and what's left of Piscary's old camarilla resisting Constance, but a few witches have joined in."

"Witches? Really?" I blurted, and Edden nodded. "I thought the witches hated me."

"Not all of them." He frowned. "Why am I not seeing people? I smell coffee."

I could smell more than coffee. The floor hadn't been empty for long. Minutes, maybe, and a bad feeling began to tighten my spine, one vertebra at a time. "You shouldn't be down here," I said, voice soft. "Constance is targeting my friends."

"Nah. I'm small fish." Edden slowed when Jenks distantly bobbed for us to stop. The corridor split, and he wasn't sure which to take. "She's targeting the Cincinnati factions who refuse to acknowledge her sovereignty. Funny how they all seem to be your friends, though." He chewed on his upper lip, making his mustache bunch. "Are you going to do something about her soon?"

Crap on toast. Him too? My breath slipped out in a tired huff. "Like what? DC sent her here. She's the designated master vampire."

Jenks came back, his dust a brilliant silver. "And you're the subrosa, Rache. If you want to be in the front seat, you gotta either drive or hold the shotgun."

"Subrosa?" Edden glanced at me. "What's that?"

I grimaced. "Demon mob boss who controls everything under the table. And I'm *not* the *subrosa*," I added, louder, as Jenks grinned and dusted a cheerful silver.

"Left," the pixy said, and Edden and I pushed forward. "And be careful. He's hungry."

"Who's hungry?" I turned the corner, jerking to a halt so as not to collide with Pike.

"Me," Pike said, his hand up to keep me from crashing into him.

My eyes jerked from the dull pewter band around his finger to his brown eyes. They met mine, and his pupils widened to an aroused black. Sensation plinked through me, and I almost lost my balance when Edden pulled me back. My air came in with a rush, and I felt warm. Two people were behind him, a woman with a clipboard, her black hair back in a tight bun, and a man with gray hair in a suit a size too big for him. Both were living vamps, both were unfamiliar, both looked . . . ill, as if they had been awake too long.

"Tink's panties, Rache. Why don't you take out an ad," Jenks grumbled as he landed on my shoulder. His sword was out. I could smell his dust sparking on the metal.

"Wh-where is he," I managed, chin rising as I shoved everything down. Pike was in a gray suit today, gray shirt, dark gray tie. I was a sucker for men in suits, especially tailored ones, and his was exquisite. "You have no right to hold Zack," I added, and the two behind him lost their amusement in a quickly hidden flash of worry.

Pike's clenched jaw eased, and the ring of brown around his eyes grew as he got control of his bloodlust sparked by my flash of fear. "Captain Edden. Ms. Morgan," he said, and I jumped when Jenks poked my ear with his sword. It helped, and I exhaled slow and evenly, trying to find my cool. "Jenks," Pike added, his lips twitching in amusement.

"I heard you were in the building. Can I help you find the door?"

"Where's Zack?" I said again, stiffening when his eyes came back to mine.

"Waiting to chat with Constance." Pike smiled to show his small, pointed canines. One had a tiny chip in it. He hadn't gotten it filed smooth and I'd be willing to bet he liked it that way—sharp and mismatched.

"Waiting?" Jenks snorted. "He's locked in an office. You'd better check on him. He's almost through the wall. Amazing what you can do with a busted chair and lots of testosterone."

I pushed forward to get between Pike and Edden, knees wobbly. *Damn vamp pheromones.* "I understand the meeting wasn't his idea. Let him go. I'll get him home safely."

Pike shrugged, his fingertips touching to make a cage right about where his chi would be. "He was given a choice. He decided poorly. Consider this a time-out to change his mind."

Time-out? Eyes narrowed, I leaned in until Jenks darted off my shoulder, discomforted. "If there is so much as a scratch—"

Edden pulled me back with a gentle touch, his eyes flicking from Pike to the two vamps with him. "We're here to escort Zack back to the dewar," Edden said. "If you could take us to him, that would be very appreciated. Mr. Welroe."

Welroe? That must have been hell in school, I thought. *Welroe. Where's my Scooby snack?*

Pike's eyebrows rose as if hearing my mocking thoughts, and I warmed. "Involving yourself in Inderland matters, Captain Edden? This is out of your jurisdiction."

"It's a city matter," Edden said gruffly. "Half the city is human. I say that makes it my jurisdiction."

"You do." Pike's voice was flat, but his eyes were going black again, worrying me.

"Hey!" I exclaimed, breath catching when he turned those dark pits to me. But years of living and arguing with

Ivy stood me in good stead, and I used my anger to smother the fear he was trying to instill, and my smart mouth to distract him from his instincts. "Are you going to give him to us or not? I still have to clean my bathroom today."

Pike's bloodlust vanished in surprise. He hesitated, and then, with half of his mouth rising into a smile, he motioned to the woman behind him. Her red lips moved soundlessly as she spoke into a radio, and almost immediately, a soft commotion grew in the hall behind them.

Jenks's wings rasped a warning when two more vampires in dull suits and shiny office shoes came around the corner dragging someone between them. "It's Nash," the pixy said, and my lips parted. His head was down and he appeared comatose.

"You don't get Zack." Pike didn't move from his central space in the hall, and the two vampires dragging Nash had to laboriously work past him. "But since you're leaving, take his bodyguard." Pike sniffed, and the two dropped him between us and backed off. "Such as he is."

"Nash . . ." I pulled on him, but it wasn't until Edden helped that I was able to move the heavy man out of Pike's reach. As Jenks stood guard, I crouched to feel his pulse and measure his breaths. He was out cold, but it was probably a charm.

"Sir?" the woman with the clipboard said, and I looked up, shocked at the fear in her voice. The three with her were pale. "She's coming," she whispered.

CHAPTER

10

THE WOMAN BACKED SIDEWAYS UNTIL SHE HIT THE WALL. Head down, she hardly breathed, fingers shaking as they held her clipboard in front of her as if it was a shield.

Jenks shrugged, and I rose to stand before Pike, Nash behind me. Edden was trying to pat him awake, and I heard Nash snort at the snap of smelling salts. *Not a charm, then,* I thought, not sure if I was glad they hadn't gotten the help of a witch, or unhappy because it meant they'd probably hit him too hard.

"I told her I had this," Pike whispered, his furtive glance returning from the mouth of the empty hallway. "You should have left," he said louder to me as Nash sat on the floor and tried to find himself. "Some advice. If you're going to spout demands at her, I suggest you couch them with platitudes. Here." He drew a necklace from an inner jacket pocket and extended it to me. "I don't know why I'm doing this, but you've got nothing," he added. "If you want to keep that ring of yours, hide it."

I instinctively covered my hand, confused. *Hide my ring? What is she? A pickpocket?* "Thanks, but I've got my external bling at the level I'm comfortable with." In vampire circles, the more you drew attention to your neck, the more you were looking for trouble, and my estimation of

Pike went down for such a lame attempt at getting me to trigger Constance.

"I'll take it." Edden leaned past me, and Pike let it coil up in his palm. "It was in the information packet," he whispered as he dropped back to show me the simple, fake gold strand. There was no magic in it for all its shine, and it probably cost all of five dollars. "She's got a thing for jewelry," he added. "It wouldn't hurt to put it on."

"I'm not wearing that piece of cheap crap, and not for her," I said, and Pike snickered.

"You try to do something nice for someone . . ." Pike drawled.

I stiffened, my next words lost when Nash shook off his daze and staggered to his feet. "Rachel," he rasped, his fingers finding my arm. "Thank the Goddess you're here. They have him. They *stole* him."

"Whoops!" I said, grappling for his arm when Nash wobbled, threatening to go down and take me with him. "Up you go," I wheezed. "Got your balance? Edden, some help here?"

"Next time hide when I tell you to," Jenks said to Nash, and then I gasped when a growl of rage erupted from Nash and he lurched forward.

"Nash!" Edden tackled the man in a sliding thud. "Knock it off, or I'll down you myself!" the captain bellowed, almost sitting on him. "You don't rush vampires. Ever!"

I looked up, my own anger swelling.

It was Landon. My lip curled in distaste as he came down the hallway at the back of an entourage of beautiful people, both men and women, all vampires, evidenced by the grace they showed, all living by their subservient cast. The former leader of the elven dewar was in a suit as usual, the high ribbon of office around his neck and that same flat-top hat that seemed to mean status in both the elven and the demon world. The living vampires with him were in professional-looking office dresses or tailored suits, none of them as nice as Pike's, though. *And the women are all wearing ugly jew-*

elry, I mused, my thoughts going to the necklace in Edden's pocket.

"He gave Zack to them!" Nash cried out, his frustration and helplessness obvious as Edden dragged him back behind me. "He *gave* him to them! You are a traitor, Landon," he all but raged. "And you will be held accountable!"

"We're not at war. There can be no traitors," Landon said as Pike shifted to make room for them, though he did not plaster himself against the walls as did the others. "Constance wanted to speak with the head of the dewar is all, and since she can't go to him, he came to her."

Against his will, I thought, face warming as I checked to see that Edden had Nash.

Landon drifted to a halt, clearly content to stay at the back. I thought the smile he wore wasn't nearly worried enough for the number of vampires down here. Just because living vampires didn't need blood to survive, it didn't mean they didn't like it.

"I should have let you die on my church floor," I said, and Landon's smile vanished. He was probably betting he would get control of the dewar through this little stunt, and as I glanced over the vampires coming to a slow halt between us, I vowed that wouldn't happen.

There was only one person before me besides Pike and Landon who didn't have his or her eyes downcast. She had to be Constance, and my suspicion grew as I took in the small woman standing before me with a neutral, pleasant expression, her rings and jewelry draped about her in an overdone, clinking show.

Constance had died in her mid-thirties, maybe, being somewhat short and small, with her dark hair loosely curled and oiled to a shine. Though her smooth features and small chest made her look childlike, her wide hips and sultry stance said otherwise. Her dark skin glistened, lots of it showing under a low-cut dress that stood in sharp contrast to the professional suits and office dresses around her. The tiny, metallic print gave the illusion of moving as she did.

Her face was painted to a china-doll perfection, and her brown eyes were mostly pupil black. Even with the two inches of hidden lift in her slip-on shoes, she looked small beside Pike, and I grimaced as I tried not to imagine them together.

Pike smiled, his pupils widening as if he knew my thoughts, and a shiver shook me.

"Wow, Rache," Jenks smart-mouthed. "I didn't know you could do slutty-casual, but vamp-girl here nailed it."

"Mmmm," Constance said, clearly seeing what Pike's flash of teeth had done to me. "Is this the witch who had been living in my new apartments?" Her high voice was soft, and the woman with the clipboard excused herself and hurried down the hall as if fleeing. "The scent of her is everywhere," Constance continued, her manicured nails playing with her jewelry. "The walls, the floors." She sniffed, making it an insult. "At least it was until that lily. Introduce us."

Pike turned toward Constance and I stepped forward.

"Where is Zack?" I said. My fingers tingled with the unfocused magic that I'd pulled from my chi. The line was out of reach, and I had one, maybe two good pops. Landon knew it, and as the stray strands of my hair began to float, he edged away, hiding his fear behind a haughty sneer.

"Yes, that is the smell of her." Constance's gaze traveled over me, lingering at my ring, and I made a fist of my hand. "An odd sort of tang, isn't it?" she said conversationally to Pike. "I wonder if it shows in her blood."

Eyes narrowed, I shoved everything I could back into my chi, where it burned and bubbled. "I'm told it does not," I said.

"Pity." She smiled, eyes pupil black, sharp canines showing. "Someone take a picture of her for my album."

Excuse me? I thought, lips pressing together as a man dutifully raised his phone and took a shot. But their thinly veiled threats fell flat. I'd heard it too many times. It might have been better if I had been afraid as Pike seemed to shudder—trying to tamp down his hunger. Seeing it, a fond smile crossed Constance's face.

Pike took a slow breath, and, with a force of will that probably hurt, he shoved his instincts down and his eyes returned to almost normal. He stepped forward, glancing at Jenks's warning wing snap as he took my arm and leaned in close. Sensation spilled down my entire side. To tease him now might set him off, and that would do neither of us any good.

"Behave, witch," Pike said, and a slip of breath spilled from me. "Don't fuck this up for me." He let go and turned to Constance. His back was to me, but he was close enough to intervene if necessary. Not that I was going to assault the new CEO of the I.S. in her tower.

"Rache."

Jenks hovered, the draft from his wing setting off my scar. "Can you park it somewhere else?" I muttered, and he made a frustrated noise.

"Stuff your libido for five minutes and check out the woman in the back," he said, and I followed his gaze, my stiff smile dissolving. "Maybe Constance likes her meals on the go," he added, but it wasn't funny.

The pale, empty-eyed woman half hung in the grip of two attendants, both stone-faced as they supported her like male dancers supporting a ballerina—not really there, not to be seen. My gaze shifted to Constance and back again. Yep, it was the same low-cut, high-slit dress, looking even more wrong as someone had cut discreet slits to allow for her more ample figure. Same overabundance of cheap jewelry, same shoes, too, minus the lift to keep her closer to Constance's height. The woman was wearing a wig, the relaxed dark curls askew to show blond hair beneath. Red rouge and garish red lipstick gave her an ugly color, and thick, fake eyelashes almost hid her dull stare. Badly mismatched makeup covered a bruised jawbone. There were no new visible bite marks, but someone had been at her. She looked too out of it for it to be otherwise.

I had heard of the ugliness that went on behind closed doors, seen it firsthand and through Ivy. But this was different. It was as if Constance had made her current favorite into a doll, dragging her along for emotional security. It was the kind of wrong that makes you recoil even as you stare—as if finding the sense behind it was the only way to come to terms with it. But there was no sense. At least, not if you were sane. I couldn't help but wonder if the woman had been randomly selected or had petitioned for the "honor" of being Constance's latest drain. Either way, I was betting she hadn't expected . . . this.

"Constance," Pike said, and my attention flicked to him. "This is the witch Rachel Morgan, formally the scion in waiting to Ivy Tamwood."

"It's demon, actually," I said, and the bevy of vamps behind her stirred and whispered. "Or witch-born demon if you like."

Constance stiffened. Pike's jaw clenched as she pushed past him, her hand outstretched as if she wanted me to kiss it. "You are shorter than I expected."

Jenks's wings rasped in warning, but I was way ahead of him. "Not even a handshake," I said, not caring if my smile looked insincere, and Constance's hand dropped. Behind her, two more people fled as the scent of fear thickened. It wasn't from Constance. No, it was from her entourage, all of them afraid she might start a bloodbath in the lower floors of the I.S.

Constance's smile never wavered as the spicy tang of vampire incense grew stronger, demanding I flee and give her something to chase. "You were abandoned by the last of the Tamwoods," the small, powerful woman said, red nails playing about the gold and silver strands as she moved to block my view of her doll. "She should have known better than to try to take a witch. They can't be turned. No matter how pretty. You were no scion. You were a toy."

If she touches my hair, I'm smacking her, I thought. She was trying to make me feel inferior. Being abandoned was the worst thing that could happen to a living vampire; sometimes it resulted in a long, slow, humiliating decline, but more often it was a quick death at the hands of another un-dead, given as a gift. "She didn't abandon me," I said as the pheromones lifted through me, demanding I do something, anything. But I stood still, and I could tell it irritated the hell out of her. "And I was never her scion. I was something far more dangerous. Still am."

"Oh?" Constance came closer, and I didn't move as Edden pulled Nash back and the woman began a slow, unnerving circle around me. Pike was wire-tight, and two more of her entourage slipped away. "Tell me," she said from behind me, and the hair on my neck pricked. "What's more dangerous than a blood toy wanting to be more?"

I turned to face her, my pulse pounding. She was really short—and I was not going to underestimate her. "I'm her friend." I paused to let her figure that one out. A friend was an equal. "Enjoying the view of the river?" I said, trying to get in a dig. "I'm told that Piscary's quarters were originally hollowed out from under *a barn.*"

"Mmmm." She finished her circuit beside Pike, smiling to show me her long, deadly teeth. "That might account for the dampness." She turned to her entourage. "Joni, love, aren't we tired of the damp? It does so make our hair misbehave."

The woman shuddered at her name, head hanging and black wig trembling until one of her handlers adroitly lifted her chin, his finger taking on a smear of makeup. Her eyes never focused as her red lips parted in a mindless haze.

"Tink's titties, she's totally gone," Jenks said as he hovered by my shoulder, and behind me, I heard Edden's quick intake of breath. I didn't think he'd seen her until just then.

"Joni agrees." Constance turned to me. Again her hand came out, her multiple rings reminding me of Hodin. "Accept my authority. The city is unsettled. You can end it."

Is she certifiable, or is it a show to keep her people in line? I wondered as I looked from Joni to Pike. But he had closed down, absolutely nothing on his face. Her entourage, too, had quietly ignored the exchange. Only Landon looked uncomfortable, skulking at the back of the group as more of her followers began to slip away.

"That's right, I can end this," I said, still not taking her hand. "I'm glad you realize that. And I'm truly glad to have met you." *Even if you are crazier than a June bug fighting a porch light.* "Give me Zack, and I'll leave."

"Mmmm," she said again, hand dropping. Behind her, Pike's foot scraped the tile floor, and I swear, her eye twitched. "Don't underestimate me. Those who do—"

"Don't live long," I interrupted, causing a gasp from her followers, but I was tired of catering to the egos of the undead, especially the crazy ones. "I have the same problem." I allowed a tinge of my own anger in my voice, but only a hint. That doll of hers had pegged my weird-shit-o-meter. "But when people underestimate me, they usually end up in jail, not a hole in the ground." I retreated to give her the illusion of control. That, and to hide my pounding heart. "It's still illegal to kill people in Cincinnati, Constance. Even those who can come back from it. Even those who deserve it. We're taking Zack. Where is he?"

"Ah, Rachel?" Edden said from behind me, but my hands were fisted, sparks of energy from my chi dancing about my knuckles.

Jenks's wings hummed as he swung between me and Edden. "If you want to walk around the corner for plausible deniability, that's okay. Nash, Rache, and I got this."

"I'm not leaving," Edden muttered, but he was vulnerable, worrying me.

Constance's eyebrows rose. Her chin trembled as her temper began to fray and the scent of frightened vamps thickened behind her. Pike looked both aroused and concerned, and when he made a small, pained noise, Constance smiled with an icy coolness. "Joni thinks you need to reconsider before she decides to teach you some manners," she said, spinning to the woman at the back of what was left of her entourage. They all flattened to the walls, heads down as if not wanting to see what was coming. "Your promises are empty," she said in her high voice, passing them slowly, stopping to finger the necklace of one of her followers pressed against the wall, head down and hardly breathing. "You have no power but what's between your hands," she added as she lifted the single strand of gold from around her neck and continued on. "And that's not enough to hold a city."

Smiling beatifically, Constance stopped before Joni, and the once beautiful woman stiffened, a soft, unhelped noise of fear making it past her suddenly clenched jaw.

"Look who you surround yourself with," Constance said as she draped the necklace she'd just taken around Joni's already overloaded neck. "A pixy? An elf and a human?" Making a soft hum of contentment, she tugged Joni's wig back in place. "There you go. All pretty."

Insulted, Jenks rasped his wings, and I flicked a finger to tell him to stay. Constance was whacked. No telling what she'd do.

"I say my choice of who I surround myself with makes me versatile, not weak," I said, and she turned, a new anger creasing the small woman's brow. "And I don't need to hold the city. The city holds itself."

"Cities do not hold themselves." More people fled, but Constance was oblivious as she arranged Joni's jewelry, patting each strand as if it was precious. "Joni, dear, you know I don't like you sad," she said, and the guard holding Joni tightened his grip as her eyes cleared. Suddenly terrified, she went pale under the makeup, pressing back into the man holding her as Constance used one finger to smear her lipstick into a perverted smile. "Much better."

Tears spilled from the woman as Constance returned her attention to me. I couldn't smile back. Not even in pretend. Not even if it might save my life. There wasn't enough vampiric incense to drown out the fear and dull the reality that Constance heaped upon them.

"You!" she suddenly barked at the woman she'd taken the necklace from, and Pike made a frustrated sound, his fingers touching his inner jacket pocket. "You know I will not have animals surrounding me. Where is your jewelry?"

Everyone behind the poor woman fled, leaving only her

obvious bodyguards, Joni, Pike, and Landon, the elf looking more and more as if he'd realized he had made a mistake.

"I—I'm sorry, ma'am," the woman stammered, eyes
wide and scared out of her mind as she stood alone in the
hall. "I had a necklace this morning. It must have broken.
It fell off!" she suddenly screamed, dropping to crouch at
the floor when Constance stepped toward her, fingers bent
to gouge. "I had it this morning! It fell off! It fell off!"

My eyes shot to Pike as he jolted forward. "Meg, is this
yours?" he said, a necklace twin to the one he had offered
me now dangling from his hand. "I found it in the hall. I
should have known it was yours. I'm so sorry for not giving
it to you sooner."

Constance's hand fell, and the woman on the floor
shook, head down and cowering.

"Here you go." He dropped it over her head, and the
woman gripped it, hand trembling as she quietly sobbed. I
understood her quandary. Wear one and risk it being taken,
or wear two and look as if she was asking for a bite. Chin
high, Constance nodded.

"Tink's little pink dildo," Jenks swore, and Pike glanced
at us as he helped the woman to her feet, clearly having
heard him. His expression was a neutral nothing, but I
could see the frustration in the back of his eyes, the anger
that this was the woman he looked to, deranged and out of
touch.

"Get out of my sight," Constance said, and the woman
fled. "Next time don't lose your jewelry. It's all that sepa-
rates us from the animals!" she shouted after the woman as
she ran, back hunched and heels clicking as she turned the
corner and was gone.

I wondered if I should spin my ring back around, or
leave it hidden. I'd fight her before letting her have it.

"My rooms stink," Constance said as she walked to
where Pike waited, as if the last five minutes hadn't happened. "Break the spell you put on them, or I break the
young elf." She lifted an eyebrow, then confidently turned

away. "I'm done here. Bring Joni to my quarters. She needs a new dress."

Maybe it was the terrified woman standing before us with three pounds of jewelry around her neck and a red-smeared, painted smile on her face. Maybe it was because all I had was a pixy, an elf, and a human backing me. Maybe it was Landon, his eyes wide as he only now realized what he had promised his loyalty to. Or maybe it was because the only reason I got down here was because a Were I didn't even know had sacrificed his health and freedom. But I'd had enough.

"Hurting Zack would be a mistake," I said as her guards fell into motion behind her. "Almost as big as buying up property from under me."

That stopped her, and she turned, her guards shifting out from between us. Even Joni was pulled to a halt, the woman's wet eyes finding mine. "Get her out of my tower," Constance said, and for an instant I thought I saw a hint of fear in her. *Because I stood up to her, crazy and all?*

Nash stiffened. "What about Zack?" he asked, his fear and hate obvious as he looked at Landon.

What about Zack? echoed in my head, and I opened my hands to let energy drip from my fingers to hiss on the floor. I wasn't attached to a ley line so what I had was finite, but I was mad, and that tiny hint of fear in her voice gave me courage. Sure, she was batshit crazy, but I had a rep for taking suicidal stands on hills just to irritate people.

Sure enough, Constance's guards closed in about her, their fear of her as scary as all hell. Jenks flanked my one side, Edden and Nash the other. The tension rose until the pheromones made me dizzy. The small woman stared at me from behind them, fingers playing with her jewelry as she weighed her options. Maybe I'd gone too far.

"Constance?" Pike's raspy voice made us both jump, and Jenks's dust on my shoulder seemed to burn. "I'd like to speak to Morgan alone. With your permission of course."

For a moment I thought we were done for, and then finally Constance flung a ringed hand into the air as if she didn't care. I allowed myself a shallow breath. Pike's eyes had gone black and his clenched jaw showed the strain he was under. He was clearly suffering, but his control was almost as good as Constance's. *Rachel, your middle name is Fool.*

"I'm confident . . ." he added as he looked at me and a thrill of unhelped sensation dropped to my groin, "that this can be settled without the *needless* spilling of blood."

Constance's lip twitched. "You are too gentle," she said, but the calculating madness behind her eyes remained. "Get her out. Landon? Tell me again about your species' magic."

Landon jumped forward, but his stammering words went unheeded, as Constance had already shifted her attention to Joni, promising the zoned-out woman a pretty new dress and some chocolate.

"What about Zack?" Nash said again, desperate as Edden put a hand on his chest to keep him from moving. "Rachel, if they bite him, he loses everything."

Back hunched, Pike closed in on us, and I jerked away when he tried to grab my elbow. A rim of brown around his pupils was beginning to show, but they were still too black for me, and when his reach missed, the black shrank even more in surprise.

"I didn't say you could touch me," I said hotly. "And not with your eyes that black."

Pike leaned in. Behind him, Constance was almost to the end of the hallway, and Nash groaned in frustration. "You're fast," Pike whispered, a new thought obvious in his gaze.

"Not really," I said. "I just knew you were going to do it."

"You're leaving now." Pike reached for me again, and this time I let him. *Fool,* I berated myself as my vamp scar flamed to life, almost buckling my knees. I'd known it would happen. I was playing with him. With myself. Worse, I think he knew it. *God, it felt good, though.*

"Rache, you want me to follow them?" Jenks asked, but

I could hardly look past the delicious sensation tripping through me—until it reminded me of Kisten and I snapped out of it.

"You need to leave before she changes her mind," Pike added, hesitating as he let a slip of tongue wet his lips. "She does that," he whispered. "Frequently."

"Let go before I hurt you," I said, and his lips quirked into a smile. "I do that frequently."

"You don't have enough to hurt me."

"You might be surprised," I said, then glanced at his fingers around my arm.

"Rache . . ." Jenks said tiredly when Pike let go, and I pulled myself together, shoving down my libido.

"What about Zack?" Nash exclaimed. "Get me in with him. I'll keep them off him."

Not a bad idea. I stepped from Pike, satisfied that I'd given him something to hang his out-of-control, Constance-inspired, vampire lust on. *Was she doing it intentionally?* I wondered as I remembered the unusual response in the I.S. lobby. Maybe the flood of bloodlust pheromones was deliberate, goading those around her into doing her work and leaving her hands clean. No wonder everyone was scared of her. She was like the youngest child instigating bad behavior in her older siblings, then sitting back with a cookie to watch, the only one not sent to her room. And Joni? And the jewelry? Was it all an act to instill fear in her people, or was it real?

"Jenks," I whispered, thoughts spinning. "Get me a hair from Nash. Make sure it's his."

Jenks looked at me, eyebrows high as he figured it out, then darted off.

"Constance, I'd ask a favor," I said loudly as they reached the end of the hallway, and Pike turned to me, shock blanking his expression. Edden, too, seemed to take pause, and Constance spun to make her guards scatter from between us.

"A favor?" Her voice almost dripped sarcasm as she stepped forward. "Are you serious?"

Smile in place, I pushed past Pike to take the center of the hallway. "I grant that me walking down here and demanding Zack wasn't the smartest thing I've done this week. This is the I.S.," I said, nose wrinkled as I looked at the ceiling. "As you say, he's under your hospitality as he considers what's best for his people."

Nash inched forward, his bulk hunched and hopeful. Behind him, Jenks gave me a thumbs-up. I had my sample to make a tracking amulet.

"Nash is his guard," I said as I drew the big man forward to stand beside me. "Let him join Zack." I hesitated, then, with more weight to my voice, added, "To be sure his value as an elven leader stays intact. He's nothing if he *accidentally* gets bitten. You understand."

Landon scowled at me from behind them all, his height making him easy to see.

"Smart," Pike whispered, his voice icing over me like a cool wind. "She'll like you owing her a 'favor.' Probably more than the favor Landon will owe her if she damages Zack's value."

Constance came forward, motioning for her guards to stay behind. Her fingers played with her jewelry and Nash paled as she looked him up and down. "I've never tasted elven blood," she said, chilling me. "Cinnamon, is it?" Her eyes came to me. "He must be strapped."

Worry slammed into me, and my eyes went to Joni, once again dull and vacant. *Damn. This isn't a good idea.*

"Agreed," he said, and one of her guards skulked forward, fastening a zip-strip around Nash's wrist with an unnecessary tightness. His arm was so thick, the strap almost didn't fit, and I knew the instant it took hold when Nash made a soft, uncomfortable sound.

"Nash, be careful," I said as Edden palmed the large elf the necklace Pike had given us. "Don't get anyone angry. She's wound them past their limits. She uses it as a way to control them."

Hearing me, Constance gave me a real smile, shifting to look behind her at Joni before turning back to me. "One of he ways. Pike, let her find her own way out," she said over her shoulder as she began to walk away. "If she doesn't leave, I'll bleed Zack's bodyguard dry."

Double damn. I stood there, helpless, as Nash joined her entourage, two vampires as large as himself bracketing him.

"Not bad," Pike said, and I started, almost having forgotten he was there. "Not good, either, but not bad," he continued, his smile mocking. "Did you mean to make Zack a bargaining chip or was it an accident?"

"Do you always carry jewelry to keep her from assaulting her own people?" I said, feeling ill. Pike's stress was well hidden, but after living with Ivy for so long, I knew the tells. "Try not to hurt whoever you spend that bloodlust on."

Pike's smile vanished. Eyes empty of emotion, he tapped his finger against his nose before turning away, steps long as he caught up to Constance's group. His arm went over the shoulders of a blond man at the rear, and after a moment, the man dropped back, probably to see us to the surface.

Edden sighed. Jenks had parked it on his shoulder, and the FIB captain dabbed at the sweat on his face. "Wow, that was intense. I don't know how you do it, Rachel. No one got bitten." Edden's eyes flicked from our escort back to me. "I suppose that's good."

"So far, anyway," I muttered, steps slow as we retraced our path to the elevators. I didn't like leaving Nash behind, but he knew the risk. He'd asked for it. And who was I to stop him from protecting what he thought worth risking his life for? Besides, after I made a tracking charm, Jenks and I would find and rescue both him and Zack. Once we had them, I'd be free to talk to Constance on a more even footing.

She didn't deserve Cincy. Because for all her death grip on Cincinnati's vampires, Constance was not only troll-shit crazy, she was afraid.

CHAPTER

11

THE SANCTUARY HAD GOTTEN WARM, THE NOT ENTIRELY unpleasant scent of wet dog rising. No surprise as three Weres had just trotted through on the way to my bathroom. It was nearing sundown, noisy now as the displaced pixies had ventured in from the garden in search of Jenks to settle something or other—and they were investigating. Everything.

"This should help," I said as I sat cross-legged on the floor and shuffled through my purse for a finger stick. A beaten and bruised Were sat on three layers of blankets as a makeshift cot, his back propped up against the old church wall and his long legs stretched out before him. His name was Garrett, and he'd been the one who had distracted an entire floor of I.S. vampires for me. I was grateful that David had found him. An uninvoked pain amulet hung around his neck. It seemed far too little for what he'd done. "You sure you don't want a healing charm?"

Garrett grinned through his obvious pain. He was as scruffy as David was polished, clearly low on the pecking order, but his heart was larger than life. "No, I want the scars," he said proudly.

"Okay . . ." But there were more bruises than potential scars. If there was one thing vampires were good at, it was inflicting pain without leaving permanent damage. Their special skill. I was just glad they'd retained enough professionalism to keep from breaking his skin other than a busted lip. Beaten up was bad enough. Beaten up and bound to a nameless vampire was life-altering.

My eyes flicked up to David standing at the foot of the "cot," Rex in his arms and his duster brushing the floor. Seeing his smile, I snapped open the finger stick, pricked my pinky, and smeared a drop of blood on the amulet. Immediately Garrett's expression eased and the pain he'd been trying to hide vanished in the scent of redwood.

David had found him in the gutter where the I.S. had left him. His three roommates, all bachelors, were the Weres in my bathroom tidying up. They'd been evicted two days ago and still hadn't found a place.

"You and your roomies can stay here until you find something, okay?" I said as I gave his knee a light pat and stood. "I don't want you furring it under a bridge anymore."

Garrett looked up, his breath now going in and out without pain. "Did you get in to do what you had to do?" he asked as he gingerly felt his ribs.

I glanced at David, my thoughts on Zack. "Most of it. We're doing the rest come sunup."

"Then it was worth it." Garrett carefully eased himself down, stretching until he went beyond what the amulet could cover and winced. His three roomies came out together, noisy and cheerful after having used my bathroom to change back to two legs. David seamlessly insinuated himself into their group, crouching down to talk to Garrett and his friends about their next move. They'd be okay now that they had a place to catch their breath.

And yet, as I smiled and backed up, I wished I had more to give him than a place to sleep on the floor and a hot meal. *Though dinner is starting to smell really good,* I thought as I breathed deep and looked at the back wall as if I could see through it to the garden.

Garrett and his friends weren't the only refugees to have shown up on my doorstep while I'd been talking to Constance. Three emotionally drunk vampires who had once been part of Piscary's inner circle were outside grilling steaks for everyone. I had no idea where the meat, potatoes and baked beans had come from. Actually, I didn't know where the beat-up grill had come from, either, and I was pretty sure the makeshift connection of solder and pipe to the broken gas line wasn't code. The contractor's paint-spotted boom box outside was loud with "Sexy Thang," and the tiny fridge was full of stuff. Two more coolers were tucked under Kisten's pool table, a faded taped sign saying *Take one now, leave one later.* My small church was starting to look, sound, and smell like a frat house six weeks before exams—meaning everyone was partying except me.

David rose from the small group, his eyes fixed to mine. Smiling cat in arms, he ambled over, duster shifting about his ankles.

"Thanks for finding Garrett," I said, liking how they all clustered about the beat-up man to bolster his mood. "They're all welcome to stay until the city serves me a warrant to vacate. I feel responsible for what he did. A pair amulet hardly seems enough."

David said nothing, amusement quirking the corners of his mouth as he peered at me from between Rex's ears.

"I didn't ask him to do it," I added defensively, and David silently petted the content cat. "Damn it, David, say something," I demanded, and he chuckled.

"Get used to it?" he offered.

"I'm not getting used to that." Flustered, I went to the coolers, digging until I found a Coke amid the beers.

"And maybe do something about Constance," he added.

"She's Cincy's master vampire," I said as I snapped the pop open and took a slug. Bubbles burned my eyes, and I blinked at David through the tears. *And a bully.* I hated bullies. Four-fifths of my scars were because of them. "And I am doing something," I added, though I had to admit that the stink spell had only been to irritate her.

"Soon as we get Zack and Nash back, I'll talk to her again." Worried, I leaned against the table and watched life unfurl around me. "I'm sure we can work something out. I don't want to be Cincy's master anything, and she does," I said, gesturing with my can of soda. "All I want is to live here and rescue a few familiars out of trees."

Arm over my middle, I sipped at my drink, my gaze going from the four Weres on the floor to the pixy dust in the rafters. *The Turn take it, those steaks are smelling good.*

David hadn't quit grinning, as if he knew something I didn't, and it rubbed me the wrong way. "And all I wanted was to have a witch for an alpha so I wouldn't have the responsibility of a real pack," he said. But then his good mood faltered and, sighing, he rested against the table, his shoulders square with mine. "I'm not sure talking to her will accomplish anything. She's . . ."

"As crazy as a dehydrated troll?" I finished for him, thinking it totally inadequate for what I'd seen that afternoon. Scary, dangerous, unpredictable, and lethal would have also worked. "Lifting Zack and Nash from under her nose will help." I took another sip, feeling the sugar and caffeine take hold. "She might be certifiably blood-crazy, but she's not stupid. Once she realizes she can't push me around, she'll back off and leave me alone like everyone else. The city will settle down. She's already afraid of me." *I think.*

"She is?"

I turned to David, drawn by the sudden worry in his voice. "I stood up to her," I said, and his brow furrowed in concern. "The dead don't like anything out of their control."

"Steaks are done!" Stef called, her bright voice echoing against the rafters to make the Weres all but howl. Two of them bolted to the back door, leaving one to help Garrett sit up.

Her arms swinging confidently, Stef went to check on Garrett. The two remaining Weres went solemn at her professional questions, but they were smiling by the time she stood and headed our way. A pixy was on her shoulder, and the tiny woman darted off when I smiled at her. She was afraid. *Of me?* I thought, not liking that.

"I told them to save two steaks for you," Stef said as she halted before us, looking far more comfortable in jeans and a lightweight tee than she had in her scrubs. "Rare," she said, pointing at David. "Medium," she added, gaze coming to me. "Is Jenks around? There's a clan of fairies out in the garden sitting on one of the tombstones. They want to know if they can hunt for grubs."

"Ah, he and Edden are driving around with a finding amulet," I said, now realizing why the pixies had come inside. "What are the pixies doing about them?"

Stef came up from the cooler, beer in hand. "So far? Watching them. It's weird. I thought pixies and fairies hated each other."

"They do," I said. "But it's not their garden to defend. It's Jenks's." I hesitated, not wanting Jenks to come home to a battlefield. "Tell the fairies they can wait in my room."

"Okeydokey." Smile wide, Stef headed for the makeshift back door, clearly startled when that female pixy dropped down to her. There was a wooden sword in her hand, and I winced, hoping I wasn't too late.

"Nicely handled," David said, and I gave him a sour, askance look.

"And tell them to stay out of my stuff!" I shouted after Stef, getting a raised hand in acknowledgment.

"Hungry?" David draped a heavy arm over my shoulders and angled me to the back door. "I'll give you some pointers on handling mixed-species arguments over dinner."

"I'd rather talk about how we're going to free Zack and Nash," I said, my steps slowing when I realized my phone was ringing. I dug it out of my pocket, coming to a halt when I saw it was Trent. "Ah, you mind?" I asked, and David smiled knowingly.

"Take your time. I'll save you half my potato."

I nodded, phone still ringing as I looked around. My room was going to be full of fairies. The backyard was noisy with vampires and music. The sanctuary was turning into a Were retreat, and I didn't want to sit in my car. That left the belfry, and I hustled to the foyer, juggling my drink as I hit the accept key.

"Trent," I said, trying to cover the phone so he couldn't hear the noise. "How are you?"

"Tired." His voice came thin through the speaker, and I eased into the even darker, cramped stairway and headed up. "You think jet lag is hard when you sleep every sixteen hours, it's murder when you sleep every twelve. Where are you? Sounds like a party."

"Church," I said shortly as I came into the belfry and shut the door but for a crack. It was brighter in the belfry, but not by much. The sun was down, and I didn't turn on the light, not wanting to advertise where I was. The music from the backyard echoed up into the small room, and I quickly shut three of the overlooking windows.

"And you're having a party?" he asked quizzically.

"No-o-o." I hesitated, failure a tight twinge. I didn't want to tell him about Garrett, either. It made me uneasy, the way he'd sacrificed himself for me, not even knowing why. "Constance is evicting people and I've, ah, got a couple of refugees. I'd find somewhere else for them, but they're making me dinner, so . . ."

He chuckled, and I sat on a box, grateful he was who he was, and that he knew I was who I was. "Hey, I'm glad you called," I said as I set my drink down and dusted the toe of my boot. "I met Constance. At the I.S." I hesitated, trying to put into words the horrors that she was responsible for. *And they thought they loved her.*

"And?" he prompted.

I stood, going to look out a street-side window to make sure the Volvo vamps weren't there. "She's not going to be easy to live with. Not only is she certifiable, but she's controlling them by fear." The image of Joni rose up, red lipstick smeared into an ugly, clown smile, and I stifled a shudder. The long undead saw people only as a way to fulfill their needs, but they were usually better at disguising it so as to convince their followers that they loved them and maintain a constant source of blood. Constance, though, seemed to have made a bizarre, unhealthy jump of thought, her narcissism twining with her need to feed on someone whose identity had been stripped away and supplanted with her own.

"Vampires controlling their camarilla by fear? That's nothing new," he said, yawning.

"True." I sat back down, enjoying the dim cool of the small room. "But they're afraid because she's using their instincts against themselves," I said, not wanting to bring up Joni. "She intentionally pushes them past their limits. They're terrified of her." *Except for Pike,* I thought, wondering why.

"And you aren't," Trent said, a heavy thread of worry in his voice.

I exhaled as the contented sounds and smells from the garden rose up. It was home, and I soaked it in. "No," I finally said, not sure if that made me brave or stupid. "I totally respect her abilities and what she can do, but I'm not afraid of her. What would be the point?" I hesitated, then added softly, "She abducted Zack this morning."

"What!" he exclaimed. "Why didn't you tell me? It's not on the news!"

I winced and rubbed my forehead. "For which I'm extremely thankful," I said. "I didn't tell you because I don't want you coming back," I added, liking him two thousand miles away and sort of safe. "Landon let them in." *The bastard.*

"Quen?" I heard faintly, and the snapping of Trent's fingers. "I need a flight out. Now."

"Hey!" I exclaimed, my face warming. "Did the words 'come home' pass my lips? No. David, Jenks, and I will free him soon as the sun comes up. Constance didn't see fit to release it to the news, and I'd like to keep it that way. She knows the creek she'll be up if she harms him. We have time. Nash is with him." I hesitated, Joni's freakish smile flitting through my memory.

"He's the leader of the dewar," Trent said, his voice strained. "I should be there."

"I know." I looked at the black window, wondering if I'd seen a hint of pixy dust in the dark. "But you aren't and we have this. Jenks is out in the streets with Edden and a finder amulet. We go in, get them both, and fall back. I will *not* let Constance think she can abduct people to piss me off. This is between her and me."

Trent's breath shook on the exhale. "How do you figure that? It's my religious leader who's been taken."

"I figure that because I'm the reason she abducted him." I stood, then got on the box so I could check on Bis. "She threatened you, and David, and even Ivy," I said as I touched the comatose gargoyle, my heartache swelling. "Zack would have been safe except that Landon gave him up. The kid is refusing to acknowledge her authority over him, and now she knows he's important to me. He'll be okay. Nash won't let anything happen to him," I added, but it sounded like a hope, not a certainty. Constance's actions shifted on forces I couldn't fathom.

"We should have let Landon die on your church floor," Trent said, and I got off the box.

"That's what I told him," I said, remembering Landon hiding behind a bevy of frightened vampires. A quiver rose through me as my thoughts turned to Pike, and I shoved the sensation down to deal with later. *Damn vamp pheromones.*

"Trent, I'm serious about you staying where you are," I said when I heard the frustration in his silence. "You're doing what you need to do. I'm doing what I need to do, and maybe once I get Zack, the enclave might realize I have their interests front and center and ease up on me." *Us.* "I'm not going to kill her," I added, though that would make everything both easier and harder. "Just get her to back off. There's no reason we can't both live in Cincy. I don't want her job, and once she realizes she can't push me around, she'll do what everyone else does and ignore me."

Trent chuckled, and I relaxed at the familiar sound. "It's very hard to ignore you. You know that, right?" and then, softer to Quen, "No, I'm staying, but keep everything on standby."

"Trent . . ." I cajoled.

"Is there anything I can do to help?" he said, and I knew by his tone that "standby" was the best I'd get. "The estate is yours to plunder. You know the code to the rare-items vault, right?"

"I do, thanks." A bead of condensation rolled down the side of my pop, and I moved it before it left a wet ring. Twin feelings of relief and disappointment fought for supremacy. I was glad he was staying, but damn, I missed him. "So far, the church has everything I need." My lips pressed as "Bury Me Face Down" echoed up. "Except a quiet place to spell."

"Okay. Keep me in the loop." His tone had changed. He was working the problem, and I loved him for it. "Call me when you have them. Whatever the time. I don't think the enclave knows this has happened, and you're right. Proving your intel is better than theirs might be useful. And don't take off your ring."

I looked at it, missing him even more. "I won't," I said softly. "I love you."

"I love you, desperately," he returned.

I couldn't end the call, and I sat there with the phone in my hand, becoming more and more miserable.

"Are you going to hang up, Sa'han?" Quen said faintly, and then the connection ended.

I set the phone down. Knees to my chest, I sat in the growing dark and listened to the vampires and Weres at my picnic table eating steak and potatoes. The unexpected camaraderie they'd found was both beautiful and unexpected, hitting me hard. *Crap on toast, I miss him.* And with that my throat closed up.

"Rache?"

It was Jenks, and immediately I straightened and wiped my eyes. I wasn't embarrassed, but I didn't want him to feel as if he had to cheer me up. "Oh, hey," I said, seeing him hovering just inside the screenless window. "I didn't hear you come in." I flipped open a box as a distraction. It was full of my books, and my gaze went to the empty shelving unit. It had been here since even before Wayde had made the space into a snug attic room. "Did you find Nash and Zack?"

The rasp of the amulet I'd given him was loud as he took it off and set it on a nearby box. It was tiny for an amulet, about as large as his head, and I hadn't been sure it would work, much less that he'd be able to carry it.

"They're not at the I.S.," he said, and my eyes flicked to his. "They're at Piscary's. Edden and I got a good triangulation. It's faint, so I'm guessing they're downstairs."

I reached a thought to the nearest ley line and, with a whispered phrase, invoked a small glowing sphere resting on the old floorboards. "That would be my guess, too," I said as I used the faint light to shelve my library. I'd alphabetize them later. *Who am I kidding? My books have never been in order in my entire life.*

"Hey," I said as I arranged the books from tall to short. "There's a faire of fairies in my room. They want to talk to you about clearing the grubs out of the graveyard. I think it's a good idea if they can tell the difference between a firefly larva and a June bug. Maybe you can get Baribas to help so they don't tear everything up getting to them."

Silent, Jenks landed atop the books I'd just shelved. His hands were at his waist, and his sharply angular, young face was creased in worry as he dusted a faint blue.

"So . . ." I said slowly, not sure what he was upset about: Zack, the fairies, or the paths the Weres were making in the tall graveyard grass. "I've been thinking about the charms we're going to need for tonight."

"Rache, are you okay?" he said unexpectedly.

He saw me almost crying. Shoulders slumped, I sank back to sit on the box. "I miss Trent," I admitted, head turning when Rex stuck a long paw under the door, reaching until he pushed it open and came in. I waited to make sure David wasn't following, then added softly, "When he's gone, no one touches me. I mean, I'm glad he's doing what he needs to do, but someone to—" I stopped, forcing a smile. "Someone to hold me for just a little while and tell me that I've got this goes a long way."

Jenks's wings drooped, and I added, "But hey, I've got you to tell me that, right?"

He nodded, clearly not convinced, and I picked up Rex and cuddled him. I could smell David on him, and somehow that helped.

"Um . . . Rache? I've been thinking about the church," Jenks said, and then my grip on Rex tightened as a tomcat growl came from the suddenly tail-twitching cat.

Jenks's attention flicked up, and from the bell, a slow peal rolled out.

"Ow!" I exclaimed as Rex dug in his claws and pushed from me, skittering to hide behind the boxes. My ears hurt, and Jenks cowered, hands over his head. Ticked, I scanned the small space, looking for anything from a dark-haired pixy to a crow. "Hodin?" I said angrily. "I told you to stay the ever-loving hell away from me."

Jenks straightened, and I followed his gaze to the small sound of a shoe scuffing by the stairs.

The door was still open a crack, but standing before it already within the room was a ruddy-faced, red-eyed, Victorian dandy in a crushed green velvet frock, lace at his cuffs and neck, and blue-tinted glasses perched on his angular nose.

"Al," I breathed, relieved to see him, even if he was stiff and cold, eyeing me over his blue-tinted glasses as if I'd been smeared in troll muck, rolled in corn flour, and served on a plate as dinner.

The tall demon's lip twitched as he looked over the small space lit by my magic. "Dali wasn't lying," he said, his low, almost gravelly voice seeming to fill the room and push on me from behind. "You are *talking* to Hodin."

He was so angry he wasn't yelling. That wasn't good, and I stood. "No," I said, and when Al raised a single eyebrow at me I added, "I mean, yes, I talked to him. He showed up and I told him to go away. But I'm not working with him." Guilt and annoyance fought for control. "You haven't, ah, made up with Hodin?" I said in a small voice, and he made an angry-sounding, guttural guffaw.

"Don't lie, Rachel. You aren't good at it. You're obviously working with the little runt." The lace at his cuff slipped as he reached to still the faintly resonating bell. He was wearing gloves again, and my heart hurt. "*That* is an *elven* spell." His thin lips curled into a sneer. "I despise that charm."

I looked at Jenks, and the pixy shrugged. "I made it. Not Hodin," I said, not knowing if that would make it better or worse. It was, as he said, an elven spell.

"You've learned nothing," Al said, his expression sour. "You will die following Hodin's foolishness. As they all did. I'm wasting no more time with you."

"Hey!" I exclaimed as he tugged his sleeves down, a sure sign that he was about to leave. And that "wasting no more time" comment was bull. He was angry, and this was the only way he could show it. "I said I'm not working with Hodin, and I'm not. It was a tiny elven charm, and I only did it so I'd know when Hodin showed up so I could tell him to go away. Did you not hear the first words out of my mouth when it rang?"

Jenks's wings dusted a hopeful gold, head bobbing. Al's brow was furrowed, but he hadn't left, and I took a step forward, pulse fast. "You know I do elven magic. If you want to leave, fine, but don't leave because of that." I hesitated, then added, "I'm *so* glad to see you."

His eyes narrowed to slits and a scent I couldn't name tickled my nose, trying to make me sneeze. I'd hurt him badly by refusing to condemn Hodin as the rest of the demons had done. I'd gone on to hurt him even more by demanding they quit feuding. It was a demand I was beginning to rue making. But he was here now, and I was talking with him, and my shoulders eased when I saw Al's clenched jaw relax.

It was a start.

"A joke spell, Rachel?" Al frowned at the window when

"Magic Carpet Ride" began to echo up. "You need to do better than that." My hands were damp, and I caught back a protest when he plucked a book off my shelf and tossed it aside, the volume hitting the floorboards in a cringeworthy thump and slide. "This is for babies. I'll get you something suiting your abilities."

"Thank you," I said, feeling as if I was walking on egg-shells. *Thanks a hell of a lot for tattling on me, Dali.* "Can you stay for dinner? I've got vampires grilling for me. It's going to be epic."

"No." He took a book from the box, flipped through it and put it on the shelf. "I didn't say you could sit down," he added when I went to do just that.

I hesitated, then made a point of settling my ass on the cardboard box, shifting to find the most comfortable spot until he grimaced. "This is my spelling lab, not yours," I said, then took a pointedly slow sip of my pop. "Constance—"

"Is your problem," he interrupted. Al closed the book he was looking at with a snap and set it on the shelf with a little tap. "I'm here . . . to say thank you for what you did for Dali."

My lips parted in surprise, and Al glanced at my globe of light when it brightened.

"*Do* not repeat this, but Dali *is* the better teacher. He hasn't taken anyone to study for too long. Instructing the boy might fill a hole in him that has been eating him alive." Again he hesitated, inclining his head in a formal gesture. "So . . . thank you."

My focus blurred as I remembered how Dali had stammered his way through his request for my help a few months back. Though they seemed singularly focused on domination, they all had lives I didn't know about, a history that didn't revolve around revenge. Dali asking to teach a child was the first I'd seen of it outside of Al. I'd do anything to fan that ember to life. They all seemed so . . . lost.

"I only hope he doesn't do anything stupid," I muttered, and Al harrumphed.

"The teacher is never stupid." Al continued to shelve my books, stacking the discards in a growing pile. "It's the world that is behind in understanding."

At the window, Jenks rattled his wings. "They're setting up battle lines," he muttered, more to himself than us, though how he could tell that from the faint glows of light darting about the graveyard was beyond me.

"I call the teacher stupid when he doesn't respect the desires of a toddler's parents," I said, rising to collect the discards. "They have him for twenty, maybe thirty years. Dali will have him forever. Tell him that again for me, will you?"

Al turned, his expression empty. "I'm your message boy now?"

I looked at the books he'd arranged, my eyebrows rising at the new spines amid the old. "No. I was hoping that maybe you could help me with Constance."

"Not likely." Motion stiff, he took up the stack of discards.

"Because Dali told you not to?" I said as I took the books from him to see what he was getting rid of. "Great. That's great. The one time I *really* need you, you decide to play by Dali's rules. Swell."

Jenks spun in the air, laughing as he turned his back on the window. "One time? Try a dozen."

"I happen to agree with Dali in this matter." Al flipped his coattails out of the way and sat on a stack of boxes, eyeing me over his blue-tinted glasses. "She's a vampire, Rachel," he cajoled. "A flimsy shadow splintered from our most perverse angers and lusts. If you can't bring her to heel, you deserve her mucking up your life."

"Bring her to heel?" I echoed, remembering what it was like when we hadn't had a master vampire keeping the lesser houses in line. "I don't want her job, and if I get rid of her, DC will only send someone uglier." I shuffled through the books, not wanting to discard them. There were things in there I liked. Needed. "Besides, there's no rule that says there can only be one powerful force in a city." I reshelved the castoffs, and Al almost growled. "Piscary and I managed to ignore each other."

"Really?" he said mockingly. "Are you saying you *didn't* arrange for your roommate's girlfriend to kill him for you?" Al grinned to show me his wide, flat teeth. "That was beautiful, by the way. You were so far from suspect that your name never came up, and the I.S. *wanted* to blame you."

"I did not arrange that," I said hotly, and his smile widened even more.

"Exactly!" Al exclaimed, snapping his fingers to make a pop of sparks. "I think that you becoming Cincy's subrosa is a grand idea. Personally, I could do without the stress. It's nothing but fix this, kill that, party, party, party until you can't stand the sight of your tie. But you're young and I understand the need to exert your influence."

"I'm not Cincy's subrosa," I ground out from between my teeth, but he was on a roll.

"If you want to delegate control of the vampires to Constance, fine, but bring her in line. Her continued harassment of your *miles gloriosus* has become an embarrassment."

Glorious soldiers? Did he mean Ivy, David, and Trent? "I am not the city's subrosa," I said again, and he winked at me, slow and long.

"Of course not. Some advice. If it were me, I'd off Constance and be done with it." He shuddered. "You can't manipulate crazy unless you are crazy. Newt taught me that." His red, goat-slitted eyes met mine over his glasses. "Newt taught us all that." He hesitated. "Unless the insane little bloodsucker is playing on your libido? I know how difficult it is for you to kill what your groin is longing for. That tiresome elf of yours, for instance."

"Al . . ." I complained, but he only closed his eyes and groaned, the earthy sound diving to my core, unhelped.

"Someone put you in a state," he said wickedly. "If it's not your elf, and it's not Constance, who is it?"

My gaze shot to Jenks. "Shut it!" I demanded, and the pixy laughed in a sound like wind chimes.

But then Jenks's head snapped up and he looked at the bell, expression cross. "Tink's little pink rosebuds, not again," he muttered, and the bell let out a much louder, painful bong.

"Oh, for God's sake, now what?" I said, wincing at the noise. Dali. It had to be Dali.

Eyes wide, Jenks flitted to land on my shoulder as a hazy mist rose between Al and me, lengthened, and solidified into not Dali, but Hodin. Behind him, Al stood, his hands fisted and an ugly red magic seeping from between his fingers. *Crap on toast, this is not what I need.*

"You put in a *bell*?" Hodin griped, but his goat-slitted eyes were bright, and he was clearly oblivious to Al behind him. "I have an idea about Bis."

My demand that he leave died. Torn, I looked past him to Al, then up to where Bis lay comatose.

Hodin's eyes narrowed, clearly confused at my lackluster response. "I thought you'd be pleased."

"Look behind you," Jenks said, and Hodin spun.

"You have gotten better at lying, itchy witch." Al dramatically shifted his fist, and the books on my shelves slid and collapsed, the new tomes suddenly not there. "We are done."

"We are not done!" I said, frantic. *Damn it all to hell. Hodin, your timing sucks dishwater.*

The thinner, younger demon in his black leather and jeans backpedaled, almost falling over a stack of boxes as he put space between him and his older brother. "You said he wasn't talking to you!" Hodin exclaimed as he found his balance.

"I'm not," Al intoned.

Oh, yeah. Now I remember why I threw down that ultimatum. "That's right," I said, pulse fast as I got between them. My hair was beginning to crackle and float from the unfocused energy echoing between the close walls, and Jenks took off, the smell of burning dust choking. "We're all not talking to each other," I said. "And the Goddess help me if *either* of you throw *one* spell," I almost shouted. "The belfry is the *only* room in the church that is *mine*, and I swear on my *mother's life* that I will eviscerate the first demon who makes so much as a smear of magic on the walls! I've had it with both of you barging in and breaking my stuff!"

Jenks's wings were the only sound as Hodin and Al stared murderously at each other, and then, miraculously, their fisted hands opened, and the magic dripping from them vanished.

"Rachel?" floated up from the stairway. "Are you okay?"

It was Stef, and I shot them both a glare to stay right where they were. "Fine! I'm fine!" I shouted, and there was the soft sound of her steps going back downstairs.

"Rache." Jenks bobbed erratically beside my ear. "He said he could help Bis."

Oh, God. My bluster fell to nothing. Almost panicked, I sent my eyes first to Hodin, who was now smiling in a confident, not-nice way, then to Al, standing with a stoic, awful stillness. I needed them both, and neither would give. I couldn't make a choice, and I hated that they couldn't find a way to live with their differences so I wouldn't have to live without both of them.

"Nothing can help him," Al said. His tone was rock-hard, but there was pain in his eyes, pain that I might choose Hodin over him, pain that I might already have.

Jenks rose up to Bis, then down, his dust crackling in the magic-charged air. They'd been best friends. *Were* best friends.

"He is bound to the baku," Al continued when Hodin opened his mouth to say something. "It eats demons. You will not be allowed to free it, Hodin. For any reason."

"You never change," Hodin said bitterly. "Your thoughts always in a box. That's why you'll never be anything other than what you are now, Gally. A pathetic—"

"Stop!" I said as the air crackled and Al's hands clenched. "Al, we can at least hear what he has to say."

I had said *we*. I wanted it to be we. Us. *Don't make me choose. . . .*

"Elven whore," Al spat, finger pointed at Hodin. "You

think to save him with elven magic. You will *die* at the hands of the Goddess, and you will *deserve it*!"

Jenks's wings rasped as he sat on the shelf beside Bis and stared down at all of us. "I don't care if I have to piss on a peach pit if it will help Bis."

Hodin looked at Al's overdone, Victorian finery, his lips curled in disdain. "Says the rebel living in the woods on acorns. You have no concept of the power held by elven magic. How do you think they enslaved us for thousands of years? We let them do it, willfully ignoring what lay at our fingertips. Don't condemn me for working within the system to find a way out of it."

"You didn't work within a system," Al barked. "You sold your body for food and a silk robe!"

"Nice," Jenks said, feet dangling from Bis's shelf.

"As if starving in the mountains did you any good!" Hodin shouted. "I was *trying* to find a way to bring them to heel!"

I looked up at Jenks, who shrugged. At least they were talking.

"Al," I interrupted, and they both jumped as if having forgotten I was there. "It was elven magic that captured the baku. That is a fact. Maybe elven magic can help Bis. That doesn't mean I have to do it. Maybe Trent could. Can you live with that? I just want him back."

Slowly Al nodded, but his jaw was clenched and I didn't like Hodin's smug look.

"I will not tell you my idea with Gally here," Hodin said petulantly, and Jenks clattered his wings in impatience.

"Get over yourselves." Tired of them, I went to fix my books. The gap where my new ones had been hurt. "Al is my teacher. I run everything past him." *Usually.*

"If he's your teacher, what am I?" Hodin asked, clearly trying to make trouble.

"You are a plaything," Al said. "A man whore."

"He is not a plaything!" I said, voice rising. "Will you stop bickering long enough to hear Hodin's idea? Can you separate Bis's soul from the baku or not!"

Hodin seemed to fall back in on himself, eyes flicking from Al to me. "No," he finally admitted, and Al gestured as if he'd known it all along. "But I'm fairly confident I know how to affix a new soul to him."

His last words hung in the air. I looked up to Bis, and Jenks dropped down, his small features furrowed in worry. "Would it still be Bis?" I asked for both of us, not sure.

Gaze flicking to Al and back, Hodin pressed his lips. "I don't know. But he wouldn't be comatose. And with that, he'd be able to teach you how to jump a line." He hesitated, one hand nervously spinning a ring on his other hand. "I think," he added.

Al made a rude noise. "That is the worst idea I've heard in an eon."

"Because it involves elven magic?" Hodin snapped, and the two faced off again.

"No, because it won't give the desired effect." Al eyed his fingernails, hidden within his gloves. "It's Bis's soul that has bonded to Rachel. Not Bis's body. Not Bis's mind. His soul. If you drop another in him like a row of candy in a PEZ dispenser, you will get nothing but a confused, bewildered gargoyle who doesn't know why he's living with a demon in a church filled with refugees from a vampire war that she is refusing to fight."

"I'm not fighting a war with Constance over Cincinnati," I said quickly, and Al tugged the lace in his sleeves down.

"No, you aren't," he said, his impatience obvious. "And that's the problem. Joke curses?" he said derisively, his gaze going to Hodin as if it was his fault. "If you desire to remain my student, don't ever talk to him again."

Hodin stiffened. "The lily wasn't my idea," he said, but Al had vanished. There were three books where he had stood, and relief spilled into me as I lurched to get them before Hodin could so much as see the titles. "The lily wasn't my idea," Hodin said again, softer this time.

But I was proud of what I'd done with the lily, and Al's words hurt even as I hugged the books he'd left to me. It had been my own magic: a mix of demon and good old-fashioned witch spells. Even Dali had been impressed.

"Hodin, will you please leave?" I said, the books to my chest as if they were a plea Al couldn't mouth.

Hodin was gone when I looked up, and I sank down on the boxes, still holding the books. Maybe they were a promise. A promise that Al would be there even when others told him not to, even when his own soul and hurt said for him to walk away.

"Hey, uh, I should probably check on those fairies," Jenks said as he hovered before me. "Baribas told his kin to leave them alone, but accidents happen."

"Sure, go," I said, head down. "Tell David I'll be down in a few minutes." I needed a moment. Hell, I needed a couple. Hodin had an idea to help Bis. It would alienate Al, maybe for good, but Bis . . . If it went right, he would be back. If it went wrong . . . well, he'd at least be alive. He could start over without me.

But Al . . . I thought, miserable. He trusted me, even now he trusted me, and to betray that? I couldn't do it.

"Rache?" I looked up to see Jenks hanging before me as if not knowing what to do with his hands. "Never mind," he finally said, and then he was gone, Rex trailing along down the steps behind him.

CHAPTER

12

THE DELICIOUS SCENT OF WERE WAS HEAVY IN THE DAMP, predawn air as David crouched beside me behind the abandoned car. His complex, rich aroma of strength and temperance almost overpowered the petroleum stink of the nearby river and the reek of burning rubber rising in a black plume from the railyard half a city away.

Piscary's lay before us, the two-story tavern turned residence dark in the early-morning haze. Not a hint of light shone in any window, and as I watched, the security light in the parking lot went out. To my right was the river, and beyond that, Cincy herself, her lights gone as the first of the sun found the top of the Carew Tower. Kisten's boat lay quiet, the water lapping softly. Eyeing it suspiciously, I worked the last of the steak from my teeth.

It had been a hard night in Cincy, though the Hollows had fared better. Smoke rose from more than the railyard, and though I'd been cloistered upstairs spelling, Stef and Jenks had kept a running tally of what had been coming in over the TV that one of the refugees had set up atop Ivy's baby grand. I was pretty sure the smaller smoke plume was from the multispecies brawl at the Grab-and-Bag on Vine. There'd also been a bonfire burning Constance in effigy at Eden Park, quickly extinguished by the I.S., but not before the news crews had gotten there. The tunnel under Central

Parkway had been forcibly opened by displaced people seeking shelter, and the I.S. caused a second riot by trying to clear the protesters/refugees out. I still didn't know how that had ended.

But the worst of the smoke came from the derailed train left to burn. Fortunately it had been freight and no one had been killed, but it had happened at a critical point on the line and the entire rail system in and out of Cincy had been shut down. Local services were still working, but I-75 both northbound and southbound was slammed as people tried to leave. Worried, I squinted up at the empty skies. It was weird seeing them without any jets. Everything was being diverted to Dayton, and no incoming flights meant no outgoing.

My brow furrowed as David rose, grit grinding under his boot. A thin trail of pixy dust was arrowing from Piscary's to us. Jenks, obviously, and if the pixy wasn't trying to hide, it was likely there was no reason for us to do the same.

I slowly got up to stand shoulder to shoulder with David, pulse quickening as I searched my bag for the vial of potion that I'd made while I waited for the earth to turn and the rising sun to force the undead belowground. I'd found the knockout curse in one of the books that Al had left, newly dog-eared and with a penciled-in adaptation to change it from a word-invoked curse taken from the collective to a painstakingly crafted potion with a much larger reach. True, a shouted curse was handy, but it had to be invoked anew each time. And there was the payment to consider, too. A potion, however, could be dropped into the air system, putting out everyone lacking the antidote. *And all without ever setting foot or wing inside,* I thought, increasingly flustered as I looked for it.

"Problem?" David asked. The vial was intentionally small so Jenks could carry it, but it wasn't *that* small.

"I can't find the vial," I muttered, setting my splat gun on the roof of the abandoned car with a soft click. A wad of zip-strips followed it, then a handful of saltwater vials to break any earth charms. My phone, now set to airplane mode so my mom wouldn't call and give us away, was next. Key ring glowing a faint red. Couple of uninvoked pain amulets. *I know I brought it.*

The sun was coming up, and the need to move made my fingers slip and fumble. I'd had to wait until sunrise despite my worry for Zack and Nash because I couldn't risk knocking them all unconscious until the dead had been driven underground. Damage wrought while rescuing an elven priest could be smoothed out and overlooked. Killing an old undead could not.

"Cameras are looped." Jenks came to a dust-laden halt before us, wings rasping. "I think they're expecting you," he said, and I looked up, blowing a strand of hair from my eyes. "There's only one living vamp aboveground, passed out drunk in Piscary's front room."

David made a grunt of surprise and stopped checking his big-ass rifle. I'd never seen him shoot at anything other than the ceiling, but it was a major conversation stopper.

"Just one?" I asked for both of us, and Jenks shrugged, his soft-soled shoes slipping on the dew-wet car roof as he landed beside my splat gun. "Even the boat?"

"Boat is empty," he said, and my gaze went to the amulet glowing fitfully around Jenks's neck. Nash was here. They must all be downstairs, waiting. If I was holding an elven holy man, that's where I'd be. But I would have had an army upstairs as a buffer.

"What about downstairs?" I asked, and Jenks flushed.

"I'm not going down until I need to," he said. "Tink loves a duck, Rache. You overdid the lily. I can't breathe in there."

I grimaced, but it didn't matter. The potion would work on a hundred as easily as one. We were going in no matter what was downstairs.

"Do you want more people?" David's gaze lifted to the three guys a block down going through a dumpster.

"Not with Rache's potion." Jenks's sharply angled features slipped into a smile.

But only if I found it, and, growing more concerned, I dug deeper. *Jeez, Rachel. How unprofessional can you get?* But I finally spotted the red-tinted vial under the plastic bag of lilac clippings. The wilting flowers were the only part of the curse that I hadn't had in the garden. Stef had gone out to get them, making a special trip to one of the local florists specializing in out-of-season blooms. They were decidedly sad looking after being dunked in salt water and then again in the antidote for the knockout potion. Trying it out at the church hadn't been an option, seeing as it was rapidly filling up with refugees coming in by ones and twos. I trusted my skills, but troll turds, everything was new, and I had no idea how long the potion or antidote would last.

"Here, keep this on you," I said as I opened the bag and gave the largest sprig to David. "Jenks?" I said, extending a drooping bracket of flowers to the pixy. Jenks darted close, using his garden sword to lop off a flower, which he then tucked into his bandana. "And one for me," I added, pinning the remainder to myself like a wilted nosegay.

Pulling myself straight, I faced the coming sunrise. The damp rising off the river filled my lungs, and I breathed it out, praying I'd be this side of the grass when the sun went down. *"Ad dormit,"* I whispered, the simple phrase invoking the already primed demon curse and shifting the potion color from red to black.

Nothing else happened, and Jenks's wings clattered. "Er, Rache?" he asked as I cracked the lid and a whisper-thin haze spilled out. The scent of lavender and apples rose—bread and autumn leaves. My eyelids fluttered. Knees weak, I fumbled to recap it as I slumped to lean against the car. But then the scent of lilac blossomed and my eyes flashed open. Pulse fast, I stared at David, then Jenks. The pixy was fine. David was yawning but looked okay.

"Your aura wavered, but it's back. Did it work?" Jenks asked, and then we all jumped when a mourning dove hit the ground, sliding three feet to a halt in the scrubby weeds.

"I'd say that's a yes." David yawned again, then lifted his lapel to breathe deep from the faded lilac. "I'm glad you're a good witch. That could be fatal in the wrong situation."

"Don't I know it," I muttered. It fit the parameters for a white curse—but only until it killed someone and the I.S. in all their selfish zeal labeled it black. Which was kind of why we had to wait until sunup to use it. No way would I knock everyone in Piscary's out before sunrise and risk trapping an undead aboveground.

"Sweeter than pixy piss," Jenks said as he darted back from the bird. It worked. Now all we had to do was get it into the air system, rescue Nash and Zack, and get out before it wore off.

"Okay, let's do this," I said as I rechecked the cap and extended it. Jenks came close, his wings humming as he took the vial in both arms. It was almost as tall as him, and I watched, worried, when he flew a sagging beeline back to the tavern. Like most vamp air systems, it would work from the lowest level up, pacifying everyone without them ever knowing it. We could be in, out, and no one the wiser.

"Talk about a light footprint," David said. "How long until we can go in?"

I glanced at the downed bird, then turned to shove everything back in my bag. "Jenks has the cameras on loop. We can go now." The distant tinkling of a bottle pulled my attention up to three scavengers. "Yours?" I said, and David nodded, his head down over his phone.

"Yep. They'll keep our exit open," he said, reminding me of Trent in the way he coolly handled old business while making new.

"Good. The fewer people involved, the better." Satisfied, I gave my bag a shake to settle everything, and together we headed to the tavern, my vamp-made boots silent beside David's soft scuff. The place seemed deserted with only one rental car out front, but the finder amulet and Jenks's intel said otherwise. Behind us, the dove woke up, flying away with a soft wheeze.

"How about them?" I said, hands in the pockets of my green leather jacket as I gave a chin lift to the two middle-aged living vamps washing the night's ash from the boat tied up across the river. They'd made a point to notice us when we had arrived, and I'd been watching them watch us for almost ten minutes while Jenks had done his above-ground recon.

David squinted across the river as he put his phone away. "Not mine. I don't think they belong to Constance, though." His eyes half closed, and he took a slow breath. "They don't smell scared, and all her people do."

The man could smell fear from across the Ohio River, I thought, impressed. He met my step, stride for stride, and as I glanced sidelong at him, my thoughts went to Trent. I liked kicking ass in a team, but doing this with David was easier than with Trent. The answer as to why was obvious. I loved Trent. I would fight to my last breath to save David, but Trent? I would fall apart and do angry, unforgiving, vengeful things if anyone did lasting hurt to him. Not having that risk sandwiched between my worry and reason made things a lot easier.

Which could make things really difficult, I thought, as I looked at the ring he'd given me. All it would take would be someone hurting Trent for me to do something really stupid.

"You okay?" David's smooth voice folded into the morning like fog over water.

"Thanks for doing this with me," I said, not answering him, and he grinned.

"Wouldn't miss it." His smile rose to encompass his eyes. "The hard part was convincing the rest of the pack to hold off. They'd do anything for you. You know that, right?"

"Which is why they aren't here," I said, not comfortable with people I hardly knew risking so much for me.

But David was clearly in a good mood, grinning at my slowly dissolving enthusiasm. The closer we got to the old tavern with its no-downstairs-windows theme and weather-beaten façade, the less I liked it. We had to get Zack and Nash without leaving any evidence of having been there. If we were caught, Constance would be within her legal rights to bring charges, even if she'd been illegally detaining Zack. It was home invasion, pure and simple, and the more well-known I became, the more scrutiny I was under, and the more finicky the I.S. was about me breaking the law. David might get a night in jail and probation, but I'd be dropped into a high-security prison, wrapped in so much red tape that even Ivy couldn't get me out.

"Jenks," David said softly, and my wandering, worried thoughts focused.

We were almost to the front door, and I swung my hair from my shoulders to give him a place to land. "Good to go?" I asked, more nervous, not less.

"Good," he echoed. "I did another aboveground sweep. There's only the one guy." He fingered the finding amulet around his neck, still glowing a faint red. "They must be downstairs."

Boots scuffing, we went up the wide, shallow steps to the large porch where vamps had once relaxed and flirted while waiting for a table. Boxes and furniture were stacked almost to the roof, left as if the people had simply vanished. "You think it's a trap?"

David fingered his rifle. "Anytime you're entering a vampire's home, it's a trap." He paused. "Front door, eh?" he said, squinting in worry.

"You want to shimmy up to the roof and come in through the second story?" I asked.

"I'm telling you, it's one guy upstairs, and he's in a drunk stupor," Jenks insisted. "The cameras are tripped. You're a ghost, Rache."

But that was kind of what I was afraid of. Pulse fast, I took Ivy's spare key from my pocket. My chin lifted at the faint scent of lily as I fitted it into the lock, but the door was open, and I hesitated, my misgivings thickening. This was too easy. We were being played.

Breath held, I nudged the thick oak door open.

The scent of lily rolled out, nauseatingly strong. Under

it was the tang of frightened vampire. I froze, unable to step forward, my neck tingling in memory.

"I'll check it out," David said as he edged past me in a hush of sliding leather.

Jenks followed, his dust a weird orange.

I should have moved, but every instinct said go. Turn around. Flee. My shadow lay long across the oak floor, scuffed and dirty from people moving things in and out. The bar looked about the same as it had for the last sixty years, with dark mirrors, darker bottles, and a light rectangle on the wall where the MPL license had hung. The large, open living room that had once held booths and tables was messy with unfamiliar move-in clutter, couches and chairs mashed up into an unusable pile before the seldom-lit fireplace. Open boxes covered the floor and the huge coffee table. It was as if everyone had been called away in midtask, and the feeling of impending disaster strengthened.

As Jenks had said, there was one living vampire, slumped unconscious in a chair facing the door, his hand around an empty bottle of whiskey.

Rifle ready, David went to check out the kitchen. "Is no one listening to me? The kitchen is clear, Mr. Peabody," Jenks complained loudly as he followed him. "The upstairs is empty. It's just Mr. Jim Beam here. And he ain't going to wake up without some help."

I forced myself to step over the threshold, eyes watering at the scent of lily. *No wonder Constance is ticked.* "He doesn't look like a fighter," I said, feeling as if something was crawling up my back. No, the man slumped in the chair with his mouth hanging open was thin, almost malnourished, the scars on his arms ranging from thick and old to red rimmed and brand-new. A thick stubble coated his face, and his nails were worn almost to the quick. He was in casual pants and a dress shirt, stained from dust and sweat. Clearly not one of Constance's favorites.

She left him for me to find. A disposable vampire so scared he drank himself senseless on cheap whiskey.

David's foot scuffed the stairs to the upper floor. The sound shot through me, and my gaze went to the camera in the corner. The little red light was on, winking at me, but Jenks had it on a loop. We were, as he had said, ghosts.

"Downstairs," I whispered, and David halted, his head even with the upstairs floor. Turning, he silently came back down to peer in through the swinging doors to the kitchen. My senses tingled, overloaded by the reek of vampire, and I held my breath against the stink of lily as we went into the kitchen to find the only way down.

The kitchen was slightly more organized. Open boxes sat on the counters and packing peanuts littered the floor. Unfamiliar glasses in the sink held drops of wine. Dishcloths I'd never bought hung from the oven handles. My shoulders hunched, I followed David to the almost anticlimactic entrance to Piscary's lower levels.

"When did Ivy put in the staircase?" David asked, hesitating inside the stark, ten-by-fourteen room. It had probably been a butler pantry at one time, but now it was empty apart from the enormous wall clock facing the elevator and the spiral staircase going down beside it. The wide, triangle steps looked like teeth, and the fading hint of pixy dust told me Jenks was running vanguard. The smell of lily was getting worse.

"Ivy found it under the floor two weeks after taking possession," I whispered, not wanting to hit the call button and possibly leave a record of our being here. "It's original." I looked at David, my gut tightening. This was too easy. Constance wanted us here. "I'm taking the stairs."

I pushed forward before David could, my steps silent on the worn wood as I descended. My bad feeling was getting worse, and not all of it was because that lily stench had become gaggingly thick. Glasses in the sink, the lack of cars out front, one disposable vamp upstairs: someone wanted us here, and I was wound tighter than a troll on her wedding night by the time we reached the lower floor, well below the level needed to ensure safety to the undead.

As Jenks had said, the main room was empty. Once

white and stark with Piscary's lack of imagination, it was now soothing grays and blues, evidence of Ivy and Nina. More open boxes and furniture were scattered about, and my heart hurt.

David scuffed to a halt, a hand over his nose. "The smell probably drove them out," he said, muffled.

I reached for a ley line, already knowing that we were too deep to manage it. Piscary had chosen his lair carefully, and though he was dead—truly dead—the place still stank of him and his paranoid preparations.

"Jenks?" I whispered, turning to the fitful sound of his wings. My face went slack at his silver-gray dust, his flight low and halting as he came from the downstairs kitchen.

"Rache," he rasped, face white as he landed on my hand. "Nash . . ." he said, voice breaking.

Fear slid cleanly through me, dividing thought from action. I strode to the tiny room, David's cautioning reach pulling from my arm. My hip nudged my bag, pushing it in front of me, and I reached for my splat gun.

"Rache, it's not your fault." Jenks's flight paralleled my motion. "It was his choice."

His words dropped down my spine like ice. The familiar cool feel of my splat gun lit a fire in my chest. Images of past vampire cruelty flashed through my mind, and I lurched to stay in front of David as we entered the small kitchen where Ivy used to make popcorn.

Fear and anger spiraled into confusion and shock. My expression blanked, and I stared, trying to figure out what I was looking at. "Oh, God," I whispered, shocked to stillness.

The masculine frame tied to the table had to be Nash. It was too big to be Zack. His body was smeared with blood, but his face was eerily clean, and his yellow shock of hair stood out bright. His head hung off the end of the table to bare his untouched throat. His clothes stuck to him, black with blood. Ivy's huge popcorn bowl sat under the table, bloody rags to the brim. Blood had dripped from the table, and a swath of it decorated the ceiling, now dried to an ugly brown. One wall had been entirely smeared with blood, the outline of a lily rubbed into it as if it had been finger-painted.

My splat gun drooped; the silence hammered on my ears. The scent of lily and decaying blood choked me.

"Sweet bloody Jesus," David whispered from behind me.

"Is he alive?" I asked as I inched forward. "Nash?" But he had to be. Jenks's amulet was still glowing, and he wouldn't dust the wounds of a dead man.

"Don't," Jenks said as I reached for the sprig of lilac pinned to me and ripped a piece free. "Rache, don't wake him up. Let him die in his sleep."

But Zack was missing, and Constance had clearly made Nash his whipping boy. He wasn't going to die if I could stop it. *How am I going to get him out of here?*

"Nash?" Hands shaking, I placed the lilac on him, thinking the flowers looked demented amid the blood and stink. A string of pearls hung from his neck, red and ugly, the shine lost under the dried blood. "Nash, can you hear me?" I added as I took his head in my hands and lifted it even with his body. Under him, the necklace swayed with an ugly stiffness.

Nash's breath came in with a sudden, terrifying rattle. Startled, I almost dropped him. His eyes opened, but they were filled with blood, unseeing as he stared at the ceiling. "Nash?" I called again, and Jenks hovered closer.

"Don't give her anything, Zack," Nash rasped, his ragged voice clear in the utter silence. "Don't make this for nothing."

"Nash?" I shifted his head, his anguished cry filling me with panic. "It's me. Rachel!" I said, trying to hold his head even. "We're going to get you out of here. Where's Zack?" *Al. Al can pop us to a hospital,* I thought. He said he wouldn't help me with Constance, but he'd left me books. . . .

"Ask him where they went," Jenks said, but then Nash's blood-caked eyes found mine, and from behind me, David took a shaky breath.

"Rachel?" Nash's cracked lips smiled. "Now you're in for it, you cold bitch. Rachel . . . will mess you up."

I thought I was going to be sick, but I couldn't do anything if I was holding his head. "David," I whispered, flushed with indecision. "Take his head so I can invoke a pain amulet."

"You can't move him," David said, and my anger flared at the Were's pinched, agonized expression. "The pheromones down here turning pain to pleasure are the only thing keeping him alive," David insisted. "You take him out of here, and he'll die of shock in ten seconds. I don't care how many pain amulets he's wearing."

Jenks nodded, and my jaw clenched. "Take. His. Head," I ground out from between my teeth, and, shoulders slumped, David shifted to stand beside me. Nash's eyes widened and his breath came fast as the Were's hands slipped in under mine. My fingers went cold, and I took a shallow breath as I backed up. I was afraid to look at the rest of him, afraid that I'd realize that David was right and there was nothing I could do.

My stomach churned as I invoked two amulets, listened to Nash's pain-etched breathing, then invoked a third. I set them on his chest, and Jenks dusted an odd gray when Nash took a deep, rattling breath in relief.

"Nash?" I bent closer, trying to smile. Constance had tortured and left him for me to find. She had wanted to scare me. But I wasn't scared. I was pissed. Enough to do something stupid. Stupid enough to actually make a difference, maybe. "Nash," I whispered again, and his eyes found mine. "Where's Zack?"

He licked his lips, hands fluttering at his sides to touch the ropes that held him. "She took him and left. They all left," he said. "After they were done with me." His eyes went to the ceiling and the pattern of blood. "Oh, God," he moaned. "You're a demon. Can you put it back? She took everything out."

"Where did she bite you?" I said, feeling his neck with gentle fingers as he pushed at his bloodstained middle. I could see no bite marks. What had she taken if not blood?

And then I followed Jenks's ashen expression to Nash's hands, still moving at his middle.

I felt the blood drain from me. Constance had opened him up and taken out what she could without outright killing him. Those weren't bloody rags in Ivy's popcorn bowl. They were his insides.

"She made him watch," Nash was saying, tears making clear paths down his bloodstained face. "I'm sorry, Zack. I'm so sorry. Can you put it back?"

David held his head steady, his jaw clenched and his eyes averted.

My gorge rose, and I kept my breaths shallow, the scent of lily filling me with a perverted contrast. She'd tortured Nash to force Zack to accept her authority, doing it such that he'd be alive for me to find. David was right. To move him would kill him, and Al . . . *Damn it, Al,* I thought, remembering both his anger at Hodin's appearance and his slyly given help even as both he and Dali insisted Constance was my problem. Giving me spell books was simply supplying resources. Healing Nash was far more, and I didn't think he'd save an elf even if I asked.

"He didn't give in," Nash whispered, pride in his voice. "Don't give her anything, Zack. Don't give the tiny bitch the satisfaction," he moaned, lost in memory.

"Rachel . . ."

It was David, and my fear deepened. He'd known there was no happy ending as I blithely ignored reality. "I can't fix this," I whispered, panic and frustration welling as I fixed on his dark eyes. "Al won't help me. David, Al won't help." *Even if he left me those books. . . .*

"That's okay." Nash's grip on my hand tightened. "It doesn't hurt anymore." He was blinking fast, tears spilling from him as he gave up hope that I could save him. "She's so mad at you. She wants you dead, but she's scared of you. Stark raving terrified that you stood up to her in the I.S. tower." His lips made a pained smile. "She can't find where the flower smell is coming from. You drove her out of her own daylight quarters. Zack. Zack laughed at her, and she killed three of her people when they tried to explain it's not really here. They'll do anything to appease her, Rachel."

My gaze flicked to the perverted finger-painted lily on the wall, and I all but gagged on the rank scent of blood and perfume. This was my fault. My fault, and I didn't have the skill to save him. He was going to die.

"Nash, we'll get you out of here," I said, lying to myself. If I didn't, I'd go insane. "You're going to be okay."

"Rachel, don't," David protested as I reached for the rope holding him to the table, but as I tugged at it, Nash shrieked, filling the air with his pain.

"Not that one!" Nash sobbed as David struggled, torn between holding Nash's head and trying to stop me. "That's the one keeping me closed."

I clenched my teeth, refusing to cry as Jenks helped me figure out what I could and couldn't cut.

"She's insane," Nash gasped, eyes on the ceiling as I took David's knife and began sawing at the blood-soaked ropes. "You have to get Zack away from her. She took him back to the I.S. The flower is driving her mad. She can't stand that you pushed her out of her new place. She had to spend the day at the I.S. She is so angry. She's making mistakes. They're trying to tell her, but she just keeps killing them. Rachel . . ."

I jumped when his newly freed hand grasped mine. The zip-strip blocking his access to the ley lines glinted behind the blood.

"He's okay. Zack is okay," he burbled, blood bubbling at the corner of his lips. "But she wants you dead. She's going to hurt everyone you care about to get you to come to her."

His hand fell from mine and his eyes closed. For a moment, I thought he'd died, but then his chest moved. "Leave me here. Go get him," he whispered, and then louder, lost in a memory: "Don't hurt him! *Don't hurt him!*"

David didn't move as he held Nash's head even with the table. Teeth clenched, I went to Nash's feet, grasped his ankles, and, eyes closed at Nash's shriek of pain, pulled him down the table until his feet hung over and his head rested on the Formica.

"Sorry," Nash panted, bright-eyed from the adrenaline

surge. "I'm sorry. I know you're trying to help. It doesn't hurt anymore. Please. Leave me here. Go find Zack."

I took his hand again, but the strength was gone from his thick fingers. Trent's ring had become a blood pearl, a swirl of bright red and dead brown as it dried. I couldn't stand before Zack and tell him I'd walked away. Constance had tortured Nash, murdered him to scare me, to scare Zack. But despite his few years, Zack wouldn't be scared into anything. His mind was young, but his soul was old. He'd suffer crushing guilt—but he'd never give in.

I'd always ignored the corruption in the I.S. because I'd never been able to do anything about it. But now, seeing Nash beg me to leave and find Zack, I decided that had been an excuse. I'd always been able to do something. I just hadn't wanted to deal with the fallout. I was a coward. Nash was paying for it.

Never again, I thought as I looked at the blood-lily on the wall, tears blurring my vision as my guilt and anguish almost swamped my anger.

"I'm sorry, Rachel. You can't save him," David said, and my lips pressed. Though he still breathed, Nash was gone. I couldn't save him. Now, it was about saving me.

"Jenks. Watch my back," I said as I took Nash's hand more firmly, then closed my eyes, stretching my awareness out for the demon collective, funneling every last ounce of rage and frustration into a single, solitary cry.

Algaliarept! I shouted into the swirling chaos, searching for the collective, not sure if I'd be able to reach it or not. Al said I didn't need the mirror anymore. *Algaliarept, talk to me!* I shouted again, gasping when my awareness seemed to sort of slip sideways and drop two feet. I was in.

Good God. She's using his full name, I caught, the anonymous thought mocking and bitter. Frustration-not-mine rose up, a nameless demon's anger that I hadn't killed Hodin when I first saw him, then another demon's amusement that I was trying to reach Al, a mocking surety that I wasn't up to the task of taking on Constance on my own, and hadn't everyone said as much?

But the barrage vanished when the smallest afterthought annealed tightly to mine. *I'm a little busy right now.*

Al's thought slipped through me as if it was my own, seeing as it sort of was at the moment. My grip tightened on Nash's hand, and I latched a thought into Al's psyche as he tried to slip away. *I need your help.*

When don't you? he thought, but I had only the teeniest fraction of his attention, and I wormed my way deeper into his mind. He was arguing with someone. No . . . someone was yelling at him. Someone other than me.

Dali? I questioned, my grip on Nash spasming when Al sort of jerked, enveloping my mind in an annoyed presence, spiraling us down to a level of conscious so low it was almost sleep. *Al, I need your help. Now,* I thought, trying not to notice the dark shadows of guilt and shame. I couldn't tell if they were mine or his.

"Rache?"

The spoken word zinged through me, ignored. It was Jenks, but Al had finally focused on me, Dali's ongoing tirade fading into a background nothing. *I'm trying to explain to Dali where his books went,* Al thought in annoyance.

The ones you gave me? I thought, and Al's smug pride swelled almost into a laugh. Somewhere, I felt Dali become choleric.

"Rache?" Jenks's wings tickled my ear, and I stifled a sneeze.

Crap on toast, he gave me stolen books? But my private thought was anything but, and I felt Al steel his thoughts, hiding mine from Dali's. *Al, she eviscerated Nash,* I thought, frantic. *She did it because I drove her from her daylight quarters with that lily smell. I can't fix him. I can't move him. Please! I need a healing curse.*

"Rachel!" Jenks poked my ear with his sword, and I jumped. "He's gone!"

I blinked, trying to focus, my mind splintered between the hellhole of Piscary's downstairs kitchen and the swirling confusion of Al's thoughts. My sight cleared, and I felt Al's mirth vanish as he saw through my eyes. Agony filled

me, and I didn't care that Al knew the pain of my soul. He'e
seen it before.

Rachel? Al questioned, our minds suddenly empty o
his thoughts of Dali.

And somehow, as I felt Nash's hand warm in mine, I
knew it was true. I couldn't tell you what was missing, bu
Jenks was right. Nash was gone. That awful, awful still
ness. I'd seen it before in a cruddy little hospital when my
dad died.

Blinking fast, I stared at Nash's face, gripped his hand
tighter as I held my breath. I tried to pull my thoughts from
Al, but he clung to me. Grief raked my soul, leaving it open
and raw, and I staggered, almost unable to bear it. It wasn'
all mine. Some of it was Al's.

Never mind, I thought, and a deep, hot, dangerous ange
flashed through us both.

Now you may survive, he thought, and I jerked from
him, stumbling as I found myself entirely in the present, my
feet sticking to the floor, Nash's hand still warm in mine.

Surviving wasn't exactly on my mind at the moment
and a hot anger drove everything else out.

"Rachel, I'm sorry," David said, and my head went up a
if I could see through the layers of dirt between me and tha
disposable vampire Constance had left for me.

"Rache?" Jenks questioned, but anger had tightened my
chest until it was all I could do to breathe.

"I'm sorry," I whispered harshly as I set Nash's hand or
his chest. "I'll see Zack safe."

I would cry later.

"Bring him," I said as I turned and walked out of the
room.

"Rachel? Think before you act," David called after me
but I was already halfway across the large room, my fee
leaving smaller and smaller bloody prints. I hit the call but
ton for the elevator, catching the door and holding it as I
waited for David. I wasn't worried anymore about Con
stance crying foul for me having found and taken Nash

There would be no reprisal for this. Constance wanted me to find him. Wanted me to see her blood-lily.

But even so, I'd exhaled in relief when the doors had opened and the elevator had been empty. A part of me had expected Constance to be in there, smiling and happy to make my bad day worse.

"She did this hoping you'd do something rash," David said as he staggered into the elevator. He held Nash like a baby, wrapped in his long duster.

"Yeah. I'm easy to read, aren't I," I said, then smacked the "close door" button to hurry this along.

Jenks hovered uncertainly over my shoulder. I knew David was right but I couldn't stop myself. I didn't *want* to stop myself. If I had been able to jump the lines, I could've popped Nash into emergency. If I had been skilled enough, I could have done a healing charm. Or put him in stasis. Or something! But I hadn't been able to do any of those things.

David leaned into the corner of the elevator, using the walls to help him hold Nash. Finally the doors opened and I strode out. "Put him on the couch," I said as I stormed through the kitchen and stiff-armed the swinging doors open.

I could hear David talking, but the words flowed over me without meaning as I stood beside the vampire sleeping off his whiskey, my hands shaking. The couch, though, was full, and I shoved everything off, sending boxes flying as David staggered closer. Jenks hovered close as David knelt, exhaling as he gently settled the coat-wrapped elf down, his head on a flat pillow.

My gut twisted and grief flowed up as I saw him, swamping the anger. Throat tight, I gently arranged Nash's hair from his eyes and took that damned necklace off, shoving it into a pocket to maybe choke Constance with. Constance had taken everything, not just from him, but from everyone his life would have touched.

"Rachel, slow down and think," David said as I touched Nash's face before rising with that scrap of lilac.

"I am thinking," I said as I dropped the sprig on the snoring vampire. "You. Wake up," I demanded, but nothing changed. It wasn't the charm that had him out now. It was the whiskey.

"Easy, Rache," Jenks cautioned, and I shoved the vampire's feet off the ottoman.

They hit a box and slid to the floor with a thump, and finally the slumbering man woke, his rheumy eyes darting over the room to find David and me standing over him. My breath shook as I exhaled, hands becoming fists as he awkwardly pulled himself up in the chair until the flower slipped to land in his lap. "She said you'd come," he said, voice rough and ugly as he fingered the lilac.

"She was right," I said, then gave in and slapped his face with my open hand. Hard.

His head rocked back, and when his eyes met mine again, there was hatred in them. That was okay. I was going to do hateful things.

"He's not worth it," David cautioned as I stood before him, my hand fisted and the power of the ley line cramping all the way up my arm.

"No, but Nash is," I said, jerking back when Jenks flew too close, dusting an unreal green and red, his face tight in anger. "Relax, I'm not going to kill him," I said, and David's pinched expression eased. "I'm just going to hit some more."

The vampire's eyes widened, but I was faster, and my open hand hit his other cheek with a startling pop of sound. Pain throbbed in my palm, and I shook it away, not caring that it probably had hurt me more than him.

"I'm glad I'm a pixy," Jenks said. "No one cares if we kill someone."

Expression sullen, the vampire touched his face. Clearly he was low in his camarilla's hierarchy and he knew better than to complain. "Zack, Zack, tied to a rack," he bitterly half sang, infuriating me. "Say you'll behave, or Nash will lack. Where *is* that flower hiding?"

My God. He's goading me, I thought, wanting to give in.

"Where is Zack!" I demanded, shaking David's sudden grip off me. "Did she touch him? Did she?!" I shouted, but the drunk vampire only giggled, high-pitched and ugly.

"He's scared," the vampire said. "He should be. He's so young." His grin widened. "Skin so smooth, and so close to being of age that it doesn't matter if he gets a little nicked."

"Did she touch him!" I screamed, my throat going raw.

Jenks's wings clattered by my ear, and the drunk vampire looked at David, then me. "One of them was going to die," he almost slurred. "She's so pissed. She finally got a city of her own, and you forced her to sleep in the I.S.? Oh, that was sweet, so sweet." He smiled to show a chipped fang. "Someone had to die for that. The big guy volunteered."

I turned away, wanting to throttle the man. If I killed him, I'd be brought up on wrongful death charges. Probably end up paying for his undead living expenses for the next fifty years.

"She told me to tell you som'thin'," he said, words slurring as the alcohol took hold again, and I spun to him. "You have until sunset tomorrow to publicly announce your fealty to her, or Zack will be next." His eyes went to Nash on the couch. "Then you will have a matched pair." He tittered, the sound raking over me to make me shudder. "And if you still don't come to heel, you will have three. Three pretty elves, all in a row. Six feet under the rain and snow."

Trent? My fisted hands ached as I shoved the ley line power back into the ground. Slowly I unclenched my jaw, and Jenks's wings clattered nervously. "I'm fine. I'm fine!" I said when David leaned close. Constance had found my soft spot and jammed her knife to the hilt. But I smiled as I stood over the vampire, leaning down until I could smell the week-old blood on his breath. "I have a job for you," I said as I put a hand to either side of him on the chair's arms. "Think you can do it?"

The man's expression went ashen, thinking he saw his death in my eyes. But it wasn't his death he saw, but rather the death of who I wanted to be. The sun was a luxury. Ignorance was too expensive for me to afford, and peace too far for me to travel to. I couldn't be the friendly neighbor-hood witch living in a church rescuing familiars. Hell, I couldn't even pretend that was what I was, or everyone I cared about was going to die.

"Tell her . . ." I hesitated. "Tell her I'm going to let her live."

"Live?" the vampire said, confused.

"Live," I said again, enunciating it carefully. "She's go-ing to live with the knowledge that she was given Cincin-nati and failed to keep it because I said no. You think a stinky flower is the limit of my abilities? This is *my* city," I said, feeling ugly, angry, powerful, and vindictive. "Not hers. I gave her both a warning and a chance, and she chose to ignore them. I'm the effing demon subrosa, and if she doesn't know what that is, she can look it up. I'm in charge, not her. If she wants to stay, it's by *my* rules."

"Uh, Rache?" Jenks questioned, eyes wide as I mentally cringed at the enormity of what I'd taken on. But it was inevitable and Al was right. I might not be that good at it, but when something bad happened, I was the one who stepped up. If I wasn't going to get paid for it, I might as well have a shiny title.

God help me. How am I going to do this?

"Wait!" the vampire shrieked as I reached for him, but I was going for the scrap of lilac, and with a sigh, his eyes closed and he fell asleep.

One day, one crisis at a time. And right now, it's Con-stance. Taking a deep breath, I dropped the lilac on the floor and pulled myself straight, shaking as I glanced over the room. It looked like I felt, the familiar gone and the boxes of the new open and scattered in a chaotic, unusable mess. I was cold and wanted to put myself in the single patch of sunlight coming in the open door. "My city, my rules," I said softly, an odd, unexpected strength pulling me straight. It was born in a hard-won decision. Nash had paid for it with his life. But it was the right one.

"Rache?" His eyes pinched in worry, Jenks hovered so

close I had no option but to look at him. "We gotta go. What do you want to do with Nash's body?"

I turned, throat closing as I saw him there, peaceful and unmoving. *I hate the smell of lily.*

"Bring him," I said, and David paced slowly to the couch. "We'll bury him in the graveyard." I made a laughing cough, but it sounded more like a sob. "What's the point of having a graveyard if you don't use it?"

Maybe I can plant Constance in it, too. Six feet, face-down.

David hoisted Nash again. Somehow he looked lighter, as if the weight of the world was gone from him. It had all fallen to me, and as I followed David and Jenks back out into the sun, I vowed to become a better demon even if it killed me. The people of Cincinnati deserved it.

CHAPTER

13

"SHONOOK COO *TA RA RIAN*," HODIN SAID, HIS LOW VOICE even and his eyes turned to the earth. *"Umbringe un ta na shonookey."* His head lifted, and I stifled a shiver at his red, goat-slitted eyes, so alien in the sun. The cool spring air shifted my hair into my face, but I didn't touch it. I hadn't known you could be angry and depressed at the same time.

Nash lay on the unbroken earth between us, the winter-beaten grass dull and brown with only the first hints of green poking up through. There was no hole. Hodin had said there wasn't any need, and I took him at his word. I stood at Nash's feet. Hodin was at his head looking like a priest in one of his auratic spelling robes, the little bells on the sash jingling as he gestured over Nash's body wrapped in one of Ivy's black silk curtains. David was to my right, and Jenks on my left, standing with a row of pixies on the top of a nearby gravestone. There was no one else, though eyes were watching us from the church's backyard.

Nash was the last of his family. He'd had no significant other. The dewar had been his life, and he had given it to protect Zack. The man deserved far more, but perhaps being laid to rest with an elven burial tradition that hadn't been enacted in thousands of years might make up for it.

"For all return from whence we spring," Hodin contined, though I didn't know if he was saying anything new or echoing what he'd just said in elven. "Accept our fallen, failed in body but not deed. Take now his light, so he may illuminate our thoughts and comfort us when we are alone and in darkness. Receive him as we loved him, fully and forever until the two worlds collide."

The two worlds had collided last year, but the sentiment held true, and I stifled a surge of sorrow that swamped my anger. I could be angry later.

Jenks's wings were a tight rasp as he flew to my shoulder. His sigh of fatigue was barely audible though he was inches from my ear. "I don't think even Trent knows the ancient elven funeral rights."

David leaned close as Hodin crouched to make sweeping gestures over Nash that looked like communication glyphs. "They probably haven't been spoken since the demons turned the tables on them," David muttered, and Hodin grimaced, clearly having heard the Were.

Which was interesting all in itself. The demons might revile Hodin, call him weak and ineffective, but he probably knew more elven lore than the last three dewar leaders combined.

My head dropped as I clenched the paper holding the spell that Hodin had given me to recite. Hodin wouldn't contact the Goddess for the final invocation, so it was up to me. My throat grew tight, and the lingering scent of lily made me want to gag. Under it was the cloying stench of vampire fear. Or maybe it was my fear. I'd told Constance that Cincy was mine. I was in charge. That she looked to me, not the other way around.

And yet, the need to take action was growing in me, rising from Hodin's softly muttered words. My pulse quickened as Hodin stood to gesture at the sky and earth, drawing enough latent energy into the graveyard to make my hair snarl. If Al hadn't been pulling his acorns out of the fire for stealing books to give to me, Nash might still be alive. The thought preyed on me. I had needed him, and he hadn't come.

So when Hodin had unexpectedly shown up at th church again, I had started yelling, seeing in the intro verted, angsty demon a bitter reminder of my inabilities Hodin stoically took my misplaced abuse as if he deserve it: my anger that I hadn't gone to him first, and then m frustration when I found out that even if I *had* called Ho din, Nash would have died. Apparently the demon didn *know* a healing curse.

But eventually my angry tirade had disintegrated t leave a growing shame. Seeing him now, elegant and sur as his multi-ringed hand gestured and words I didn't know passed his lips, I began to wonder if maybe *this* was th demon I'd rather be: studious, apart, holding wisdom n one else did. Snappy dresser.

Not everyone has to be all-powerful, I thought as Jenk rasped his wings, uncomfortable as the latent energy con tinued to build. Though admittedly only the powerful ha survived the demon/elven war. My eyes went again to Ho din. *Mostly.*

Regret finally began to push out my anger where sorrow had not, regret at what I'd said to him, that he lacked, tha he was useless. He wasn't useless. *This,* I thought as h sprinkled herbs atop Nash's body, *is not useless.* Healin was not useless. Finding how to live with what had hap pened was not useless.

With a sudden ping of understanding, I realized that Ho din embodied what was missing from the demons: he knew the way for them to forgive if not forget, a way to find peac with themselves if not everyone else. Hodin, I decided, ha far more to offer than at first glance.

My grip tightened on the crackling paper, and I vowed wouldn't let the demon collective literally bury him in hole again so they could go on being broken—as comfor able as they were with that. Forgiveness was hard. Lettin go was hard. Staying a sullen, angry-at-the-world, all powerful, poor-me demon was easy.

I almost panicked when Hodin nodded to the assemble pixies and they began to sing. I'd heard the tune when Ho din taught it to them while David and I had wrapped Nash for burial, but hearing their voices now twined in heart-aching harmonies struck me to the quick. Elves and pixies went together like demons and gargoyles, and I caught back another sob before I could give it voice.

Bis . . . I was losing too much. I had to find a rock to cling to, and as my fingers began to tingle from the rising power, my watery gaze went to the nearby tombstones. *How fitting.*

"Tal Sa'han?" Hodin prompted.

I blinked my wet eyes and shoved my heartache down. I had one thing to do, and I would do it for Nash.

My breath came in slow, the power-filled air tingling in my lungs. Head dropping, I tucked a staticky strand of hair back and looked at the paper. Exhaling, I felt a welcome drop of power.

"Rache?" Jenks questioned, and I shook my head, sending crackles of ley line power snapping. I was fine. The Goddess didn't recognize me anymore, didn't even see me. At least, not any more than she saw anyone else.

"Ta na shay, cooreen na da. Sone dell cooms da nay," I whispered, recognizing the last phrase as one Trent had used to send a soul to rest. *"Sone favilla, suda conay."* I hesitated at the tingling sensation rising through my feet to flow to my hands. Quashing my unreasonable fear, I crouched to take a handful of earth. The tingles became pinpricks, and I looked at Hodin.

He gave me a single nod of approval. I was doing it right, and my pulse quickened. *"Sa'ome, sa'ome,"* I intoned, shuddering when the rising power collected and dripped from my hands.

"Rache, it's mystics," Jenks whispered, his voice holding fear.

But even as they sparked in my hair and made my aura flare, I knew they weren't interested in me. There was no buzzing in my head or whispered thoughts-not-mine. They were just there, latent energy called together for a task.

Chin trembling, I gently tossed the power-imbued dirt

over Nash's silk-wrapped body. *"Ta na shay, sa'ome,"* I whispered, gut clenching as the spell spilled from me, the earth flaring brilliantly as it arced down to him, pulling magic and mystics from me in a shivering wave.

The charm settled over Nash like a haze, brightening to make me squint and the watching pixies cry out in alarm. When I could see again, Nash was gone.

"Holy pixy piss. They took him!" Jenks swore.

David shot him a dark look at his vulgar language, but I could tell the Were was surprised, too.

I licked my lips, my hands still humming with the last of the spell. The grass where Nash had lain was alive with flowers, and the pixies dropped to flit above the new little bronze blossoms. The scent of green rose to drive the stink of lily and fear from me, and I breathed deep, feeling refreshed. I didn't recognize the flowers with their bloodred stamens. Maybe Hodin knew what they were.

David bent to pick one, his head bowed to hide his grief as he breathed it in. Hodin's dark eyes, too, were lost in memory. I dusted my hands free of the last of the glowing earth, wondering how many times he had stood at the outskirts, silently mouthing the words and watching those he cared for put to rest. For though elves lived long lives, demons could live forever, and despite their lingering hatred for the elves, there was a path to peace. They just had to remember it. Or perhaps . . . find the courage to act on it.

The pixies darted away, drifts of their new song trailing behind them like audible solace. Somewhere, my anger had turned to ash, but my resolve that Constance wouldn't be allowed to ride roughshod over Cincinnati remained—stronger now that the hate had been extinguished. "Thank you, Hodin," I said, feeling tired and spent.

Hodin looked up, visibly quashing an old panic. His attention flicked to David, then settled on me. "You did it, not me," he said gruffly. Tugging his spelling robe free of the clinging winter-dead weeds, he stood unmoving, his shoulders slumped in a memory.

I refolded the paper and tucked it in my jeans pocket. "You gave me the knowledge," I said. "Thank you."

Hodin grimaced, his solemn mood broken. "I'm surprised I remembered the words." Head high, he strode forward, and Jenks made a wing chirp of shock when the demon walked right over where Nash had lain. "Here." Hodin bent down and came up with a flower. "You wear it to show you're in mourning."

"Oh, ah, okay." I felt funny as Hodin tucked the tiny flower in my hair. "Hey, uh, I'm sorry for what I said to you. Earlier? That rant of mine was totally out of line."

Hodin froze, then dropped back, his ringed hands clasped and hiding in his sleeves.

"I was angry at myself," I added before he could speak, my face warming. "And Al, maybe. And I took it out on you. No one knows how to do everything, except maybe Newt, and it drove her crazy." I tried to smile, but I was sure it looked sick. "You aren't useless. You know things that no one else does, stuff that would otherwise be lost. I had no right to say what I did, and I wish I could take it back."

The demon's expression became cold. "Because you want something from me."

"No, because I was wrong," I said, and Jenks, standing on David's hand to look at his flower, snickered.

Hodin turned to go. Desperate for him to understand, I took a breath and lurched after him, grabbing his arm and taking his hand. Hodin stopped stock-still, shocked as our energy balances shifted and equalized. "I said I was wrong," I said, my tone taking on a hint of anger as he pulled his hand away. "You have amazing skills and knowledge, but even if you didn't, I'd stand beside you, whether Bis is returned to me or not."

He stared at me, not seeming to know what to do. There was pain in him, though, and I bent to pick a flower. Not knowing why, I extended it to Hodin.

Blinking in surprise, he almost smiled. "I'm not sorrowing for the dead," he said as he took it from me. "They are gifts from the deceased, given by those who care for the bereaved. Something to show they're not alone." He leaned close again, and the scent of burnt amber reached me as he settled the second flower beside the first.

"Oh." Flustered, I felt myself warm. "Thanks."

Hodin cocked his head, an unknown emotion flitting behind his eyes.

"Here, Rache." Jenks hummed close, a flower as large as his head in his grip. "I want you to be happy, too," he said, gruff and embarrassed as he darted up and wedged the flower next to Hodin's two.

"And me," David said, and Hodin dropped back when the smaller Were came forward, smelling of earth and growing things as his nimble fingers tucked a fourth flower beside the rest.

"Thanks, guys." Flustered at the attention, I looked at the ground where Nash had lain, and blinked. *I will not cry. I will not cry.*

But it was hard when David pulled me into a solid, warm hug. The scent of lily was finally slipping from me, masked by the complex scent of Were and pixy dust, and I felt loved. Brow furrowed, I gave David a tight squeeze and rocked back. Sure enough, Hodin had distanced himself, but he hadn't left, and I hoped he wouldn't before I could talk to him again. He had come. Al had not. Sometimes, it was that simple.

"You are a good person," David said, recapturing my attention. "Don't let Nash's choice turn you from that."

"I . . . How can I not let this change me?" I said, gesturing at the carpet of flowers as all the ugly returned. But this time I knew I wasn't alone and I could handle it.

David touched my hair as he stepped back, his smile faint but real. "We all change. But that doesn't mean you have to lose what makes you, you." His eyes flicked to Hodin. "I'll be inside." Giving my shoulder a squeeze, he turned and walked away. "Jenks!" he shouted, and the pixy hovered, his dust a conflicted silver and red.

I leaned against a tombstone and Jenks landed beside me, wings snapping. Together we looked at the graveyard and witches' garden as David made his way to the back door, trailing the new pixy clan.

"Hey, ah, I'm letting Baribas and his kin stay if they can work around the fairies," Jenks said, though that was clearly not what was on his mind. "Same thing with the fairies."

I glanced sideways at Hodin. The demon had gone to sit on a nearby fallen tombstone, his eyes closed, basking with his metal rings and demon bling glinting in the sun. Little trills of pixy song rose up like life-giving rain in reverse. Maybe he wanted to talk to me. "That's great, Jenks," I said. "I know how hard that is for you, but if you didn't, they probably wouldn't survive. Any of them."

His wings hummed into motion, then settled. "It's the damndest thing," he said, clearly confused. "Baribas is helping the fairies find grubs and spiders to eat so they don't have to clear-cut the garden to reach them. They're working together." He hesitated. "We can hold the same ground together," he added softly, still trying to make sense of it.

I turned to Jenks, his head nearly in line with my eyes as he perched on the stone I was leaning against. "Are you trying to tell me to find a way to work with Constance?"

Jenks blinked, a flash of dust lighting him. "Tink's titties, no!" he exclaimed, and from Hodin's distant rock, I heard a snort. "That bitch needs to die twice."

"Okay. Let's forget for a moment that it's illegal," I said, attention dropping to my hands. Nash's blood lingered in the creases and had turned Trent's pearl a muddy brown. I curled my fingers under to hide it, but it was still there. "If I kill her, DC will send in someone worse. Someone even more depraved and cruel, with a better chance of killing me. And that's if by some miracle I don't land in jail."

"So don't kill her," Jenks said, as if that was all there was to it. "You don't have to fight all of them, just her. You best her, and everyone who looks to her will fall in line. Guaranteed."

He was right, but it would be a constant battle. I'd have to become as savage and extreme as her to keep her playing by my rules. "We were spoiled by Piscary," I whispered.

"Seriously?" Jenks rose up as David stood on that fifty-five-gallon drum that was now my back porch and yelled for him. "Get your head out of the wasp nest, Rache. Piscary was just as bad as Constance. He only looked less cruel because his children were conditioned to take the abuse instead of rebel at it."

My thoughts jerked to Joni with her red-smeared smile, then to Meg, terrified and cowering because Constance had taken her necklace and was about to punish her for its lack. And finally to Ivy and Kisten. Kisten had died when he tried to be the person he wanted to be instead of the one Piscary needed. Ivy had nearly done the same. She said I'd saved her. I hadn't been able to save Kisten, though.

"Convincing Constance to play fair might be easier if she hadn't found my soft spot," I whispered.

"You mean that you care about people?" Jenks rose up and down, flashing at David to wait, and the Were went inside, the temporary door thumping shut hard enough to hear out here. "That's called being normal, Rache. All you have to do is find what's important to her, jam your sword," he said, pantomiming it, "and twist. She'll come in line."

Blackmail. My frown deepened and my focus blurred. I wasn't against blackmail, but it was a short-term solution. I'd seen what happened when Trent's blackmail turned and bit him on his lily-white ass. I had to find a way to get her to accept my authority, or, at the very least, our equal authority. But after meeting her, I was pretty sure that Constance wanted me dead or gone. If by some miracle she did agree to coexist, I'd find myself in a never-ending battle to control her bloodthirsty ways and keep the I.S. from hauling me in for jaywalking.

"Hey, could you excuse me for a moment?" Jenks said as a timid pixy darted up to hover at a respectful distance, clearly wanting to talk to Jenks.

I looked at Hodin in the sun, and a flicker of warning

rose and fell. "Sure," I said, missing Trent, and Jenks hummed away, his dust vanishing as the young buck spoke so fast and high it sounded like another language.

Wary, I pushed from the stone and angled over to Hodin. It was frustrating. The only people who wanted Constance in Cincy were the I.S. and her own clearly terrified camarilla. Together they were a small but powerful population of vampires who could use the borrowed teeth of the I.S. to bully the rest.

I need to talk to Constance, I thought as my thumb polished the blood from Trent's ring. Unfortunately, all Constance had to do was sit in the safety of the I.S. tower and make my life hell one friend at a time. I couldn't talk to her there. I needed neutral ground if I was to even have a chance.

"Rache."

I jerked to a halt when Jenks was suddenly facing me.

"Tink loves a duck," he muttered, brow furrowed. "These pixies are no smarter than newlings sucking on nectar. You tell me *before* someone gets in the church, not after."

Boots scuffing the weeds, I sighed. "Is it the city with an eviction notice?" That would round out my day nicely.

But Jenks had lost his frown, his dust an excited silver. "No, it's that contractor Sharron told us about. She must have cashed in all her Realtor favors to get someone to come out here." He rose up, hands on his hips, yelling, "And they should have told me she was here *before she got to the front steps!*" He dropped back down. "It's going to take me all summer to whip them into shape," he muttered.

"Cool." I turned to ask Hodin if he could wait, but he was gone. Disappointed, I put my hands in my pockets and began to pick my way back to the church. "I can't wait to get that hole in the floor fixed," I said as I stepped over the shallow wall and into the backyard/garden. The scent from the previous night's steaks lingered, and as I rose up the makeshift steps, I realized I'd be able to see Nash's "grave" from my bedroom window. *Swell.*

Jenks landed on my shoulder as we went in and the sudden noise of too many people pressed on us. I got nods and shy smiles from people I'd never seen before, and a feeling of having lost control tightened my chest. Light chatter came from my old bathroom, and steam slipped out from under Ivy's bathroom door. Two vamps waited in the hall, towels over their arms.

"Oh, no," I whispered as I edged around them and into the sanctuary. I hadn't gone through the church with Nash's body for obvious reasons, and I'd had no idea that the number of our refugees had swelled in the few hours I'd been gone. They were everywhere.

A big pot of soup was simmering on the twin burner set up on a cardboard table. The unreal-fast *tink-tunk, tunk-tink* of sound drew my eyes to the vamps playing Ping-Pong on Kisten's de-felted pool table, more coolers making a significant row under it. Cots took up one corner, some of them holding shrouded bodies trying to sleep through the noise. As I watched, someone came crawling out of the hole in the floor and tossed a beer to someone else. *I suppose it's cooler under there. . . .*

"Where did they all come from?" I said as I spotted a woman standing beside Ivy's baby grand, ignoring everything as she shone her laser measuring light at the corners and made notes into her electronic clipboard.

"Edden." Jenks laced the word with annoyance. "Every last one of them. I think Constance's game is to kick as many people out as she can, knowing they'll come to you for help. Sort of a nuisance attack."

I edged around a trio of witches clustered at the small slate table, practicing their pentagrams in colored chalk and comparing notes on proper glyph positioning. "But why would Edden send them here?"

"Jails are full?" Jenks guessed. "The I.S. won't help, and they have to go somewhere. But if you ask me, he's sending them to you to get you up off your, ahem, 'lazy ass' and do something about Constance."

"Yeah, okay. I get it," I said, and Jenks lifted from my shoulder, his chuckle sounding like sunshine.

"It kind of brings the situation home, huh?" he said, turning to track the wad of wet towel arcing through the air to fall with a sodden splat on the witches' table. One rose with a shout, and I felt a tweak on the ley line when he threw a spell across the room, where it exploded in a shower of sparks and laughter. "Not just a story on the news that you can turn off and ignore for another day."

Crap on toast, this is awful. "I haven't been ignoring anything," I said, scowling when someone fell into the crawlspace with a whoop. It was real all right. Really noisy. Really smelly. Really . . . in my way.

I knew I was still wearing my frown when I finally got to the woman Sharron had sent over. She was about my height, but that was where any resemblance to me besides her curves ended. I was well toned, but *she* had muscles showing in her arms and wide shoulders. Her straight brown hair was cut below her ears, and her smile was toothy. She looked comfortable and casual in her worn overalls and faded Howlers cap, and I was willing to bet her boots had steel toes under the scuffed brown leather.

"Hi," I said as the woman shifted to take me in with one long up and down, lingering on the flowers in my hair. I kept my smile in place to hide my dismay at the impression I was making. My church was a mess, and it was beginning to spill out both the front and back doors. "I'm Rachel. You must be Finley?"

Immediately the woman stuck out her hand. It was calloused and strong, and I met her firm pressure with my own. "Rachel. Yes. Sharron said you had a unique property."

Her voice was low and strong, fitting her. "Ah, it's usually just me and Jenks," I said, and the pixy bobbed his hover in greeting, unusually reserved around the woman. "But there's been several forced evictions, and apparently we're a paranormal city shelter." That I would have let them stay regardless didn't need to be said.

"Yo!" Jenks said, keeping his distance. I could tell she wasn't a witch or an elf or a living vampire, which left human—a human who was confident enough about herself that walking into a church full of Weres and vamps and working for a demon didn't faze her. Either Finley knew enough about Inderlanders to hold her own or she blissfully knew nothing at all. And as I eyed her strength and her slight twitch at a loud howl, I was betting it was the former.

"A shelter without a kitchen?" Finley glanced at the temporary burners, plastic silverware, and big trash can overflowing with waste.

I sighed, wincing when someone came in and three people called to him by name. "We, ah, lost it last year when the vampires blew the addition off the back."

"Oh." Finley turned on a bootheel, her gaze lingering on the vamps playing cards before the blaring TV. "Well, tell me what you want to see. New windows? Maybe something that opens?"

Yeah. It was starting to smell in here. "That's a start," I said, and Jenks's wings hummed.

"Do you think you could find some replacement colored glass?" Jenks blurted, surprising me.

Finley smiled, her head down over her clipboard-style tablet. "I can try," she said as she typed into a list. "My supplier makes the odd foray into the abandoned stretches for materials."

"Cool," I said, fidgeting as I looked past the noise and mess to the bones of the church. "Maybe you could find a match for the floor and we could get that hole fixed."

Nodding, Finley came up from her clipboard. "That's odd," she said as she looked closer at the perfectly round hole. "It looks as if it was burned out." She hesitated when neither I nor Jenks said anything, finally looking up at the ceiling to see the matching, repaired hole. "Oh."

Can I possibly make a worse impression? I wondered, eye twitching as two damp vampires padded past smelling of my shampoo, nothing but towels draped around their waists. "Ah, ideally I'd like the back of the church rebuilt," I said, trying to turn Finley before she saw them. "But we don't have the money for that at the moment. Our goal is to bring it to resale condition. You're the only one brave enough to come out."

Jenks's wing pitch dropped, and I could have kicked myself.

"That's right." Finley bobbed her head. "Sharron told me you were blackballed. That kind of behavior puts tacks in my tea. You just got yourself a ten percent discount."

Tacks in my tea? I thought, but Jenks's wings had brightened in hope.

"Well, in that case," I said, looking over the sanctuary, "we'd like an estimate on the hole in the floor, new windows, and maybe turning one of the bathrooms into a kitchen for resale."

Jenks returned to my shoulder as Finley gazed appraisingly at the floor, then the ceiling. The pixies had come in, and the rafters were glowing. "It seems to me as a paranormal shelter, you need an open area for gathering, two separate rooms to accommodate the various Inderland sleep schedules so you don't have people sleeping in the foyer, and, as you say, a kitchen."

"True." *Good God. Are people sleeping in the foyer?* But she was moving, and I jolted into motion to follow her. "But we have only what you see. You can't invent space." Not to mention we wouldn't care what the church was used for after we sold it.

People were getting out of her way, impressing me. "No, you can't invent space," she said as she took another measurement. "But you can use it creatively. You have two separate bathrooms already, yes? One for boys, one for girls. You could do the same with the bedrooms. They're small, but I could do bunk cots with minimal storage."

Jenks's dust slipping down my front was a coppery color of indecision, but he wasn't saying anything. "Actually," I said, not sure what was up with Jenks, "if I was dividing it up, I'd have one for the vampires and the other for everyone else. But one of them is my room."

"Until we leave, Rache," Jenks said, voice small, and I winced. In the excitement of having someone come out to fix the place, I'd forgotten. I wanted to stay, but Jenks's feelings meant more than my desire for lots of room and a kick-ass garden.

"Right," I said, glad I couldn't see his face. "You know, I could move up into the belfry short term. That would open up my room and alleviate a lot of this."

"Sure." Finley bent her head over her tablet, making notes.

Jenks's wings rasped a warning, but it was only David with Garrett and his packmates approaching. They had their stuff with them, and I smiled. *Thank you, David.* Four less Weres would help.

"Excuse me, Rachel?" David interrupted. "If you have a second. Garrett wants to say good-bye."

"You mind?" I asked Finley, and she shook her head.

"I'll give her the tour," Jenks said, and Finley started when his dust blanked her screen. "I've got ideas, and Rachel's busy trying to keep Cincy together. Can you take a look at the backyard and tell me what you think we could do besides putting in steps? All it takes is one drunk vampire to fall off and crack his head open to set everyone else off. We don't even have an MPL."

Finley smiled, clearly charmed when Jenks lit on her clipboard. "You don't need a mixed-population license if you're nonprofit."

"Profit?" Jenks snorted, his usual cocky attitude beginning to slip back. "This here is a runner firm. I can't tell you the last time we made a profit."

I lifted my brow as they walked away. Jenks's plans sounded like overkill on resale repair, but his dust was cheerful, and I wasn't going to mess with that. "You have a place?" I said when I turned back to the Weres.

"David found us somewhere," Garrett said. "We just wanted to say thanks. This was better than the mall bathroom we'd been looking at. If there's anything we can do to repay you, let David know. He'll tell us."

Suddenly all the noise and confusion seemed worth it, and I gently shook Garrett's bandaged hand. "Thanks, but you got me out of a tight spot at the I.S. I feel as if I owe you." Giving in, I tugged Garrett closer for an earnest hug. He was red-faced when he pulled back, grinning as he ducked his head, not knowing what to say.

"No retaliation against Constance or her people, okay?" I said, and they jostled elbows, worrying me.

David looked at the door, then me. "Go ahead. I'll be right there," he said, and the quartet wove their way to the front, fist-bumping everyone as they went.

"I'm going to have so much hair in my sink," I said, and David laughed. "Thanks for finding a place for them," I added, wondering who I could call to locate somewhere for the witches. I didn't know who to talk to about the displaced vamps, either.

"Not a problem. They're a good pack." He hesitated, then put a hand on my shoulder and turned me to the wall. "Before I go," he said, making sure no one could read our lips, "I need to hear the words come out of your mouth that you are not going after Constance by yourself, either."

The pleasure of seeing the four Weres find their feet vanished. Life rushed back, and I stiffened at the reminder of Nash. "If I don't tell her what she did was wrong, no one will, and that was wrong no matter how you smell it," I said, angry. "You think I should accept her authority like everyone else?" My voice had risen, and I didn't care. "She's a bloody monster preying on the living and the dead!"

David's hand came up, placating me. "I was there. I saw what she did. I agree with you taking control. All I want to know is that you aren't going to try to bring her to heel alone." He smiled. "You have friends, you know."

"Oh!" I blurted, and Jenks, who was showing Finley the detail in the moldings, spun in midair to look at me. "Um, I haven't thought that far yet," I admitted, warming.

"She's tearing the city apart because half of it would rather follow you than her," David said. "They're looking for direction. I know asking for help isn't your modus operandi, but you need to use all your tools this time."

Scowling, I ran a hand over Ivy's baby grand. There

were at least six open bags of chips and pretzels on it, tantalizing me with salt and carbs. "This is between myself and Constance. The more people are involved, the more people will be hurt. Not getting hurt is the point."

"True, but that includes you." David put his hat on, clearly ready to go. "The Weres and vamps are frustrated," he said. "I don't know how long I can keep distracting the more fed-up packs with chaining rats to flagpoles." He gave me a fond grin when I looked up, adding, "Why do you think there are so many people here? Finding a place to sleep isn't that hard. They're here because they want to help. Either you use them in a way that won't get them hurt, or they will escalate their own actions until they do get hurt."

Be the subrosa, echoed in my thoughts as I spun on a slow heel to look at the refugees. Furtive, expectant glances met mine between the soft talk and sudden bursts of laughter. I could feel the tension they were hiding behind the apparent cheerfulness, the anger. I could see it on the news and in the street. I'd get no help from the demons, that was obvious, but I didn't need them to prove to Constance that even without the backing of the I.S. I was stronger, more resilient, and had a longer reach than her, a reach that was not only in resources or power, but also in the simple ability to get large and small things done. If I couldn't impress her with that, I'd be playing her game of "let's see what will piss Rachel off" until she killed me. The problem was, all she saw was a witch-born demon living in a broken church. I had to get her away from the I.S. to where my skills would work.

"I need Pike," I said, the beginnings of an idea drifting about the folds of my brain.

"Constance's scion?" David asked, suddenly uneasy. "Ah . . . are you sure? I was thinking more along the lines of staging a howl-in or maybe a transportation strike."

My back to the piano, I reached for my phone. "Pike."

David took his hat off again. "Um, abducting Pike might buy Zack a day or two, but it's more likely that blackmail will convince her to find your family."

I stifled a flash of anger. *If she touches Trent or his girls . . .* "I'm not abducting him. I just want to talk," I said with a false lightness. "He's her gatekeeper, and if I'm to have any chance of getting Constance outside of her I.S. turtle shell, I need to convince him it's in her best interests to do so." *Where are you?* I mused as I ran through my list of contacts to find Zack's number. If anyone had Zack's phone, it would be Pike. "Though if I find out she's hurt Zack, I will carve my initials into his forehead before I send him home." I hit the connect icon and smiled at David. It felt good to have a plan.

"Mmmm." He sounded worried.

"She's been listening to Landon," I said, remembering the elf's look of horror when Constance drew a smile on Joni's face. "Landon still thinks he lost control of the dewar because I was lucky. I'm going to have to force a face-to-face where I can use my witchy—hang on a sec. I want to talk to you before you go," I added when the call went through.

But David had leaned close, clearly wanting to listen in. I angled the phone and stifled a quiver at the silence on the open line. This felt good. *Damn it, Al. Right again.*

"Pike?" I said, hearing only a soft breathing. "It's Rachel."

I waited, but there was nothing, and my eyes flicked to David.

"Ah, I want to talk to you," I added, hand over my other ear to try to block out the noise. Still, there was nothing, and I began to get peeved. "Pike?" I tried again, voice sharp, and this time, a clear intake of breath sounded.

"Are you at a party?" Pike's gravel voice said in wonder, and I grimaced.

"No, but my church is full of your boss's refugees," I said, feeling good about them for the first time. They trusted me, and I needed that show of support, even if being in my church was the extent of it. "They're blowing off some steam."

"I didn't agree with what she did with Nash—" he said.

Anger flushed hot through me. "I don't care a floating

troll turd what you agree or don't agree with," I said, interrupting him. "I want to talk to you about finding an agreement with Constance. What she would expect from me and what I can expect from her in return." Giving in, I reached past David and took a pretzel. "She made her point," I said around my crunching. "We should be able to come to some arrangement of shared power." *Ha-ha. As if.*

"You're taking this surprisingly well," Pike said, but his suspicion was obvious.

"You'd be surprised what and who I've had to make deals with before," I said, and David scrubbed a hand over his stubble in concern. "So . . . You. Me. Eden Park Overlook. Twin Lakes Bridge. Five tonight. I need some time to whip up a few curses so I'm not a pushover to your vampiric charms." Not to mention the sun went down right before seven and I wanted Constance out of it for the moment. She'd get her turn. Half of any battle was won in the mind, and fear worked best when it had some time to fester.

"Ah, Twin Lakes Bridge isn't coming up on my GPS," he muttered.

"It's that teensy footbridge over the two recirculating ponds by the parking lot," I said. "I assumed you'd want to meet over water so I can't reach a ley line, but if you want to do this on a park bench, I'm good with that. Oh, and come alone."

Pike chuckled. "Alone won't happen."

I glanced at David as he frowned. Yeah, I'd probably have Jenks with me, too, and I took another pretzel. "Then keep them back, okay? I get nervous with too many people around."

I hung up before he could answer. David was eyeing me in concern, and I shrugged.

"You're not really talking to him about finding an arrangement with Constance, are you?" he asked.

"Not the way he thinks, no." I pulled the bag of pretzels closer and searched for unbroken ones. "She'll send Pike, whether to find out if I'm serious or simply to try to kill me and be done with it. Either way, I'll impress on him that if

Constance wants me dead she'll have to come out of the I.S. and do it herself." My words were light, but yes, I was worried. "Whereupon I be-the-demon and convince her of the need to play nice in my sandbox. Life goes back to normal."

I crunched through a pretzel, searching David's expression for a hint of agreement as he leaned back against the piano. "He's stronger than you, faster."

"That's why I'm spending the rest of the day in my belfry spelling," I said, forcing a smile. "Relax. I work best when I'm improvising." But David's words were well-taken. I was playing with fire. Again. Too bad I'd lost my fireproof gloves when the demons decided not to help me.

"That you do." David had his hat back on, and I felt a surge of relief. He thought I could do it. "I'm coming with you."

"Thank you," I said, my gratitude heavy on me. "But just you. No pack."

"Agreed." He looked over the sanctuary, his smile going tight. "I'll call you by four so you can tell me where you want me. Are you going to warn Edden, or should I?"

"Can we keep him out of it?" I asked, almost whining, and David grinned.

"We can try. But you *will* call Trent!" he said over his shoulder as he turned to the door, and a romantic-based "ooooooooh . . ." rose up from the witches clustered at the table.

I waved my agreement, but my hand curved around my middle in worry as David left. Calling Trent was probably a good idea. I might need bail money before this was over.

CHAPTER

14

"CAN'T PUT IT BACK, BLACK COIN ILL SPENT. TEN THOUSAND years, at detriment," Takata sang, his low, rough voice ragged through my MINI's speakers, and I wondered if black coin was a metaphor for magical smut or oil. Maybe it didn't matter.

"Down in the earth, buried deep. Down where the demons sleep," I spoke/sang with him, our voices eerily similar. "Down where God can't speak. Black coin spent, our soul to keep. So as you sow, so shall you reap. So as you sow, your children weep. Just killing time, as black coin seeps."

I sighed as my birth father wound up from the low monotone into a healthy, headbanger howl for the last five seconds of the song, screaming the chorus, "Just killing time. Just killing time. Just killing time," over and over until I clicked the radio off. Seemed I came by my rebel tendencies naturally.

"Bet he can do that song only once a night," Jenks said from my rearview mirror, and I nodded, my mood slowly evolving into an angry depression as my thoughts swung back to Nash. Maybe if I had womaned up sooner, he wouldn't be dead. The pixy's dust shifted and settled as I made the tight turn into Eden Park Overlook. I took the spot at the end so if I had to leave fast, I could drive over the grass and be gone.

I cracked the window for Jenks, settled back, and reached for my coffee. I was early, but that wasn't why I stayed in my car, carefully scanning the park spreading between me and Cincinnati. That Nash had died in so much needless pain pissed me off, and the more angry I got, the more I questioned my motives for meeting Pike. Was I looking for an excuse to hurt him? *Do I care if I do?*

David was already here, looking sharp in his expensive go-to-church duster since the one he'd wrapped Nash in was at the cleaners. Confident and smiling, he encouraged the few people taking advantage of the late afternoon to shift to another, less dangerous part of the park. I appreciated his efforts, seeing as, if he was doing it, I wouldn't have to—possibly finding the thugs Constance had most likely sent in an assassination attempt.

"I can't believe you brought him coffee," Jenks said, and my eyes went to the rearview mirror and the steep drop-off to the Ohio River behind me. It wouldn't be unheard-of for someone to come up that way, but why when you could simply drive up here with a gun?

"It's more for me than him," I said, licking the sugar and caffeine from my lips—though I sort of agreed with Jenks. Pike had to have been there while Constance gutted Nash. He had been there and done nothing to stop it. My fingers drummed in angry anticipation.

Twin Lakes Bridge was before me, the small footbridge once a picturesque proposal hot spot from when Cincinnati was the fourth-largest city in America. Now, straddling recirculating copper-blue water and surrounded by grass and the noise of the encroaching city, it was still a good place to pop the question, but it was used more often as a place to feed the ducks without getting mobbed by them.

The quiet spot of green had been one of my favorite places in Cincy long before I knew the nearby ley line had been scraped into existence by Al. My dad had brought me up here to look down upon the Hollows when the weight of his secrets lay heavy on him. He had known. Somehow he'd known that by saving my life he was unleashing a rebirth of demons upon the world. And when I say *dad*, I don't mean Takata. I mean Dad, the man who raised me.

"You want to check in with David?" I said, and Jenks nodded, his wings humming as he took a red bandana from his back pocket and darted out the cracked window. His dust glinted, and then he was gone.

I gave him a few seconds before shrugging my bag over my shoulder and getting out. The low sun was warm, and I felt a flash of vulnerability as I leaned back in to get the two coffees. The caramel smoked-salt latte was for Pike. Most vamps liked smoked salt.

I shut the door with my backside, keys and phone in my pocket in case I had to ditch my bag. Coffees in hand, I headed for the bridge, my bootheels soft on the grass, then thumping on the old cement walk. The breeze was nice, shifting my hair and making me wish I came up here more than to smack heads.

The scent of lily seemed to cling to me and I stifled a grimace. Using the church's shower was too uncomfortable an option, but I *had* changed into a short white skirt, black leggings, black tank top, and a lightweight jacket. All the black seemed fitting seeing as I'd just put someone in the ground, or the ether, or whatever. The unusual ribbon of black lace around my throat was to torment Pike, and I felt mean as I strode to the bridge.

Al had redrawn his ley line out of the pond, meaning I could reach it now without actually being in the water. Even when I was standing on the bridge, the two man-made ponds were no longer enough to cut off my access. I was hoping that little nugget hadn't gotten around and Constance thought I'd be vulnerable. I tapped the line now, feeling a staticky lift in my hair, but as I walked to the center of the bridge, an uncomfortable tickle tripped down my spine. Other than David talking to a woman with a dog, the park was eerily empty for such a nice early evening. *Thanks, David.*

My breath came in slow, and I set the coffees on the elbow-high cement railing and did a slow spin to show I wasn't packing, even if I was. I had a couple of new pain amulets, my splat pistol, and that spoken immobilization curse that I'd used on Landon last November.

I hoped I wouldn't need any of it, but after seeing Constance with Joni and the terror she filled her own people with, I was guessing that her decisions wouldn't be made on dead-vamp logic, which made a perverted sense once you picked it apart. Rather, she'd move on tiny shreds of memory triggered by God knew what, making her erratic and unpredictable. All I wanted right now was Zack.

A wing rasp from the branches high overhead turned out to be Jenks, and my shoulders eased. "Hey, Jenks," I said as his dust sifted over me with little pinpricks of sensation. "Why do I feel as if I'm being watched?"

"Because you are." He dropped down, his red bandana making an unusual splash of color. "David's got your back while I see what's got the local pixies in a snit. I need a few minutes and some of that whip on Pike's coffee. You good?"

I glanced into the harsh-blue water and nodded. It was inches deep on one side of the bridge, a few feet on the other, the drop-off somewhere under the bridge. "Yeah. I'm going to check if Sharps is around. I doubt the I.S. has had time this week to evict bridge trolls."

"Gotcha." Jenks hovered over Pike's coffee, using the chopsticks from his back pocket to gather some foamy whip before darting off.

The breeze coming up from the Ohio River suddenly felt chill. Sipping my coffee, I rested my elbows on the railing and did a scan, my eyes narrowing at the four vamps coming in over the grass.

I hadn't seen them arrive. They were just suddenly there, strolling in from all corners with a sultry casualness. David was watching them, too. Even from this distance I could tell they were not the three vampires from the Volvo. *Constance upped her game,* I thought, noting the steadfast, dark confidence that her other thugs had lacked.

I felt the outlines of my splat gun through my bag, pulse

quickening as, one by one, they settled themselves at a near distance, blending into nothing as they leaned against a tree, slipped behind a utility building, or sat on a bench and pretended to sleep.

Interesting, I mused. If I was their target, there was nothing stopping them. Perhaps Constance wanted to hear what I had to say before unleashing her professionals.

Concerned, I leaned over the thick railing, my hair swinging as I peered into the filthy water. The memory of Trent and my first meeting here rose to make me smile. A lot had changed since then, but a lot hadn't. "Hey-de-hey, Sharps," I called softly. "You here?"

The water bubbled and boiled, and a long, water-melting face pushed up from the blue. "Hey-de-ho," the wispy-thin troll burbled, his words sounding like water over rocks. "Rachel. I should have known. No one bitch-steps over the bridge like you. You in trouble?"

I smiled, remembering my early I.S. runs sent to drive him out from under the bridge, and the lies I'd told claiming that I had. The I.S. hated bridge trolls, but I didn't see the harm. You patched up the mortar they ate and dealt with it. "What makes you say that?" I said, surreptitiously checking to make sure the four vamps hadn't moved. If anything, they'd blended deeper into the park to become almost invisible.

"You're not here to feed the ducks," he said as he reached a thin, algae-covered arm up to pluck off a tiny chunk of the bridge and eat it.

My smile was short-lived as my eyes again rose, barely picking out the vamps. Damn, they must have a spell working. If I hadn't seen them settle in, I never would have spotted them now. "No," I said. "I'm trying to convince Cincy's newest master vampire to play nice."

David was still talking with that lady with the dog, but she finally left and David settled himself on her park bench, his duster brushing his ankles and his wide-brimmed hat pulled low. It was a position I liked, relaxed and far enough away that I was basically on my own.

"If you need me, whistle," Sharps said.

"It's pretty cut-and-dried, but thanks." I pushed off the railing and eyed the park, brow furrowed. *Where are you, Pike?* "If anyone goes in the water, could you keep them there without drowning them?"

"Sure. I don't like it when the I.S. dredges the ponds. They always make me leave." With a bubbly gurgle, the troll eased into the water. He might look thin and weak, but, like Bis, he could increase his mass considerably with an instant water intake. Get slammed once with ten pounds of spit water, and you never tease a troll again.

My head rose at the roar of a black sports car coming up the park's drive. David pushed up his hat, eyed the car, then settled back down.

Pike, I thought, then stifled a jump when Jenks dropped down, wings rasping.

"We got four vamps keeping their distance," the pixy said, dusting heavily on my shoulder. "And that's Pike in the Jag. David's pack blocked the road with a fender bender after he came through so you're good for about twenty minutes. I think the four svelte-and-sexies are there in case you do anything like . . . I don't know. Try to kidnap him?" Jenks laughed, the sound like wind chimes. "Where do you want me?"

Pike had put his car three spots down from my little red MINI, aggressively revving the Jag to make the sparrows flee. "Close," I said, and Jenks silently darted up.

The thump of Pike's door shutting sent a pulse of adrenaline through me, and I set my bag by my ankle, where I could reach it if I had to drop. He was alone, and as he made his careful way to the bridge, I wondered if he'd seen Jenks. Angry at him or not, I could still admit that he looked good, if a little tired, in his slacks and gray button-down shirt, the wind in his short hair and his brown eyes squinting at me. There were two cups of takeout coffee in his hand, and my eyebrows rose.

"Great minds think alike, eh?" I called out, and his pace bobbled when he saw the two cups already cooling on the thick cement railing. Then he gathered himself and strode up the wide footbridge without hesitation. I tightened my grip on the ley line.

"Thanks," he said, finally slowing to stop a too-close five feet back. "But I don't drink what I don't bring."

I looked at the grande in his grip, suspicion rising high in me. "Ah, I don't drink what I don't bring, either," I said, and he chuckled and set one cup on the railing.

"You sure? I dropped your name, and the guy said to get a skinny demon latte. Smells good."

Like you? I thought, my gut tightening at the scent of vampire incense rolling across the bridge to me in the light wind. It was sure and strong, having none of the fear that the rest of Constance's people had. Kisten had smelled like that. Especially at the end. Which was probably why Piscary had killed him.

"What guy?" I came closer with a fake casualness. "Was he a witch? My height, brown hair? Or was he a demon, few pounds overweight and graying at the temples?"

Pike's eyes widened. "*That* was a *demon*?"

I knocked my coffee against the one in his hand. "Welcome to my world," I said, then eased back, wondering if I'd overstepped. My gaze went to the park, and both of us were silent, each of us reading the air, each of us sensing something we didn't like.

"You know, just once I'd like to meet someone out here without worrying about landing in the water," I muttered, and from under the bridge, I heard a bubbling laugh.

"This is one of your *special* spots, eh?" Pike squinted as he continued to look over the park. "To be up-front, nothing you say except that you submit to Constance's authority will free Zack." He chuckled, head dropping. "She is *pissed* that you drove her out of Piscary's."

My anger flashed, quickly stifled, but I knew Pike had caught it when the rim of brown around his eyes shrank. His pupil-black eyes lingered on me to make my breath come shallow.

He'd be hard to down, I thought, then wrestled my anger

back and shoved it away. "Actually, I was thinking more along the lines of a little tussle where we settle a few things and then both go home to get stitched up," I said lightly. "You didn't really think I asked you out here so I could capitulate to her demands, did you?"

Pike sighed as he put his elbows on the railing, looking out over the water and showing off his long torso in a languid ease. "You think you could last ten seconds with me?"

I mirrored him, only a foot between us. "Here? With a pixy and troll to back me up? I could last . . . forty seconds. And that's without magic. *With* magic, you don't stand a chance."

Pike's gaze followed the sifting pixy dust up into the overhanging tree. "Thirty," he countered.

"A full minute." I pushed off the railing and faced him. "Because now you think you're better than me."

His head swiveled, and I held my breath as he took in the sun in my hair, his lingering gaze reminding me that I'd forgotten to take the flowers out. Eyebrows high, I touched the lace around my neck, teasing him. "You think you're better than me?" he said, low voice raking over my thought and reason like delicious claws.

Damn it, why do I always go too far? "No, but I'm not a pushover, either." I put a few more inches between us, disguising it by taking another sip of coffee. "I've got three years of living with Ivy Tamwood to back me." I sipped again, the caffeine a welcome jolt. "She only bit me once, and I wanted her to. She was Piscary's scion, and if you think Constance is warped, she's got nothing on him." I turned, smiling with no emotion. "I learned how to say no from the best."

I could feel his gaze on my neck, his expression empty. I knew he was looking for and not seeing the scar that was hidden under my curse-new skin and that tiny wisp of lace. I'd put it on because I'd been angry. In hindsight, maybe not such a good idea.

The idle chitchat was over, and I set my coffee on the railing. "Killing Nash was a mistake," I said, letting some of my anger show. "Hurting Zack would be another. One I won't forgive." Pike made a soft harrumph. It pissed me off, and I added, "So did you hold him down, or did you do the cutting?"

Pike pulled himself straight, his focus blurred as he turned to lean against the railing to watch the other side of the park. "I wasn't there."

I faced him, hand on a hip, a risky three feet between us. "That's hard to believe."

"I wasn't there," he said again, but I could see a hint of guilt, and my eyes narrowed in accusation. "I ran some errands after she said she would only cut him a little. Scare the kid."

"His name is Zack," I said loudly when Jenks's wings rasped from the overhanging tree. "And I'm not buying your 'not my fault' crap. You know her better than anyone. You left knowing it would happen and that Nash wasn't going to get off that table."

Pike's gaze flicked to mine, his black eyes making the sun feel cold. "I was on an *errand*," he insisted, and when I said nothing, his shoulders slumped. "Which I left to do because I knew it was going to be bad."

My pulse quickened. *How can I look past that cold indifference on his scarred face?* And yet, he carried necklaces in his pocket for when Constance stole one from her own followers. "You could have stopped her," I muttered.

Pike laughed bitterly. "You don't know much about the long undead," he said, voice ugly.

Eyebrows high, I stared. "You're afraid of her?" I said, not believing it. I mean, I'd seen him in the tower's lower halls. He hadn't been afraid. Cautious, maybe respectful even as he was disappointed at her failure to be the powerful master he wanted to look to. But not afraid.

Pike leaned back to put his elbows on the railing behind him, his attention on the bathrooms across the upper pond. "Yes and no," he said, as if he'd never admitted it before.

I pressed my lips together, angry for even thinking to

give him a pass for this. "You could have done something," I insisted, and he looked at me as if I was stupid.

"I did. I convinced her to leave him alive." He returned to scanning the park. "I assumed the great and powerful Rachel Morgan could save him," he mocked.

Guilt flashed through me, and I hated that he knew it. "I—I'm not that good," I admitted, flushing. "And I had a falling-out—" My voice cut off. *Why am I telling him this?* "Hey, don't tell her I said that, okay?" I said, giving him a weak but honest smile.

He stared at me as if in disbelief, and my flush deepened when his attention dropped to the lace at my throat.

"Hurting people with the sole intent to piss me off is not a good idea," I added, and he almost rolled his eyes before turning his focus back to the park. "Your job is to protect her, right? Then convince her to let Zack go so we can talk this out. We can find a way to live in Cincinnati together. This should be between me and her, not everyone we care about."

"Then perhaps you shouldn't have made her daylight quarters unlivable," he said, a cross expression bringing his features tight. "With the sole intent to piss her off. She thinks that if I kill you, the spell will be broken."

"Ah, it doesn't work that way. It will be harder to break if I'm dead," I said quickly.

"That's what I told her," he said, ruefully rubbing his ribs, his eyes still scanning. It was starting to get on my nerves, and I risked a look behind me at the seemingly empty park. Maybe he thought that Were pack at the front gate was coming up to swamp him.

"She still wants you dead," he added, smiling as he lifted his cup. "But not with coffee."

I couldn't help it, and my lips curved up in a smile as Jenks's soft "told you" drifted down. *That's why the charms, Jenks.*

"So." I leaned my back against the railing and set my thoughts lightly in Al's ley line. "Are you going to kill me?"

We were shoulder to shoulder and, eyes closing, I let my head loll and my hair spill down in an open invitation, exposing my neck, knowing he wouldn't dare, knowing if he did, I'd be able to evade him for a precious three seconds to circle myself—then smack him halfway to the Hollows. *One minute without magic becomes my advantage with magic.*

"Not yet," he said, and I made a small sound, half nonchalance, half enticement. "Not if I can convince you to tuck tail and leave. And you should leave. They're talking about you in the lower levels of the I.S., not her. She's so angry now that even if you publicly humiliated yourself and begged for her forgiveness, she'd kill you the week after."

"As if I'd ever do that," I said. But he said nothing, and I finally opened my eyes. He had moved, standing with his shoulders hunched and jaw tight. Embarrassed, I pulled myself straight. "Sorry," I said as I took the lace off and stuffed it into a pocket. "It's not fair to push your buttons like that."

"You have no clue where my buttons even are," he muttered, and I flushed again.

"So, just for gits and shiggles, what are Constance's terms?" I asked.

Pike eyed me, clearly annoyed. The rim of brown had returned, but I'd thought it important that he knew I wasn't afraid of him. Cautious, yes. Afraid, no. "She has no terms," he said flatly. "She *wants* you dead. Gone will satisfy her. I suggest you take it."

Thinking, I sipped my coffee. My foot was touching my bag, but I didn't need anything in it if he moved. All I needed was in my fists, feet, head, and that ley line nearby. "Say I leave. Will she free Zack? Stop trying to subjugate the elves?"

Pike's wandering attention returned to me. Something was distracting him, something that had nothing to do with the lace I'd stuffed in my pocket or my short white skirt. "Are you going to leave?" he asked, and in that instant, I thought about it. Really thought about it. I could abandon Cincy, go out to the West Coast where my mom was. Trent could probably find something to do out there, seeing as his holdings here were being picked apart one lawsuit at a time. And Jenks? He could make it anywhere.

"No," I finally said, and Pike slowly nodded as if knowing this was real, not posture and play. "I like the Hollows. My dad is buried here, and it's where I went to school. I finally found a place that cuts my hair the way I like it, and I have a few spell shops that will sell to me again." Melancholy, I slumped against the thick railing and thought about the church. I really wanted to talk to Jenks about staying, but damn . . . his face went awful every time I brought it up.

"You'd live longer if you left," Pike said, jerking me back to the present.

But he wasn't looking at me, scanning the park over my shoulder, a rising tension pulling him straight. "Will you relax?" I said, annoyed. "I'm not trying to kill you. There's no point to it."

Eyes empty, he looked me up and down. "I never said you were trying to kill me."

"Then what is it?" I said. "You're hardly listening to me."

"It's nothing." But his jaw was tight and his eyes continued to track the passing cars.

My arms went over my middle. There was little that irked me more than taking the time out of my day to threaten a city power and having them be more concerned about the tour bus driving by than me. "Good God. You'd think having four vamps watching me would be enough," I said flatly, and his eye twitched.

"There are five," he said, grit grinding under his foot. "And they aren't watching you."

"Jenks counted four."

"You saw them? They're here?" Pike jerked forward. "Shit, you need to leave," he said, his attention going to my car. "Now."

"We haven't settled anything yet," I said, stepping out of his reach when he made a grab for me. "I want to talk to her, but she has to release Zack first as a goodwill gesture. I want a meeting. Just her and me. Somewhere neutral and public. Not the I.S. You're the only one who can get it for me."

"Get in your car," Pike insisted. "Damn it, I never should have told Constance to pull her people back, but I didn't think you'd show if I had anyone with me."

He thought a few vampires would spook me? I thought, then realized what he'd actually said. "Ah, those aren't Constance's people?"

Pike's eyes narrowed. He opened his mouth, but I never found out what he was going to say, as his expression shifted to an icy, abiding anger and he shoved me so hard I went flying, my backside hitting the concrete with a painful jolt before I slid to the far end of the bridge.

"Hey!" I shouted, angry as I stared at him. Until I saw the quivering knife embedded into the cement railing where I'd been standing.

"Rache! Get off the bridge!" Jenks shouted, and my lips parted as Pike threw someone dressed in black into the pond. Water fountained up, followed by a bellow of anger and a gurgle as Sharps took him down.

"Get off the bridge!" Jenks exclaimed again, hovering so close I couldn't focus on him. And then he was gone.

What the hell is going on? I scrambled up, half crawling until my feet were again on solid ground. David was out, looking asleep on the park bench. My eyes widened. Two vampires were headed right for me, unearthly fast like shadows before the storm. *"Rhombus!"* I cried, still crouched as my bubble rose up, gold and red in the sun.

But they raced right past me. My jaw dropped.

"They aren't after you, Rache," Jenks said, and I let my bubble fall. "And they aren't Cincy vamps. They smell like coal. David's okay. His aura says he's only knocked out."

I glanced at David, reluctant to leave him to fate, but he was down and Pike . . .

Pike wasn't. Not yet.

I stood, trying to follow Pike's living-vamp-fast motions as he blocked and kicked at the two vampires facing him.

He clearly had some martial arts to his credit. *Ten seconds without magic,* I thought as I watched, reevaluating my chances as two more joined the first. *If I'm lucky.*

As Pike had said, there were five total. The one in the water had freed himself of Sharps and was slogging ashore only to fall back when Pike threw a second attacker at him. That left three on the bridge, and they all went at him at the same time. No movie-magic, wait-your-turn here. They were out for blood.

Scar-marked face twisting, Pike yelled, yanking the first past him to slam headlong into the concrete railing. Jaw clenched, he upended him, tossing him into the water to land facedown and unmoving. But the other two had scored on him in the interim, and I winced as the savage sound of flesh on flesh rose with the grunts of pain.

Once in the gut was all it took, and two grabbed his arms, fighting to keep Pike upright as two from the water finally regained the bridge.

He was caught, and I took a step forward at the familiar snick of a katana being pulled.

Not here, I thought, anger and adrenaline a hot mix. *Not while I'm watching.*

One of the vamps stepped forward, blade shining, his expression ugly with greed.

"Hey!" I shouted as I pulled heavily on the line. "I'm talking to him! Wait your turn!"

"Stay out of this, witch!" Pike shouted, and then, with a savage yell, he pulled one of the vamps restraining him into the katana's descending path. An angry bellow thundered out as it thunked heavily into his attacker's shoulder. The sword's wielder yanked it out, and with no consideration of his comrade, he swung again.

"Look out!" I shouted, wincing when Pike took the hit on his arm before kicking out and sending the sword-toting vampire pinwheeling back. He must have been wearing Kevlar as there was no blood. Clearly it hurt, though, as Pike held his arm close and followed the man down to wrench the katana from his grip.

"Pike!" I exclaimed, aghast when he jammed the swor(d) in the downed vampire's gut.

And then the other two were on him, pulling him awa(y) and trying for the katana. Pike lashed inexpertly out wit(h) the blade, taking a hit but swinging to keep them at bay a(s) they circled him. It was three against one, and my puls(e) pounded as he struck forward, then back, keeping the(m) off-balance and on defense. He wasn't good with it, but h(e) didn't need to be.

One of them jumped atop the railing. I gasped in warn(-)ing as he flipped over his comrades and crashed into Pike(.) They went down. Two lurched forward, fingers crooked an(d) savage.

"Should I do something?" I said as Jenks hovered besid(e) me, sword bared.

"No, he's got it," Jenks said as two vampires went flyin(g) across the bridge. Pike rose, the third still clinging to hi(m.) Howling, Pike fell to the bridge floor, knocking the ma(n) atop him senseless.

It was two to one, and I inched closer, ley line powe(r) itching under my skin. I could hear sirens, and the need t(o) flee began to grow. The I.S. would put me in jail unde(r) suspicion of riot, and with no charms to back me there . . (.) I'd be Constance's toy.

Blood dripped from Pike's face. The two men facin(g) him were slick with it. One had bones sticking past hi(s) skin, and the other was bleeding from his eye. But the(y) were gathering themselves for another go, and my breat(h) caught as one scooped up the abandoned katana and the(y) attacked together.

"This is *my* day!" Pike screamed, but, focused on th(e) sword-wielding vamp, he missed the second vaulting ove(r) them both.

"Behind you!" I shouted, but it was too late, and thic(k) arms wrapped Pike from behind. Eyes savage, Pike back(-) headbutted him, then screamed in defiance, shifting unde(r) the descending katana.

It struck his shoulder instead of his head. Blood flowe(d)

and, howling, Pike freed one hand, pushing himself forward with that vamp still clinging to him. Fingers crooked, he grabbed the man's head and jammed his thumb into his remaining eye.

Screaming in pain, the vampire lurched away, katana falling.

There was still a vampire on his back, and as the man hammered at Pike's ear, Pike reached up and pulled him over his head as if he was taking off a shirt. The vampire hit the bridge and rolled. He rose with that broken katana in his grip. The half-blinded vampire had gotten upright as well, and a third, previously knocked out, had regained consciousness. It was back to three against one.

And they weren't stopping.

"Yeah, you might want to help him," Jenks said as I stepped forward. I'd had enough. Not in my city. Not while I was talking to him, anyway.

"Hey!" I shouted, but they had gotten him against the railing, and Pike struggled as one slowly approached, murder in his remaining eye.

"I said, knock it off!" I yelled as I strode forward. Power grew in my palm, itching.

Pike's low growl rose into a howl as, with an inhuman strength, he got a hand free and smashed one of their faces. Blood gushed, but the attacker didn't let go, and the one with the katana lashed out, burying the broken blade into Pike's shoulder.

"*Stabils!*" I yelled as I physically threw the curse to immobilize at his attacker, then yelped, ducking when it ricocheted off the low wall as Pike threw the man off him, crashing into me and sending us both tumbling over the railing.

I hit the water with a shocking smack. Copper-infused water flooded my nose, and I came up gasping. Mad as hell, I stared up at the ugly sounds as I got to my feet and sloshed to the shore. Damn it, I'd never get the blue out of my clothes.

"Hey!" I shouted when I reached the bridge, but the

vampires weren't paying me any attention. They'd finally gotten Pike down, his neck bared and ripe for slitting.

"Hold him. Hold him!" the one with the broken katana panted, the blood dripping from his remaining eye. The blade was only four inches long, but if you knew what you were doing, size didn't matter.

Pike's lips pulled back from his teeth, his bloodshot eyes focused on the vampire with the sword. "You should have brought more," he said, voice rasping.

"Let him go!" I exclaimed, ignored as they pulled Pike up and the vampire jammed that broken blade at him again.

"Detrudo!" I shouted, my knockdown curse hitting nothing when Pike moved, slipping his bloodied hand free from his attacker and deflecting the knife into the other guy's arm.

Howling, his attacker yanked his hand away, and with that, Pike was up and free.

In one move, he twisted and broke the vampire's hand as he shoved the knife deeper into him. Spinning, he knocked the second man out, catching the falling knife and slitting the throat of the third with one smooth, practiced motion. Grinning, he lurched to catch the last man, knocking his head into the cement until he collapsed with a sigh.

And just like that, it was over.

Shocked, I stared at the carnage, Jenks's dust warm on my shoulder. "Ah, are you okay?" I said. But Pike wasn't listening, grunting in pain as he levered the bodies over the railing and into the water, where they floated to the middle of the pond, ducks pecking at them.

Limping and trailing blood, Pike lurched to the last vampire. He was beginning to regain consciousness, and I inched closer as Pike hauled him up, propping him against the thick railing. Pike's eyes were black, and there was blood everywhere.

"When you wake from death, tell whatever brother of mine who sent you that he came in a little light."

The man nodded. Satisfied, Pike took that broken blade

and, with one smooth, unhurried motion, opened up his neck and tipped him over into the water.

"Pike!" I cried, horrified. I mean, fighting for your life is one thing, but they were down.

Pike turned to me, blinking as if having forgotten I was even there. "I . . . don't need . . . your help," he said, and then he collapsed.

CHAPTER

15

"DUST HIM, JENKS!" I SHOUTED AS PIKE SLUMPED AGAINST the railing, his eyes closed and his hand going to his lower chest. Blood dribbled from his upper shoulder, but it was the lower stab wound that worried me.

Jenks darted down, the sound of his wings shifting as a peculiar dust sifted from him to clot the flowing blood. "You want to keep him alive?" he said as he looked quizzically up at me.

I glanced across the grass toward the sound of sirens. "I do when I'm the last person who saw him alive," I muttered. "He's my ticket to Constance." I hesitated, torn. "You got this?" I asked, and when he nodded, I ran to David, dodging the blood slicks so I wouldn't leave prints.

David was sitting up, his hat in his hand as he held his head, nursing a small scrape from where someone had hit him. "David," I called, relieved when his focus was sharp and rueful.

My attention flicked to the three I.S. cruisers across the park, hitting the curb hard and bouncing over the grass toward us. Holy crap on toast, they were driving on the grass! *"Elerodic!"* I shouted, my palms aching as I funneled a crapload of line energy through them, focusing it with a charm I'd gotten from Trent. They would blame me for this. I knew it.

The spell hit the three cars with a dramatic pop, wrenching the hoods up in a screech of metal and plastic and stopping them dead. One hood broke free, pinwheeling over the ground until it stuck in the soft earth to quiver upright. Behind them, the passing cars in the street shorted out with a gentler bang, and the traffic light blew with a shower of sparks.

"Damn, Rache," Jenks said as he hovered at my shoulder. "I think you got 'em."

Flustered, I knelt to hold David's face and force him to look me in the eye. He was focusing properly, but he probably had a concussion. "We have to move. Can you walk?"

"Sure," he said ruefully as he took my hands from his head. But he wasn't standing, and we had to go. "Jesus, what did I miss? You're blue. And wet. Did you fall in?"

I turned to Pike. He was sort of standing, but he didn't look much better than the dead guys floating in the water. "We have to go. I can get us into the ever-after. Can you walk?"

He nodded, and I looked across the grass. Shaken I.S. agents were getting out of the cars. They were coming closer with a hesitant slowness. The ley line was between us, and as I watched, a third car arrived, late as it wove through the stalled traffic. Three agents got out, and I frowned when one pulled a wand.

Crap on toast. They brought a witch.

"Go." David hauled himself up, wavering until he found his balance. "I'm staying. Someone has to keep the resistance informed. They might think you're dead if I don't tell them otherwise. No telling what they'd do."

He was grinning, and I stared at him blankly. *Resistance?*

Jenks's wings rasped in impatience. "Go, Rache!" the pixy said, bobbing up and down. "Get to the ever-after. I'll get David out of here. Keys!" he directed.

I dug them out of my pocket and dropped them in David's hand. Grinning, the Were put his hat on his head and wobbled to my car, worrying me when he reached for a tree.

Resistance? Does he mean the refugees in my church? I thought as I looked at the bridge in a near panic. I couldn't leave Pike here. Not broken the way he was. Constance would lie and say I'd done it, and with the I.S. actively after me, I had, like, zero chance for my plan to work.

"Damn it all back to the Turn," I swore as I glanced at the approaching I.S. officers, then ran to the bridge. One of the witches threw a spell, and I yelped, ducking when it hit the concrete and slid, sparks flying up as it rasped across the rough stones. Tendrils wound out from the mass of purple magic, shattering the column it had latched onto. *That doesn't look like a white spell. . . .*

"Let's go!" I tugged at Pike, jerking back when he flung out a hand, almost hitting me. "It's me!" I darted in again, pulling him to his feet. "You want to get caught? Move! If someone is trying to kill you, the last place you want to be is the hospital."

Pike wobbled upright, a hand pressed to his middle. He wasn't bleeding out thanks to Jenks, but he obviously hurt, and his eyes weren't focusing right. "What are you doing?"

I put an arm around his middle and began walking him to the end of the bridge. "Keeping you alive. You want to move your feet a little? We need to get to that statue of the lactating wolf."

He blinked, head rising. "That's a wolf?"

His lean body was heavy on me, and the scent of vampire incense was growing stronger. Images of Kisten flitted and died. The I.S. agents had organized, and that witch was winding up again, his hands dripping with a sinister red. *"Rhombus,"* I whispered, imagining a huge circle enclosing us and a nice section of the line. The energy sprang up, pissing off the I.S. agents as they skidded to a halt, four hundred yards back. Behind me, I heard David and Jenks roar off in my car, and I breathed easier.

"Go around!" I heard. "Triangulate it!"

Pike stumbled and I lurched to catch him. We weren't moving fast enough, but we were off the bridge, and I strengthened my circle. The head witch gestured for the other two to move behind me. If they made a triangle, they could take my circle down. It wasn't drawn, and it lacked permanence.

"Hey." Pike twisted to look over my shoulder. "My car is the other way."

The line was just ahead. I could feel it pressing against my skin. I might not be able to jump the lines without Bis, but if I stood in one, I could shift to the ever-after—taking anyone I wanted with me whether they agreed or not. It was a demon thing, and I shoved the flash of guilt down. I was saving his life. I didn't care if he forgave me or not.

"Car?" I said as we limped forward. "Where we're going, we don't need no car."

"Stop her!" the witch shouted, gesturing wildly. "She's got access to a ley line!"

"Ley line?" Pike's pale face went whiter. "Ah . . ."

But I grinned as we stepped into it and the red and gold of my circle flared brilliantly. I was standing in the line. Nothing could break my bubble of protection now. "Sorry about this. It's a moment of weird, and then it's okay."

"Morgan, I don't want to . . . arrgh!" he gurgled, voice cutting off as I shifted our auras to match the line, and we were suddenly . . . gone.

The sounds of Cincinnati vanished with a shocking suddenness. My heart beat once in the new silence, and then the soft hush of wind in the tall grass replaced it as we were there with only the barest sense of disconnection. Eyes closing, I took a deep breath, shoulders easing as the low sun seemed to soak in. This wasn't my parents' red-smeared, hellish ever-after. It was brand-new. And it was . . . beautiful.

"You crazy witch! What is wrong with you?" Pike pulled away from me, staggering until he fell to his hands and knees. Shaking, he felt the tall grass as if it was unreal. "Grass?" he questioned, squinting up at the lowering sun. "I thought the ever-after was a sun-ruined hell."

"Not anymore," I whispered. My smile took on a pleased softness. The damp, spring-green meadow ran for miles,

and the sun looked closer to setting without the buildings
in the way. The obvious rain had left the air clean, really
clean, and I pulled it deep into my lungs and let it go with
a sigh. I could see black clouds in the distance, but here it
was nice.

Far at the horizon were mountains that never ringed
Cincinnati. The original ever-after had been created by the
demons as a mirror of reality to trick the elves into believing they hadn't been plucked from reality and dropped into
an elaborate cell to die. Sort of like a magical holodeck. Al
said it had once been green and cool, but when the elves
imprisoned the demons in turn, the smut from their eons-
long war turned it into a red ruin.

When Landon had destroyed the ever-after last year in
an effort to kill the demons, Bis and I had made another.
Since there was no need to mimic reality anymore, we created what we wanted: trees, grass, cool pools, and high
mountains now pink with the setting sun. There was supposed to be a beach here somewhere, but I'd never seen it.
Bis, I thought, slumping as I gazed at the tall mountains. *I
will find a way. I promise.*

One thing was sure. There were no I.S. agents. Smiling,
I turned to the distinctive *thump-thump-thump* of a drum,
not altogether at odds with the pastoral setting.

Pike lurched upright, his knees damp and his eyes
squinting from the low sun. His hand pressed into his side,
and his face was splattered with someone else's blood.
"Why am I here?"

I'd never seen that mix of anger and unease on him, and I
wondered if I'd made a mistake. I couldn't tell if it was the trip
through the line, or just being away from concrete and skyscrapers. "So you don't die," I said. "And you're welcome."

He took his phone from a pocket, frowning at the
cracked screen. It deepened when the phone powered up
and found no towers. "Are you serious?" he said as he put
it away. "Maybe you didn't notice, but I killed them."

"I noticed." The thumping drum had been joined by
masculine singing, low, loud, and kind of beautiful. There'd

been no music the last time I'd been here, no drums. Dali must have opened his restaurant. "You hungry?" I said as I took a step toward the sound of the drums. "My treat."

Hunched in pain, he carefully used two fingers to shift his torn shirt to see a slowly oozing, pixy-dust-caked puncture. "My God. You are crazy," he said, apparently satisfied that he wasn't dying today.

The music was coming from behind a gentle rise in the land. Hips swaying, I flicked my blue-wet hair back and started that way, pushing through the tall grass and glad I'd put on my butt-kicking boots that morning, even if they were now squishing. "How's your shoulder?" I asked, turning when he didn't answer.

He hadn't moved. He was staring at the empty meadow, and I could almost see the moment when he realized he was trapped.

"I think Dalliance is over the hill," I said, trying to be nice. "We can get you stitched up if someone puts in World War Two Paris."

Jaw clenched, he pushed forward, a hand pressed to his middle. "I hear words coming out of your mouth, but they don't make sense."

"I'm sorry, but all my pain amulets are on the bridge," I said, wincing as I thought of the I.S. impounding my bag. My wallet. Cash. ID. *And I was worried about leaving footprints?* Fortunately, cash wasn't the usual mode of payment where we were headed. "Are you going to be okay?"

"Odd time to be asking me that," he muttered as he came even with me.

"So," I said as we angled up the low rise together. "If they weren't after me, who were they?" I wasn't exactly sure how I felt about this. I mean, I'd watched him kill every single one of them, the last with a ruthlessness that left me cold. But he hadn't initiated the fight—that I could tell, anyway—and that was important. Still . . . his brother had sent them?

"The fab five, back there?" I prompted when he remained silent.

Pike took an extra-long step, clenching in an unexpected pain. "None of your business."

"Okay." God, I was dripping blue water. Not exactly the impression I wanted to make as we strolled into Dalliance. If I was lucky, Dali would have a gangster theme going. That was the only way we were going to fit in with Pike bleeding the way he was.

Breathless, Pike came to an abrupt halt. "What's your thinking?" he said, pain etching his face and his good hand gesturing at nothing. "Are you trying to kidnap me?"

I couldn't help my grin. "Trying? I think I am."

Pike's expression emptied.

"Sorry. Bad joke," I said, though kidnapping him was exactly what I'd done. "This was not my intention. But the I.S. would have taken me in under suspicion of whatever they felt like, and me running is better for everyone than me destroying Eden Park to get them to back off. You were bleeding out, and I kind of owed you one."

"How do you figure that?"

I shrugged with one shoulder. "You saved me on the bridge. How come?"

Pike's eyes narrowed, and then he blinked, remembering. He had shoved me out of the way of a knife thrown at him. "I didn't like you taking my hit," he said, and I nodded.

"Exactly. And if I left you on the bridge, the I.S. would have taken you to the hospital. Not a good place to be when someone is trying to kill you. Believe you me."

Pike's lip curled. Head down, he started forward again.

"I did you a favor, fang boy." I jumped to follow, easing the gap between us.

"Fang boy?" Pike muttered, slowing as we reached the crest and looked down.

My smile returned as I saw the expected open-air restaurant nestled at the bottom of a perfectly round divot in the earth. The grass thinned to nothing, and there were no trees, just scrubby bushes. It looked how I'd imagine Mesopotamia might have been three thousand years ago. There were even some magic-derived camels tied to a highline, groaning and spitting.

The large area was already in the shade of the surrounding earth as the sun neared setting. It held several tents and fires, but it was the center I focused on, where the musicians drummed into the lengthening day. Bearded men who were really demons sat around it, waited on by who had better be a paid extra, not an indentured familiar. And they were singing, the unearthly sound mixing with the drums to send a shiver through me.

As if someone had flipped a switch, the drums ceased. The singing stopped, and, as one, the gathered demons turned to us, silhouetted against the blue sky at the top of the rise.

"Hey, hi!" I called loudly, making a stupid sort of a wave, and they looked away, heads leaning to one another and talking. About me, obviously. The drums made a *thump-thump-thump* and began again. The singing, though, did not.

Flushed, I looped my arm in Pike's and tugged him into motion.

"Not exactly popular here, are you," he said flatly.

"It's been worse." I leaned back to handle the steep incline. Beside me, Pike half stifled a groan. The grass became more sparse, shifted to dirt and finally sand. Even the air felt drier as we came under the influence of the magical restaurant, and my nose wrinkled at the stink of unwashed bodies and animals. Dali thought it important to maintain as close a tie to reality as possible at his multi-themed eatery, which sort of begged the question of what they liked about sand and camels when they could be in suits and ties, smelling of cologne and eating caviar.

I searched for Al's disapproving glare, but he wasn't here, and I sighed.

"Expecting someone?" Pike pushed my hand off my arm as we reached level ground.

"No." I beamed at the demon waiting at the archway leading into the restaurant. He was either the host or the bouncer. Either way, I'd have to get past him, and he looked me up and down in disgust, safe in his dusty purple robe. "I know you're a mess, but try to make a good impression, okay? It's usually demons only, but they're probably bored enough to make an exception for you." I looked askance at Pike, seeing his ugly, pained look. "Can you smile a little? Pretend you're my date, and we might get in."

"Yeah, I'm always going out with women covered in blue water, stinking of duck shit," he muttered, adding, "Those aren't demons. They look like extras in a bad Arabian Nights movie."

Damn it, they'd heard that, and red, goat-slitted eyes turned to us. My smile froze. "You know what? You really need to get off my case about how I look, smell, or act. You are a bloody, effing mess, Pike."

Someone laughed, and my jaw clenched. Suddenly I knew how Newt must have felt. They had barely tolerated her, too, even if she could best every last one of them.

But Mr. Purple Robe was facing me, barring our way, and I forced a smile. "Good evening," I said loudly as my boots squished to a halt. The word DALLIANCE glowed in the dust hanging over the archway like a banner, sparkling and out of place. It was the only visible indication of magic, but I could feel it everywhere. "A pillow for two, please."

"Hold up. Don't let her in!" a loud voice demanded, and my hope both rose and fell when Dali pushed the host out of the way to bar our entrance. His arms went over his ample middle and his red, goat-slitted eyes narrowed. His robe was a flat brown, stained with dust and grease, but seeing as he was the cook, that was probably okay. "Go mind the roast. I've got this," he said, and the bouncer nodded and left.

"Hi, Dali." I drew Pike back a step and moved to stand before him with a sheepish determination. "Two, please. Somewhere at the bar, maybe?" My eyes went to where a handful of demons sat around a fire, using their hands to eat from overflowing bowls. "That's the bar, yes?"

"What is that smell . . ." Pike said in disgust, and Dali stiffened.

"We call it lamb," Dali said shortly. "You're not sitting at the bar. But if you can manage to dress yourselves appropriately, I'll find you somewhere in the kitchen turning the spit."

My eyes narrowed, and I put a hand on my hip. "Look, you—"

"No, you look," Dali interrupted, pushing forward until I backed into Pike, who swallowed a groan of pain even as he kept me from falling. "You know the rules. You either *fit in*, or you don't *come in*."

Several demons laughed, ticking me off. "Let her in, Dali!" one shouted. "It's the first time the rain has quit in two days!"

Apart from the rain comment, the entire situation was eerily reminiscent of the first time Al had brought me to Dalliance, and I cringed.

"No dinner?" Slumped, Pike held his middle. Blood leaked from between his fingers. Jenks's first aid was good, but there were limits. His face was starting to swell, too.

But Dali was right. If we couldn't fit the restaurant's current motif of ancient Mesopotamia, we couldn't come in. Still, there were ways around that, and I looked behind me at the bales of sheep fleeces wrapped and stacked like a waiting area. "Sit down before you fall over," I said to Pike. "I'll be right back."

"I haven't been asked to wait outside a restaurant since I was five and on a field trip," Pike muttered, wincing as he sat. "And never on anything that smelled like this," he added as he wiped his hand off on his bloody slacks.

Dali settled more firmly before me. "Is that toilet water dripping from you?"

"I'll change the theme so we do fit in," I insisted, and Dali shook his head. "I've got to have coin on account," I said, sure of it when Dali's expression went empty. "I know you've been using that picnic tulpa I made," I added, and he cringed.

Yes! I thought exuberantly. It had been ages since I'd made my memory of the hot, Arizona sun real to prove that

I was a demon. Every time one of them "replayed" the tulpa on Dali's jukebox, I was supposed to get a royalty. Al had helped me make it, because, though only a female demon had the mental stamina to coalesce a memory into a solid form, it took a male demon to successfully disentangle a tulpa from her mind and "code" it into a curse so anyone could access it. The experience had humbled both him and me. I'd trusted him to keep me alive and forgive me for what lay in my deepest thoughts, laid bare to him.

And now he wouldn't talk to me because I wouldn't condemn his brother.

"You can float me a coin for the machine until I can make Al cough up my percentage," I said, and Dali's expression twisted into a sneer. The easygoing babysitter was nowhere to be seen, and I wondered if things were going badly on the student/teacher front.

"You have credit," Dali admitted. "But it's no good here or in the collective if you are still taking study from Hodin." He reached out and I lurched backward, warming when I realized that all he was after was one of those flowers still in my hair. "He's elven filth," he said, apparently knowing what it was. "And it's beginning to cling to you," he added, flicking the dilapidated, blue-stained flower to the sand.

"Hodin isn't teaching me squat," I said, the hair on the back of my neck pricking as I felt the demons behind him listening. "And you need to get off his case. He knows things you don't."

Dali laughed. "Oh, trust me, Rachel. I know how to use my genitals to gain food, and that's all he is good for. You will cease talking to him or you will find he's the only one who *will* talk to you." Dali spat, the heavy wad making a dark splat atop the flower. "Elf magic."

"Which you know I practice . . ." My words trailed off when two demons pushed past me, halting to stand over Pike, wicked grins on their faces. "Ah, I mean elf magic, not the other thing," I added, surprised when Pike looked up and they shifted to silk suits, their hair slicked and smelling of musk. Eyes narrowed, Pike stiffened in a wary threat as they sat beside him, talking smack about him as if he wasn't there. They looked like living vampires, and I grimaced, unable to help him at the moment. *God! Demons are such bullies.*

"You didn't sit out the war eating raspberries and wearing silk," Dali said, and I turned back.

"So you admit you're angry about how he survived, not the elf-magic issue?"

"He did not survive the war," Dali said. "He *relished* it. Leave."

"Because I talked to Hodin?" Ticked, I stood toe to toe with him, refusing to back down. It was more than not getting a table, now. "You think you can sling me out of here? I made this," I said, gesturing. "All of it!"

Dali's eyes flicked to Pike, then returned to me. "Tell me true, Rachel," he said, a new wariness in his voice. "Is Hodin helping you best Constance, or are you here on your own?"

"Hodin is not helping me." I stepped back, knowing this was important by his sudden lack of bluster. "He is not helping me!" I said again when Dali's eyes narrowed. "He made a cloche to cover the lily I'm using to stink up Piscary's. Big whoop. That was between him and Jenks. And he helped me bury Nash. Again, more of a sanitation issue than anything else. But other than that, no. He's not much good with anything but passive stuff," I admitted, and Dali eyed me.

"You only angered her with that lily," he said.

"Yeah? I drove a master vampire from her day quarters with a *joke curse*!" I said proudly. "Forced her and her camarilla to bunk at the I.S. I *humiliated* her," I said, then winced when Pike pointedly cleared his throat. Flustered, I tugged the hem of my soggy skirt. "And just so we're clear, I'm standing up for Hodin because out of all of you, he's the only one trying to help me recover Bis." My voice began to rise, and I let it. I was mad at them, and I didn't care if they, or Pike, knew it. "*Out of all of you*," I shouted, "he's the only one willing to concede that reconciling with the Goddess might be the only way to survive the rebirth of the elves!"

Dali's face screwed up in an ugly expression. "The rebirth that you engendered."

"Damn right." I pushed forward until I could've bumped forehead to chin with him. "I worked with a Kalamack elf to save them. And then I stood up against the elven dewar and saved each and every one of your asses. I don't know why." I retreated, gaze going past him to the rest. "None of you like me. Come to think of it, the elves aren't that fond of me, either."

My gaze hot on Dali, I put out a blue-tinted hand. "Float me. A coin. For the jukebox. I am not leaving."

"Crazy. Batshit crazy," Pike muttered from the bales of fleece, and I shot him a quick look. The two demons to either side of him smiled with their long teeth as they arranged his hair, laughing when Pike slapped their hands away. They were playing with him, but it was only play. Apparently he was scared of his brothers. No doubt if they were trying to kill him.

Dali shifted from foot to foot. His eyes went to Pike, then back to me. He owed me big for introducing him to baby Keric. I hadn't seen the need to remind him of it. He knew.

And finally . . . Dali slumped. "We're at a limited selection right now due to a lack of materials," he said, and I snatched from his fingers the flat, dented coin that appeared.

"Stay here," I shot over my shoulder at Pike as I strode past Dali. Sometimes I thought the demon liked being a few pounds overweight because he'd known a bone-aching hunger for too long. *And maybe he found respite from his thoughts in cooking for others for the same reason. . . .*

Head high, I skirted the largest fire, moving quickly to avoid the grumbling demons trying to down me with a surreptitious spell flung out like a tripping foot. There was anger in some, amusement in fewer. The air reeked of lamb, and I couldn't fathom why they were camped out around a fire. Unless it was because they were well and truly under an open sky, one that was theirs and not toxic from the waste born in their war with the elves.

"Touch me, Tron, and your nose is a snake," I muttered as I aimed for a canvas-draped shape that had to be the jukebox, and a ripple of laughter rose up. Spine stiff, I turned my back on them and flipped up the stinky tarp to find the expected modern, bubble-and-light jukebox. It didn't stock music but tulpas, memories of times and places made real with demon magic. With the symbolic payment of coin, I could shift Dali's restaurant from camel and donkey to electronic disco, and with that, Pike and I would fit in and could stay.

Slowly my exuberance began to fade. Dali was right. There were only a handful of options where there had once been hundreds. There'd never been many tulpas from the current century, as only female demons had the mental stamina to make one and Newt hadn't trusted anyone to pluck it from her mind to make many. But I didn't even see the upscale New York power bar. It was all ancient Rome, China, and Mongolia. Old stuff. I needed something that had antiseptic, jeans, and maybe a cheeseburger. But then my eyebrows rose. *American Gigolo?*

"Ah, not that one," Dali said, suddenly at my elbow.

"Why not?" I dropped the coin in, and he shifted uneasily.

"Newt made it when she was in one of her more strange moods," he said, and my eyes narrowed, hearing a half-truth. "No one likes it."

"Sounds like fun," I said, then pushed the right button.

Dali groaned, dropping back when everything but the demons became hazy. The drums shifted to suggestive, canned music from the seventies. The sky darkened to a low ceiling, and the sand became a dirty, scratched floor. Dingy walls appeared, and the lights, what there were of them, were low. Small round tables made a half circle around a stage. I could smell cigarettes and bad Brimstone. The bar was big enough to dance on, with hundreds of bottles and one disgusted demon in a purple robe behind it. As I watched, his robe vanished into a pair of bondage shorts and a halter. He even had the kohl-lined eyes and blue-dyed hair. Good God, it was a strip bar.

"Wow, even a trapeze," I said, seeing it swaying behind the man onstage. There wasn't much between my eyes and his skin, and as I watched, there was even less.

The demons in their Mesopotamian robes made ugly noises. Most popped out, but three moved to the stage, their clothes shifting to modern, sleazy businessman as they waved dollar bills and tried to lure the male stripper closer.

"You're going to ruin me," Dali said, and I beamed. He looked like a bouncer now, and I brushed a flake of glitter from his colorful vest. Pike and I matched the decor. If he wanted to refuse me a table, he'd have to be honest about it.

"I see a quiet spot in the back," I said as I gestured for Pike, and he stood. Behind him, the bales of fleece turned into a hard bench sporting carved names and numbers. "We'll have three cheeseburgers, a couple of beers, and the first aid kit. There's bound to be one in a sleazebucket place like this."

Nose wrinkled, Dali watched the memory of a man gyrate on the stage. "I remember the day she made this," he said, focus distant. "It was a bad one. Minias pulled it from her psyche. He never did tell me what triggered it. I had no idea she'd been going reality-side. Neither did Minias. He swore she hadn't slipped him in a hundred years, but you can't make a tulpa if you haven't been there. I'll get your order in." Dali turned from the stage. "I've only got three staying. Shouldn't be long."

"Thanks, Dali," I said, grateful as I looked over the low-ceilinged room. I had a feeling the jukebox held only a few themes because Dali didn't have the magical funds to support more. They'd lost nearly everything but their lives and what curses had been in the collective when the original ever-after had gone down.

I shoved my flash of guilt away, frowning at the three demons in their cheap suits shouting out catcalls and waving dollar bills at the stripper. Chances were, he wasn't a paid extra but part of the tulpa itself, a solid illusion from Newt's memory. Even so, I felt myself warm as the tall, imagined vampire blew me a kiss and gyrated just for me. There was a scar on his neck in the shape of a sickle, and his bottle-blond hair reminded me of Kisten. Flushing, I headed for a table.

Pike slid heavily into a chair. His back was to the wall, and I took the one next to him, the stage to my left. The pain creasing his scarred face made him look old, and my guilt thickened. He could be in a hospital right now, doped up on vampire pheromones and feeling nothing. But then again, him in a hospital would have left him vulnerable to his brothers' plan B.

"A strip bar? Is that what counts as a night out for you? Nice."

I quirked a smile at the sarcastic humor in his voice. "It was either that or a picnic in the Arizona badlands, and I don't think there was a first aid kit in the car."

Pike carefully shifted to a more comfortable position. "Someday, you're going to have to explain this so every other sentence out of you doesn't sound crazy."

I jumped when Dali came up from behind me and dropped a first aid kit on the table followed by two beer bottles, dripping with condensation. "Burgers will take some time. Unless you want ground lamb?" he said hopefully, and I shook my head vehemently.

"Thanks, Dali," I said, then clinked my bottle against Pike's and took a swig. Slumped, Pike stared longingly at his, and I wondered if he was worried about tampering. "Your brother can't reach you here. Unless your brother is a demon."

Pike reached for the bottle, looking pained as he tipped it up and downed it, his Adam's apple bobbing. "Damn, that's cold," he said when he came up for air, a swallow or two left in the bottom. Glancing at the bar, he held up two fingers, and the bouncer turned tender nodded.

Somehow that made me feel good. Quashing it, I flipped

open the first aid kit and began rummaging. "Shirt off," I directed. "Let's see the damage."

Again he hesitated as if reluctant to make himself vulnerable, but at my expectant stare, he carefully, painfully, took his shirt off. I had been right: it was lined with Kevlar, the fabric having done much to minimize the damage. The stripper made a catcall, and I looked away from the stage, blanching.

Pike's chest was a mess of old and new scars, blood and caked pixy dust holding him together. Or at least it had been, and new ribbons of blood dribbled down as he blotted them with a wad of napkins.

"Hey, can I have a bowl of warm water and a couple of towels?" I called loudly. The stripper had finished, leaving just us and the three demons at the stage nursing their drinks and listening to bad seventies music. "Okay," I said, reluctant to run my fingers over him. His abs were more than nice, and his body trim. I scooted my chair closer, and after hesitating to make sure he'd let me, I prodded his swollen nose to see if it was broken. There was a scuff on his cheekbone, and a scrape at his hairline, and a nasty gouge under his eye, but compared to the old scars, they looked hardly mentionable. "Your face looks okay."

"Swell," he said sourly.

"But you're going to have an ugly bruise tomorrow. How bad does your head hurt?"

Pike finished his beer when the bartender brought over the new ones. "Tolerable," he said, drinking one down as if it was medicinal.

"Headache?" I asked, but he didn't answer. "Headache?!" I shouted, and his wandering gaze found mine. "You shouldn't have more than one beer. Actually, you shouldn't—"

"This isn't necessary," he said, and I made a scoff of a laugh as I wrung out the cloth.

"Necessary doesn't enter into my decision-making process most days." I dabbed at the blood under his ear, my motions turning rough when I realized it wasn't his blood, then stopping when I discovered it hid an old puffy scar. *Nice going, Rachel.* "But some of this is my fault. If I'd known someone was trying to kill you, I would have let you bring a second."

"I'll finish if you don't mind," he said, and I put the cloth into his bloody-knuckled hand.

What am I doing? I wondered as I watched him work his way down to the new knife wound, dabbing the blood from his smooth, broad chest, revealing scar after scar. Some were old, some were new. Some were just scratches, but others . . . others looked as if they had been hard to survive.

"How long have your brothers been trying to kill you?" I said as I uncapped the antiseptic. "That one looks really old."

Pike was silent, stiffening as I gave him three healthy squirts of the antiseptic spray. The one wound needed to be stitched, but I knew without asking that he wouldn't let me do it. A butterfly bandage would do.

"Is that why you're with Constance?" I guessed as I rummaged for the biggest Band-Aid I could find. "Is she protecting you?" It would explain why he saw to her needs when there was clearly no love between them. Most scions were dangerously infatuated with their gnomons.

Saying nothing, Pike finished the second beer and started on the third. Vamps generally had a high tolerance for alcohol, but he'd lost a lot of blood and neither of us had eaten yet. I couldn't cart him out of here if he passed out.

"It is brothers, yes? Plural?" I prompted, and his grip on the bottle tightened, his gaze going to the stage, empty under a single, ugly spotlight. "You told that last assassin to tell your brother he came in too light." *And then you killed him.* "Five against one, and they were good." I hesitated, the sound of the bandage's wrapper loud as I opened it. "Expensive."

"My dad is a bastard," he said, wincing when I pulled the cut shut with the bandage and stuck the free end down. "This is none of your business. Why do you even care?"

Good God, I was taping him together with Band-Aids

when he needed a professional. "I have no idea. Jenks would say it's a Rachel thing." Finished, I wiped my hands clean, then opened an antiseptic package to try to get the blue out from under my nails. "I can't stand bullies. They've been at you for a long time. How did you get a bounty on your head?"

Pike gingerly put his bloodstained shirt back on. "I was born."

I waited for more, but he was silent. Worse, that blue wasn't coming out from under my nails. "Sibling rivalry sucks." Disgusted, I threw the wipe on the table with the bloodied rags.

He chuckled at that, choking it off when his face screwed up in pain. "So true. So true."

I could smell our burgers cooking, and my mouth began to water as I put everything away. Pike slowly sipped at that third beer, his thoughts almost visibly beginning to shift as the immediate danger of him bleeding out grew less. "If I don't call her, Constance will assume you kidnapped me to exchange for Zack. Are you sure that's how you want to play this?"

I set the first aid kit on a nearby table to make room for the coming burgers. "Convince her to meet with me outside of the I.S.?" I offered, and he shook his head. I took a breath to protest, catching it when Dali headed our way, two bags of takeout in his hand. "Oh, come on!" I protested. "We fit in. We more than fit in."

Dali put the bags on our table and frowned. "I can't lose an entire night at the strip club because your vampire got stabbed. Take your burgers and go."

"I'm not done with my beer yet," I complained. *My vampire?*

Pike sighed and rubbed at his swollen cheekbone. "Kicked out of a strip club. Story of my life."

Dali smiled in a not-nice way. "Would I be correct in assuming you don't have any funds to pay for your meals?"

My wallet was probably on Doyle's desk by now, but they didn't take coin in Dalliance regardless. The entire demon realm ran on a complicated account system of favors and royalties from curses. I'd all but depleted Al's considerable fortune ages ago, but I knew I had a little dribbling in. "Al has my money," I said as Pike opened one bag and took out a handful of fries. "Get it from him."

Dali pulled the bags out of Pike's reach, the burgers smelling good enough to die for. "Get it from him yourself."

Pike frowned, the beer and the blood loss clearly hitting him. "Worst date ever."

"Tell you what we're going to do." Dali slammed the kitchen knife that had been tucked in his waistband into the table between the bags and Pike's reaching hand. "You can give me a week as a waitress—"

"No," I said, and Pike looked up, surprised at the vehemence in my voice.

"Then I've got an order that needs to go out." Dali smiled to show his teeth. "Deliver it, and we're even." He turned to Pike and pulled the knife out.

"Done," I said, pleased for about three seconds. Two meals and a tulpa shift for delivering a meal sounded as if we had gotten the better end. That was usually when the rug was pulled out from under me. "Why is everyone here, anyway?" I said as I peeked inside the heaviest bag to see two burgers and fries. "The curse is broken. They don't have to stay in the ever-after." I looked up from the moist warmth, worried. "What did they do? Are their auras that smutty already?"

Dali shook his head, a flicker of regret in his eyes. "No. Worse," he said softly, his attention going to the trio by the stage. "They got overwhelmed. Al is the only one coping well. Probably because he has been the most active in the affairs of reality. Dalliance has always been a place to connect and resolve issues." His attention came back to me. "Which is why I am trading two meals for a delivery of a third. Go."

They needed me, I realized, but I wasn't sure if that was good or not. "How far is this place?" I asked as I rolled the bag down to seal in the moist heat.

Dali turned to the front, drawn by the loud complaints of the four demons who had just popped in, their disgust shifting to loud suggestions of what to put in the jukebox. "Everything is close in the ever-after," Dali said as he took a ley line amulet from around his neck and extended it. "Red is hot, green is cool," he said. "Five-minute walk. It's very close to the ley line near your church. Your vampire should be able to handle the travel."

"His name is Pike." I took it, feeling the warmth of his body lingering in the metal disk. *The demons are suffering from culture shock?*

"I'm not her vampire," Pike said, and I stood, ready to go. The restaurant was going to change, and I wanted to be out of it when it did. Sometimes the food on your plate shifted with it.

"You will be," Dali said sourly. "Rachel never brings anyone here unless she's culled him from the herd."

My lips parted, but Pike chuckled, apparently finding a compliment in there. "Come on," I said as I grabbed the two bags. "We need to get out of here before our burgers change to lamb."

Pike slowly rose, and as Dali shouted at the demons to get off the stage, I hustled us out.

The sun had set while we'd been inside, spreading gold and pink over half the sky. There was a breath of exhaust, the hint of a dark parking lot, and then it was gone as the shack behind us evaporated. Palm trees whispered back into existence, and the calls of an exotic bird.

"Five-minute walk. We'll take it slow." I peered at the darkening sky, not seeing enough stars to know if they were the same.

Pike jerked his attention from the jingling of tiny bells and the laugh of a woman coming from the oasis behind us. "It would take twenty to cross Cincinnati in a car this time of night."

"Everything is closer in the ever-after. We walk across it here, and pop out there."

Pike sighed, his shoulders shifting. "One of those is mine, right? I'm starved."

I handed him a bag, and he opened it up, giving me the top burger before going back for his own. So much for his "if I don't bring it, I don't eat it" rule.

"Huh," he said, glancing over his shoulder toward the fading music. "You're better at this than I expected."

"This being . . . what?" The paper crackled in the dusk as I opened it up, and my mouth watered at the fragrant steam. God help me, it had Gouda cheese on it.

"Getting your way in an antagonistic situation with minimal friction," he said as he limped beside me. "Constance wouldn't have been able to walk in, get what she wanted, walk out with no yelling, no screaming, no blood on the floor."

"Well, I am a demon. What did you expect?"

"Not this," he muttered as he took a dripping bite, and I found I couldn't argue with him.

CHAPTER

16

I WAS GUESSING PIKE WASN'T MUCH OF A NATURE PERSON by his perpetual grimace and his periodic mutters of disgust when he slipped on a root or misjudged the depth of a rut in the path. That the sun was down and we were walking by reflected light probably didn't help. I had fallen into the steady yet variable pace I'd learned at camp, one that allowed for both bad terrain and periodic bites from my burger. I thought it interesting that the green and white paper the burger was wrapped in was from Junior's coffee shop. That the finding amulet was leading us from the open grassland and into a looming, dark forest was even more so.

But my stomach was happy and I was almost dry apart from my underwear and socks. My feet still squished, and my hair had dried in tight ringlets sporting that *lovely* shade of blue at the tips. Dali, though, knew what to do with hamburger, and I was content as I chewed, swallowed, and repeated—even if Pike did keep slipping on damp roots. Dress shoes. Sheesh.

"Want me to carry the bag?" I said, worried he was going to fall and squish it.

His gaze went from the trees to me, eyeing the half-eaten burger in my one hand, the amulet in the other. "I've got it," he said, having finished his burger and fries in the time I had eaten half of my own.

"Okay." I slowed, eyeing the faint path. The sun was long gone, and though it still illuminated the upper sky, it was dark under the trees. Thoughts of Little Red Riding Hood meets Hansel and Gretel flitted through my mind. My hands were full, but Pike was done. He could hold a flashlight.

"Lenio cinis," I whispered, and a glowing, fist-size ball of energy materialized, hanging in the air at chest height to send a cheerful glow a few feet into the woods. "Could you carry that, then?" I asked as I moved around it. "It will go out if I touch it. It's basically an undrawn circle filled with energy, and my aura will break it."

I wasn't sure why I was explaining it to him, other than he was staring at it as if it might knock him out. "Sure." He hesitated. "Neat trick," he added as he gingerly took it.

I stifled a shiver as we slipped under the first of the trees. Clearly the burger and fries had done him good. But the farther we got, the less I could tell which smelled better: Pike, or the dinner we were delivering.

Pike had gone silent, probably to concentrate on his footing, and a slow unease began to steal over me. My eyes dropped to my hamburger and the few bites left. *I'm eating in front of a vampire. . . .* "Ah, I'm eating because I'm hungry," I said, and he looked up, the glow from my magic seeming to smooth the scars on his face.

Pike eyed me. "Okay . . ."

"Not because I'm coming on to you," I added. "I want to make that perfectly clear."

He laughed, the honest sound falling short in the trees. But then surprise brought him up, and he took an extra half step to catch up. "Good God. You've read the book."

I flushed. Appetite gone, I dropped my unfinished burger back in the bag and wadded it up. "Cormel's dating guide? Ah, yeah. Ivy gave it to me so I'd quit pushing her buttons." Eating, especially crunchy things, was a vampiric dog whistle inviting a bite. Washing your clothes together to mingle your scents, hiding your throat, conversations about family ties . . . Yeah, I had been a vampire hussy until I learned better. *Crap on toast, I asked him about his brothers.*

"I'd be willing to bet you haven't given it back yet, have you."

My gaze rose to the new leaves whispering in the dark. It was eerie here under the spring-green trees—I thought they were oaks—but peaceful, too. Alone. Apart. "I'm not sure where it is, actually," I said, and Pike smirked. "Maybe I should find it," I kidded him. "Start a little library in my church, seeing as it's filling up with Inderlanders."

I had said the last somewhat sourly, and Pike stiffened, gaze going to the sighing branches. The woods *had* gotten noticeably darker, the path all but vanishing until it was merely a hint, weaving through the large trees and around deadfalls. It was the amulet now that guided us, and I picked our way through the fallen branches, wondering how there could be so much leaf litter when the trees hadn't even existed last year. But seeing as the entire forest had sprung from my memory of camp, it made sense.

Slowly a bright spot ahead of us became more obvious. "I think that's it," I said as the amulet in my hand began to pulsate a vivid green. "When we get there, we drop off the food, then walk to the ley line by the church. I can feel it from here. I'll shift us back. It's only a few blocks to the church from there."

"Oh, get off it," Pike said, and I looked up from the glowing amulet. "You're really going to let me walk away? That innocent Midwestern-girl vibe you cultivate doesn't wash with me. We both know holding me might insure Zack's life for a few days. That's why you hijacked me."

"It is not," I started, and Pike cut me off, the brown rims of his eyes shrinking in the light.

"Don't lie to me. You might be crazy, and blind to reality, and foolish with the company you keep, but you aren't stupid."

There might have been a compliment in there. I wasn't sure. "Holding you hostage for Zack's return won't make my life any easier," I said, then pointed for him to go left around a huge fallen tree instead of over it. "I don't want to live by way of blackmail and threat."

"Oh. You want to die young. Sure, I get it," Pike said, but he didn't get it at all, and I tried not to care that he didn't believe me.

"There's a bus stop at the end of the road where we're going to come out," I said blandly. "But you're welcome to sit at the church and wait for Constance to pick you up. I'd rather you did, so there's no claim of foul play when your brothers' assassins pick you off."

Pike slid a sidelong glance at me. The trees were black behind him, outlined in silver from my light in his grip. "I can handle myself."

"Five to one, sure, but that was an exploratory team. Now that they know you're not sheltering under Constance's wings, they'll spend the big money." I cocked an eyebrow, curious. "My brother used to hide my stuffed animals in the yard when I pissed him off. What did you do to warrant so much *brotherly* love?"

His jaw clenched, and a wave of angry-vampire incense rolled over me.

"Or I could escort you home," I offered, making it worse. "Aww, come on, Pike . . ." I wheedled. "I want to talk to her. Explain a few things I couldn't bring up with Edden behind me. Get her to talk to me. I won't kill her. I promise."

Seeing him work so hard at keeping her alive was beginning to make sense. She was giving him protection. The why was worth asking. Though high in the hierarchy and sipping on her blood, he was clearly not one of her original children. He'd been "adopted." What was she gaining from the arrangement? He couldn't be that good in bed.

Could he?

Stop it, Rachel. Grimacing, I slowed to a halt at the edge of the trees to give whoever lived here a chance to see us. The sky was marginally brighter, making the shadows deeper. Some of the small trees at the edges were flowering, and a drift of white brightened a corner of the glen. A narrow, grass-edged stream wove a serpentine path through the middle of the wide area. Parked beside the stream was a huge horse-drawn van with enormous wheels and heavy timbers. Everything was painted vivid red, gold, and purple, almost glowing in the light from the fire between it and the stream. It was singularly beautiful, but demons never did anything by half measures. Always over the top.

"This is it," I said, tucking the amulet away in a back pocket. "Hello-o-o-o at the camp!" I called. "Got a delivery from Dalliance!"

Pike's nose wrinkled. "A demon wouldn't live in a wagon."

"Why not? You had dinner with one who lives in a church." Before he could say anything, I pointed to the very old gargoyle perched on top of the van, her yellow eyes slowly blinking in suspicion. "That says we're at the right spot," I said, and Pike frowned, not getting the connection.

Bis, I thought with a pang as I compared his cat-size form to the veritable Kodiak bear on the roof. Bis had hardly been old enough to be away from his parents. He had been my responsibility and I had fallen short. But how could I have guessed he'd do something like that to save me?

I should have known, my guilt insisted.

There was a tongue attached to the van, but the wagon was too large for horses. Maybe oxen. Really big oxen. The cheerful fire snapped and popped with a blackened cooking rack over it and a single, blanket-draped log beside it. *All alone in the woods. Someone is having a pity party.*

"Just drop it off and let's get out of here," Pike said.

"Hold up!" I yanked him back as he stepped forward. "You can't just walk into a demon's lair like that," I said as I took the takeout bag from him. It was still warm. Clearly a spell was in use.

Pike looked from me to the peaceful setting. "You're serious, aren't you."

Frowning, I eyed the crackling fire and sent out a little rill of exploratory thought. *Ley line is close. Lots of power here.* "I know you won't listen, but try not to say anything,"

I said, and Pike's eyes narrowed. "No matter what the jack-ass does."

I stepped into the glen, senses searching. No one had responded to my hail. That didn't mean he didn't know I was here. The entire place was circled. It wasn't invoked, but I didn't want to get trapped in it, and I stopped, toes edging a toadstool ring. It had to be forty feet in diameter, but that was small for a demon-held circle.

"I thought you didn't know who it was," Pike said, and I pointed at him to stop.

"I don't," I muttered. "They're all jackasses." I took a breath, bag crinkling in my grip. "Hello in the camp!" I shouted again, not knowing what else to say. "Delivery from Dali. You want me to leave it this side of the circle?"

There was a muffled thump and bellow from the van. On the roof, the gargoyle's tail twitched. And then the door burst open, slamming into the side of the van and making me jump. But my stilted smile became real when I saw Al standing there in a robe so black it was hard to make out, trimmed in gold brocade and with tiny bells on his sash.

"Al?" I whispered. A hundred thoughts tumbled as he stared at me, none of them lasting long enough to act on. He had given me, no, stolen for me the book I needed to rescue Zack. But he hadn't come in time to save Nash. He hadn't helped me bury him. *Hodin did.*

My grip on the bag tightened. Dali had done this on purpose—the busybody. *Al lives in a painted wagon in the woods?*

Al's goat-slitted eyes narrowed, his confused anger shifting to a frightening fury. "How did you find me?" he said from atop the stairs, the hem of his robe shaking, making the bells on his sash ring. "Did Dali tell you?" he snarled. "Get out of my house."

"I'm not in your house," I said, not sure why he was mad. I was the one dealing with everything. *Why does Al live in a wagon? Maybe it's because he doesn't feel welcome anywhere.* "I'm in your yard, delivering your takeout. You want it?" I added, flushing as the wind picked up, clouds boiling out from nowhere. My feet were wet, my fingers were blue, and now I was warm in embarrassment.

"Huh," Pike mocked as he looked up at the clouds forming overhead. "Worldly cosmic powers, living in a trailer in the woods. Who would have guessed?"

Al clenched his hands. I could hear his knuckles crack from twenty feet away.

"Did I not say to keep your mouth shut?" I muttered, then smiled weakly at Al. "Ah, I didn't know it was you," I said, glad that I hadn't crossed the toadstool ring. "I'm working off my dinner. Should I just leave it? I'll leave it."

There was a roll of thunder. Al stared at me from the van's door, his lip curling in disgust. "I heard what you did," he said, and I strengthened my hold on the ley line. He was pissed. *Because I talked to Hodin.*

"Dali told me!" he shouted, and I took a step back. "You stink of Hodin. Lie, Rachel. Lie and tell me you've not aligned yourself with him. A suckling nothing of a traitorous elven whore."

Dali, you son of a bastard, I thought. That was why we had gotten our dinner so cheap. Dali had sent me to Al knowing he'd have to do something about me talking to Hodin if I showed up on his doorstep. As my teacher, it was Al's place, and only his place, to mete out punishment.

"I'm not working with Hodin!" I exclaimed, my toes edging the toadstool ring, then added, "Okay, he helped me bury Nash. But he offered. I didn't ask. And it was easier than digging a hole. Jeez, Al. Give me a break! I've decided to bring Constance to heel, but I don't need his help." No, I needed Al's.

But Al only grimaced at the threatening skies as a soft patter of light rain began. On the roof, the gargoyle sighed and hid under her wings. "You and Hodin summoned the Goddess's mystics to ascend an elf!" he shouted over the distance, and then, softer, far more threatening: "Get. Out."

Pike reached for the bag, probably to help himself to Al's dinner. "Yeah?" I said as I pulled it away, frowning at he annoyed vampire. "Maybe you should have shown up instead of him."

Al moved. The wood ladder creaked under his feet, and I backpedaled three steps before I could stop myself. Pike's expression emptied and he retreated, slipping deeper into the woods until he was a shadow beside a tree, eyes black and shining.

"You admit that you took instruction from him!" Al shouted as he strode forward.

I forced myself to stand firm, scared as I was. "No! We buried Nash," I gushed. "Al, I'm sorry about that ultimatum," I babbled. *Stay out of this, Pike. Stay where you are.* "I shouldn't have told you both to get along or stay out of my life. I was wrong, and I'm sorry."

"Get out!" he bellowed, and my shoulders came up to my ears as I felt him tap the same line my thoughts were in. "He's dangerous, and manipulating, and you are not listening to me!"

"But he's not that bad!" I coaxed, pulse fast as the distance between us narrowed to ten feet, five. "He wouldn't even do the charm to bury Nash. I had to do it."

"He is *using* you!" he shouted, his black slippers edging the toadstool ring. "Twisting you to him with little gifts and small favors," he added, voice breaking. "And you will die like all the rest who followed him. He will betray you, Rachel. That's what he does. He's the Goddess's bastard. Her toy. Her sword we die on. Elven magic does not make us stronger. It makes us vulnerable. Celfnnah . . ."

I watched, horrified, as he choked in grief, his face drawn and his breath ragged. *Celfnnah?* I wondered. Had his wife followed Hodin and died? Or maybe the Goddess killed her. *Or the elves?*

My pulse quickened. I wasn't Celfnnah. I had no hatred for the elves or their magic. Hodin wasn't using me. He was trying to bring us together. *I* was trying to bring us together.

"Al," I whispered, my own heartache growing. Whatever had happened, he couldn't forgive. He could not let go.

"I will not do this again," Al said, voice empty. "I am done. Get out."

"Al. Please. Just talk to me." I reached for him, more than that toadstool ring between us. "I can't tell you how sorry I am about Celfnnah. But things have changed—"

"Get out!" he demanded again, pulling on a line to vanish in a haze that exploded into a tall, glowing, burning form. Golden streamers flowed like hair from a willowy-thin, wasp-waisted figure towering over me. A haze of energy circled his head like a halo. "Get out!" he demanded, his voice now feminine and echoing with thunder.

It was Newt's voice, and I lurched backward, tripping and falling. He'd turned himself into an image of the Goddess, my greatest fear, to scare me away. It was working. My pulse hammered. It didn't matter that I knew it was Al; I was scared spitless. She had nearly killed me. Several times. Newt had become her to save me.

"Get out, or I will kill you where you stand!" he said, a hand rising to the black and boiling skies as if to draw down hell itself.

Lightning flashed, and as my heartache swam up, it began to rain in cold, heavy drops.

I got up. My eyes teared. I told myself it was from his glare, too bright to look at. I lifted my chin, my grip on the line strengthening. "No, you won't," I said, then pulled a wind-whipped strand of hair from my mouth. "You need me, Al. No one else trusts you. Except perhaps Ray and Lucy, and don't you *dare* ruin that so you can wallow in your pity party alone. We know you're a good person. Please. Let me stay. Let me try to find a way—"

"Arraggge!" the figure howled, stretching to the sky.

My expression emptied. "Pike! Get down!" I shouted in real fear as the energy built. Turning, I lunged, knocking him down. We hit the earth and I looked up as Al threw a tantrum, streamers of Newt-inspired energy flowing from him to strike the trees and crawl along the bottom of the clouds.

"Leave me!" he shouted, his voice an eerie blend of Newt's insanity and his steadfast roar.

"I will not!" I shouted back, and then yelped as I felt myself shoved into a ley line.

Pike, I thought in panic, but he was still with me, and I snapped a bubble of protection about us, cowering as the roar of thunder became the echoing of the line.

Al had dropped me in a ley line. I had let him, trusting that he wouldn't leave me here to try to claw my way out without Bis. The last time I had, I'd scraped a ley line across Loveland Castle and burned my synapses to a seared state that took three days to recover from.

But nothing shifted. Nothing changed, and I felt the pinch of worry as the line hissed and echoed in my thoughts. Heartache swamped me again. He'd left me. He'd dumped me in a line and left me!

Al? I thought, fear shiny and bitter like bright silver.

And then, just as I steeled myself to try to escape the line, I felt my aura shift. Fire flickered over my soul as I was pushed out. My knees hit a cold cement pad. I gasped for breath, head down and staring at that stupid takeout bag in my grip. A thump and soft groan of pain beside me was Pike.

My pulse hammered. *He could have killed me,* I thought. And my trust in Al would've let him do it.

But he hadn't, and I looked through my stringy hair at Pike. His eyes met mine, pupils black in anger.

I heard a seagull crying. There was salt in the air—it had to be more than my tears on my lips. I could smell dead fish, and the light was almost painfully bright. There were people surrounding us, some talking in whispers, some shouting, but all of them wearing the same flat white shoes.

I sat up on my heels, Al's bag of takeout in my hand.

"Oh, shit," I whispered, and Pike lurched to a stand, a swollen, scraped hand pressed to his side.

But I half knelt there, staring at the thick, heavyset woman pushing her way through the ring of orange jumpsuits surrounding us. I knew the sound of the surf. I knew those ugly uniforms. I knew the feel of those charmed silver bracelets around their wrists and the scent of rotted redwood. Hell, I even knew the woman, and as she stood before me, Auntie Lenore's beefy arms going over her chest and a cocky look coming in her eye, I slowly got to my feet.

"Somehow I knew you-all'd land yerself back he-e-re," the woman drawled in a thick backwoods accent, her flat face jeering. "I jest didn't think it was gonna be this soon." Hands clenching into fists, she never took her eyes from me. "Mary, keep them guards busy. Sunshine and I have sometun to finish."

I sighed, a hand up to try to talk my way out of this. Al had done more than send me away. He wanted to hurt me, as I had apparently hurt him. And as I looked across the desperate, eager faces, I decided he had succeeded.

"Where are we?" Pike said, and then I lurched, dancing back as Auntie Lenore swung.

"Alcatraz," I said, wincing as the surrounding witches shouted for my blood, content to let Lenore find it for them.

CHAPTER

17

"ALCATRAZ, SAN FRANCISCO?" PIKE SAID IN DISBELIEF, though we were surrounded by orange jumpsuits and an appalling lack of hairstyling products. I'd never been in the yard, but that was where we had to be, the shadow of the walls from the setting sun cold on the cement.

Lenore swung again at me, and I ducked, darting to the left. If it was anyone else, I'd kick the woman, but Auntie Lenore was like a wall. "Yeah," I said as a faceless inmate shoved me back in, shouting for me to kick her ass. "Soon as I'm done here, I'll give you the tour."

"Why did you bring us here?" Pike said, then glared at the man jostling him until the guy paled and found somewhere else to stand and shout at me. "Alcatraz is coed?"

"This wasn't my idea." I jerked to the right and ducked. "One flight-risk facility is a money sink, two is cost prohibitive when holding witches. We can get out of almost anything."

"Stop moving yer skinny ass!" Lenore drawled. "Arrrgh!" she exclaimed, coming at me with her muscular arms spread wide to give me a deadly bear hug. Her thick feet stomped in an impressive display as she rocked back and forth, coming closer in six-inch steps designed to intimidate. It was working. "Y'all stand still, now," she drawled, her accent a harsh backwoods rasp. "I'm gonna pulp yer spine, Sunshine."

"Sunshine?" Pike echoed, and I shot him a glance. He'd sandwiched himself between a red-faced man shaking his fist and a frightened thin woman.

Mary? Monkshood Mary? I thought, recognizing the distressed man beside her with the basketball as Ralph. And then I lurched back as Lenore swung a meaty fist. Grabbing the woman's arm, I flung her into the surrounding people. Lenore crashed into them, taking three inmates down. But there were more to lift her up, spin her around, and shove her back at me.

Anger and relief were an ugly slurry in me as my thoughts churned: anger at Al for dropping me in Alcatraz, relief that he hadn't left me in the ley line to scrape my way out by myself. I knew Al still grieved for his wife, but that Hodin might have had something to do with her death was new.

Clearly I'd hurt him. And yet, as I stood on the cold cement and evaded another of Lenore's swings, I knew that he hadn't abandoned me completely. He could have dropped me two hundred yards to the right and into the straits to drown, or in an oubliette to starve, or at the top of Mount Fuji to freeze. But no. He had dropped me here, in jail for uncommon stupidity.

"Knock it off!" I shouted, but the woman kept coming, and I finally slammed my foot into her middle in a spinning back kick. The crowd yelled for more and Pike politely applauded as Lenore rocked. Frustration fueled my anger, and I flicked my foot up, snapping her head back.

Arms pinwheeling, Lenore fell into the circling people. She'd felt that one, though, and she stood there, blinking, as the crowd urged her on.

"Some help here?" I said to Pike, and he grinned, head shaking.

"No way am I getting near that," he said, and I evaded Lenore's next clumsy swing. "Besides, you're a demon," he yelled over the loud shouts. "Do your demon stuff!"

But I was a demon on an island surrounded by salt water. There was no ley line here, and my purse with all my toys was two thousand miles away.

"Rachel, look out!" Mary shouted, and Lenore's fist slammed into my head, knocking me flailing into the crowd.

Ow . . .

"We gonna see what color black witches bleed, Sunshine," Lenore drawled, and I scrambled up at the glint of metal in her meaty fist. She had a knife. *Of course she does.*

Mouth wide in an ugly howl, Lenore came at me, knife slashing the air. Pulse fast, I ducked under and in from her first swing, grabbing Lenore's arm and using it to yank her down so my knee hit her solar plexus. Lenore's breath whooshed out. I danced back, shocked when her thick fingers encircled my wrist and jerked me to a stop.

The woman wasn't breathing, but she swung at me anyway, face red and eyes angry.

Good God! I thought as I evaded the first swing, deflected the second, then used my grip on the woman's own arm to walk up her leg and flip over her head, dislocating her arm as I landed behind her.

Lenore screamed in angry pain, arm dangling useless as he came at me again.

I spun to the right, then left, hammering on her ear until Lenore rocked back, disoriented.

The crowd began chanting my name, which was both gratifying and disturbing. Pike was laughing, but I felt sick. Beating up Lenore was not fun.

"Rachel, look!" Mary shouted, and I followed her frantic pointing over the surrounding people. Guards. Lots of them, all with drawn wands. The yard was becoming empty as people peeled off from the fight and ran for all corners. Those who were too close to the guards knelt with their hands behind their heads, waiting until they were past before scrambling up and running for the gates.

"I'm gonna pulp your pretty little head!" Lenore screamed, oblivious.

"Crap on toast," I whispered. The last time I'd had a fight in Alcatraz, the guards had busted my knees from behind, threatened me with a lobotomy, and thrown me in solitary.

Brow furrowed, I looked from the guards to the fleeing people and then to Mary pulling a grinning Ralph down to a kneel. I could feel the latent power in the wands growing, arcing from one to the other. We had seconds, maybe. Desperate, I ran at Lenore, jumping to slam both feet into her chest. I had to down her long enough for the guards to get here. The solid thump of impact seemed to rattle all the way to my brain . . . and then I hit the cold, salt-stained cement with a painful thud.

Howling, Lenore scrambled up and started my way, her one good hand opening and closing.

But the guards were close, little arcs of power stringing them together as they shouted at everyone to get on the ground.

"Pike, get down!" I shouted as I sat on my heels. "Hands behind your head!"

"What?" he said, but his eyes were sharp on the oncoming guards as the circle of onlookers broke up, half running as if hell was after them, the rest cowering on their knees.

"Do it!" I shouted, and he laboriously knelt down, his hands laced behind his head.

This is going to be close, I thought, wincing as Lenore, still oblivious, came at me.

"Rigor!" the closest guard shouted, and with a whoosh of power that lifted my hair, a wave of magic rose straight up from the previously spelled cement, latching onto the tips of the raised wands and then condensing into a bright hot light that arced out and struck every inmate whose knees were not on the ground.

Lenore jerked in a widemouthed, silent scream and fell.

The scent of ozone and dead fish rolled over me as it carried by the groans and sobs. I stood as the guards approached, and Pike rose as well, stiff and uneasy. "I'm Rachel Morgan!" I exclaimed, hands in the air and spinning in a slow circle as they screamed at us to get back down. Our street clothes were obvious, and I flushed, wondering if they thought we were here to break someone out. Which was stupid. Who tries to break someone out of prison in the middle of the day wearing black tights and a short skirt stained blue from copper sulfate?

The ring of inmates slowly thinned as the wary guards moved past them and they retreated, hunched and afraid. "I'm Rachel Morgan!" I said again, and Pike grimaced, clearly not having fun anymore. "I'm here by accident. I just want to make a call and get out of here!"

"On your knees!" the nearest one said, that wand aimed right at my heart. "Now!"

But I couldn't do it. I could not kneel down and submit. I'd been that person before, and I wasn't going to do it again. And as I stood there, knowing it was only my street clothes and attitude that kept me from being shot with a spell, Pike moved closer, his eyes dark and his expression hard as he put his back to mine.

He didn't owe me anything, especially his trust, and his presence there hit me hard.

We didn't move as the guards wove through the downed inmates, closing in. One shoved Mary and Ralph toward the yard's door. It was hard to tell who was helping whom as Mary clung to Ralph, crying as the simple man gave me a thumbs-up. The ball that had been in his hands rolled away, forgotten. Lenore lay there and drooled, eyes unfocused.

"On your knees!" the largest guard shouted again, his aimed wand dramatically propped up on his crooked arm. I could see the Möbius strip glinting silver on his insignia. They were the coven of moral and ethical standards' personal guard, caretakers of their private prison for witches so the rest of the world wouldn't know how dangerous we could be when cornered, and as I stared at him, unwanted memories flooded up, memories of being hurt, bullied, and threatened to be magically neutered. I'd been helpless to stop them.

Fear swamped me, and I heard Pike take a ragged breath. My emotion had hit him hard, but his soft groan gave me something to anchor myself with, and I shoved the fear down deep.

"We didn't mean to come here," I said, but there were twelve of them now, two coming forward with silver-spelled cuffs.

"Get the vamp first," one said, and Pike made a warning growl.

"Let them cuff you," I said, and then someone tried to touch him, and he was no longer at my back. "Pike, knock it off!" I shouted, torn between watching him and not dropping the eyes of the grinning woman facing me, cuffs in hand. Sighing, I held out my hands, feeling my headache worsen as they snicked over my wrists. Behind me, the scuffle grew louder as four witches fell on Pike, forcing him facedown onto the cold cement and aggressively cuffing his hands behind him. A small sound of surprise rose when they realized he was bleeding, but that didn't get him any consideration as they held him there and searched him.

I jumped, startled when a guard began to roughly pat me down. My attention flicked from her to the head guard still holding that wand pointing at my eye, and I did nothing as she took my phone, Dali's finding amulet, and finally, my ring. The white pearl turned black as it left me, and I frowned. *Trent, it's okay. Don't freak.*

Pike was still down, making half-hearted kicks at the guards searching him to find a second knife, a pistol I didn't even know he had, his cracked phone, and his wallet. Finished, they rolled him over and backed off so he could get up. If he hadn't been half-dead, they never would have downed him, and I saw his frustration, maybe even anger, that I'd done nothing to stop them.

But they were Alcatraz guards. They answered to no one, and I knew what happened in the medical wing.

Only now did the lead guard lower his wand. The yard had been emptied, which made me even more uneasy. "Who are you?" he asked, suspicion hard in his eyes.

"None of your damn business," Pike said. "Take off the cuffs, and tomorrow you might still have a job cleaning toilets."

I gave Pike a weary look, but the lead guard had already

decided I was the one to talk to, seeing as I was standing confidently passive and not throwing a hissy-girl tantrum. "I told you," I said, letting a little impatience show. "I'm Rachel Morgan. That's Pike Welroe. We didn't mean to come here. All we want is to leave."

The guard looking into Al's takeout bag frowned in confusion. "It's a hamburger," he said, and the lead guard's eyebrows rose. "And fries."

"Ralph asked me to bring one by the next time I was in the area," I smart-mouthed. And then I gasped as a heavy, wet wash of salt water hit me from behind, almost knocking me down.

"What the *fuck*!" Pike exclaimed, now dripping as well, but I totally got it. It was to break any earth charms we might be under, exposing us if we were trying to escape by impersonating someone who wasn't supposed to be here.

"Oh, for little green troll turds," I said, disgusted as I looked at the guard with the empty bucket. I was wet again, and the breeze off the bay was suddenly cold in the setting sun. "I took a wrong jump from a ley line and ended up here by mistake. We aren't here to break anyone out!"

But one of the guards was staring at me, snapping his fingers in recognition. "I know that hair," he said, and I slumped, not sure if that was good or not. "That's Sunshine." He turned to everyone, face cracking in a rude smile. "Sunshine! Remember?"

"Your jail name is Sunshine?" Pike chuckled, using his shoulder to wipe the salt water dripping from his chin.

I felt myself warm despite the cold water running into my underwear. He was *laughing* at me. At least until one of the guards gave him a shove and told him to shut up.

"You know . . ." I inched closer to him as they tried to decide what to do with us. "Rachel. Ray. Ray of sunshine?"

"The one who escaped while talking to the coven's high priestess?" the lead guard said.

Yeah, Brooke had been pretty pissed, but I'd had Bis with me, and Ivy had summoned me out. Bis was now comatose, and you couldn't summon a demon anymore. I had to get out of here on my own. *The Goddess?* I wondered, then dismissed it. Way too risky when I hadn't exhausted my true talent of talking myself out of trouble. But if that failed, she might be the only way to access magic on an island with no ley lines and surrounded by salt water. *And wouldn't Al be pleased?*

"You escaped Alcatraz?" Pike said, clearly impressed, and I shrugged. He had flicked his head to get his dark, wet hair out of his eyes, and it looked bad-boy nice.

"Yep," I said as the guards moved in. "So clearly I'm not supposed to be here." Shit, they just kept getting closer, and I backed up into Pike. "I was pardoned!" I exclaimed, adding, "Stop shoving," when they pulled us apart and gave me a push to the door. "Damn it back to the Turn, I was pardoned. I didn't mean to come here! Give me my phone and I can clear this up."

But they weren't listening, hemming us in and herding us to the yard's gate. According to the news coming in over the radio, everyone had been accounted for, and they didn't know what to do. That could be good, or really bad.

"We should put them in the warden's office. Let him figure it out," one guard said.

"I'm not getting salt water on his carpet." The head guard flicked his arm out to look at his watch, adding, "Put them in the lunchroom. He can talk to them there."

I leaned toward Pike. He'd fallen into a sullen silence. Maybe he didn't like his threats not being taken seriously. *Welcome to my world, bud-dy.* "Trust me. It's better than a cell," I said, then stopped stock-still at the door and the wave of sour redwood that poured from the opening. Fear bubbled up from nowhere, and I shoved it down, almost panicked when Pike gave me an inquiring look. He'd smelled my fear.

"Move," someone said, and Pike stumbled, shoved from behind.

"Easy," he said, eyes dark and knowing as he caught himself. "I've got a stab wound."

"Did Lenore do that?" one of them asked, but I was concentrating on my breathing, trying to convince myself that I was not walking into a jail cell. We'd talk to the warden, explain things, and if he didn't listen, I *would* call on the Goddess to sink this rock into the sea, because I was not going behind bars again.

Pike turned to give me a shitty grin as he willingly went through the door, seeming to be pleased he'd found something that scared me. "No," he drawled, and I forced myself to follow him into the dark, cold, stone and metal ugliness. "I'm not supposed to be here."

There was a chuckle from one of the cells we were passing. "None of us are," a man behind bars said, then spat at the guard who ran his wand over the metal and told him to shut up.

And still, my gut twisted as we were paraded into the lunchroom. I'd had one meal here. It had been breakfast, ending with egg in my hair and me in solitary. The only reason they hadn't lobotomized me was because Brooke wanted to talk to me first, offering me a way out that required me to become a baby factory and Brooke's private soldier at need.

"Sit," someone said, giving me a shove forward.

But that's not what is going to happen here, I vowed as I went to the nearest table. Satisfied, the head guard walked out, presumably to brief the warden.

Pike sighed, somehow managing to be graceful as he sat down with his hands cuffed behind his back. His eyes were fixed on the guards pawing over our stuff two tables away. Apparently Pike's pistol had a few modifications that weren't legal. My ring was of little interest, and a sliver of relief washed over me when the woman guard who tried it on couldn't get it over her pinky.

"Your prison name is Sunshine?" Pike said, his long face creased in amusement.

My eyes jerked from my ring. *God, my head hurts.* "I'll take care of this. Don't worry."

"Worried?" Pike beamed, showing me his sharp canines. "One call and I'm out of here. You, though." He paused. "Kalamack will get you out eventually, but not until Constance well and truly has Cincinnati. You, Morgan, are the small bite at the end of a big meal."

Vampire idiom? I wasn't exactly sure what that meant, but it didn't sound flattering. My attention shifted at the sound of clicking shoes. The guards stiffened, and, as one, they quit messing with our things and came to stand obnoxiously close. It was the warden, obviously, and I gave Pike a look to stay quiet so I could hear what was being said.

"Everyone has been individually accounted for. Twice," the guard was saying as he and a man in a suit strode in. "They were de-spelled in the yard. Neither of them were charmed. Sir, I think it's really her. We're still waiting for a positive ID on the man."

"Did she say why she was here?" the warden said, and I gave him a stupid smile and little wave when he stopped eight feet back and stared at me.

The guard shifted uneasily. "She said she was bringing Ralph Laron a hamburger."

"Her cell was next to his, right?" The warden's gaze went to our pile of stuff.

"I'm here by accident," I said, then frowned when a guard gave me a smart smack on the leg with her wand. I'd had enough, and my eyes narrowed. "I may be dripping wet and blue, but I am not an inmate," I said to the guard, my jaw clenching when she dropped a heavy hand on my shoulder. "And if you keep treating me like one, I'm going to stop being nice. Got it?"

No one was impressed, and Pike chuckled. "Small bite," he said, and I felt myself burn.

"Hand. Off," I muttered. "Or I take it with me when I leave. You know who I am," I added, and the woman cleared her throat and stepped back.

Brow furrowed in concern, the warden went to our soggy pile of things. "No, you're not an inmate," he said, holding an amulet over our stuff before peering into the flattened takeout bag and wincing. "Which leaves you here to break someone out and it went bad, or . . . you got lost in a ley line? I'm not buying that." He put the bag down, and my pulse quickened.

"What's this?" he said, ignoring Pike's pistol and going right to the amulet. "A finding charm? Who were you trying to break out?"

"No one," I said, and Pike chuckled, his expression smug.

"Her demon teacher got pissed and dropped her here," Pike said. "I'm along for the ride. If I could make a call, I can clear this up."

"Pike!" I exclaimed, embarrassed until he mockingly licked his lips, and then I was just mad. *Small bite.*

But the warden was nodding. "That, I might believe," he said, then grimaced when his phone hummed. "Excuse me. That's probably about you." Dropping the defunct finding amulet back on the pile, he turned away, phone to his ear.

"You are amazing, Pike," I almost growled as everyone but me tried to listen in. "I'm not a small bite. I'm a full-course meal that Constance is going to choke on. I'm trying to get us out of here, so shut up and let me talk."

"Yeah. Okay. Have fun with that." Pike confidently shifted on the bench, but discomfort was beginning to show in his scarred face again as the balance of adrenaline and pain turned.

"You need to listen and watch how grown-ups play," I muttered. But this was really bad.

"Wow, that hurts." Pike pressed a hand dramatically to his chest. "If I've learned one thing surviving Constance, it's that crazy only works when your hold on them is based in fear, and if you think you can talk your way out of breaking into Alcatraz on your own merits, you are certifiable— Sunshine."

My lip curled, but the warden had ended the call, his head shaking in disbelief. With a curt gesture, he told the guards to release us, and a breath I hadn't known I'd been holding slowly slipped out. He was letting us go?

"Your story checks out," he said, and Pike blinked in shock, a stunned silence gripping him as he rolled his shoulders after they opened his cuffs. Mine were next, and

I scrambled for my ring when a guard dropped our stuff on the table. Well, most of it. They kept Pike's knife and pistol, which didn't sit well with the man. *Small bite, eh?* I thought as I slipped the cool ring back on my finger, worried when the pearl remained that ugly black. I'd been banned from San Francisco for a reason, and it had everything to do with the unexpected rebuild of downtown.

"Who vouched for me?" I asked, wanting to know who to add to my Christmas card list.

"Vivian Smith," the warden said, and I couldn't help my smile. All but one guard had filed out, taking Pike's weapons with them and leaving the promise he'd get them back. I knew from experience that the entire prison would know what had happened in three minutes, bare minimum. "Head of the coven of moral and ethical standards, and hence, my boss," the warden continued. "She said, and I quote, 'That sounds like Rachel,' and then advised me to let anyone with you go as well, as a courtesy to you."

Pike's head snapped up from where he'd been prodding his stab wound. "Didn't the coven banish you to the ever-after?"

"Yep." I beamed at him, the need to call Trent rising as I tucked my phone in a damp pocket. *Not here where everyone can hear.*

The warden wore a faint smile as he stood at the end of the table and waited for us. "Sorry about the salt bath," he said. "We had to be sure someone hadn't smuggled in a doppelganger charm. Would you like to shower? The next boat isn't due until midnight."

God. Midnight. At least I had my phone.

"That would be great, thank you," Pike said, but thoughts of that communal shower room were thick in my mind, and I stifled a shudder. I was free, but it was still Alcatraz.

"No, thanks," I said, and Pike stared at me, his gaze running down my wet, dripping hair to my blue-tinted skirt and my soggy boots rubbing a hole in my heel.

"You can use the guard showers," the warden said,

seeming to understand. "Do either of you need medical assistance? A meal?" He looked at the takeout bag, thoroughly flattened.

"I could do with something to eat," Pike said as he stood. "Aspirin . . ."

He just ate! "Nothing for me, thanks," I said, fidgety. All I wanted was a quiet moment to call Trent and assure him I wasn't dead. Not to mention the food here was laced with magic-ending amino acids.

But again, the warden seemed to understand, and he turned to the remaining guard. "Round up some quarters for the vending machine," he said softly as he beckoned for us to follow, and then louder, to us, "I'll get you to the guard lounge. Showers are off it if you change your mind. I'm sure we can find you something that isn't orange to fit you. But as I recall, you made Rock-orange look good, Ms. Morgan."

He was playing with me, but there was no background threat lacing it, and I managed a smile. "Thanks." I looked at my ring. "I need a quiet place to make a few calls is all."

"Right this way," he said, and I hustled to follow.

Pike already had his cracked phone to his ear, distracted as he walked beside me smelling of vampire incense and salt water. Vamps at the beach. Go figure.

"No, not yet," he said slyly to whoever he was talking to, making me think it was about me. "Ran into a little snag." He looked at me, his expression unreadable. "Nothing that won't heal. Rachel took me somewhere to get cleaned up." He hesitated, then added, "I have no idea. Perhaps she didn't like our meeting being crashed." His eyes fixed on mine, he said, "No. I'm free to go. I'm waiting a couple of hours until it's easier to move."

But we were over two thousand miles away. A "couple of hours" wasn't going to put us appreciably closer.

"You wouldn't believe me if I told you," Pike said as the warden led us down a hall holding light office chatter and the scent of printer ink. "No. It isn't prudent at the moment." Pike's eyes found mine again. "Too many people around," he said, and the warden perked up, worry showing at the corners of his eyes. "Of course. Talk to you when it's done."

"Do I need to remind you to stay out of San Francisco?" the warden said, and I shook my head. "Good. Here we are," he added loudly, slowing at a frosted-glass door and punching a code into the panel beside it. The door buzzed a harsh warning, and he opened it, waiting for me to go in first. "The staff knows you're here," he said as I went in to find the expected blah-colored corporate sofa, white laminate table, crumb-laced counter with a water-stained stainless steel sink holding half-rinsed coffee cups. It even had the notice-stuffed board. Two doors led off it, one said MEN, the other WOMEN. Showers, presumably, and I felt ten times more filthy.

"Rachel, one of the guards, Mandy, is about your size," the warden said, adding, "She has a pair of running sweats if you change your mind about the shower. I'd call a boat for you, but it won't get here any earlier than the usual midnight run. Vending machine is there. Quarters are on the way. Good?"

I turned at Pike's sigh to see him gingerly settling himself at the table. "Yes, thanks," I said. The sooner he left, the sooner I could call Trent.

"Oh, and I'd appreciate it if you stayed here." He smiled, but it wasn't nice this time. "No fraternizing. Pike, someone from med will come up when your tray is ready. Lasagna okay?" he said, and I shuddered.

Pike looked from me to the warden, clearly noticing my abhorrence of Alcatraz cuisine. "Thanks. And coffee?" he asked. "Lots of it?"

The warden nodded. "You got it," he said, then left, tugging the door shut behind him.

There was a click of a lock, but it didn't seem so bad when there were almost a thousand people in cells within shouting distance, all of them being slowly neutered of their magic abilities through their breakfast, lunch, and dinner.

"Huh." Pike winced as he carefully shifted position. "It

would have been easier for me to go to medical than bring medical to me."

"They don't want you to see what they do down there," I said, and his gaze flicked to mine, suddenly interested. "What did you mean by 'when it's done'?" I prompted. "Were you talking about killing me?"

A wide smile came over his face, showing me a slip of tooth. "I've revised my estimate. You could last one minute against me. Maybe more. But you'd be hurting at the end."

Not so small a bite, eh? I thought. "Thanks for not telling Constance where we are," I said, hand on the ladies' room door, and he shrugged.

"It wouldn't have made a difference."

But it did. She would have taken advantage of it, threatening Zack when I was too far away to do anything.

Eyes down, he rubbed his wrists, now free of charmed silver. "You're still two thousand miles from Cincy. Maybe you should stay here on the West Coast. You lost."

"Have I?" I didn't move, still trying to figure out where I stood with him. He'd put his back to mine in the yard, but that had been self-preservation.

"Funny," Pike said, eyes closing as he let his head drop into his cupped hands. "I haven't felt this safe since I was seven and living with my aunt." He chuckled, in a memory he wouldn't share with me. "That woman was one tough bitch. I miss her."

I pushed the door to the women's showers open. The scent of shampoo was strong, and somewhere water dripped. "I know how you feel. The best sleep I ever had was when I was trapped in the ever-after with a demon who wanted to make me his live-in slave."

Pike's head came up. "Seriously?"

I searched his expression, breathed the air, and decided that he wouldn't try to kill me surrounded by the coven's personal guard. "The I.S. assassins couldn't reach me there," I said. "Al had this weird idea that I was too important to spoil with frivolous bedroom play." I hesitated as my hurt rushed back. "Excuse me. I need to make a call."

Pike waved a dismissive hand, and I practically bolted into the bathroom.

"Hello?" I called loudly to confirm I was alone, and when no one answered, I peered under the stall doors and into shower cubicles to make sure. Knowing firsthand how well a vampire could hear, I turned on one of the showers. Steam rose, and seeing it there, bright and inviting, I decided I could chance looking like an orange if it meant I'd be clean.

I scrolled through my phone for Trent, hesitating before hitting the connect button when I caught sight of myself in the long mirror.

"Good God," I whispered, appalled when the dripping monstrosity did the same. My hair was in stringy ringlets, the dried salt blue at the ends from the copper sulfate. My skirt looked as if kindergartners had finger-painted the sky on it, and my tights were torn. *How long until* that *wears out?* I wondered, gazing at the blue in my cuticles.

But it was better than Nash's blood, and, sighing, I turned my back on the mirror and hit connect. A feeling of failure rose up, and my grip tightened on the cold plastic. I didn't want to be rescued. I didn't *need* to be rescued. I had a boat coming at midnight, and from there, I could jump a plane back to Cincy. Or at least Dayton. I had this.

But I needed to hear his voice and tell him I was alive.

The phone's ringing cut off, and I heard a muffled "It's Rachel," then, louder, "Rachel? Are you okay? My ring went black."

Eyes closed, I slumped against the counter. The heavy warmth from the shower was creeping up my legs, and I held an arm around myself, refusing to let the tears come. I could hear his love for me, and it hit me hard. "I'm sorry," I choked out, then cleared my throat, forcing a smile though he couldn't see it. "Some idiot took the ring off me. I just got it back." I looked at it, still black on my finger, then made a fist.

"Thank the Goddess," he said around a soft breath. "Are you okay? What happened?"

I turned to the mirror, shocked again at my state. "I'm fine . . ." My voice rose at the end, and I put a fist to my mouth, eyes closing.

"You don't sound fine. What happened?"

Don't you dare start crying, I thought, trying to push the headache away. "I'm fine. I'm sorry it took so long for me to tell you I was okay, but they took my phone, too."

"Rachel?" Trent questioned, and I took a breath.

"I'm fine," I said for the third time, but it was beginning to sound ridiculous, even to me. I didn't want him to come to my rescue, but damn it, I wanted to see him, wrap my arms around him, and breathe him in to remind myself that I was still alive and that everything would be okay.

"Is it Zack?" Trent asked. "Rachel—"

"Zack is okay," I blurted, not wanting to tell him about Nash yet. "So far." I took a slow breath to find a sliver of professionalism. Calm. "I'm still working on it. I called to tell you I was okay. Sorry about the ring. Is it a one-shot deal, or can we set it up again?"

"What's the matter?" Trent insisted. "You're upset. Is Ivy okay? Jenks?"

"All good!" I said with a forced cheerfulness. "I'm sort of stuck until midnight, when I can get a ride to the airport." *Don't tell him where you are. Don't!*

"I thought Hollows International was shut down," Trent said, and I slumped.

"It is." I turned to the mirror, telling my reflection it was too dumb to try to lie.

"Rachel, where are you?"

My eyes closed, and a lump thickened my throat. Sure, I was mad at Al, or guilty, or something, but I hadn't wanted Trent to know how badly I'd effed this up. "Alcatraz," I whispered, but I knew Trent heard me when he didn't say anything. "Al dropped me here. As a joke." My eyes opened, and I held my arm around my middle. A joke, I had said. But it wasn't a joke, and it hurt. "I'm fine," I said again. "The warden has been great. Vivian vouched for me. I'm waiting for the next boat so I can get to the airport and get back home."

"I'll be there in forty minutes," Trent said, and I heard him snapping his fingers for Quen's attention . . . and then the scratching of a pen on paper.

"Trent, I've got this," I said, but I was three seconds away from crying. "I didn't call because I needed a knight on a white horse. I've got money for a ticket home."

"Good, because my horse is black and I'm a little short on cash. You might have to buy me dinner," he said, and I wasn't sure if he was serious or not. "I'm coming. I need to get out of here before I smack Ellasbeth. She's . . . I'll tell you when I see you. God, Rachel, coming out here without you was a mistake. You'll be okay until I get there?"

I blinked back the tears, feeling loved. Loving him. "I will. Pike is here with me."

"Pike?" he said, clearly caught off guard, and then he ended the call.

He hadn't said good-bye. He hadn't said he loved me. They were both pretty obvious. Sighing, I locked my phone's screen and smiled at the bedraggled woman in the mirror.

After I called Jenks and David, I was going to run the hot-water tank cold.

CHAPTER
18

"DAVID IS FINDING PLACES FOR THE WERES, BUT THE witches have set up a tent in the backyard," Jenks was saying, his tiny voice louder than usual through the phone's speaker. "Stef moved all your stuff except for your bed up to the belfry so Finley could set up some temporary cots and storage. The mattress wouldn't fit up the stairs, so we put it in storage. The fainting couch is still up there, though. Are you good with that? I can get you a cot."

"The couch is fine," I said as I drew a strand of blessedly clean hair from my mouth and looked out over the blue and gold water tinted with sunset. The scent of Mandy's detangler was heavy despite the stiff wind, but we'd gotten word that Trent was on his way, and the warden and two of his officers had joined us on the dock to wait for him. It was the only place on the island where I felt remotely comfortable. Even in the shower surrounded by perfumes and soap, I'd felt the presence of the ancient ghosts who'd held the island long before the Europeans.

"I went ahead and okayed Finley's plan so she could buy some stuff," Jenks was saying as I scanned the stiff waves. "The lumberyard pushed back the delivery for two months when they found out where it was going, but the vamps went out and got it after the demo." He laughed. "And then some."

Demo? "I don't want to know, do I . . ." I said.

"Not when you're two thousand miles away."

I gripped the plastic grocery bag holding my blue-tinted clothes tighter and rocked from foot to foot, grimacing when my boots squished. Putting on the size eight inmate sneakers I'd found beside the sweats hadn't been an option. The guard-emblazoned sweats, though, I'd accepted, and the stiff breeze was going right through them.

Pike seemed warm enough in a long, borrowed rain slicker, the heavy black fabric and classic cut giving him a gangster look as he chatted with the warden in the gathering dusk. Two officers lurked behind us with Pike's weapons. There were two more guards in the small skiff tied to the dock, and my pulse quickened when I followed their sudden pointing to a tourist boat cutting through the waves. *Trent.*

One of the officers blew an air horn, and immediately the boat slowed, its wake rolling out before it. The two guards in the skiff pushed from the quay, a spotlight playing over the tourist boat as they went to check its credentials. Even in the twilight I could recognize Trent in the huge, covered cockpit, and I waved, getting an enthusiastic wave back.

"It's a good thing they did, because the stores are beginning to empty out," Jenks said, but I really wasn't listening and had no clue what he was talking about. "You can't find a roll of toilet paper or loaf of bread unless you go into the Hollows. Hey, you owe Edden big."

"Edden, why?" I asked, and Pike's conversation with the warden faltered.

"He got to your purse before the I.S. did," the pixy said with a laugh, and I glanced at Pike to see if he was listening. Two thousand miles away, someone was playing their music too loud. Cutting through it was a rising argument about chip dip and the sound of a nail gun. Which, when you put it all together, made standing on the dock at Alcatraz almost pleasant.

"I had Stef put it in the belfry," Jenks continued. "So far, you aren't being blamed for the five dead vampires, just fleeing the scene and blowing out three blocks of electronics. He worries about you, Rache."

I exhaled, wishing the guards tying their boats together would hurry up. There were two deckhands and a captain clustered in a spotlight on the rafted boats, and one of them couldn't find his wallet. "Tell Edden thanks, and that I'll be in to tell him my side of it when I can," I said as I looked at Pike again and the vampire returned to his conversation about handguns with the warden. "It might be a while."

"You got it. So you'll be back tomorrow?"

"Absolutely," I said, relieved. Maybe eight hours to get home including layovers, another four to prep to talk to Constance, because I wasn't going to let Pike go until he agreed to arrange a meeting with her. Sleep somewhere in there. "I'm trying to get in tonight, but it will likely be a red-eye into Dayton. Sunrise, maybe?"

"Good, because the city is hunkering down as if they expect squids to start crawling from their toilets," Jenks said dryly.

Finally the officers on the skiff handed everyone's ID back. There was a *toot-toot* of an air horn, and the spotlight flicked off. "Thanks for handling everything," I said. "I have to go. I'll text you when I know my flight info."

"Trent's there, huh?" Jenks said with a chuckle, and I smiled.

"Bye, Jenks." I closed my phone down and dropped it in my grocery bag with my damp clothes. It was easier to see now with only the natural light. Trent was standing at the bow, and I grinned like a fool as he moved to the boat's off ramp, not yet extended as the large tourist boat eased to the dock. He looked different in a thick coat and wool hat, probably purchased for this single trip onto the bay.

"Wow," Pike said as he left the warden and eased up even with me. "You really got a thing for knights on white horses, huh?"

I gave him a sidelong glance, my gaze lingering on the blood- and salt-stained jacket visible behind his raincoat.

"He's not rescuing me. He's getting me to the airport so I can get home before Constance digs her claws in any deeper," I said, not caring if he knew how much I loved Trent. It wasn't a secret—which made it more than a potential liability.

My stomach rumbled as the two boats approached the dock. I was starving, but it was a good feeling. I'd managed to bully my way into a real sit-down conversation in the lunchroom with Mary and Ralph after my shower, and I had given them everything out of the vending machine. Mary was still avoiding eating anything from the cafeteria, and Ralph just liked chocolate. Mary had a few years left to go, but Charles had gotten out and was apparently working at an animal rescue clinic in San Diego. The frightened cats and dogs didn't care that he couldn't do magic anymore.

Ralph was doing okay, clearly glad to see me though he couldn't verbalize it, and as I felt the little carving of a rabbit he'd given me, laced on a bit of twine he'd stolen from the shop, I couldn't help but wonder who he'd been before they had lobotomized him. Probably someone amazing since they only cut inmates who tried, and failed, to escape. I was the only one who'd succeeded since the coven had taken control of the island. And that was only because something I had thought was a liability—subject to being summoned against my will—had been turned to an asset.

But that was beginning to feel as if it was ages ago, and I touched my hair, smiling at Trent's eager lurch up onto the dock even before they finished tying up.

"Hasn't anyone told you falling in love is too expensive in this business?" Pike said.

Peeved, I glanced at his bitter confidence, his coat open and his thumbs in his pants pockets as the warden went to talk to the boat captain. "I told you I wouldn't kill her, but if Constance touches him or his girls, she won't survive the night," I said, all the while smiling at Trent. "The ever-after is an up-and-coming neighborhood, and best of all, there's no extradition from it."

"I can see why you like him," Pike continued, as if I hadn't said anything. "Great body. Money. Powerful magic on both sides of his bloodline. I bet he's good with kids, too."

I broke eye contact with Trent to frown at Pike. The guards were checking their IDs again, and Trent waited impatiently as they ran a spell checker over him and shone a light in his face. Finally they let him pass, and he bounded up the last of the stairs.

"Rachel," he said as we came together, followed by an earnest kiss. But it was the hug that I was waiting for, and I could feel his strength even through his thick coat as his arms wrapped around me. My eyes closed, and I breathed him in, thinking the scent of salt water on him made him different even as he was the same. Cinnamon and wine joined it as I reached up and touched his hair, feeling its silkiness in my cold fingers. I felt complete, and it was hard to pull back.

"I'm so glad to see you," I whispered, and he nodded, his attention flicking to the warden.

"Me too. Look," he said as he took my hand in his and lifted it to show that both our rings were again white. "I was hoping that would happen."

I beamed, and when Pike sighed, I remembered we weren't alone.

Not at all embarrassed, Trent gave me another sideways hug and a kiss. I wasn't surprised when my slight headache eased. Trent had tapped one of the lines running through San Francisco through Tulpa, who was not only his horse, but his familiar. Bis wasn't my familiar, but I could tap a ley line through him when I was over water or too far below-ground. At least until his soul had been separated from his body.

Blinking fast, I gripped Trent's hand tighter, appreciating the soft energy flow restoring my internal balance. It would end when our hands parted, but for now, it was more than nice. It was home.

"Thank you for letting me bring a boat across," Trent

said as he turned to the warden. "I know you must be bending the rules."

"Not at all," the warden said sourly. "Frankly, the sooner Ms. Morgan is off my rock, the better I'll feel." The warden looked up from handing Pike his knife and pistol, and I wondered if the vampire would give me any trouble as he tucked everything where it belonged.

Trent, too, eyed Pike with a new suspicion, but I wasn't worried. Much. He didn't know it yet, but he needed me to get back to Constance alive. I was looking forward to seeing him realize it. *Small bite, my ass.*

"Trent, I don't think you've met Pike," I said, and Trent's hand went out. "He's Constance's scion, and he's going to try to kill me at some point."

The warden's eye twitched, but Trent's reach never flinched as Pike grinned to show his small, sharp canines and shook Trent's hand.

"Not until I get back to Cincy," Pike said, but it wasn't very reassuring. "Since I've met with Rachel, I've had burgers at an ever-after strip joint, then a late dinner at Alcatraz. Is shifting realities, jumping time zones, and prison food normal, or am I just lucky?"

"It depends on who's currently trying to kill her," Trent said, and I frowned as they laughed. They thought it was funny. It was *not* funny.

"Ms. Morgan," the warden said, his face shadowy in the buzzing hum of the dock light flickering on. "I'd appreciate it if you don't come back."

Trent's arm was still around me as I shook the warden's hand. "I can't promise that as long as I have someone who thinks it's funny to fling me across the continent. Thanks for your hospitality."

The warden's eyes narrowed. "Once is an accident, twice and I'll lock you up until a court order tells me otherwise. Understand?"

Trent stiffened, and I tugged him closer. "I told you I'm having a problem right now and that I appreciate your understanding. If you try to lock me up, I'll tear a hole in your is-

land so big it will sink." My smile widened. "Hey, I appreciate
the shower and change of clothes. Is there somewhere I can
send them when I get home?"

The warden's gaze went from me to Trent, probably trying to decide if I was being serious. "Ah, keep them," he
said when Trent hid a smile behind a cough.

Pike shifted impatiently, and I pressed into Trent, enjoying his warmth. I could almost pretend we were leaving a
behind-the-scenes tour. A little too much behind the scenes.

"Sir," Trent said as he leaned past me and shook the warden's hand in farewell. "If this happens again, call me." He
slipped him a card, adding, *"Before* she sinks your island."

Turning away, Pike stomped down the light-spotted
dock to the boat.

"Bye! Thanks again for the shower!" I called out as
Trent tugged me into motion and we followed Pike, clasped
hands swinging. Leaning in, I gave his hand a squeeze. "I
can threaten people all on my own," I said, and Trent
chuckled.

"You can't begrudge me some fun, eh? It took me an
hour to get here."

I couldn't seem to bring myself to let go of his hand as
we made the easy move to the boat and the two crew members in their thick wool coats and gloves pulled the ramp
aboard. The engine was a heavy thrum, and we went to the
back of the boat and out of the way as the boat was cast off
and we pushed from the dark dock.

Pike had already put himself up front by the captain, out
of the wind, and Trent and I sat on the cold, water-splashed
seats at the back. It was a sightseeing boat, and I wondered
how much it had cost to rent it and the crew for the late-
evening jaunt.

But the island was already shrinking behind me, and I
didn't even care that my seat was wet. "I shouldn't have said
all that," I half shouted over the roar of the engine. "I mean,
he could have locked me up or held me for trespassing."

Trent leaned in, lips brushing my ear. "True, but he
didn't. You must have done something right."

I laughed somewhat sourly as I remembered my fight with Lenore. "Busted the Rock's bully is all. Held my ground. Stayed calm." I shifted into him, appreciating his warmth as the boat hit the heavier waves and began bouncing. "Followed the rules," I added, softer. "Let them make themselves feel safe." *Didn't use elven magic.* "Thanks for coming out here. I might be able to get an earlier flight now. I wasn't looking forward to trying to snag a spot on a red-eye. People without light restrictions always get bumped." I smiled up at him, glad he was here. "How on earth did you get here so fast?"

His gaze was on San Francisco, the city's lights beginning to glow in the early night. "I was at the Jetway ready to head home when you called."

I rubbed my ring, a dull gray in the dim light. "You don't think they're going to give me any trouble about being in San Francisco, do you?"

He smiled to show his teeth and gave my hand a squeeze. "I won't tell if you don't," he said, but it was likely the local police knew where I was. "I should be thanking you. I needed to get out of there. Ellasbeth is driving me crazy. I hope you don't mind, but I've arranged for our flight home." His gaze lifted to Pike. "All three of us."

"Wait. You're coming, too?" I stammered, and from beside the captain, Pike met my eyes. Yep, he was hearing everything despite the loud engine and being fifteen feet away. "No. I've got this. I can't do this and protect you at the same time. Besides, you have to stay here and get your Sa'han status back."

"As far as I'm concerned, I never lost it," Trent said, his expression cross. He wasn't angry at me, but the people he'd been politely and politically arguing with the last few days.

"You know what I mean." I gave his hand a squeeze, and Pike closed his eyes again, napping in the lee of the wind beside the captain.

"I might return after it's settled," Trent said, face tight. "Pick up a few things from home first. Like my sanity. I believe I left it in my sock drawer."

I stared at him, never having heard quite this brand of sarcasm from him.

"The Goddess help me, I missed you," he said, leaning to kiss me though the jostling of the boat made it awkward. "Believe it or not, the enclave wants me to go back to Cincy," Trent whispered as he tugged me closer.

"Maybe they're hoping you'll get caught up in everything and die," I whispered, and he made a soft "mmmm" of agreement.

"Perhaps," he said. "I told the enclave about Constance taking Zack and refusing to let him go until he agrees to do her bidding. I can't tell if they're more upset that a vampire is breaking tradition by trying to wield power over them, or that their intel didn't know about it. I told them you were handling it, but when word got out that you were in Alcatraz, I stretched the truth to let them think that you were there checking out a lead." He smiled with half his mouth. "I'm officially here to learn what you found out."

"That Lenore still has a mean right cross," I said, and he tugged me closer. But at least I didn't look like a flake to the entire elven enclave, and I rested easy against him despite the boat thumping into the black waves. Pike was pretending to be asleep again, but I saw one eye open when a deckhand went past him to go below.

"I've been asked to accompany you until he's safe," Trent said. "Truth be told, I think they want me on the other side of the continent so they can talk about me."

"Gawd, it's like high school," I said to lighten everything up, but Trent's jaw tightened.

"Actually, there's a good chance they're going to use this conflict to evaluate us."

"Oh." I hesitated, thinking that over. "Us as in an effective team in promoting elven issues? Or us as a couple?"

"I'd say that's about right." Trent was clearly peeved, and his attention went to the second deckhand going below as well.

"So . . . I guess that precludes me asking you to sit this out, huh?"

Trent grinned and gave me a light kiss. "I'd say that's about right as well."

Sighing, I snuggled deeper against him. He was pretty good at defensive magic, but honestly, for as well as we worked together, it was sometimes easier without him. Now I'd be worried about him twenty-four/seven. "So, how are the girls?" I said to change the subject. The deckhands had come back up, standing with impeccable balance as they untangled a long length of docking rope though we were nowhere near the shore yet.

Trent's head shook ruefully. "Fantastic," he said, surprising me. "I doubt Lucy will ever be the same. Everyone dotes on her, treats her like a little princess." A frown crossed him, his focus going distant. "Unfortunately."

"And Ray?" I pressed.

"Making waves in her own way." He hesitated. "You look cold. Do you want to go belowdecks?"

I shook my head, not knowing how the deckhands could stand there between Pike and us, totally at ease with the bouncing boat.

"Ellasbeth is driving me crazy," Trent muttered. "I know I've said this before, but thank you for preventing me from making the biggest mistake of my life."

I grinned. "So smacking my head into a tombstone no longer tops the list?"

Trent chuckled and held me closer. "The Goddess help me, I was such an idiot. I'm so sorry about that. No. I swear, I'm going to spell her, Rachel. If I have to spend one more dinner party with her and her dad and listen to their back-and-forth slights at everything from Cincinnati art to the color of my tie, I'm going to spell her with chicken pox."

I laughed because I knew it wasn't true. And I needed to laugh. Mary's gaunt form and Ralph's slow humor haunted me: one starving herself to avoid the magic-stunting amino acids the coven laced the food with, and the other lobotomized for trying to escape. I needed to talk to Vivian. She'd said she was going to stop their practice of magically neutering their inmates.

"We can be back in Cincy before sunup," Trent was saying, and I pulled my wandering thoughts back.

"If we can get a flight, sure," I said, rubbing at the blue staining my cuticles. "And then a car rental from Dayton. Can Jonathan come pick us up?"

Trent's expression went positively smug. "No need. We can land at Hollows International. My car is in the lot. It's only the big carriers that are being diverted."

I pursed my lips, trying to figure that out—until I remembered his earlier remark about being on the Jetway when he got my call. "You still have your private jet?" I said.

"Of course. Why would I sell it?"

"Because—" My words faltered. "Because you're trying to be more environmentally conscious," I said instead, but I was pretty sure he knew where my thoughts had been.

"Pike, there's a seat for you as well," Trent said, and the vampire opened his eyes, peering at us from between the two deckhands coiling that rope. I didn't like his smirk, not knowing where it stemmed from.

"No, thanks!" he shouted over the roar of the engine. "I'll find my own way home."

Ah, innocence, I thought smugly. I had zero concern that he'd walk away when we reached land. I'd once escorted Trent across the U.S. with a price on his head. Pike wouldn't get twenty feet from the dock before an assassin tried for him and he decided he'd be better off with me until he got back under Constance's protection.

"I don't trust him," Trent said, the words a whispered breath on my ear.

"Me either," I said. "But he's got my kind of problems, and he won't do anything until he gets to Cincy. He'll take you up on that flight home. Guaranteed."

"What makes you so sure?"

But my expression emptied when the captain turned from the wheel, nodding sharply at the two crew members.

"Rachel?" Trent prompted.

Pulse fast, I lurched to my feet when the two deckhands

snicked the ends of the ropes through their hands and, with an assassin-like quickness, twisted them into snares.

"Pike!" I exclaimed, and his eyes flew open. Gasping, he flung a hand up. One noose landed about his neck cleanly, but the other caught his wrist, pinning it to his neck.

The ropes hissed and water jumped as they snapped them in a neck-breaking yank.

Pike hit the floor of the boat, red-faced. Spinning, he braced himself and pulled.

Both his attackers lurched, yanked off-balance. The captain stepped forward, the boat on autopilot, presumably. His expression held no remorse, and a knife was in his hand, long and thin for gutting fish.

"Stay back!" Trent shouted over the roar of the engine, and a wave broke over the bow, soaking us. "You can't tap a line!"

Damn it back to the Turn. I'm wet again.

No, I couldn't tap a line, but I could slam my foot into the captain's gut, and I sent him staggering back to the wheel.

Pike was scrabbling on the floor of the boat, one hand pinned to his neck, the other trying to reach that knife in his ankle sheath. He wasn't going to make it, and the two crewmen held him steady, unmoving between them like a lion staked for the kill.

"Leave *off*!" I shouted, hammering my foot into one of the crew members' kidneys. He never even felt it, shoving me away as Pike got to his knees. The captain had regained his feet, his eyes on Pike and only Pike. Their intent was obvious: gut him and throw him overboard.

I'm not taking the blame for this, I thought, teeth clenched. But if I was honest, I just didn't like someone trying to kill Pike, even if he had been told to kill me. Maybe it was because his vulnerable confidence reminded me of Kisten. Maybe it was because he didn't freak out when I yanked him into the ever-after and then got us dumped in Alcatraz. Maybe it was because I'd been there myself and knew how it felt. Jenks would say it was the vampire pheromones, but I *liked* him. I didn't want to see him dead.

"I said leave *off*!" I exclaimed, ignored as the two crew members held Pike, red-faced and choking, between the ropes as the captain advanced. *Son of a bastard!* Spittle came from Pike's mouth, his eyes unfocused as he tried to breathe and reach that knife in his ankle sheath.

"Stay out of it, Rachel!" Trent yanked me back when I made a lunge for the captain.

Peeved, I shoved Trent's hand off me and dove at one of the men holding the ropes.

I tackled him, slamming him into the low wall. Heavy hands gripped me, and I gasped, wishing I could vanish into the ever-after like a demon when his thick fist slammed into the side of my head. I went sprawling, and then I was alone, facedown on the deck.

Another wave soaked me and, head shaking, I looked up at the savage shouting over the engine's roar. Only one rope was taut. Pike held the other, still around his neck as he flicked the free end at the men like a whip. His knife was in his other hand, and he fended them off until the two deckhands ganged up on the one rope and yanked him off-balance.

He went down, and I got to my feet, lurching with the boat's motion, unable to stop the captain from stomping on Pike's wrist. Pike howled in anger. The knife was loose, and the captain kicked it away.

I went for it, having been forgotten or simply dismissed, and I spun when the smooth feel of Pike's knife fitted into my hand.

They had him stretched between the ropes again, held against the low wall of the boat. Spray flew up, drenching them as the captain came forward with heavy, sure steps.

Not on my watch, I thought, jaw set. "Tell Pike's brother he came in too light!" I snarled, jumping between them to cut one of the taut ropes.

The knife went through the wet cord with a shocking give. Pike gasped as he lurched, his fingers loosening the noose even as he spun and headbutted the man holding the last rope, knocking him right over the side of the boat.

The man screamed as he hit the water and was gone. And then Pike choked, bracing himself against the low wall to keep from being pulled over in turn.

Bellowing, the captain rushed him. I lunged, knocking the older man over before swinging the knife and cutting the rope angling into the water.

Pike fell inward and hit the boat's deck. His bloodshot eyes darted behind me. "Down!" he rasped, and I dropped, hitting the old planks hard.

I spun, breath catching when I saw the thrown knife stuck in Pike's leg instead of me. It had been the captain, and I butt-scooted to Pike, still trying to breathe around his crushed throat.

"Stay down!" Trent shouted, and my gaze snapped to him at the threat in his voice.

Trent stood there, balance perfect as the boat lurched and crashed, water spraying over us. His jaw was set, and magic, pulled from a line through his familiar, dripped from his fingers. Shit, he was going to do something.

"No! Stay down!" I whispered, grabbing Pike's lapels and holding him where he was.

"Cease, or die," Trent intoned, and the captain turned to him, motioning the last assassin to finish us off. "I will not warn you again."

"One more body will make it that much more convincing," the captain said. Then he took a step to Trent, fish knife brandished.

"Detrudo!" Trent shouted, and I jumped as a bubble of line energy exploded out from him, sending the boat's tackle rattling and flattening the waves. The two men went flying, crying out as they hit the low rails of the boat and tumbled overboard.

The boat bobbed and settled in the eerie, spell-flattened water.

Pike sat where he was, exhausted and fingers fumbling to get the last noose off. His expression dangerously empty, he tossed the rope after them. The knife he took out of his leg he kept, and I pressed my hand down on the wound when he pulled it out.

"You should have told me you were marked," Trent said, and Pike stared at him.

"Yeah. Maybe. You know what?" Pike rasped, a shaky hand coming up to cover mine holding his stab wound closed. "I think I'll take you up on your offer for a ride." His eyes went to mine. "Huh. Maybe a minute ten," Pike slurred, then his hand atop mine went slack and he passed out.

CHAPTER

19

"TELL HER I'M ASSESSING MORGAN'S POSSIBLE COMPLI-ance through a secondary means," Pike said into his cracked phone, and my gaze flicked from the vampire crammed into the back of Trent's sports car to Trent sitting beside me in the passenger seat. He was on the phone, too, the light glowing on his face in the predawn haze to make him look dangerous. He, though, was using texts to keep his conversation private. Hence me driving. I loved driving Trent's car, and I angled the vent until my hair blew back to mimic the top being down. Which it wasn't. *The things we lose when there's a price on our head . . .*

"On a jet," Pike said, his voice rich with undertones as it came from the dark back seat. "Coming in from San Francisco. She's a demon. She knew a great place for Italian out there, and she wanted to treat me to dinner."

Trent looked up from his phone, and I shrugged. I appreciated Pike stretching the truth, but it begged the question of why he was doing it—other than possibly for the pure enjoyment of it, telling them to go to hell and handing them a window-seat ticket.

All in all, Pike was looking surprisingly better, but I thought it was due more to us being back in Cincinnati than to the first aid I'd stitched him up with on the five-hour flight back. We'd flown out of darkness and into a predawn glow, and I hoped the metaphor of leaving the dark for the light was apropos. Even with the rest and the metabolism-upper, Brimstone-laced cookies he'd bought at the airport, Pike was pale. Early morning clearly wasn't his time. Mine either. I was bone-tired. It was a good thing we hadn't needed to fly commercially. They never would have let him on the plane leaking blood and looking like that.

"If I can't convince her to leave Cincinnati," Pike said ominously. "Sure. I'll know better by the end of today." Then he added, somewhat cross, "Then convince her. I know what I'm doing. Half the city is enamored with Morgan. God knows why. She's certifiable. But why throw that away when you can use it first?"

Eyebrows rising, I cracked the window to try to get rid of the vampire pheromones. They hadn't been bad until he started talking to his peeps.

Trent leaned over the console, the light of his phone glowing on his face. "What happens if he can't convince you to leave Cincinnati? Oh, right. Kill you."

I met his smile with my own, but now that we were back under Constance's influence, the chance he might try was a possibility—even if Trent and I had saved his life. Vampire rationales sucked.

"Trent Kalamack," Pike said, probably answering the question of who had spoken. "It was his jet that got me home." He hesitated, then added, "Why do you think? You've got his holy man in her back bathroom. I know she's hell when she doesn't have her own stuff around her, but try to get her to consider not touching the kid. He's important to the elves, not just Morgan."

My grip tightened on the wheel as I took the exit off I-75, dumping us almost insanely fast into a band of light commerce. I slowed, shocked at the lack of traffic. It was almost seven in the morning, and though most Inderlanders would still be sleeping, we were in Cincinnati and the humans would be up fighting Monday-morning traffic. As it was, we were almost the only car on the road.

"It's her game," Pike continued, idly looking out the tiny

back window as I eased down to a careful thirty-five mph. "But the elves *are* up-and-coming." He hesitated, clearly listening, then added, "Fine, but tell her she needs to take them out first, not after."

"Take out who?" I said loudly.

"After what?" Trent added, and Pike ended the call.

"The elves out of Cincinnati before deciding to bind their adolescent holy man to the vampires." Pike smiled at me from the back of Trent's car, eyes black in the predawn gloom.

Trent snapped his phone case closed. "That's not going to happen."

I frowned, not liking the threat, empty or not. We'd gone through the Hollows via the expressway, but now that we were again on the side streets, I could see the damage the night had wrought. According to the news I'd caught at the airport, there'd been sort of a half-prayer, half-spell-gathering bonfire at Fountain Square that started peacefully and ended bad when the I.S. showed up. Which might account for almost all the streetlights being shot out. Abandoned cars with little yellow I.S. stickers on them loomed out of the dim light to fall behind us like dead elephants. What traffic there was, was furtive and fast. The I.S. was traveling in packs of three, and I had yet to see any FIB vehicles despite it being the hour when they usually were in force.

"You want to drop him at the hospital, or a vampire safe house?" Trent asked, and Pike stiffened, his foot hitting the back of my seat to make me jump.

"Either one will end with him dead," I said, not caring if I was being crass. *See? I can drop idle threats, too.* "The first from his brothers, the second from angry, displaced citizens." I had told Trent about Pike's situation on the flight home. I still didn't know why I'd helped him on the boat other than it went against my grain to sit and watch someone killed in front of me when I could stop it. Maybe I was making a mistake, but I'd already put myself on the demons' shit list for standing up for Hodin. Adding an already disgruntled master vampire probably wasn't smart, and if I returned from San Francisco with a dead scion, Constance wouldn't care who killed him; I'd be blamed.

Trent's brow furrowed. "Piscary's?"

Again, I shook my head. "Abandoned. I drove her out with a stink bomb of a lily. I'll take him to Constance after she agrees to meet with me outside of the I.S. She's going to have to talk to me. He's my ticket in," I said, shooting a "No offense, Pike," over my shoulder to hear "None taken," slithering up like fog from the back.

"Church," I said firmly, and Trent slumped in the seat. "She wouldn't dare send her people to pick him up. Not with half of Cincy camped out in my sanctuary."

"So I'm a hostage?" Pike said. "Make it official, now. Let's hear the words."

I smirked at him through the rearview mirror. "You want me to drop you at the corner?" I said, and he shook his head.

Trent ran a hand over his new stubble. "I don't understand your logic here."

"That's because she's crazy," Pike muttered, clearly not happy.

We were almost home, and I was glad to see the graffiti tags had gotten less numerous and not as aggressive. The last time I'd talked to Jenks, we still had refugees. Bringing home the scion of the person who'd evicted them was going to cause some waves.

I tapped a line as I pulled onto my street, immediately feeling better. Trent smiled as he sensed it, his frown lines easing as he touched my knee and sighed, and our energy balances swirled and equalized with a little trill of sensation. I'd caught some sleep on the way home, but Trent hadn't, and I could almost feel his fatigue through the energy sifting between us.

But the closer we got, the more I slowed until we were hardly crawling.

There were three food trucks parked illegally across from the church, the burrito van sporting a short line as earlier risers got their breakfast tacos and hot coffee. A contractor's truck and trailer was parked right out front between orange cones, and three guys in jeans and mismatched tees were unloading cinder blocks from a nearby station wagon, taking them through the gate and into the backyard.

Steps? I thought, concerned at the number of them. The narrow strip of yard between the street and graveyard wall had all makes and models of cars parked in a tight order, making it look as if church was in session. My breath caught at the two gargoyles asleep beside the steeple, the first of the light turning them red and orange. They were too big to be Bis, though, and I slumped, depressed at the reminder. Perhaps they'd been keeping Bis safe while I was away.

The unfamiliar people milling about were bad enough, but the black Crown Victoria with the city plate had me downright worried. *The FIB?* I thought. *Please let it be Edden. . . .*

"I'll help you get Pike in, and then I need to go home and pick up a few things," Trent said, clearly reluctant to leave at all.

"Thanks for the ride," I said, beaming across the car at him. "I have no idea where to park," I added, distracted as I rolled the window down and whistled with two fingers in my mouth.

"What the hell?" Pike muttered, then jerked, pain flashing over him at the sharp movement when Jenks darted into the car.

"Rache!" Jenks exclaimed, his dust an excited silver in the new light. "God, you stink like dead fish and bad cheese. Slumming it in Alcatraz again? Piss on my daisies, I'm glad you're back. I've got, like, six fires I'm trying to put out and we're out of chip dip." He bobbed up and down, adding, "Hi, Trent. Thanks for giving Rache a ride home."

Pike snickered, and Jenks put his hands on his hips. "What's fang boy doing here?"

"Surviving." I smiled, feeling a tingle where his dust had

landed on my hand. "Is there anywhere to park, or do I have to circle the block?"

Jenks rose up and down. "Trent's car should fit behind yours in the carport. David brought it back."

Relieved, I put the car into drive. "Did the I.S. give him any trouble?" I asked, not liking that I'd fled into the ever-after without him. It had been less than a day, but it felt like forever.

"They would've if they had *seen* him," Jenks said, his pride obvious. "He'd make a good runner. *He* listens to me."

The ribbing felt like home, but my good mood faltered when my gaze went to Pike. He was listening, too.

"Wait until you see what Finley has done, Rache," Jenks said, his good mood obvious as he flitted from Trent's shoulder to mine. "We've got real dormitories now, and rules. Everyone in the church is helping because Finley can't get anyone to come out."

"Really?" I scanned the people at the food truck, but they all seemed okay, some of them waving shyly or taking pictures. *Gawwwd . . .*

Trent waved back, and a titter-fest broke out. "Jenks, what does the FIB want?" he asked, and Jenks looked up from running a hand down a wing to smooth a small tear.

"It's just Edden."

He'd brought my purse back, but that wasn't why he was parked at my curb at seven in the freaking morning. "Is he picking up or dropping off?" I asked, and Trent chuckled.

"Ah, right." Jenks's wings clattered as he rose up. "Hey, there's a couple of assassins on the far side of the grave-yard. You want to share with the class?"

"Those are for me." Pike cleared his throat. "Probably."

"You?" Jenks hovered, stock-still as I hesitantly pulled in behind my car in a start-and-stop motion that made Trent's head shift back and forth. "You want me to run 'em off, Rache?"

I nodded, and Pike made a scoffing sound. "Sure, you do that, little man," he said, and both Jenks and I frowned.

"Hang on," Jenks said when I jerked forward another two inches. "I'll spot you."

"Yes, please do," Trent muttered, his hand braced on the dash.

Wings rasping, Jenks darted out the window to hover high over the front bumper. "I don't want to hit my car," I said, creeping forward until Jenks's dust flashed red.

Trent sighed as I put his car in park and, grinning, I turned the car off and handed him the keys. Jenks gave me a salute and darted over the garden wall. Three seconds later, he rose up with four more pixies, all of them headed to the far corner of the graveyard.

Little man, I thought, frowning at Pike as Trent got out and stretched. If I had a dollar for every time Jenks had saved my life, I could probably buy Constance off. "Are you good to walk?" I asked Pike, groaning as he tried to shift his feet out from under the seat.

"Yep."

"I really wish you would convince Constance to meet with me," I said, tracking Trent as he went around the back of the car to get to Pike's door. His shoulders were hunched, and his pace looked weary in the new morning.

"You'd rather have her kill you than me?" Pike said, and I turned sideways to face him, making no move to get out of the car. "Ahh, maybe later," he amended with a faint smirk. "I'm still assessing your possible threat."

"I thought it was my *possible compliance* you were evaluating. Are you seriously still considering trying to kill me? In my own church? After I saved your life twice?"

"Why not? I saved yours." Pike turned as Trent opened his door, a hand at his middle as he swung his long legs out and put his salt-stained dress shoes on the cracked cement. He hesitated when Trent held out a hand to help him up, finally taking it and rising to a pained stiffness.

Tired, I got out and carefully shut the door with a thump. Okay, I was home and surrounded by my friends and . . . refugees, but Pike remained a threat. The tingling running through me was from his vampire pheromones, not the ley line I had rested a light thought in. Him finding a way to make me compliant was a real possibility—if I hadn't had three years of practice saying no to Ivy.

A delicious shudder ran through me, and I frowned. "You got him okay?" I said, arms over my middle as Trent and Pike headed slowly to the sidewalk. People had noticed Pike, and an angry whispering was rising.

Chin high, I strode to the church, my toes cold in my still-damp boots. The smoke from the graveyard was nice—as was the sound of the piano coming from the open windows. My steps bobbled and I continued forward, a small smile beginning. The plywood at the windows was gone, and the stained glass was open to let in the morning air.

"And a banister," I said, feeling its smoothness as I went up the stairs.

But I stopped still, breath catching when I saw that someone had not only polished the plaque over the door, but engraved my pack's dandelion tattoo in the corner.

Blinking fast, I pulled the door open.

The smell of new paint rolled out with the sound of the piano. Jenks had said that the refugees were supplying the labor, but we still needed to pay Finley, and this? This was a lot.

"You got the stairs?" Trent asked Pike, and I went inside, a smile finding me.

Despite the chaos of people outside, the mess I'd left the sanctuary in was showing signs of order. Unfamiliar people in jeans and tees were moving sheets of wallboard to the back of the church. A woman with a broom was sweeping up behind them. The cots were gone, and with them, the tired people sleeping in them. A beautiful circle of inlaid wood made the patched hole in the floor look intentional. The makeshift kitchen remained, bigger now with an additional folding table. Kisten's pool table was still covered with snacks, but at least it had a red-and-white-checkered cloth on it now. A faded, unfamiliar couch sat across from

Ivy's old one, and that and a small ring of chairs gave people a place to eat. Most, though, seemed to be taking their plates of eggs, chili, and bacon outside.

People I didn't know were smiling at me, and it was noisy. The sounds of hammering and a nail gun came from the back, luring me. *A real deck?* I wondered, remembering the plethora of cinder blocks. That would be a great selling point.

Immediately my mood crashed. I had to talk to Jenks. I didn't want to leave anymore.

"Is that chili?" Pike said. "For breakfast? You mind if . . ."

"Don't ask me," I said sourly. "I didn't make it."

Pike limped over to the table. Hand outstretched, he smiled a toothy grin at the woman, but when she realized who he was, she dumped the bowl back in the pot and walked away. Undeterred, he scooped a portion out for himself before using his foot to open the cooler under the table and painfully taking a pint of apple juice from it. Food in hand, he started for the couch. Seeing him coming, everyone picked up their plates and left. The woman playing the piano quit, and they all walked out.

"Ah, this looks great," Pike said as he gingerly sat down, exhaling in relief.

"Better than a skunk for clearing a room," I muttered.

"My secret power," Pike shot back, completely unbothered.

Trent gave me a sideways hug, the lingering scent of vampire making a curious mix. "Do you want some breakfast?" he asked, expression hopeful.

I shook my head. "Help yourself." I'd snagged a doughnut at the airport. It was enough.

Trent indeed went to help himself. Chili in one hand, the entire, huge serving bowl of crackers in the other, he pointedly sat right next to Pike. The vampire looked at the empty couch across from him and chuckled, clearly recognizing Trent's protective stance even as he continued to tuck in.

I didn't blame Trent. Though the assassins were real, all

Pike had to do was call in Constance's people to fetch him—if he was willing to cause a bloodbath at 1597 Oak Staff Street. No, he was finding it far more useful to linger, either to kill me or, more likely, to gather information.

But then Pike seemed to choke, staring at the bowl as if in horror. "My God! Someone put chocolate in it!"

Chin high, Trent crushed a handful of crackers into his bowl. Somehow he made the simple act into a threat, and after a moment, Pike began eating again. He was clearly not enjoying it but just as obvious was his need to eat whatever Trent could stomach.

The high-pitched chatter of pixy wings drew my attention as Jenks flew in, a contented gold dust falling from him like an early sunbeam. Edden was right behind him, and my shoulders slumped. I was honestly glad to see the man, even if he probably had a cease and desist habitation order in his pocket.

"Hi, Edden," I said, and Trent swallowed a spoonful of chili and stood.

"Rachel, Trent." The somewhat squat, older man hesitated as he took in Pike. "Mr. Welroe. I didn't expect to see you here."

Pike dabbed a napkin against his lips. "Captain."

Beaming, Edden stopped before me. "Rachel, next time you leave your purse next to five dead vampires, please call me."

"I know. I'm sorry." I gave him a hug, and his hand awkwardly patting my back felt like home. "Thank you for keeping it out of evidence. Did the I.S. give you any trouble about it?"

He shook his head, shifting to make room for Trent. "No, and that was what had me worried. Trent. It's good to see you. Nice trip?"

Trent smiled as he took his hand. "No, not really. I'm glad to be back in Cincinnati."

Edden cocked his head, a question in the slant of his eyebrows. "Al-l-lcatraz?" he drawled, and I felt myself warm.

"It's not a long story," I said as I glanced at Pike. "But it's embarrassing."

The last of the wallboard was being moved out, and I suddenly realized that though it was noisy outside, we had the sanctuary to ourselves. *Thank you, everyone.*

"Assassins are off the grounds." Jenks lit upon my shoulder with the scent of oiled steel and daffodils. "They won't be using their hands for anything other than scratching their asses for a while," he added, laughing.

"I don't want to know, do I," Edden said with a sigh.

"Thanks, Jenks," I said, and together Jenks and I stared at Pike. "Who were they?"

"What part of 'I don't want to know' didn't you get?" Edden said.

"Vamps." Jenks's wings shifted to tickle my neck. "Out of state."

Pike leaned to grab a handful of crackers from the big bowl. "And you'd know that by looking," he said, his smile pained as the new stitches on his chest pulled.

Jenks left me in a burst of sparkles. "I'm on a first-name basis with all the assassins in a fifty-mile radius, moss wipe," he said, hands on his hips and dust falling into Pike's chili bowl. "Yours are not only not from around here, but they're not that bright." He flew closer until Pike squinted and leaned away. "And if you get Rachel killed, I'm going to cut every tendon you have, and leave you for the neighborhood Were pups to play with. Got it?"

Pike clearly wasn't impressed, dramatically slow clapping in a mocking insult.

"Are you sure you need him to arrange a meeting with Constance?" Trent said sourly.

"'Fraid so."

Edden scrubbed a hand over his chin, frowning. "I know you just got back, but I could really use your help on something."

Worry unrolled in me like a fog, made worse when Pike snickered, seeming to know what it was already. "What?" I said, and Jenks came to hover between Trent and myself.

Edden glanced at Trent, clearly worried. "You know the planes aren't running, right? And the trains have been stopped?"

Trent reached for his phone. "That's not cleaned up yet?"

"No. Delay after delay." Edden frowned, making his mustache bunch. "This is way out of my jurisdiction," he said, eyes lifting from Pike. "But if I don't do something, I'm going to be up to my eyebrows in misery in three days, and frankly, we don't have the morgue space."

"What did she do now?" I said. It had to be Constance.

Attention on his phone, Trent pressed his lips together and shifted his weight to one foot. "She stopped the incoming Brimstone."

Edden winced. "She stopped the incoming Brimstone. And where I normally wouldn't worry if the families of the recently undead are having difficulty keeping their blood production adequate to supply their elders, the I.S. is turning a blind eye to it."

Okay. This was bad, but I failed to see why it was Edden's problem. Brimstone was basically a metabolism upper, enabling one or two people—instead of a dozen—to safely produce enough blood for their deceased undead. Trent was a major supplier, taking great pains to make the drug safe as well as remove the psychedelic side effects that kept it technically an illicit drug instead of the maintenance medication it really was. "And you're concerned, why?"

Edden's expression shifted to a deep disgust as he looked at Pike. The vampire was grinning broadly, reclining in the couch as if whatever trouble we were in was his doing.

Trent closed his phone and tucked it away. "If the undead can't find enough blood within their kin, they will go looking for it elsewhere."

"Humans are easy prey," Edden muttered.

Horror parted my lips, and I turned from them to Pike, and back again. "She can't do that! Do you have any idea what that might lead to? Not just in Cincy, but everywhere?"

Edden looked pained. "I do. That's why I'm asking you to help."

But this didn't make sense. Constance wanted to rule Cincinnati. Why was she breaking it? "You mean to tell me that the I.S. is going to let Constance hold the entire city's, no, our entire society's state of peace hostage? For what?"

Pike stretched to lace his hands behind his head. "She doesn't like you. You drove her out of her first real home in over a hundred years." He grinned. "She is so pissed at you for that. You have no idea."

My little joke curse is making big waves, I thought. Brow furrowed, I spun, hand on my hip. "You think *she's* pissed? We were all fine until she showed up." *How am I going to work with someone who puts her own people at risk because she doesn't like me?*

Edden looked nervously resolute. He must have an idea, or he wouldn't be here.

"Too much of a local celebrity to be ignored," Pike was saying, clearly enjoying himself. "And not enough real clout to be an effective leader. Rather egotistical of you, isn't it? Risking an entire society so you can stay thirty miles from where you were born. You should leave."

A memory of Nash burst in my thoughts, and I quashed a flash of anger. *Save Cincinnati by walking away and giving a blood-crazy bully of a master vampire control? Not happening.* Turning, I grabbed a handful of cheese curls from Kisten's pool table buffet. So I was a stress eater. That's when you need the calories.

Jenks's wings rasped as he landed on the piano. "Rachel has street clout."

Pike took up his chili bowl. "Not where it counts." He began eating again, and I started to hate his unshakable confidence, his ass sitting on my couch, him eating chili out of my bowl—even if it was made of paper and I hadn't bought it. "Oh, you have an in with the Weres and the demons, for what it's worth," he said, spoon scraping. "One is too disjointed to be a threat, the other simply doesn't care. Listening to you and Trent on the way home tells me the elves would just as soon see you dead. Clearly the witches are trying to ignore that you exist." He frowned. "That in you have with the coven leaders notwithstanding," he said softly in thought.

I pushed off from the table and wiped the orange cheese dust from my fingers.

"I admit a few vampiric camarillas are splintered by indecision," he was saying, head down over his bowl. "Torn by a promise you made to them, one that the long undead will never allow to come to fruition. All of which can be overlooked or worked out if you were capable of taking control of the city. But you don't have the influence in the I.S. to get things done." He hesitated, moving spoon faltering as I came to a halt before him. "You can't control a city without an effective police force backing you," he said, looking up at me. "Constance could savage someone on Central Parkway at midnight, and no one could stop her. You?" He chuckled. "You can't even find a place to live. The I.S. doesn't like you, and they are the major law-enforcing unit in the city." He looked at Edden. "No offense."

"None taken," Edden grumped back, his long-standing frustration obvious.

I stood before Pike, the hammering of nails and the pixies singing outside a surreal backdrop. "That depends who you ask and what the I.S. feels like enforcing on any given day." *Influence? I don't need influence. I need a plan.* Frustrated, I turned my back on Pike. "Don't you have a store of Brimstone somewhere?" I said to Trent. "I mean, you clean it up. Make it safe. Reliable."

Edden winced and pressed his fingers into his forehead, but it really wasn't a secret.

"I used to." Clearly peeved, Trent went to the table and sat down across from Pike. He drew his bowl across the table, but didn't pick it up, staring at Pike. "My refining facility was raided last night. It's gone. The I.S. impounded it."

"For distribution to the houses who bow to her," I said, slumping. Bribery and blackmail. Not how I wanted to live my life. Tired, I sank down beside Trent, my toes blue and green from the new stained glass.

Edden stood at the end of the low table, fidgeting. "The

city has maybe two days left, and then the scions of the newly undead will either begin to die from blood loss, compounding the problem, or begin to bring their masters' people off the streets."

"Or go for door number three and kiss Constance's ass," I whispered. It was a ducky of a choice. Rebel and prey on your neighbors, or submit to a clearly warped and toxic master vampire. Eyes narrowed, I looked at Pike, hating his smug satisfaction. *Why did I save your ass?*

It was becoming painfully obvious that even if I did manage to meet with her, I wouldn't be able to bring Constance around to simply play nice—not if she was ready to destroy Cincinnati to control it. Frustrated, I pushed back into the couch smelling of Were, witch, and vampire. Trent's shoulder pressed into mine, and I took his hand, not caring if Pike thought I was weak and looking for support. I'd been gone not even one day, and the city was falling apart.

It burned my toast that even half the vamp population were looking to Constance. They did fine looking to their own houses. Constance was toxic and cruel, and I had severe doubts that her sanity was sufficient to make stable decisions. She would ultimately destroy Cincinnati. Why the Turn had the old ones in DC sent the whack-job here? *To kill me?*

Nash's sacrifice, Zack's defiance, Vivian's steadfast trust, David's ready presence, fear in the lower levels of the I.S.: thoughts plinked through me, bringing me back to the ugly realization that I'd been avoiding. Jenks's idea of controlling them all by controlling Constance wasn't going to work. I had only two options. Kill her or drive her out, either of which had its own set of consequences. One was illegal, the other would be really, really hard to maintain, especially without the backing of the I.S.

Damn it back to the Turn, I thought, quashing my flash of fear before Pike could recognize it. I was going to have to do the hard thing. I was going to have to drive her out. And then I was going to have to do her effing job at keeping the vampires in line because I was not going to allow the DC vamps to send another.

A sigh slipped from me, and I gave Trent's hand a squeeze. "Okay," I said softly, and an eager smile came over him. "Your cleaned and prepped Brimstone is at the I.S. lockup, right? We'll go get it. Edden, you know where it's needed the most, yes?"

Pike snorted, and I beamed a nasty smile at the spy sitting among us.

"Er, Rache?" Jenks prompted, but I wanted Pike to hear this. I had pull. I had so much pull I fell over from it three times a week.

"I'll drive the car," Edden said, eyes alight. "I probably shouldn't go in."

"Rachel!" Jenks shouted, and I turned to him, surprised he'd used my full name.

"What!" I exclaimed, then followed his gaze to Pike grinning at me.

"Oh. Right." I held out my hand. "Pike? Phone. Now."

"Sure," he said, clearly unruffled as he slid it across the table to me, but it was Trent who picked it up, a noise of dismay slipping from him at the unfortunate mix of new technology and cracked screen.

"You knew this was coming," I said, not liking what I was going to have to do. "I'll prep as fast as I can, but if she harms Zack between now and when she agrees to see me, I will send her your ears. And then your nose, and your tongue, and then your manhood."

Pike chuckled and I leaned forward over the table, careful to keep out of his easy reach. "I buried in my graveyard yesterday what you allowed to happen to Nash," I said, and his mirth vanished. "I'm trying to work within the law. But if Constance takes everything important away from me, I will have no reason not to step outside it."

Pike's eyes flicked to Jenks, Edden, and Trent, and the last of his amusement evaporated. "Blackmail?" he prompted, somehow coming across as disappointed.

I stood, feeling strong when Jenks landed on my shoulder. "Promise," I said. "Thanks to your call in the car, Constance won't expect you to contact her for—what? Eight hours?" I smiled down at him without warmth. "I can do a lot in eight hours." *I might even be able to sleep. . . .*

Pike leaned back, his expression unreadable. "Maybe you do have what it takes."

Edden shifted from foot to foot, clearly eager to go. "Great. Thank you, Rachel. I knew you'd be able to help. I'm going to clock out and pick up a few things. Back in two hours." A hint of a smile threatened. "There's bound to be a van in impound that needs to be run to keep its battery from going dead."

That would help, and the beginnings of true confidence replaced my cold anger.

"So . . . are you good here?" Trent said as he stood. "I need to get something for tonight as well." He took my hand, hesitating until I looked at him. "Promise you won't go without me," he added, and Jenks snickered.

I leaned in and gave him a hug and a quick but earnest kiss. "You know me too well."

Trent's eyes were warm, and his hands around me held an unspoken feeling. "That wasn't a promise," he said, and I pulled from his hands and dropped back, smiling.

"Then don't be late," I said. "You either, Edden," I added, and the older man raised a hand, acknowledging it.

"By hook or by crook," he said, and I sighed as the two men started for the door together.

"Seriously?" Pike said, still on the couch. "You're leaving me alone with her?"

Jenks rasped his wings, the pixy having put himself on the edge of the cracker bowl. "You're not alone with her, fang boy," he said. "You're alone with me."

Nearly at the door, Trent turned to give me a smile. "Try not to damage him, okay? He might be useful before the end."

Together, Jenks and I said, "I'll try," getting a raised eyebrow from Edden and a disbelieving snort from Pike. But he was beginning to look unsure, and I went to get a bowl of chili as the door opened and closed. Suddenly the sound of that nail gun seemed really loud.

"Is this to convince me you've got the nads to run a city?" Pike said, and I calmly ladled a cup of chili into a throwaway bowl. I was dead tired, and I should eat something more than a doughnut before I began spelling.

"I've been with you for less than a day," Pike said pointedly. "And in that time you were beat up by a woman in orange, starved yourself, let a TSA agent feel you up at the San Francisco airport, and a demon throw you across three time zones. Stab wound or no, I could be out of here in . . ." He hesitated. "Ninety seconds."

"Perhaps." Thirty seconds, to a minute, to a minute ten, and now a minute and a half. It was nice being taken seriously. I turned, getting a sleepy thumbs-up from Jenks when I tapped a line and I felt my hair begin to float and snarl. "But we aren't on an island anymore, or in a jet, or even a car. We are in my church." I breathed him in, liking the sudden hesitancy behind his hard-won confidence. "You set one foot out that door, and I won't have to kill you. Your brothers will."

Pike didn't drop his eyes, but I could tell he was thinking about that. Smug, I came forward a few steps, chili bowl in hand. "I've been with you for less than a day," I said, echoing his words. "And in that time, you were stabbed twice, ate chemically tainted lasagna, nearly choked to death, flirted unsuccessfully with a TSA agent, and were thrown across three time zones to where you needed an elf and a witch to get you home alive. I don't know why your brothers want you dead. Frankly, I don't care. But unless Constance wants to risk a bloodbath trying to get you, you're here with me, pretty boy. It would be easier to convince her to meet with me. Until then, I'm keeping you alive."

"Pretty boy . . ." Pike frowned. It was the first time I'd had him on edge, and a remembered thrill from Kisten jolted through me. "You are not keeping me alive."

"I am." I breathed in the scents of the church, listened to the sounds of life it sheltered, let it fill me up. I was home, and it felt good. "You need someone to watch your back. So do I. No shame in that." I smiled at Jenks, totally at peace with myself. "Actually, there's a lot of strength in it. Being able to trust."

But my smile faltered as Pike showed me a slip of tooth. "Jenks, watch him," I said, and the pixy touched his forehead in salute. "I'll be upstairs spelling. Bring him up when you need a break. If he gives you trouble, pix him, then bring him up."

I put an extra sway in my hips as I crossed the new circle inlaid in the floor, but as soon as my back was to Pike, I let my brow furrow. *Storm the I.S. basements. Steal a van of Brimstone. Drive an undead from her daylight quarters a second time in as many days. Sure. I can do that.*

"What's pixing?" Pike asked, and Jenks laughed, sounding like crazy wind chimes.

"You don't want to know," he said. "Sit there and eat your chili like a nice vampire, or she'll pull your soul out and give it to her gargoyle."

Fatigue rose as I took the stairs to the belfry, feeling every mile we'd crossed, every hour of sleep I'd missed. I'd never pull Pike's soul out, but it wouldn't hurt to get a few immobilization curses ready for when he got stupid and tried to leave. It had been a pretty speech, but vampires never listened until you proved your strength. No one did.

I wasn't letting him out of my sight until Constance was out of my city for good. She had put the entire human-and-Inderland balance under threat because she had no real power but for what lay in fear. There was no getting along with her. It was out, or twice dead.

CHAPTER

20

THE IRREGULAR THUMPING COMING FROM THE GARDEN had been going on for a while, punctuated by bursts of cheering and good-natured groans. But it was the growing scent of roasting meat and the rattle of pixy wings that woke me, and I jerked awake, surprised that I'd fallen asleep while studying one of my demon texts. My middle was tingling from the extended contact, and when I sat up from the dusty fainting couch and looked, the faded, hand-printed curse was glowing to show an alternative text. Grimacing, I brushed the page to make the words flare and go out. I'd been hoping to find a charm or spell to prevent Al from tossing me into a line and then Alcatraz again, but the reality was, I had stupidly let him do it.

I swung my feet to the floor. The large fourteen-by-fourteen room was warm from the late-morning sun. *Almost noon, really,* I thought, gaze drawn to the sounds of the ongoing volleyball game in the graveyard where they'd strung a net between two of the higher monoliths. A fading trail of pixy dust caught my attention, and I stretched, muscles pulling. "Jenks?"

The soft rasping of dragonfly wings returned and Jenks slipped in through the cracked door to the stairs. "Sorry. I didn't know you were pushing pollen," he said, the unfamiliar pixy metaphor for sleep making me smile as he landed on my pencil cup atop the small marble-topped dresser. It had been here when we first moved in, and I'd used the smooth surface to work a few spells on before. The mug with its happy rainbow was now full of magnetic chalk, ceramic stirring rods, garden scissors, highlighters, and my secondary ceremonial knife. Beside it was a moving box holding my spelling waste, and beside that, the finished products of the morning's spelling.

"Crap on toast," I said as I stood to look out the window at the sunlight. "I didn't realize it was that late. How long have Trent and Edden been back?"

"That's kind of why I'm here," Jenks said.

Panic washed through me, better than three cups of espresso. "Pike . . ." I said, eyes wide, and Jenks's tiny features bunched up in amusement.

"Is fine," he said, and I exhaled, slumping to sit back on a stack of boxes. "Trent and Edden are fine. Hell, even Zack is fine." Jenks rose up to check on Bis, safe on his shelf. "But I don't want Pike around when Edden and I go over the escape routes. Trent called. Said he was going to nap before coming back if that's okay, but Edden's been here for about twenty minutes." Jenks dropped, right through his sifting dust. "You mind babysitting Pike for a few?"

I forced my arms down before they could wrap around my middle. "Sure. Bring him up." I stood from the boxes and covered a yawn.

"Great. Thanks," Jenks said, stifling his own yawn. "How much do you have left?"

"Not much." I stretched my hands to the ceiling and groaned. I was beginning to understand why demons had kept familiars and forced them to make all their charms and curses. This was tedious. "I've already made the counter-charm to de-stink Piscary's," I said, looking at the ley line amulet on the marble top. "And a couple more pain amulets."

"Because we can always use pain charms." Jenks's wings started and stopped.

"I made a few more for you," I added as I pointed them
out, proud that I'd managed it. Modifying spells was tricky,
and I'd been afraid I might deaden the pain to the point of
stopping his heart the first time.

"Sweet. Thanks." Jenks took his red bandana and
twisted it into a bag to carry them.

"Restocked my splat gun with sleepy-time charms," I
added, very glad Edden had brought it back to me before
the I.S. could tamper with it. "Brushed up on my defensive
curses. All I have left is this little baby."

Jenks rose up to land on my shoulder as I set the book
I'd fallen asleep with on the dresser. "If I'm reading this
right, it will solidify my aura so it can't be modulated. Basically preventing anyone from throwing me into a line even
if I'm unconscious."

The pixy snorted, and the dust spilling down to light the
page turned thick. "Cool as a newling's ass on washday."
He rose up, wings clattering. "You want me to send him up
with some lunch? Someone made a stack of peanut butter
sandwiches."

Head shaking, I scanned the room, thinking it was going
to feel too small with a vampire in it. "No, thanks. I
shouldn't eat with him around."

Jenks's grin widened. "I forgot."

"I didn't," I muttered. "I'll hit him with that immobilization curse I got from Al if he gives me any trouble." My
gaze rose to the paper stuck to the dresser's mirror where
I'd written my emergency curses.

"The one you used to bind Landon?" Jenks chuckled.
"That's a good one. Hey, Etude is on the roof, if he tries to
run that way. He's asleep, but he'll wake up if you shout.
But seriously, everyone knows Pike's here and is keeping
an eye out. He won't get two feet on that sidewalk before
someone takes him down the hard way."

"Thanks, Jenks. I couldn't do this without you." I jerked
my curse cheat sheet off the mirror, folded it up, and tucked
it in a pocket. "Send him up," I said, and Jenks gave me a

salute before darting through the cracked door and down the cramped stairwell.

Immediately I went to the screenless window and leaned out to see that yes, there was a huge gargoyle sleeping on the nearby peak. I lingered, half out the window to soak in the view. The church looked nice with people scattered about, playing volleyball, minding kids, bringing in shrink wrapped firewood from a home-improvement store to keep the coals hot under the whole pig roasting at the graveyard's new firepit. Dang, that smelled good.

Toes brushing the floor, I leaned farther, stretching until I could see the new deck foundation. It was substantial, filling the entire footprint of the demolished kitchen and back living room. Finley was out there working with a volunteer crew of eight. Rafters lay nearby, ready to raise. It looked as if they might get a roof up by tonight with the amount of help she had.

"Cool," I whispered, then pulled myself back in. Apart from my spelling supplies, I had winnowed my day-to-day stuff to the bare minimum while living on Kisten's boat. Even so, the small room looked cramped with open boxes of spelling and ley line equipment against one wall, my personal stuff by another. The few clothes I'd had in my closet now hung on the tiny bar set between two rafters. A long, low bookcase stood beside the marble-topped dresser under the narrow windows. Cookbooks mingled with spell primers and demon texts in what probably invited trouble, and a nagging feeling of unprofessionalism pricked me as I knelt to organize them while waiting for Pike.

"Don't clean on my account," Pike said unexpectedly from the stairway, and I jumped, trying to hide the motion as I turned, still kneeling. "I like a room that's lived in."

"Lived in is one thing, but this is . . ." I shrugged as he leaned against the doorframe and brushed pixy dust off his shoulder. He'd showered at some point, and his hair was wavy and thick, styled above his ears. He'd shaved, too, and, sensing my attention, he came in and posed for me, showing off the new slacks and dark button-down

hirt. I could detect a hint of cologne, and a warning flag
napped. "Not a bad fit," he said as he shifted to show me
his other side. "It was in the back of a bedroom closet, apparently."

"Ivy's leftover box," I said, gaze lingering on the small
ear near the shoulder. "She didn't take it when she moved
in with Nina. Have a seat." Hesitant, I inched closer, taking
up the book I'd been reading before I'd fallen asleep, my
thoughts on how soft his dark hair would be on my fingers.
Damn vamp pheromones. "Everyone being nice?"

I heard him sigh as he sat on the low fainting couch. "If
looks could kill, I'd be twice dead by now. You were right.
I might as well be on an island surrounded by sharks." He
hesitated. "Quite a setup. And it's all gratis. You aren't paying them anything."

It's not always about money, I thought as I backed to the
middle of the room. "No, I'm just giving them somewhere to
park their asses after Constance kicked them out." *Speaking
of which, where am I going to park my ass if he's on the
couch?*

Seeing my dilemma, Pike grinned and patted the fainting couch in invitation.

"Yeah. Right," I muttered as I sat on a box. Head down,
I set the open book on my lap and looked over the aura-
solidifying curse again.

Pike was silent for five heartbeats, then, "Do you have
anything to read?"

I ignored him, jaw clenching when he rose and started
for my bookshelf. "Sit," I almost growled, then stretched to
get him a cookbook. "Enjoy," I said as I handed it to him.

He looked at the title, then down at me, weight all on one
foot. Tossing the book onto a box, he went to look out the
window at the graveyard. "I'm bored." Pike bent over, his
elbows on the sill to show off his behind. "I've been here
all day, and nothing is going on."

"Take a nap," I suggested, and he pushed himself up
again, eyes going from Etude asleep on the peak down to
the book on my lap.

"Is that a spell or curse?" he said, and I stiffened when he sat on the box beside me.

My fingers running down the ingredient list curved under into a fist. "Curse. I'm going over it to make sure it doesn't violate my rules for white magic. I don't do black magic."

Pike's eyebrows rose. "I thought all curses were black."

"You and everyone else," I complained, then added "No. Most curses cause smut, which is basically a mark of how badly you are screwing up the balance of nature, but smut isn't bad. Actually, it can be useful."

He nodded knowingly. "To curse someone."

Save me from armchair practitioners. "I suppose, but it's easier and not against the law to get someone to take it willingly in exchange for something they need. The amount of smut for a curse varies by how far you're stretching the laws of nature. For example, if I did a curse to immobilize you, there'd be only a tiny fraction of smut because being still is a natural state except in two-year-olds and pixies. But one to, say, fill your lungs with water and kill you would leave lots of smut because putting water in your lungs is not natural."

Pike ran a hand over his smooth cheeks. "Death is a natural state," he offered.

"Not when it's caused by magic," I said. He was too close. Damn it, my entire side was tingling. "This curse checks out," I said, rising from the boxes and going to the marble top dresser. "Do me a favor and stay out of my way, huh?"

"Sure, okay."

It wasn't a complex curse. The hardest part was to get your victim to drink the potion and thereby be unable to jump the lines without the countercurse. But the hair on the back of my neck began to prick when he stood to follow me, standing at my shoulder as I began sifting through my ley line equipment. Some of it was brand-new, a gift from my mom when she upgraded her spell box. I was sure I'd seen a Klein bottle in here somewhere, and I almost forgot Pike was beside me as I opened boxes and unwrapped metal and glass.

"Ooh, a crystal," Pike said as he held up one the size of my fist. "Kind of hocus-pocus, new-age crap, isn't it?"

My eyebrows rose at his obvious mockery. "Crystals can accentuate vibrations to make your blood boil or freeze, blind you, or drive you mad. If they're perfectly cut as that one is, they do the opposite, letting you separate things that should never be separated. Like auras into their shells, or maybe your soul from your body and mind."

Brow furrowed, Pike carefully wrapped it back up in its silk scarf and replaced it in the box. "How close are you and Trent?" he said, catching me off guard.

My eyes rose to his. "Other than we love each other?" I said belligerently. "Sit down. You're getting in my way."

Pike made a soft sound of recognition. Taking a book from one of the boxes, he retreated to the fainting couch. His fingers were lumpy from being broken too many times, and I thought of his brothers. "I read up on you," he said, his knees almost to his ears on the low couch. "Know-your-enemy kind of thing."

I breathed easier with him on the other side of the room. "That's nice."

"You hated him," Pike said lightly as he idly flipped through the book. "He tried to kill you. Repeatedly. Word is, he put you in the rat fights. What is that a metaphor for?"

There you are, I thought, finally finding my Möbius strip, safely wrapped in a gold silk cloth. "It's a metaphor for turning myself into a mink to steal from Trent Kalamack, getting caught, and being put in the rat fights."

Pike looked up from the book, following me with his eyes as I set the twisted metal on the dresser top and returned to the boxes. "Fuck," he finally said, and I frowned.

"You're smart," I said, not liking his language. "Be more creative in your expletives."

"Fuck that," Pike shot back, and I smiled, reminded of Kisten. Kisten, though, had been far more submissive. Survivable. Pike would be . . . anything but.

My smile faded, and I shuddered at the thought of him between the sheets. Head down, I searched for my diamond dust among the stubs of candles. *Damn vampire phero-mones. Keep talking, Rachel. And maybe open another window.*

"My dad and Trent's father worked behind the law to find a cure for the elves' cascading genetic failure," I said, pleased when I found the Klein bottle and set it with the Möbius strip. "When I was born with a common but deadly genetic flaw, Trent Senior used the same illegal genetic tinkering that had been keeping his species alive to fix it, accidentally breaking the elven curse that his way-back ancestors created to commit a slow genocide on the demons. There were two of us, the first demons to survive since the curse was put on them over two thousand years ago."

Pike stared at me, his eyes an even brown. "So . . ." he prompted, clearly not getting it.

Head down, I rummaged for something of mine not DNA oriented to target the curse to me. Nothing seemed appropriate. "Witches are stunted demons," I said. "Able to breed true, but when things line up right, a demon is the result. Until Trent's dad, it was always fatal, but because he fixed the cure to my mitochondria, I can pass it on."

I jerked when Pike snapped his fingers, the light of understanding in his eyes making me grimace. "That's why you have so much influence with the demons," he said. "They can't kill you until you have a couple of brats." His lips parted, and I could almost see reality hit him as he looked at me, to the stuff assembled on the dresser, and back to me. "Holy shit, you really *are* a demon. I thought it was propaganda."

"Hard to tell, isn't it," I said sourly. Yep, that was me. A demon who couldn't travel the lines on her own or tap a ley line over water, and had to use a supplemental curse to keep from being tossed into Alcatraz by my disgruntled . . . teacher? Mentor? Frenemy? I didn't really know what Al was anymore. *Most treasured pain in the ass?*

"You're going to live forever," Pike said, his speculative tone surprising me. "Not a few hundred years."

I wasn't sure where this was going and, nervous, I got up

to open a new box. "I suppose. As long as no one outright kills me by surprise. Jenks talks a good game about me, but I'm as vulnerable as anyone else." I hesitated, suspicion rising heavy and thick. "And if you make one move I don't like, I bind you with a curse and you're drooling on the floor."

Pike smiled at that, but it looked real, setting me on edge. "Not me." He settled back into the fainting couch with that book. "At least not until Constance starts wondering why I haven't called. I can see the assassins from here." His head shook in rue. "I don't know why you don't leave Cincinnati to her. I'll admit, after seeing you in action, you have more multispecies influence than I thought, but that still leaves the I.S. You can't police an entire city of Inderlanders without them."

I shrugged, feeling as if we were back on familiar ground. "So I should be the demon and scare everyone into behaving?" I said as I pushed past an old hairbrush, unmatched socks, and stuffed toys won at Six Flags. *Why do I even have these?*

Pike laughed, irritating me. "You don't have it in you. Vampires are swayed into obedience by fear. Nothing more."

"Mmmm," I said, wondering if he had forgotten me threatening to chop him up and send him to Constance. But his opinion of me stung, and I couldn't help myself from trying to hurt him back. "Too bad you're too afraid of your brothers to stand up to them."

"I am not afraid of my brothers."

I turned, surprised to see his attention was on that slim volume he'd found in my things. "Then I'm sorry you're afraid of whoever those two vampire-looking snots in suits were who sat with you outside of Dalliance and messed with your hair." His eyes flicked to mine, and I knew I'd been right that they had been his brothers. "That's what demons do," I added as I stood in the center of the room and looked up at Bis's shelf. My pinky ring would make a fabulous non-DNA focusing object. It was in my jewelry box, which was currently up with Bis. Jenks had asked me to put it up there, and I occasionally heard the little tinkling of music from the windup dancer play sadly. "They dip into your brain and pull out what scares you." I chuckled, remembering the dog-headed god Al turned into to frighten Piscary. But I quickly sobered. At least Al wasn't turning into me anymore.

"Okay, you got me," Pike said as I pulled a closed box to the center of the room to stand on. "When I was seven, my mother made the mistake of presenting me to the family master, claiming I had lineage through his sister and grandfather to take his place when he died his second death. She only meant it to solidify her standing in his camarilla, but he took it as a threat and promised his holdings to whatever sibling killed me twice."

"Sorry." Which explained everything from the fight on Twin Lakes Bridge to the assassins on the boat to him needing Constance to survive. He was a prince with a price on his head, seeking refuge at a rival queen's domain—if you liked that kind of thing.

"So yes, I've been the object of my brothers' warped affections for a long time," he admitted. "And you are afraid of a glowing woman with lightning shooting from her hair."

"What?" I asked, then remembered. "Oh. Sure." I blew a strand of hair from my eyes as I frowned up at the shelf. "That was the Goddess. If you're not afraid of her, you're stupid."

"And being in a cage," he added, voice low.

"Of a cage?" I echoed, shoulders slumping as I remembered freaking out at Alcatraz. "No. The cage door always opens. But of being helpless? Sure. Of having my skills taken from me, my ability to protect myself and those I love? Of what makes me, me? Damn straight."

I hesitated, gaze dropping to Pike. He was taller than me, and if he'd get the jewelry box down, I wouldn't have to stretch suggestively before him. "Would you do me a favor?" I said, and he arched his eyebrows. "Would you get me my jewelry box? It's on that shelf."

"With your gargoyle?" Pike slowly stood, looking tall as he got on the box. "Sure."

My hand reached for it when he dragged it from the shelf. "Thanks." I waited, hand outstretched until he set it into my grip. "I'm going to use my old pinky ring as a focusing object," I said as I opened it up. The tinkling music played, and I swear Bis's tail twitched. My ring was right where I'd left it, but my face flamed when I saw my caps, the ones Kisten had given me for my birthday to put over my teeth to extend my canines to match his, a harmless, creative way to liven our bedroom play. I hadn't been able to throw them away, and grief rose up at the sight of them in their little vial, my sadness unwanted and unhelped.

"Rachel Morgan," Pike drawled, still above me. "Are those caps in your treasure box?"

I snapped the jewelry box closed and the tinkling music cut off. "Absolutely not," I lied. "I've got everything I need. Thanks."

But his motions were slow in thought as he got off the box, his eyes following me as I set the jewelry box on the dresser. "You *used* to have everything you needed," he said, and I shuddered at his low voice, so much like Kisten's. He wasn't talking about the curse. "But you don't anymore. Not for a long time."

I turned, taken aback at his pupil-wide stare and carefully unmoving stance. My skin was tingling again from the vamp pheromones. There were windows everywhere, but it wasn't enough to dilute the need and desire he had filled the air with.

"You miss him?" Pike said from across the room, and it was as if he was whispering in my ear. "It was him, wasn't it? Rumor has it that Ivy only broke your skin once."

I flushed, and Pike's lips curved up into a smile. A slip of fang showed, and I trembled.

"Where?" Pike said, taking a soundless, graceful step

closer, and I backed up until I found the dresser. "Your skin is perfect."

My breath caught when he moved forward, and my eyes closed in a long blink. Sensation blossomed as a light finger shifted my chin, then touched my neck.

I gasped, eyes flashing open as I smacked his touch away. "No touching," I said, and he smiled, hand raised in apology.

"I'm sorry," he said, but that was not what his eyes were saying. "I overstepped."

He leaned closer, and I held my breath, enjoying the tingling fire racing down my side. Oh, God. It had been so long.

"No touching," Pike echoed, and I didn't move. He said he wouldn't touch, and though I didn't trust him, I trusted the vampires' blood-play code—God knew why. I was stupid. *No, I am in control,* I mused, a light finger of thought resting in the nearby ley line. I was faster than a vampire's teeth.

And as he leaned forward again, my eyes closed and my hands gripped the top of the dresser, enthralled by the feeling of promised rapture plinking through me.

His breath brushed my neck, and I let my head loll, almost inviting him. I knew how it would feel, I knew the rush of sensation that would fill me, the utter belonging, the promise. "Give me this," he whispered, and I licked my lips, knowing I had a master of the blood arts standing before me.

"No," I whispered, and I felt him smile at my mild denial, thinking it wouldn't hold. "You touch me, and you die," I promised, eyes closed. "Right here."

"I'm not touching you." His words were hardly there, and my knees almost buckled. "But I could. I could draw you to the summit." His incoming breath was like a promise. "Bring you half a step from death—to life."

I held my breath as he blew, warm on me to waken my scar.

My grip on the dresser behind me tightened at the tingling wash, and my eyes opened. It was almost a shock to see him there, his pupil-black eyes holding a promised journey to somewhere Kisten never dared take me. He would pull upon every strand of desire in me, fulfilling them all.

"You know us." Pike's eyes closed, but it made him more dangerous, not less.

"I know you," I agreed. My pulse was fast, and my grip on the dresser became white-knuckled.

"You could be everything with me," he whispered, and tingles raced to my groin, his breath heavy on my hidden scar. "I could give everything to you. Everything . . ."

I uncramped my hand, fingers shaking as I went to push him away, but as my palm met his chest . . . I found I did not. "I would be nothing," I said, almost pained by what he offered. "I've heard this lie before."

Pike stepped back. I took a breath as my hand lost contact with him, bringing the scent of incense deep into me—just as he planned. "You lived it," he said, his gaze tracing my neck as he took my elbows and drew me a faltering step to the center of the room. "Live it again, but this time you will not be bound to an ill-appreciated scion playing craps while the master plots betrayal. Keep Constance fed, and she doesn't look past her blood parties. Together you and I could keep Cincinnati safe under her, you with the rabble, me with the I.S."

Again I breathed deep, searching the air for lies but only finding truth in his black eyes, feeling his earnest belief in his light touch. This was not a trick, but it would kill who I was nevertheless. I loved Trent, and what Pike offered was power and sensation. If I said yes, I would lose everything.

And so I stood before him, feeling his promise light through me like cold fire. "I will not walk this path again," I said, gut twisting. I would not take it because there was no love to make it right.

"If you won't walk it, I'll carry you."

His hand touched my jaw. A welling of line energy rose to swamp him, and I caught it back, enjoying the tingles bringing me alive. "You . . . will not," I whispered, eyes closing. "It is a lie without love."

His hand fell away, and my eyes opened, seeing his lips twisted in a bitter understanding. "There is never love," Pike said, a dangerous glint of fang making me lock my knees. It would feel so good to have them cleanly slice into me, filling me with sensation. "It's give-and-take, but mostly take. Take what I offer, Rachel. Give in to her. We can keep Cincinnati together while Constance remains ignorant."

But I knew the lie within the truth, and I shook my head. "Sometimes, there is love," I said, though he'd never believe it. "I might do this for love, but not for anything less."

Pike dropped back a step, the ardor falling from him. "Then I am sorry," he said with true regret. "You will have to die."

He moved. My breath came fast, but I was already dodging his lunge or I never would have kept out of his reach. *"Stabils,"* I whispered as he shifted direction and one grasping hand touched me. I gasped as the line I held blossomed through me, almost buckling my knees as it rolled through my vampire-incense-addled state. *Damn,* I thought as it raced from my core and was gone, leaving a soft hum of promised ecstasy to slowly fade.

Pike's eyes widened as the immobilization curse hit him, and then he dropped, groaning as he struck the box under the bell and collapsed to an uncomfortable sprawl. "You stupid fool of a vampire," he wheezed, cursing himself as I stared down at him, shocked at how fast it had happened. One second I'd been nearly enthralled, and the next, he was on the floor. "You stupid damn fool!"

"Rachel?" a gravelly voice ground out at the window, and I turned, pulse fast, to see Etude's craggy face in the screenless window.

I trembled as I stood over Pike, the last promised sensation pulsing to nothing within me. My head dropped to the vampire shuddering to a frozen stillness at my feet, unable to move, apart from his voice and what would keep him alive. Slowly my fisted hands opened. I'd made little indents in my palms from my nails, and I rubbed them out. "I'm good. Thanks."

"Mmmm, huh?" the old gargoyle said, then settled where he could see into the room, and fell asleep again.

Pike was still swearing at himself as I leaned over him, arms wrapped around my middle. Memories of Kisten were thick, and they hurt. "I told you I wouldn't be bespelled," I said, voice low, and he struggled to find me with his eyes. "You're good. Good enough to make me break my promise on a bad day. But I know what you offer, and I know where it leads, and I'm not going there. Not for you, not for me, not for anyone." Angry at myself, I rose from my crouch over him. "And not to become Constance's puppet. Got it?"

"Sure," Pike rasped, sounding pained. No doubt, seeing as his leg was uncomfortably pinned under him.

But as I stood over him, my anger shifted to worry. I couldn't leave him frozen here when we all went to get the Brimstone. The only reason Constance was leaving me alone was because she was waiting for Pike to kill me. And as I listened to his increasingly labored breathing, I realized there was something here I could use.

"Jenks!" I shouted, and from outside, Etude sighed and dropped deeper into slumber.

The pixy darted in, sword bared, but he snickered when he saw Pike on the floor. "Told you," he said as he dropped down to poke his nose with his sword point. "You can't bespell her."

I felt myself flush, embarrassed.

"I should have," Pike wheezed, and, finding an ounce of compassion, I wedged a toe under him and flipped him over. "You have caps," he said as his eyes found mine. "You've read the book. You have a binding scar. You know us."

He meant "know us" as in the carnal sense, and I warmed even more. "That's just it, Pike," I said, hands on my hips as I tried to decide what to do. "I know you. I know you better than you know yourselves. Been there. Done that. Got smart."

But guilt that I'd stood there and enjoyed his offer pricked through me. "I'm so embarrassed," I whispered as I backed up and levered myself up to sit on the dresser beside my spelling equipment.

"Why?" Jenks hovered over the jewelry box, clearly wondering why it wasn't on the shelf anymore. "He pushed your buttons, you said no. He insisted. You decked him." Landing, he strode to the edge of the dresser and looked down. "She should leave you like that."

"Doing my job," Pike said, sprawled faceup now. "Nothing personal."

But it had sure felt personal, and I slid from the dresser top, feet lightly hitting the old floorboards.

"Too bad," Pike said, eyes finding me. "It could have been fun. Constance is right to be afraid of you. Kill me if you want. She'll send someone else."

"I'm not going to kill you." I nudged his legs straight, wondering if I might be able to lug him up onto the fainting couch. His threats didn't worry me as much as the lingering question of what I was going to do with him in the interim. "I don't get it, Pike," I said as I grabbed him under his shoulders and gave a heave toward the couch. "You know she's so old she doesn't remember anything of love. Why do you work so hard to keep something like that in charge?"

"If she dies, no one will protect me," he said. "My brothers won't stop until I'm buried facedown." He made a bark of laughter, ending it with a muffled swear word. "I should have let that knife find its mark," he said bitterly, arms and legs askew as I got him propped up against the side of the couch. He was too heavy for me to lift, and I left him there.

"And miss Alcatraz?" The air still smelled of vampire incense, and I went to push open another window.

"What are you going to do with him?" Jenks asked, his dust a dismal blue as he darted from the jewelry box to Bis's shelf in a clear request for me to put it back.

"I don't know." Head down, I took my wooden pinky ring out of it and snapped it closed. "She'll send her goons when she finds out he failed to seduce or kill me."

"Then she'd better not find out, because Baribas and his kids can't handle a full assault yet."

Jenks settled on the shelf, overseeing as I stretched to shove the jewelry box back where it belonged. I hesitated, resting a hand on the cat-size gargoyle, whispering a silent promise that I'd get his soul back to him.

Depressed, I got down off the box and pushed it back into the pile. But I froze at a sudden idea, flashing warm as I looked at Pike slouched against the fainting couch and staring at his hands as if trying to get them to move. Constance wouldn't send anyone until she knew Pike had tried and failed. All I had to do was keep him with me for a few hours more.

"Jenks, do we have any mouse nests in the garden?"

"Sure." His voice came down unseen from the shelf. "Why?" His head poked over, and he looked at Pike, a wicked smile coming over his tiny features. "Oh, hell yes," he said, then flew out one of the windows, whistling for Baribas, presumably.

"What are you going to do?" Pike said, and I crouched to shift his head up.

"Congratulations," I said as I patted his cheek. "You're going to have the chance to see the world from a view very few have."

The curse to thicken my aura would have to wait and, feeling sassy, I stood and went to my spell library. I knew what I wanted was in there.

"I said, what are you going to do?" Pike said, frightened now.

"Be the demon," I said shortly, and he paled, even under the immobilization curse. "I'm going to turn you into a mouse. You do anything I don't like or stray from my side, and you will be a mouse forever. Or at least until someone sees you and feeds you to their cat." I beamed at him. "So I suggest you sit in my pocket where I put you until I get this done."

CHAPTER

21

I STOOD BESIDE TRENT AT NASH'S GRAVE, MY FOCUS
blurred on the delicate, bronzed flowers waving in the sun-
drenched breeze at our feet. It was after noon and he
smelled fresh and clean, his light aftershave going well
with the sound of the wind in the new leaves. Guilt flickered for having momentarily enjoyed Pike's attempted se-
duction, and I quashed it.

"Hodin said the flowers were gifts from the dead to the
bereaved?" Trent asked, fingering the one that I'd given
him. "To remind the living that they are loved?"

I nodded, wondering how expensive my agreement to
stick up for Hodin was going to be.

"And these are the words that cast the spell and gathered
the mystics?" Trent asked, attention on Hodin's cramped
script.

I nodded again, my sorrow heavy at what Nash had gone
through, the strength of will he had shown, the pain he had
endured to keep a young man safe—sacrificing his life to
give Zack the chance to live his from beginning to end.

"I don't know these words," Trent said softly, brow
creased. "And mystics enveloped him, and he vanished?"

My breath came in as I remembered to breathe. "Clothes
and all." God, this was depressing.

Trent shoved the paper in his pocket before taking my

hand in a comforting squeeze. "I'm sorry you had to do this, Rachel." His eyes began to swim, and tears pricked as he pulled me to him and held me. "Thank you. I'm grieving for Nash, but this is a piece of our heritage that we'd never hoped to regain. It will mean so much to so many people."

I nodded, my throat tight. Yes, this was a good thing, but it might have cost me everything with Al. Trent's arms eased and I stepped back, trying to smile as I wiped my eyes.

"I don't recognize the flower," Trent said as he tucked it in my hair. "It's beautiful."

"Dali did," I said, remembering his disgust when he flicked it to the ground and spit on it.

Shoulders slumping, I turned us away and we started back to the church. The clattering of pixy wings sounded fitting in the garden, and the bright butterfly wings of the fairies in the graveyard were a stark contrast to my mood. A few vampires lingered at the firepit, asleep with their legs outstretched to the coals. The pig was gone, the leftovers now soup simmering in my makeshift kitchen for whoever needed it.

The grounds were surprisingly quiet with most everyone either sleeping or at work. Even the construction had taken a break, and I could hear birds and distant traffic. Apparently Finley was shopping. I half wondered if Trent hadn't slipped her a check, because what I was looking at as we walked back to the church had big dollar signs attached. At this point, I was ready to accept anything, pride be damned.

The new back end had a high roof, a plywood floor, and stud walls wired for sockets and obvious gaps for wide windows. The fireplace had been left where it was, new mortar shoring up the fire damage. *A covered outdoor kitchen will be a nice plus for someone,* I thought, then sent my gaze over the garden. "Is Jenks around? I need to talk to him."

Trent stepped over the low wall and held out a hand for me. "He's watching Pike with Etude. Rachel, about your idea to turn him into a mouse . . ."

I froze, my hand in his. Then I stepped over the wall and pulled away. "I'm listening."

Trent squinted at the belfry. Pike might not be able to move, but vampires had excellent hearing. "Are you sure you're not doing it out of revenge?" he said, voice low.

My boots scuffed on the new walk of pavers now weaving through my garden like a slow river. Then I looked closer, wincing. They had names on them. Someone had stolen them from Cincinnati's benefactor walk. *Crap on toast, I'm going to hear about this.* "Revenge for what?"

"For trying to bind you to him," Trent said, his voice holding a shocking anger.

"Oh." I winced, guilt flashing through me again for having enjoyed it. But the drowsing vampires had clearly heard him, one jostling the elbow of the other and grinning at us. They knew. God, how they knew. I thought it telling that Trent was more angry about Pike trying to seduce me than him trying to kill me when he failed.

"It might be better to use, say, a binding curse," Trent continued as we made our way to the raised deck. "One that will keep Pike from straying and still allow Constance to see him with you, furthering her belief that he hasn't yet tried to seduce you and failed."

"But I already stirred the potion," I said, feeling the seven tiny vials in my pocket. Pike had watched me make them, and no way would I leave them around to be ingested by accident. "They won't be any good after a week." I pulled Trent to a halt at the wide steps. "I even have a little carrying case for him so he won't get crushed in my purse. He can breathe and everything."

Brow furrowed, Trent took my elbows, his eyes pinched in his need to convince me. "If you're out of the church, he needs to be seen with you," he insisted. "If Constance even *thinks* he's at the church alone, she'll send her thugs to tear it apart. She's afraid of you, Rachel. You're the only person standing up to her, and that makes her an extremely dangerous vampire."

Is there any other kind? A slow sigh shifted my shoulders as I looked over the sunlit grounds, remembering all the people sheltering here, filling my and Ivy's old room, the tents in the garden, catching z's and something to eat in a safe place until they could find a permanent solution. I couldn't risk Constance coming here. They wouldn't be able to stomach being displaced again. People would be hurt or killed. Not to mention Finley's work would be torn up.

"I don't have time to find, much less make a new curse to force Pike's compliance," I said, hating the hint of whine in my voice. "Hodin isn't that good, and I can't ask Al." Depressed, I stomped up the stairs to the deck, hesitating when I realized that though the deck was plywood, the steps themselves were redwood. *Nice*. It was going to be more of an enclosed porch, maybe, and that it wasn't going to be mine made my mood even worse.

"Rachel . . . we have options."

Trent had followed me, and I forced a smile when Edden and Jenks came out the temporary door Finley had put up. It had ROOM 304 on it, and I didn't want to know where they'd stolen it from. One end of the deck had six webbing chairs arranged in a circle around a huge cooler before the old fireplace. Construction equipment had been pushed into a corner, and a huge fan was bolted to the tall ceiling where my kitchen had once been, wires running to a box switch in the open wall. It looked too industrial to be decorative, but maybe that was the theme Finley was going for. It *was* an outdoor space.

"Trent's right," Jenks said from Edden's shoulder, and I slumped, hating it when they ganged up on me. "Constance needs to see him or she'll attack the church. But that mouse potion Pike watched you make will be a good carrot to keep him behaving. I can sit on his shoulder and threaten to douse him if he does anything but sit down, shut up, and enjoy the ride."

Edden ran a hand over his chin, his mustache bunching as he squinted in worry. "I have an impounded van ready downtown. Are you serious about taking Pike into the I.S.? How is threatening to turn him into a mouse going to stop him from saying the wrong thing at the right time and getting you caught? Especially when it has to be ingested, not splashed on him."

Hearing it from Edden, I wasn't sure, either.

Jenks snickered, exchanging a sly look with Trent. "*He* doesn't know that. Fear and bluff got Francis in his own trunk."

I nodded, remembering conning the hapless man into his trunk so I could take his interview with Trent, hell-bent on blackmail to pay off my I.S. contract. But then my smile faded. Francis hadn't survived, taken out by Trent's car bomb to eliminate him as a witness. We had both grown since then, but Constance was going to test that to the limit.

"Pike is smarter than that," Trent said, making Edden frown even more.

"How big a van did you get?" I asked Edden, thinking he looked odd in jeans and a FIB jacket. Just an average guy with a pistol in a hidden-carry holster. "Maybe he can stay with you."

Eyes wide, Edden put a protesting hand in the air. "No. Not even spelled or cuffed. I can't protect him against a death threat. I drove past two groups of them on my way here. You're the only reason they haven't shown up on your doorstep to finish him off."

Trent tugged me into him, smiling. "I wasn't sure until now, but that was a good decision in San Francisco to beat those three off him. They know it's not worth their effort when they can wait until you aren't with him. Constance will know that, too. Maybe it will get you the respect you deserve."

"Or maybe she'll send bigger thugs to kill me," I muttered, and I swear, I heard Etude chuckle, the faint sound of gravel being crushed coming from the roof.

But my attention went to the temporary door as Stef came out, somehow looking both relaxed and frazzled in her work scrubs with her hair in disarray. "Oh, fabulous," she said, clearly relieved as she saw us. "Rachel, I've got two men insisting—"

"Who?" I said suspiciously, going to stand with Trent as two older elves in suits and ties filed out behind her, their gaze going from us to the obvious construction, and back again. Though appreciably older than Trent, they looked remarkably similar to him apart from their docked ears, each having that wispy blond hair, a slim build, narrow face, and of course, the suit that cost more than my yearly shoe budget. Trent's dad hadn't been big on individualism, preferring to stick with something he was confident would work. It made all the elves sort of look the same, and I knew Trent hated it.

"Kaspar, Jakob," Trent said warmly as he paced forward, his hand extended. "So good to see you." He shook hands with the one in the blue suit, then gave the other a professional half hug, all the while shaking his hand. Beaming, he turned to include me. "Rachel. Edden. This is Kaspar and Jakob, two of the more open-minded high priests in the dewar."

"Nice to meet you," Edden said, and Jenks rose up and away from him when the captain leaned forward to shake the two men's hands.

I stayed where I was, forcing a bland smile. "Hi," I said, making a lame wave. Maybe I should shake their hands, but I wasn't fond of the dewar, and they weren't fond of me.

Trent jumped when Stef slammed the door as she went inside, and then he forged ahead, clearly determined to make the best of this. "I'm surprised to see you, but in hindsight, I probably shouldn't be."

The man in the gray suit, Kaspar, if I remembered right, turned to me. "We're here to see Ms. Morgan, actually, but you being present is fortuitous."

"Oh." Trent took a step back, brow slightly furrowed. It was an obvious invitation for me to come forward, but I didn't move and Jenks snickered, his sparkles a brilliant silver dusting down Edden's front as he sat on the older man's shoulder.

"It wasn't my fault that Zack got abducted," I said quickly. "Landon let them in."

Kaspar grimaced, glancing at Jakob as if I'd confirmed something they already knew. "Which continues to be a great . . . source of . . . pain," he said, his words bobbling when he noticed the flower in my hair. "Ah, Landon has been restrained," he added. "Jakob and I are here in an official capacity to ask if you'd consider helping us recover Zack and his bodyguard."

Dude, I thought, glancing at Jenks when his wings rasped in surprise. They were coming to me for help? An image of Nash, gutted on Piscary's table, flashed through me. "I've been working toward Zack's release, but it's a sensitive situation and pushing Constance may . . ." My throat caught as I took a breath to tell them it was too late for Nash.

"We've tried reasoning with her," Jakob said, his melodious voice rising like a fickle spring wind. "Coming to you is not a popular decision, but we are here. Asking. Will you help?"

I froze. How could I tell them what Constance had done to Nash? It was horrific, and it felt as if it was my fault. I'd read the situation wrong, and Nash had died. Again I took a breath, but the words wouldn't come and my eyes began to fill.

Fear that it was too late flashed over them, and Trent stepped forward, sparing me. "Gentlemen," he said, voice even and terrible in its tone of absolute. "I regret to inform you that while Zack appears to remain unharmed, his bodyguard, Nash, was killed yesterday in the service of protecting him."

"Yesterday?" Kaspar breathed, face ashen as he looked at Jakob. "He was alive when our agents stormed Piscary's and were repelled."

Shock flickered over me. "Wait. You attacked Constance?" I echoed, and I looked at Jenks, my guilt for Nash's death seeming to swirl and eddy. It hadn't been me and that damned lily that pushed Constance into disemboweling Nash. It had been the dewar's clumsy attempts. "You attacked Constance? When you knew it would make things worse? What were you thinking!"

Kaspar colored at the anger in my voice. "We thought it worth the risk."

"What do you think now?!" I exclaimed. Relief filled me. It hadn't been my fault. Nash's death hadn't been my fault.

Trent cleared his throat. "Ah, Rachel has since recovered Nash's body and laid it to rest with what I believe are the original burial rites of our ancestors, in honor to his ultimate sacrifice. What we all believe in."

My gaze shot to the back door when two vampires in work clothes came out and began puttering among the assembled tools. Tall and lean, they looked a lot like Pike, but I relaxed when Jenks saw my concern and gave me the "we're good" sign we used while on a run. He knew who they were.

"I believe the burial rites are over two thousand years old," Trent said, having noticed the workmen as well, but clearly having dismissed them as "staff" and able to be ignored with impunity. "Returned to us through Rachel's continued and ceaseless efforts to improve demon and elf relations."

Which was stretching it, but yeah. I *liked* living in reality, and the best way to ensure that continued was to keep hammering at the prejudice caused by five thousand years of war.

"Is this true?" Kaspar said. His eyes were riveted to my flower as if guessing what it was.

The workmen's clattering was getting louder, and I stifled a wash of annoyance. "I have no reason to think otherwise," I said. "It was an elven spell. It summoned mystics, and they took him." I slipped the bronze-colored flower from my hair and held it out. "This grew in the spot. A gift from the deceased to the living."

Kaspar's fingers shook, his green eyes closing as he breathed its sweet smell. They were rimmed with tears when he handed it to Jakob. "It's the *cor mors*," he whispered, naming it.

The *burrrrrb* of a power tool jerked me stiff, and I gave

the offending vampire a glare. Grinning, he showed me his fangs to remind me of Pike. When you got down to it, there really wasn't much difference in many of the vampires, either, since they'd been bred by their masters to fit a certain look: slim, sexy, tall. Scarred.

My lips pressed in thought, and my gaze went from the two workmen to Kaspar and Jakob standing with Trent, looking like relatives at a family reunion. Constance was hitting Cincinnati with both barrels. The loss of Zack would send the elves into a downward spiral as they were forced to follow a corrupt, morally bankrupt leader. The lack of the Brimstone would do the same to the vampires by way of chemical blackmail.

We needed both Zack and Trent's Brimstone back. We needed one hell of an idea. And as I looked at the vampires behind me, and then the elves before, I got one.

"I might have an idea," I said softly, but only Jenks perked up. Edden, Trent, and the two dewar representatives were deep into a conversation discussing Nash's sacrifice and the peace he found in his honor-strewn burial. Frankly, I thought Nash could not have cared less. His only concern had been Zack, and it had killed him. Any peace found in funerals was for the survivors.

"I have an idea," I said again, louder, and this time Trent turned, his stance easing. "But I'm going to need everyone's help. You're good with magic, right?" I directed this at Kaspar, and he blinked, trying to keep up with my jumping thoughts.

"It's about time," Jenks said from Edden's shoulder, and Kaspar pulled himself straight.

"I am a Kallasea scholar," Kaspar said haughtily. "I've taught ley line studies to—"

"Good. Great," I said, interrupting him. "It's basically plan B, but with some added sparkle. Constance is still camped out at the I.S. because of that lily stink, right? We can work with that. Pike is going to walk me in there under the flag of compliance. I'll tell him I'm willing to talk to Constance about, say . . . compensation for me leaving Cincinnati and the Hollows. He'll know I'm lying, but he'll take me to her if only to get back under her protection."

Jenks flashed a brilliant silver. "As if he managed to seduce the demon."

"Wait up," Trent said, worried. "If you go into the I.S., what's to get you out again?"

"He tried to seduce you?" Edden interrupted, looking appalled. "Why? Other than the obvious," he added, then flushed when Jenks whispered in his ear.

"Ah . . ." Trent said, clearly not liking the idea.

"Which will free you, Kaspar, Jakob, and Edden to retrieve the Brimstone and get it on the street where it belongs," I said to Trent.

"You want to be a distraction?" Jenks said in disbelief. Which I totally got. I was never a distraction—distracted, yes, but never a distraction.

"Mmmm, this idea has questionable merit," Trent said, clearly uneasy. "As soon as you cross that seal, you'll be searched and strapped. Helpless."

I nodded. "Agreed. It's the only way they'll let me talk to Zack to 'convince' him to comply with Constance."

Kaspar stiffened, even though I'd made finger quotes around *convince*.

"Then it's plan B," Jenks said merrily, wings rasping. "Grab the fish and run like hell."

Distraction, hell. I'm the main event. "I'll find Zack. Get him out," I said, and Jakob bristled.

"Kaspar and I will find Zack," Jakob said. "You and Trent will retrieve the Brimstone."

"Constance won't let you in to see him," I said harshly. "She owns the tower. Besides, Brimstone is *not* a distraction. The vampires need it as much as you need Zack to keep Cincinnati stable. You already tried for him and failed, getting his bodyguard mutilated and killed before Zack's eyes because you pissed her off. When there is a life in the balance, you send your best man or woman—"

"Or pixy," Jenks interrupted.

"Or pixy," I continued. "With all respect, gentlemen," I

said, hands on my hips as they stared at me in anger and frustration. "You tried and failed, then came to me because you know I can do it. *You* get the Brimstone. Jenks and I will get Zack. Everyone is happy." Except Constance, but, unlike Pike, I wasn't here to make her life roses and cream.

Kaspar took a breath, and I pushed up into his space.

"That is how it is going to run," I said, looking at his features so much like Trent's it was scary, "or it's not going to happen."

"I will *not* help vampires when our high priest is being threatened by them," Kaspar said.

"That's right." I stared up at him, my expression cross. "You're retrieving the Brimstone to help Cincinnati. I'm going to need multiple distractions to get Zack out of there, not just one. Pike knows we want the Brimstone, which is why he won't suspect our goal is also Zack." I backed off, brow furrowed at his continued ugly expression.

"You can't do any magic when you're strapped," Trent said, clearly not liking this. "And there will be too many for you to physically overpower, especially alone."

I smiled, fingering the potions in my pocket. "Jenks will be with me. And I'm not planning on overpowering anyone. Pike saw me helpless when I was strapped at Alcatraz. He'll think I'm contained, but as long as I'm not soaked in salt water, a potion will change me whether I'm strapped or not." I took out a vial and held it between two fingers. "Jenks can get one to Zack, and we will escape through the ducts as mice."

"As what?" Kaspar bellowed, and Jenks rose up, dust a brilliant silver. "That is insane!"

"Insane works when nothing else does," I said, glancing through the open rafters at the belfry and Etude on the roof. "Unless you keep shouting and tell Pike what I'm going to do."

"Rachel." Trent took my hand, pulling my attention to him. "This works on paper, but you need two potions. You will be searched, and Jenks can only carry one."

"I'm going to put them into splat gun pellet refills," I

said. "They're small enough to hide under my tongue or between my teeth and cheek. I break it when I need it. It's light enough for Jenks to carry, and it won't break if it's dropped. It needs a lot of pressure. A bite will do it."

"Sweeter than newling piss," Jenks said, wings a gossamer blur.

But Edden was shaking his head. "Everyone knows me. Rachel, I can drop you off, but other than that, I'm out."

"Not necessarily." I smiled, glad the workmen had stopped dinking around with the tools and were listening, heads tilted, an eager, waiting light in their eyes. I was going to need their help, too. "Kaspar, Jakob, this is where you come in," I said, looking first at the older elves, then over Trent's shoulder to include the workmen. "You all look close enough to be brothers. With a little magical makeup and the right clothes, an I.S. grunt won't know the difference between you and Trent at a quick glance."

Jenks rose up in excitement. "This isn't plan B. You're pulling a pearl-with-the-peas."

My eyebrows rose. "I don't know that one," I said, and Jenks grinned all the wider.

"You're going to flood the tower with fakes so the real one gets where they need to go."

"That's it," I said, and Trent sighed as if taking on a burden. "Plan C. The dewar can supply the Trents, and if some of my taller guests with fangs are willing, we have enough vampires to glamour to look like Pike. Edden?" I turned to him, and the man's eyes widened in alarm. "How would you like to be Doyle for a day? He's about your size and he's got enough clout to take anything out of the I.S. in a van."

Trent shifted from foot to foot. "Let's say we do this . . ." he said slowly. "Pike is under a death threat. What about his assassins? Anyone pretending to be him will be in danger."

"Which won't be a problem when they're in the I.S. tower," I said, hoping it wasn't a wish, but the truth. "Just make sure everyone knows how to break the charms with salt water. If they get caught, the most they will be charged with is using an illegal doppelganger charm." My pulse quickened. This was going to work. Jenks could get us out of the tower in ten minutes through the ductwork, in a car in fifteen. Back at the church in thirty.

Kaspar and Jakob stared at me as if I had lobsters crawling out of my ears, but Trent, used to my schemes, looked understandably worried.

"Sweet Jesus. I'm going to pinch Brimstone from the I.S.," Edden half whispered.

"I could really use your help," I said to Kaspar, the man clearly not sold on my plan. "But if you don't want to get involved, could you at least provide the doppelganger curses to add to the confusion?"

"I'm not afraid," Kaspar huffed. "But a bad plan is not made good by magic."

True, I thought, but it wasn't a bad plan. "A dozen or so Pikes and Trents running around will make a difference. Are you seriously going to let your pride stop me from rescuing Zack?" I said, and Kaspar's eyes narrowed. "I'm the one taking the greater risk by walking into a tower full of hostile vampires. All you have to do is break into evidence and steal a few hundred kilos of Brimstone."

"That's the problem, Rachel," Trent said softly. "You're taking all the risk."

"Maybe," I said, anxiety easing into me like poison. "But they'll be waiting for you. Pike knows we want it, and he's too smart to not know that's why I agreed to take him home."

No one said anything as the *burrrrrb, burrrrrb* of the power driver came and went behind me. "Will you do it?" I said, looking at Kaspar and Jakob. "We're a little short on time and they're counting on Pike seducing me this afternoon."

"Kaspar, I think we should," Jakob said, and Kaspar spun. Trent's expression emptied as the two men began to argue. I wasn't listening. I only had to convince Trent. They'd follow him. They'd come to me for help and Trent was their bloody Sa'han whether they liked it or not.

Frowning, Trent took my elbow and turned me away. "I don't like you being that small. The world is so big."

Jenks's wings rasped as he hovered beside us. "I've got her back."

"I'll be okay," I said, hoping I wasn't overextending myself. "Its effect will be threefold. One, if we get the Brimstone, it will alleviate the pressure on the vampires. No one should have to make a choice between what they feel is right, and survival."

Trent's head went down. Before I met him and smacked him around, he used to hang that over people to gain power. They turned on him as soon as they could. Lesson learned, hopefully.

"Two, we will get Zack free from that crazy whack-job," I added, and Kaspar looked up from his argument with Jakob.

"And the last, Rache?" Jenks asked, and I hesitated.

That it would show Constance that I wasn't a pushover? That I could handle the city? That I wouldn't stand by and do nothing if she tried to hurt the people of Cincinnati in a freaking power play? *Or am I doing this to prove I'm the bigger bully?*

"Yeah. I've been meaning to talk to you about number three," I said, and Trent's expression went flat. "This latest thing with the Brimstone . . . I can't allow her to take Cincinnati," I said, and Jenks's wings shifted pitch, an odd gray dust slipping from him. "She's ruled by her delusions, hurting the people she's supposed to protect. I'm not going to kill her," I added when Edden stirred uneasily. "But I'm going to have to force her out." I looked at Trent, wincing. "And then somehow keep the vampires in line as a demon subrosa, because if this is what the DC vamps are going to send us . . ."

Trent grimaced. "This is the last time I take a week off to go to the coast."

Edden's eyes pinched. "What's a demon subrosa?"

I glanced at the men circling me, their doubt, anger, and worry all obvious. "It's the demon equivalent of a city master vampire, both protector and enforcer, but honestly, the Cincy

vamps do a good job at policing themselves." I winced at
Kaspar's sudden agitation. "It's a break-glass-in-case-of-
emergency position."

"A demon can't be Cincinnati's master anything," Kaspar said. "We will not allow it!"

"Hey!" Jenks shouted, a burst of silver drawing all eyes
to him. "You came to her. She's already doing the job, so
sit down, *shut* up, and maybe she's got something you can
do to help get back your ancient soul stuffed in a kid before
Constance binds him!"

I winced as Edden grinned and Trent ducked his head
and hid a smile behind a soft cough. Jakob pulled Kaspar
two steps away, whispering as the older elf glared at me.
Finally Kaspar nodded, and I exhaled in relief. I didn't
want the job, but Constance could not be allowed to stay.

"My goal is Zack," I said as Kaspar tugged at his sleeves
and bobbed his head. "I can't get him out of there without
the dewar's support. Will you help? I need volunteers from the
dewar to help fill the tower with Trent and Pike look-alikes.
There are no guarantees, and if you can't pull it off, you
might land in I.S. jail. Actually, I'd count on it."

Jenks's wings rasped in the silence, and behind Trent,
the two eavesdropping vampires gave me a solemn nod. My
pulse quickened. I had a growing suspicion that most of the
vampires here were not simply looking for three meals and
a cot. David had been right. They'd been here all the time,
waiting for direction, and my breath shook in my lungs.
Damn, why me?

"Zack is our new beginning," Kaspar said, looking ill.
"I will lobby for support for this plan, but I do *not* support
you taking an official demon subrosa position."

It was probably the best I'd get. I knew they were desperate for Zack, and the return of one of their most treasured
losses—the funeral rites, given freely without expectation of
a returned favor—would probably go a long way.

"Yes!" Jenks shrilled, startling all of us. "I'll go tell the
vamps. They've been itching to do something, and vampire
jail is more fun than here. Plan C. Woo-hoo!"

I managed a smile as he darted to the firepit, and I touched Trent's shoulder. "I'll leave you to the details," I said, thinking they'd rather take direction from him than me. Squaring my shoulders, I turned to the waiting elves. "Kaspar. Jakob," I added. "I'm looking forward to working with you. If you'll excuse me. I need to see about Pike."

"Um, Rachel?" Trent asked, and I stopped, wondering at the odd smile threatening to show. "How many doppelgangers do you want?"

From the firepit, there was a whoop of anticipation, and I shrugged. "As many as volunteer. Make sure they know to break the charm before they leave the I.S. or if they get caught. Pike's assassins are still out there."

Nodding, Trent turned back to Kaspar and Jakob.

My steps were slow in thought as I went into the church. Steam flowed from under the bathroom door, and I heard the chug-chug of the washer as I went by. The entire church smelled like witch, Were, vampire, and fabric softener. A small gathering of people were clustered in the sanctuary, chatting pleasantly as they worked on preparing dinner for whoever showed up. I had no idea where the groceries were coming from, and I gave them a thankful wave as I headed for the foyer, leaving an excited, whispering conversation in my wake. It was really weird. I had no idea who these people were, but they were doing what needed to be done, and I appreciated it. *Me, the demon subrosa? This is going to go just great.*

The door to the belfry staircase groaned as I opened it, and I made a point to hit every squeaky board on the way up, not wanting to burst in on Pike and Etude unannounced, but really, the gargoyle had probably been following my progress since I left the back deck.

"Etude? Pike?" Tapping my knuckle on the door, I went in. "You both awake?"

"Seriously?" Pike said from the fainting couch. "You think I'm going to nap?"

My gaze went from Pike reclining on the couch where

Trent had moved him to Etude watching him through the window. "Thanks, Etude. Did he give you any trouble?"

"No." Etude's low voice rumbled to make the bell over our heads resonate. "We talked about sunrises and my youngest son so he couldn't hear your conversation. It's a good idea."

A flash of guilt rose, vanishing at Etude's steadfast belief in me. Back stiff, I turned to Pike, my hands on my hips. "Hi, Pike."

Pike made a low growl of unease. "I don't like the sound of that," he said, and Etude's laugh rumbled through me like distant thunder.

My hand touched the vials through my pocket, and I remembered the pain of turning into a mink to raid the I.S. files, and then, later, caught in Trent's office and tormented. *I can do this.* Uneasy, I shoved his legs over so I could sit beside him and he could see me without straining.

"Sorry about the extended immobility." *Start with an apology. Nice, Rachel. That's sure to impress him,* I thought sourly. "Congratulations. You convinced me to leave Cincinnati," I added lightly.

Pike's eyes were pupil dark, but it wasn't as if he could move. "I did, huh?"

"Yep." I grabbed his shoulders and, straining, hauled him up a few more inches. "And this afternoon, you and I are going to walk right in the front door of the I.S. and down to Constance to tell her. Your attempt to seduce and bind me failed, but you did manage to convince me to concede Cincinnati to Constance nevertheless."

"Okay. No," Pike said, clearly not liking me manhandling him up like that, even if his chin was no longer crunched against his chest. "That's not going to happen. And if you spell me to force me into it, her people will be able to tell I'm under duress. You will be her toy until she tires of you, and then you will be mine. If I can keep her from killing you outright."

My thoughts flashed to Joni, her lipstick smeared into a smile, tears of fear streaking her face. "Did you not just hear me say you win?" I stifled a jump when Jenks darted in the open window. "I see the error of my ways, blah, blah, blah. All I want is compensation for having to move." I rubbed my finger and thumb together, and Pike frowned.

"Good try," he said, his black gaze dangerous and following Jenks as the pixy went to sit with Bis. "You're a distraction so Kalamack can steal his Brimstone. Obviously."

I beamed at him, resisting the urge to tweak his chin. "Come on, Pike," I wheedled. "You'd be helping free Cincinnati from Constance."

"I want her to hold Cincinnati. The stronger she is, the safer I am."

Etude shifted his bulk, his nails scraping the new shingles. "You look safe where you are, little shadow," he rumbled, and Jenks snickered.

Maybe short term, I thought. The woman had crossed from undead crazy to can't-work-with-this crazy. "I need that Brimstone to keep Cincinnati from siding with Constance," I said, knowing he didn't care. "But if you need convincing, don't forget that you already told her you broke me. If you don't bring me in for her to gloat over and parade on TV, she's going to skin you alive and lap the blood from every inch of you."

"I never told her that," Pike said, but his confidence faltered as I took his cracked phone off the dresser, held it to his face to unlock it, and then began to scroll.

"Sure you did," I said as I studied the pictures of people he'd been talking with lately, memorizing their names in case we ran into them. There was Vince, a squat man with bulging muscles and a mustache. Someone named Kip, thin with white hair and a fresh, young face that most of the older vamps found too young to appreciate. Shawn, a muscular blond, and Leigh, who could be his brother. And finally, Constance herself, who didn't have a picture, but instead an icon of a red-hot chili pepper. It was weird. Constance's camarilla seemed to be borrowed from everyone else. There was no theme here, which was unusual for so old an undead. Perhaps she kept bleeding her children to death and had to adopt unwanted children from other lines. It might explain what Pike was doing with her. *God . . . what an ugly thought.*

"What are you doing?" Pike asked as I opened Constance's thread and began typing.

"Congratulations, Pike. You just convinced me to kiss Constance's ass through good old-fashioned threats. You did it without biting me, though. Points for me." Fingers shifting, I typed in that "I" had been successful and was bringing Rachel in at five thirty, right before the six o'clock news. "I bet she could even arrange a news conference at the I.S. to hear my statement. I'm even willing to try to convince Zack to do the same thing if she gives me enough money to relocate," I added, planting the seed that would get me in with the kid. A few more taps, and my smile widened. "A-a-a-and done!"

"She won't believe that," he said, but his phone was already vibrating.

"She doesn't have to," I said as I looked to see it was Constance. "All I need is her distracted for thirty minutes." Eyes down, I typed back that I, being Pike, was busy.

Pike's brow was furrowed when I set the phone back on the dresser and smiled. "She's going to give me hell for not taking that call," he said.

"Sorry?"

His breath came faster. "It's not too late to make that text real. Come on, Rachel. I don't know what you think you can accomplish here," he said, but I wasn't the one immobilized on the fainting couch. "Soon as you reach the I.S., you will be strapped and helpless."

"Like that hasn't happened before." I stood up, hands on my knees as I loomed over him. "Sure, Constance is a bitch and no one wants to cross her—much less talk to her—but I probably know more people involved in the nitty-gritty of the I.S. than you and she combined ever will. You have a point, though." I fixed his lapels, and his eyes darkened in anger. "I can't drive Constance out unless Cincinnati gets behind me. And for that, I need the Brimstone on the street, not locked up in I.S. evidence, doled out to only those who follow her."

"You are going to try to take the city?" he said, incredulous. "I thought you were all about the letter of the law."

"I'm not killing her, fang boy. I'm asking her to leave." I hesitated. "Politely. At first."

He stared, eyes wide and brown in disbelief. His phone dinged, and I looked at it, smiling. Constance had texted back: "Make her get rid of the stench at Piscary's."

Feeling sassy, I went to the dresser, fingering the ley line spell for a moment before pulling the pin from the ring and breaking the curse. From overhead, the bell seemed to tremble, and I stifled a shiver.

"You'd let yourself be caught so Kalamack can recover his Brimstone?" he said derisively. "He gets to sell his drug, and you get locked in Constance's bathroom."

"Yeah. Stupid idea. You're probably right," I said as I turned back around. His hair had fallen into his eyes, and I resisted the urge to arrange it. I hated it when my captors did that to me. "We have a few hours before we have to go," I said as I stood over him. Time enough for the dewar to make some doppelganger charms and me to load a few splat gun pellets with potion. "Try to get some sleep. It's going to be a busy night."

"You're going to hand me over to one of my brothers, aren't you," he said suddenly, and I blinked, lips parting. "Use the money to try to buy her off."

"Is that what you think of me?" I said, truly shocked. "No, and to prove it, I'll let you drive us to the I.S. Good?"

He stared, speechless, and in the calm, bird-filled silence rising up from my garden and graveyard, I grabbed my splat ball kit and headed out, leaving him to mull that over.

CHAPTER

22

MUCH TO MY SURPRISE, PIKE WAS AN ANNOYINGLY NER-vous driver, his usual steadfast confidence utterly absent. Slow and hesitant, he wove through Cincinnati as if he was a blood virgin going through the Hollows after midnight on a dare. His eyes were more often on the rearview mirror than out the front, making me wonder if he knew Jenks was hiding in the back with a splat ball full of mouse potion. But in all fairness, there *were* two cars following us. One had to be Constance's goons, to judge by their belligerent, on-our-bumper attitude. The other was probably Pike's assassins, as they were almost two blocks back and in a nicer car.

Still, I was beginning to regret handing him my keys. That he might think I was taking him to his brothers for the bounty on his head had really bothered me. That I was currently on the phone with Edden, basically lying to Pike via an overheard conversation that we were only after the Brimstone, did not.

At least, I was trying to. Edden had me on hold, and my tongue kept worrying the splat ball/mouse potion tucked between my teeth and gum. If I accidentally swallowed it, I'd be up a creek. I didn't know if it would pass through me unbroken, or if I'd unexpectedly find myself turning into a mouse.

"Rachel?" Edden called from my phone, and I pushed the splat ball back under my tongue. "Sorry about that. You can't get a decent signal in the parking garage, and I had to move to where I could reach a tower. Trent and, ah, his friend are glamouring the van," he said, clearly wanting to keep Kaspar's name out of it. "Holy space cats," he whispered in awe. "No wonder we can't keep up. I'd never be able to tell that wasn't an I.S. vehicle. Damn, even the plate."

His voice became distant as he asked Kaspar how long it would take to turn it back after they fled the I.S. That it was an illegal, white charm went without saying. But when had one of my runs ever not dipped into the gray?

"Remind me to get you a pair of glamour glasses for Christmas," I said when he came back. "It lets you see through just about everything."

Pike's eyes were fixed on the road, but I knew he was listening. As intended.

"Sounds like something I should already have," Edden said, his voice suddenly deeper. Clearly he'd been spelled to look like Doyle. "Trent says we're ready. We're moving." There was a hesitation, and then, "Holy sweet Jesus. Even my voice is different."

I smiled as Kaspar chuckled, and I hoped Pike would assume it was Trent.

"That, Captain, is the difference between a community college degree and a Kallasea scholar."

Yeah, yeah, whatever, I thought sourly, but Edden was clearly impressed as he said, "Never in a million years. Wait until I tell Glenn. Working with the elves to steal Brimstone. I'm going to jail. I know it." He laughed, sounding nothing like himself.

"You won't go to jail for stealing it," Trent said, and I angled the phone to try to hide the conversation. "It's the distributors who they go after. Three months, max."

"Well, you'd know," I said, and Edden grunted his agreement.

"See you at the church with the goods," Edden said. "If it's compromised, the basilica."

"Bye, Edden." I ended the call, and my smile faded. It still felt kind of slipshod to me.

"You didn't really tell me your fallback positions, did you?" Pike said.

"No, of course not." Peeved, I set my phone in the center console for Pike, seeing that as far as Constance knew, he was bringing me in, not the other way around. Reminded of our subterfuge, I dug in my bag to put Pike's phone next to mine. We were almost there, and if he wanted to call and tell them they were about to be raided, more power to him.

But as the shadow of the I.S. tower took us, traffic ground to a halt. Amber lights flashed a few cars ahead, and when I leaned to look, I decided someone was being towed. "Great. Now we're going to be late."

"No . . ." Pike casually took both phones, tucking them in his jacket's inside pocket before stretching to see around the cars. "They're making a parking spot for us."

"Seriously?" I leaned farther as well, eyebrows rising at the vampire directing traffic.

"Yep." Pike sounded tired as we were spotted, and the somewhat squat vampire dressed in black made a motion for us to sit tight while he kept all the other traffic moving— as much as they could with the tow truck there.

"You won't even need to feed the meter," I said, and Pike frowned, his scars making deep furrows. "Is that Vince?"

His lips parted in his surprise, then remembered. "Yeah," he said, hand touching his chest where his phone lay.

I would have given a lot to know what his thoughts were, but I was far more interested in the three blond men in suits currently bunched up at the revolving door, waiting to go in. Two vamps were behind them, their mood cocky and aggressive as they decided to go in through the pull doors instead. *Our doppelgangers,* I thought in a surge of anticipation. Jakob had cut off the dewar volunteers at three. We had eight vamps from the church. It would have to be enough.

The tow truck finally moved out, and Vince waved us in.

I held my bag with its distracting magic paraphernalia tighter as Pike backed into the parking spot. If this didn't go well, I was going to be up a creek. They might douse me in salt water. They might knock me unconscious. I might have done something wrong in stirring the spell and end up inside out. *Trust yourself,* I reminded myself. *Jenks is with you.* But it was hard not to jump when a second vampire in security black tapped my window.

"Last chance to make this real," Pike said, and when I shook my head, he slipped my keys in over the visor in case they needed to move the car. Pulse fast, I opened the door, gaze rising up a seriously stone-faced man.

"Hey!" I yelped when the vamp grabbed my elbow, yanking me up and out while simultaneously taking my purse. "I came to you," I said, then gasped when he shoved me against the car, then shoved me again, holding me there as he slipped a band of charmed silver over my wrist, snicked it tight, and patted me down.

Fear was an unhelped spike in my heart as my contact with the lines severed. I'd been made helpless so many times in the past, and I'd survived them all. But each had left its mark, and I stared across my car's low top at Pike and Vince grinning at each other.

"Vince!" Pike gave the powerfully built man a fist bump. "Good to see your ugly face."

"Welcome back, Pike." Hand on Pike's shoulder, Vince gestured to the tower's door. "Finally got your bitches in line, eh?"

Pike laughed. I stared at him, ignoring the man behind me, his fingers a little too exploratory as he did his job. "So how are you and Veronica?" Pike said, standing in the street with Vince. "Still getting the ice cube?"

"Nope." Vince smiled to show his short fangs. "We be as warm as sunshine now."

Good God, it's only been a day, I thought, seeing their obvious pleasure in each other's company. But that was how vampires were. Ties of found family and loyalty were all that kept them alive when their master went too far—a shared misery their masters heaped upon them that they all told each other was love. My focus blurred as I thought about Pike's probable deep-set, aching need for family, trust, and unquestionable loyalty, and I couldn't help but wonder if he had found that here or if it was just surface.

"So," Vince said, and I stiffened when his eyes landed on me. "Is it true what they say about redheads?"

Pike rubbed his jaw, squinting. "Get me drunk enough, and I'll tell you."

Vince guffawed, and I yelped when the man searching me spun me around, shook my bag into the street, and handed it back to me empty. Pike had my phone, wallet, and splat gun, but everything else was in the gutter. Good thing I hadn't put anything in it I'd really wanted.

I stumbled when the guy who'd searched me gave me a push to follow Pike and Vince. The windows were up in the car, but that had never stopped Jenks before. People were watching, and I didn't like that they thought I was leaving them to Constance's tender mercies even as I tried to find a mix of nervous anger and beaten-down shame for having given in to her.

"You need to let go," I said when the vamp took my elbow to escort me in as if I was a criminal. "You like being able to pick things up with that hand? Scratch your ass?" I said. "Then take it off me."

"Don, let her walk on her own," Vince said, and Don backed off, his gaze full of promise.

"Is she strapped?" Pike said, and when Vince nodded, Pike slowed to a stop, right there in the middle of the sidewalk, his hands at his waist and the wind from the river in his hair. Don settled in behind me, his presence heavy as I stared at Pike, wondering why we weren't going in. Behind him, a street vagrant was picking through what had fallen out of my bag. A hint of pixy dust glimmered, but there was no other sign of Jenks. And still Pike hesitated, eyes narrowed as he calculated something I wasn't privy to.

Finally Pike nodded as if having made a decision. "Morgan is here on pretense," he said, and my jaw clenched, not surprised. "She's a distraction as Kalamack, FIB captain Edden, and at least one other unidentified male try to liberate the Brimstone you intercepted yesterday. But since she's here, we'll get that promise to submit to Constance regardless."

My face warmed as Vince chuckled. Chin high, I held Pike's gaze.

"Then it's a good thing it's not in evidence but at Piscary's loading dock waiting for distribution," Vince said.

It's where? I thought, shock making me pliant when Don grabbed my arm and propelled me to the doors. At Piscary's? Across the river? Son of a fairy-farting whore!

Jenks, I thought, scanning the sidewalk. He was probably inside already and hadn't heard. I had to get a message to Trent. They were walking into a trap, and though we'd expected Pike would tell them about our plans, we hadn't known that the Brimstone had been moved and their efforts would be for naught.

My bootheels thumped as I was propelled to the door, Pike, Vince, and Don behind me. People were getting out of our way, their expressions fearful. It wasn't my vampire security. It was me, giving up, capitulating. Shaking out my hair, I lifted my chin and felt the splat ball under my tongue. Zack. I had to concentrate on Zack. But it was hard knowing that two men I cared about were risking their lives and freedom for something that wasn't even there.

Pike leaned forward to get the door as I reached for it, and I dropped back, hating his smug confidence. "Where is Constance?" he said softly as we went in.

"Tormenting the boy," Vince said with a grimace. "She wants Morgan's confession on the six o'clock news. She's hoping it will convince him to capitulate in time for the late news."

Not happening, I thought. I would have looked at my phone for the time, but it was still in Pike's jacket along with my splat gun and wallet. My mood worsened as we crossed the lobby and I scanned the surrounding people, picking out the plants among the innocents by their misplaced, sly confidence. *Where are you, Jenks?*

"Thank God you're back," Vince said as I was pushed to the front of the security line and shoved through the spell monitor, which glowed a dull green. Uninvoked potions and charms never showed, which was why there was a visual inspection as well. "She's been an unholy terror the last twenty-four. Kip took one for the team last night to keep Joni alive until she forgets about her, but—"

"Is Kip okay?" Pike interrupted, and Vince's gaze slid to me, a flicker of fear dropping down my spine.

"If we can keep her out of Constance's thoughts for a few days."

"Days!" Worry crossed Pike, and he seemed to slump into a different person. Cockiness was replaced with unease, confidence with concern for someone else. It reminded me of Kisten, this other side I was catching a glimpse of.

Vince ducked his head, concerned. "I don't know how you keep her as level as you do."

Pike frowned, his long, scarred face bunching up. "My mother was worse," he said, then put a hand to my back and propelled me forward. "This way, Morgan. You have two minutes to come up with a concession speech. You've seen what Constance will do if she has to force one from you. Best hope she doesn't catch anyone in evidence with which to encourage you."

My thoughts went to Nash, and then Joni with her red-smeared lips and soft whimper of fear. "I know where the elevators are," I muttered, and he gripped my elbow hard enough to make me try to jerk away.

"No mischief, Ms. Morgan," he said, giving me a shove into Don.

"Knock it off!" I said loudly, and heads across the lobby turned. But it was the sparkle of pixy dust that set my pulse racing. *Jenks.*

Empty bag tight in my grip, I went into the elevator. I

had to talk to Jenks. He could get to evidence and tell Trent where the Brimstone was *before* they got themselves in too deep to get out. Pike sidled up beside me, and Vince and Don flanked us.

"Congratulations, Mr. Welroe," Don said as the doors shut. "Constance will be pleased." He took a breath, muttering, "For a fucking moment, anyway."

Vince tapped a button and, seeing which one it was, I stiffened. The media floor. It was down two levels, deep enough that the undead could hang out without risk of light poisoning, but not so deep that the media couldn't get their live feeds to work. Zack and Constance would be lower. Much lower.

I didn't see any pixy dust, but I was sure that Jenks was in the elevator shaft. "It doesn't matter if the Brimstone is at Piscary's," I said as we started down. "I'm not going to make any public announcement. And you can be sure as hell I'm not going to convince Zack to, either."

"He's already seen one person eviscerated," Pike said. "You think he'll sit and watch another?"

"Fine. Put me in front of a live camera," I said with a sneer. "I dare you."

Pike frowned as the elevator dinged, and we all looked forward as the door opened and the noise and warmth of too many people in too small a space rolled in. "There she is!" someone exclaimed, and I winced at the sudden clicking and the glare of a bright spotlight finding us.

Pike leaned to push the button to close the door.

"Ahh . . ." Vince started, and Pike shook his head, eyes narrowed and black hair swinging.

"Constance," Pike said, and Don's lips parted.

Vince, too, was not happy. "She wants Morgan to make an announcement first."

Pike turned, showing some fang as he all but pinned Vince to the wall with his stare. "And I don't want to take Joni's place," he said softly. "Morgan isn't here to capitulate. You put her in front of a camera, and she'll rally the city, not hand it over."

I tightened my death grip on my empty bag as the doors opened up to a brightly lit hallway. We were deep underground now, and my skin tingled at the pheromone residue soaked into the cold tiles. *No wonder Ivy always came home hungry. . . .*

"She needs some convincing yet," Pike said, then gave me a push into the hallway.

"Will you stop shoving?" I said, glaring as I caught my balance. "I came here of my free will."

"And you will die if you don't give it to Constance." Pike pinched my biceps and started forward. His long legs struck a pace that was a shade longer than mine. He was edging into a living vampire's faster reflexes, too, and I had to hustle to keep from being dragged along. Gray and soothing, the walls and floors absorbed the sound. We went through a set of guarded double doors into the lower executive lounge . . . and then I balked as if running into a wall.

But then again, I sort of had. The pheromones were heady, hitting me as if I'd been sipping tequila all day. Instead of relaxing, I stiffened, tingles racing from where Pike held my arm. *Crap, I might be in trouble,* I thought as I felt for that splat gun pellet under my tongue and scanned the beautiful faces turning to us.

I'd never been to the lower, executive floor, but Ivy had told me it was like a perverted pleasure palace, the front looking as any luxurious Fortune 500 lounge would, with bland artwork and a low-key wet bar serviced by professionals who went home at the end of the day the same way they'd come in. Behind it was a maze of rooms, each one more unique and tailored to the undead's varying tastes. The people working there pretty much stayed there. And as I took in the crowded outer lounge, with vampires draped over every square inch as they played court to Constance sitting on the central couch, I quashed a rising worry.

Turning Pike down in my belfry was one thing. Saying no to a master vampire in the belly of the I.S. tower . . . was another.

"It's Pike. And Morgan!" I heard someone say, and Constance looked up, the surrounding conversations silencing until only the enormous TV on the wall playing a pre-news game show was left.

Her white, high-slit, low-cut dress stood out against her dark skin, drawing the eye like a beacon among the gold, black, and red clothing surrounding her. Jewelry hung around her neck, clinking when she turned to us, eyes pupil black and focused with a skin-crawling intensity. Zack sat to her left, and her arm draped over his shoulder as she cuddled him close. Someone had put him in an uncomfortably tight suit and slicked his blond hair back. His tan was obvious amid the predominantly pale faces, and when he met my eyes, his leashed hatred and frustration vanished in surprise.

A woman slumped to Constance's right, her long red hair matted as she pushed against the corner of the couch as if trying to crawl into the cushions to hide. It had to be Joni even though her clothes didn't mimic Constance's anymore. A chill dropped through me as I caught a glimpse of a red-smeared mouth and the new red-rimmed slash under her ear. Constance had been at her. Recently, by the look of it.

That's a different wig, I thought when the pale woman jerked, startled when Constance pulled her arm from Zack and rose in a tinkle of jewelry. The kid slid down the couch and away from her, and my lips parted when I realized Joni was wearing exactly what I had been the first time I'd seen Constance, right down to the vamp-made boots and the big hoop earrings. She'd dressed her doll to look like me, then brutalized her and drank her blood.

Take a picture of her for my album, echoed in my thoughts, chilling me. Crap on toast, Constance had this psychological warfare down to a science. Trouble was, I didn't think it was intentional. Intentional implied a plan, and this shell of a woman had only a savage instinct left to her.

Hands at her hips, Constance sent her gaze from me to Pike. He had inclined his head slightly to lower his eyes. It was a surprisingly obedient gesture, even if his hands were clenched. "I gave instruction for Morgan to make a statement on tonight's early news," she said, her high voice holding anger, and people at the back began to slip out the side doors. "Why is she here?"

"She came on false pretense," Pike said, voice low and oily. "To provide a distraction while Kalamack steals his Brimstone. If I put her before a camera, she will rally the rabble."

"I see." Black eyes narrowed, Constance sent her red fingernails to play with her necklaces. "Turn off the television. We will be entertaining ourselves tonight."

I doubted she meant board games or dice, and I kept my breathing slow as the soft murmur of the TV vanished. More people were excusing themselves until it was easy to pick out the hard-core security detail hiding among the wine-drinking, slit-skirt, power-tie fluff that kowtowed to her, both the living and the dead. Two stone-faced thugs settled in behind Zack, and he scowled up at them, his fingers working the band of charmed silver about his wrist.

More security began closing in around Constance, and as she berated them to stay back, my skin began to crawl. It wasn't her, and I scanned the lobby for someone not moving. *There you are,* I mused, finding one of her attending undead watching me, a faint hint of amusement and speculation on his young face. Though in a suit and tie, he didn't look like the kind who would be attracted to the chaos and blood sport that Constance clearly enjoyed.

Seeing me pick him out, he tilted his head, whispering something to a dark-skinned, hardly clothed woman draped over him. She was clearly a living vampire, and when she scoffed—at me—he dumped her off his lap and stood, tugging his suit coat down as he strode away. The woman shot me an ugly look and hustled after him, her overdone jewelry swaying between her almost escaping breasts. People watched them go, their own fear growing.

"You came to kill me?" Constance said, looking small with three guards behind her.

Pike gripped my arm again, and I let him. I was probably safer that way.

"I'm not here to kill you," I said. "I'm here to escort you to the city limits. Withholding Brimstone to force obedience shows a complete disregard for the people you're supposed to be protecting."

Constance laughed, her fingers playing amid a tray of sweets on the low table. The sound was practiced, but I could hear the madness in it. "Mmmm. We will have so much fun," she said as she bent low and chose one. "I wasn't given this city to protect. I was given it to use, and you don't have the strength to get me to leave."

My eyebrows rose. "I got you to leave Piscary's."

Pike made a soft grunt of dismay as a wave of outrage flowed over Constance, making her ugly until she gathered it to her like a cloak, shifting her shoulders to settle it more firmly about her. "So you did," she said softly, making me wonder if it had been that great of an idea after all. "The vampires who don't look to me don't matter," she said as she came forward, a chocolate between two fingers. "If they die, they die. That is how the family prospers and the rest fade to nothing."

She stopped before me, her eyes even with mine as she stood on the top of the low stair that separated us. "There's no Brimstone to be had," she said, her high voice hard. "Your lover is fighting for his life, and you are here with me. Would you like a chocolate?"

Zack had gone pale, eyes widening when I looked at him. The guards had tensed when Constance had moved closer, but it was the chocolate he was afraid of. *What has he seen? Is this one of her games?*

"No, thanks," I said as Pike's grip tightened. The candy had a little curlicue of drizzled red sugar, and I stared at it as if it was poison. "Allergies," I lied.

"I insist." Constance held it out on her palm. "Joni says I need to learn to share more." She turned to the woman on the couch. "Isn't that so, Joni, love?" she added, and the woman buried her face in the corner of the couch, pulling her legs up into a fetal position. More people were leaving, their heads down and their paces fast.

Pike's grip became ironhard. "Thanks, but no," I said, not liking the soft shake in my voice. There was a loud and certain click of a door shutting as Constance's retinue winnowed down to a handful of her followers too frightened or desperate for her attention to leave.

Constance smiled, playing up to those who remained. "You think it's been tampered with. How quaint." Small red mouth opening, Constance took a bite, her long, undead fangs showing as she closed her eyes and moaned in pleasure, a hand to her chest. "I have these flown in special. Try one. I insist."

I shook my head. I wanted to back up, but Pike wouldn't let me. Zack looked scared.

"Don't move," Pike whispered, and fear slid between my thought and reason as Constance leaned closer.

"Open your mouth," she demanded, and my knees almost buckled when she breathed on my neck. My scar flamed to life, pleasure rippling down my entire side.

"No," I ground out between my clenched teeth. God, it felt good. It would be unending ecstasy, fire and ice. I would be alive, filled with feeling. But it would be a lie, and I closed my eyes, not wanting to see myself in the black depths of her pupils. "I will not," I moaned.

"Don't eat it, Rachel!" Zack shouted, and my eyes flashed open at the sudden smack of flesh on flesh. Zack was staring at one of the guards in hatred, his hand pressed to his cheek.

Annoyed, Constance took a rocking step back, that chocolate between her fingers. "It's not your fault you failed to bind Morgan," she said to Pike. "She's stronger than you."

I jerked, shocked when her hand flashed out to painfully grip my jaw. "Open," she said as she pulled me closer. Pike held my arms to my sides. "Open your fucking mouth!" she demanded.

On the couch, Joni sobbed, crumpled and forgotten as she relived something. Zack, too, looked terrified. It hit me like nothing else and Constance moaned when fear swamped me. It soaked into her like a drug as her pupils widened to an unreal black. But I couldn't help it.

Instinct kicked in. I lashed out with my foot. She dodged it, never letting go of me. Pike hooked a foot in mine, and all three of us went down.

"I'll do it. I'll do it! Let her go!" I heard Zack say. I hit the floor hard, gasping as a fist slammed into my middle. My eyes teared, and suddenly my mouth was full of something sweet.

No! I thought frantically, but they were holding me down, Constance's dark hand forcing my jaw closed.

"Eat it," she said, black eyes alight as the pleasure of dominating me coursed through her.

I struggled, but Pike forced my shoulders into the flat carpet and I couldn't move. My eyes never left Constance. Memory swam up and I was nine again, held down on the playground dirt and forced to eat a worm. But, unlike the worm, chocolate melts.

Oh God. It's made with blood! I realized as a flat, coppery taste filled my mouth. I began to struggle in earnest, grunting in anger. Pike's jaw was set in determination as he held me there, whispering for me to just eat the damn chocolate, that it wouldn't kill me. It wasn't human blood.

It didn't matter. It was the principle of the thing. But I had to swallow or choke on it.

They knew the instant I did.

Arms pulled away, and I sprang to my feet, spitting what was left out on their perfect gray carpet. Two men held Zack to the couch. His expression was desperate and the new red mark on his face stood out like a flag. He'd seen this before. *Nash* . . .

"Son of a bastard," I choked out as I wiped my mouth. "What the hell is wrong with all of you?" And then I froze. The mouse potion was gone. I'd swallowed it.

"That depends who you ask," Constance said, a safe eight feet back. "But it does prove that Joni is wrong. I can share," she added, smiling at me to show her fangs.

"I'll do it," Zack choked out, slumped and beaten. "I'll sign whatever you want. Don't touch her again." He sat, face pale and eyes haunted as he shook off the guard's hands. "Promise me she walks out of here unharmed and unchanged, and I'll say whatever you want."

"Zack, no," I said, seeing the memory of what they'd done to Nash bringing him down.

"Mmmm." Jewelry clinking, Constance went to give his cheek a little pat. "Maybe there's something to this sharing after all. See if it's too late to get the dewar brat on the last spot," she directed, and two security agents bolted to the door.

My lips curled in hate as she settled herself in one of the side chairs as if it was a throne. I seemed to have been forgotten as everyone except Pike surrounded her as if ants around a queen. I wanted to talk to Zack, but Pike wouldn't let me move. This was not how I had envisioned this playing out, and the sweet taste in my mouth made my stomach roil. Everything that could go wrong was, and my heart sank when Vince had a hushed conversation on his phone and Constance turned to look at him behind her.

"Have they gotten her lover?" she said, voice high. "Morgan, does he like chocolate?"

"Ah, no, ma'am." Vince backed up, eyes wide when Constance stood shockingly fast. Pike's grip on me tightened, and I took it, glad she wasn't looking at me. "They, ah, fled," Vince continued. "They abandoned Morgan at the first sign of us."

Constance's anger vanished and Vince exhaled, relieved when the undead woman returned her attention to me, her chancy sanity restored. "You will make the desired concession," she said. "Leave Cincinnati. Or die here."

"You just keep thinking that," I said, and Constance's eyes narrowed. *They left!* I thought, heart singing. Jenks had gotten to them in time. Trent would never abandon me.

"They knew it wasn't there," Pike whispered, and my skin tingled when he leaned closer, whispering, "How did you get the message to them? Was it that pixy?"

"Ah, ma'am," Vince said, phone to his ear again. "Good news. We have him."

Constance frowned. "Did he leave or not?"

"He did," Vince said, his confusion clear. "We have it on video, but security is telling me they have Kalamack in custody. Ah, we also have him pinned down at records. And on the roof?"

"Which is it? There aren't three of him," Constance said, and then she frowned, her black eyes coming to me as she figured it out.

I tried not to smile as Pike sighed. The plan was working. At least, their part of it was, and I fidgeted, not liking that I was stuck in the executive lounge. But it was then that I spotted the faintest hint of pixy dust spilling from a side table lamp. Jenks.

My pulse leapt. I might be stuck here, but Jenks could free Zack. That was what mattered.

"That's impossible!" Vince said into the phone, and I beamed as the confused man looked at Pike. "He's standing right in front of me."

"What is it?" Constance demanded, and her own security dropped back, trying to stay out of the way.

"Keep me informed," Vince said as he closed out his phone. Hand shaking, he turned to Constance. "The I.S. has detained three people looking like Pike. There seem to be at least six different versions of Mr. Kalamack as well, but the numbers of each are still growing."

Constance pulled her lips back in a snarl, oblivious to the pixy dust in the lamp. "Zack isn't going to sign anything," I said to distract them from it. "And neither am I," I added as I tapped my foot in the code Jenks and I had agreed on for "go."

I would have sworn that Pike saw it, but he said nothing.

Constance's longer fangs glinted. "Perhaps I need to share more with you," she said, but all eyes were on her, and no one but Pike and I saw Jenks shoot up out of the light, flying high along the top of the ceiling until he hovered right over Zack. He made a sharp snap of his wings for

Zack's attention . . . then dropped the splat ball, right into his lap.

"Everyone, stop!" Constance said, fear flicking over her. "I hear a pixy."

Zack jumped, fingering the little blue ball, not a clue where it had come from.

"Damn right you did," I said, stumbling when Pike yanked me to him. "Zack, bite it!"

"No!" Constance exclaimed, eyes wide. "Stop him!"

But it was too late, and, chin high, Zack fumbled it into his mouth and bit down.

"No!" she shrieked, her grasping reach jerking back when Zack dissolved into a pearly white mist laced with purple and green. His suit collapsed to the couch in a soft hush, and his shoes fell over on the gray carpet. "He's gone!" Constance turned to me, hunched and eyes wild. "Where is he? What did you do to him!"

Silent, I watched the small bump in Zack's shirt move to the edge of the couch and, with a little thump, hit the floor under his pants' cuff.

"My God!" Pike said in awe. "He's a mouse!"

Constance shrieked, utterly terrified as she jumped up onto the chair behind her, her high-pitched screaming going right through my head as she pointed at Zack sitting beside his shoe, the kid clearly disoriented. Joni pulled her face from the couch, slack-jawed and blinking.

"Get your furry ass moving!" Jenks shouted as he dropped to hover right before him, and Zack fell over, arms and legs struggling to coordinate.

"Catch him!" Constance shrilled, and three agents jolted into motion, hunched and reaching. "Someone catch him!"

"Zack, run!" I shoved at Pike, but he didn't let go, and we fell back, hitting the floor together. "Follow Jenks!"

Zack looked at the three men inching forward, their hands outstretched to snare him. I lay flat on the floor, helpless, as Jenks hovered beside him, sword drawn, ready to defend him. "Run!" I shouted again, and Zack the mouse eyed me, shook his head, stood on his hind legs with his tail braced behind him, and . . . squeaked.

I gasped, shocked when a wave of force burst up and out from him, pushing the chairs, couches, and even Jenks back four feet. Constance hit the floor, tumbling into the wall where she lay, stunned. The three security personnel were knocked aside, and Joni began to laugh, raspy and pained as she held an arm to her middle.

Pike swore softly. We had already been on the floor, but the blast had shaken him, and his grip on me had eased. I found Zack's eyes and grinned as hope returned. He could do magic. He was a mouse, but he'd lost the band of charmed silver when he had shrunk down, and he could work the lines through his familiar!

"Rache. Change and let's go!" Jenks said as he dropped down before me.

"I swallowed it," I said as Pike renewed his hold on me. Everyone else was still shaking the blast off, but it wouldn't be long until they got it together. "It's gone."

"You what?" Jenks exclaimed, and I shrugged, letting Pike drag me up since I wanted to be upright anyway.

But then Jenks spun to Zack, his dust shifting to an alarmed red. "Look out!" he shouted, then darted to the ceiling.

"Squeak!" Zack said again, and I staggered, falling into Pike when a second blast hit us. They were expecting it, though, and everyone braced themselves, sliding back two feet but keeping upright.

"You need to *let go*!" I shouted, elbowing Pike and stomping on his instep. His grip loosened, and I shoved him pinwheeling back. "Zack!" I called as I broke from Pike, and the kid scampered to me. "Let's move!"

"Circle. Now!" Jenks shouted, and I dropped to a kneel as a green-tinted bubble snapped into existence around us. Zack leapt into my hands, and I jumped when Pike angrily side-kicked the circle, stymied.

Eyes narrowed, Pike dropped back to glare at us. Behind

him, Constance was in a state, screaming at her people and throwing chairs—big heavy ones that crashed into the walls to leave dents. Her security surrounded us, weapons drawn but not knowing what to do. Joni was laughing, her knees to her chest as she sat on the couch and rocked. The wig was on the floor, and her eyes were bright despite her pallor. *Damn, vampires are resilient.*

"Thanks," I said to Zack, but my lips parted as I realized he was trying to chew through my charmed silver. "Are you okay?"

He looked up at me, squeaked, and went back to chewing. I wasn't sure how we were going to get out of here if I couldn't shrink down: one hallway, one elevator, one I.S. personnel at a time until we were aboveground and on my streets.

Jenks's wings were a tight hum until he lit on my shoulder. "Thanks for telling Trent about the Brimstone," I said. Past the circle, Pike was organizing them, and I ducked, wincing when they all fired on us, bullets ricocheting from Zack's circle to make them scatter and Constance scream at them all the louder. "How is it going up there?"

"Beautiful chaos." Jenks took a strip of tape from his utility bag to fix a torn wing edge. "Someone talked, and people I've never *seen* before are wandering the streets looking like you, Cookie Man, and Pike. It's like a three-theme Halloween out there."

"Really?" I said, flushing. "Any ideas?" I added, sighing in relief when Zack finally worked through my charmed silver and it gave way with a snap. I didn't bother to reach for a line. We were too deep to reach one without a familiar. We had to move.

"Kill her! Both of them!" Constance shrieked, oblivious to Joni as she staggered to a stand, helped by a thin, white-haired woman. *Kip?* I wondered when Pike gave them a nod.

My pulse jumped when a chair bounced off Zack's circle and crashed into a table. Wincing, I looked over my shoulder at the door we'd come in. It was the only sure way out of here, and Pike stood resolute before it. The worry he had shown for Joni and Kip was gone, his arms crossed and a mean look on his face.

"Pike!" Joni called as Constance raged, and I watched, shocked, when Pike's anger turned to fear at her voice. Joni and Kip stood at a distant door. Both women were weak from blood loss and a never-ending fear. But all Joni did was look at me and nod, unexplained tears streaming down her face.

What did I just miss? I thought as Pike's determined stand before the door faltered.

"Squeak, squeak, sque-e-e-eak!" Zack said, and I glanced down.

"I can't reach a line until we're closer to the surface," I said, and Zack sat in my palm, stymied.

"Well, we can't stay here," Jenks said.

"Maybe I can teach you something," I said, and then I started, attention falling to Zack again. His tiny little hand was placed on my palm, and through him . . . I felt a ley line. "Zack, you're a genius," I whispered, then ran through my mental Rolodex of charms. There was one thing the vampire was more afraid of than anything else. "Okay, close your eyes when I do the spell. And if we get separated, run for the door. We'll meet in the hall. Ready? On the count of three, drop your circle and give me every last erg you can handle."

Zack nodded, and I moved him to my shoulder. "Hang on. One." I took a breath, looking past our circle at the vampires trying to appease Constance as she freaked. Joni and Kip were gone. "Two." I looked behind me at the door. Pike saw me, and his arms fell from his chest and a line of worry etched his brow. "Three!" I shouted, and Zack dropped his circle.

I rose up as a cry went out to catch me. *"Lenio cinis!"* I shouted, funneling the line coursing into me into a burst of light as bright as the sun. It exploded from me with a pop of sound, the heavy weight of a supernova slamming into us like a wave.

"No!" Constance shrieked, deathly afraid as she turned

and ran right into a wall. Falling into a huddle, she cowered and wept, thinking I'd opened the earth and let the sun in.

I sprang for the door, Jenks a tight hum at my ear. My charm died, and it was as if all the light in the room went with it as our spell-shocked eyes tried to adapt.

"Adaperire!" I shouted again, hand waving in front of me as I struggled to see, and I heard Pike cry out as the locked door swung open, knocking him aside.

And then we were in the hall, running for the elevators, Constance's screams going faint behind us.

CHAPTER

23

"TINK'S LITTLE PINK THONG, THAT WAS GREAT!" JENKS shrilled as I stumbled forward, hand held out to find the wall. My pulse pounded, and I couldn't see well. Zack's little nails dug into my ear, and I tried to stop lurching like a drunk. The elevator was down and to the left. Unless I'd already gone past it.

"Jenks, I can't see. Which way do I go?"

"You didn't shut your eyes? Straight," he said, and I squinted through the tears to see him hovering before me. "Pike's coming. He doesn't know when to stay down."

I lurched into a run. I was no match against a vampire's speed. I was a tiny, soft lion cub trying to outrun a hyena. I was a butterfly against a hawk. I was—

"Someone get her, or you will *all* die in my bed!" Constance screamed faintly, and I ran faster.

"Duck!" Jenks shouted, and I veered to the right, slipping on the tile and going down with an ungraceful thump as I tried to shield Zack. I looked up from the floor, shocked as a heavy stone lamp thudded into the wall and shattered. If it had hit me, my skull would have been crushed.

"Squeak!" Zack said, clinging to my hair for dear life, and Pike screamed, falling back and ripping his clothing from him. I stared, oblivious to Jenks shrilling at me to get up and run. Pike was on fire. Zack had set his clothes on fire!

"Rachel, go!" Jenks shouted, and I jumped, startled when his sword poked me.

Pike was rolling on the floor to put out the flames. Three more of Constance's people were storming after us, and I spun to my feet. Boots squeaking on the tile, I began to run.

"Left?" I said. I skidded around the corner—only to slide to a halt when the two I.S. agents waiting for us in front of the elevator looked up.

"We got her," one said into a radio, and I put a hand up to Zack before he toasted anyone else. Okay, I totally got he might have some revenge needs to work out, but setting people on fire was not a good option. They rarely died, and living with burns . . . No. That was worse than hell.

"Zack, I mean it. Do not set them on fire," I said as I kept coming forward, and the kid began squeaking at me. "I don't care!" I shouted, and the two men looked at each other as if I was crazy. "It's not just surviving that counts. It's how you survive. Pick something nonlethal."

"Fire isn't necessarily lethal," Jenks grumped.

"That's close enough!" one of the men at the elevator said. "Hands up!"

"Oh, for little green apples, fine," I muttered, fisting my hands and putting them in the air. But I was talking to Zack, and I felt the faintest zing of line energy as he gestured and a small glow took form in his hands, looking really odd since he was a mouse.

"She's not strapped!" Pike shouted from behind us, and I turned to see him loping forward, three men from Constance's personal security with him. There were six of them, and three of us. I liked those odds any day.

"Squeak, squeak . . . squeak!" Zack said, and my internal balance gave a hiccup as a bolt of tiny force shot straight up into the light above us.

Eyes wide, Pike skidded to a halt as the lights in the hallway began to glow, a high-pitched whine coming from them. "Take cover!" he shouted, then kicked in a door and dove for shelter.

"Squeak!" Zack said again, and I jumped when the

glowing lights shot out a wave of force to coat the five remaining vampires. Ozone crackled the air, and they shook, dropped, and went still. Every last one of them.

"Holy shit," I heard Pike whisper from the office, too smart to poke his head out just yet.

"Are they alive?" I asked, pulse fast, and Zack shrugged, staggering to grip my hair to keep from falling. Clearly it had taken a lot out of him.

Jenks darted to the nearest downed vampire, his dust a brilliant silver. "They'll be fine," he said, and I hit the elevator call button. "This would be easier if you were two inches tall. What happened to plan C?"

"I accidentally swallowed it," I said, arms going over my middle when Jenks faced me in disbelief. "I'm sorry, okay?" I said as we waited for the elevator. "She jammed a chocolate in my mouth, and I accidentally swallowed it!"

Zack was clinging to my hair, and I carefully gave him my hand to sit in. He looked exhausted, his ears and whiskers drooping. "And you might get your wish before this is over," I muttered to Jenks as I gave Zack the option of my shoulder again and he took it.

I felt like a time bomb with no display. I could shrink down and go mouse at any moment. I mean, sure, the charm was encased in plastic, but my gut was probably like Mount Vesuvius at the moment. Now that we were free and running, I kind of hoped it wouldn't happen. Strutting out the front door with Zack would do loads for my confidence.

Except when the elevator dinged and opened, it was full of two I.S. officers in combat gear, clearly as surprised to see me as I was to see them.

I fell back, my hand raised protectively to Zack as Jenks dropped to hover menacingly before us. The kid had just channeled a crapload of line energy and I wasn't helpless—even if they looked really big in their anticharm gear.

"You think you can bring me in?" I said, trying for bravado as I scrambled for options. "How bad do you want to go home tonight?" I said, bluffing, and they looked at each other, one shrugging as if they were trying to decide something. But they hadn't pulled their weapons, and the one seemed positively sheepish as he stuck his foot out to keep the doors from closing.

"Ah, we've been talking," he said, his voice incredibly deep and soothing. "You need to get to the surface, Ms. Morgan?"

Ms. Morgan? My lips parted, and I let my hand drop from Zack as Jenks's wings clattered in surprise. Eyes narrowed, I took a step forward to stand before the open door. They took up a lot of room in there. "Why would you help me? Your boss wants me dead."

"Morgan!" Pike shouted, and I spun, seeing him disheveled and hurting as he stood beside the kicked-in door, his clothes charred and red skin showing.

"Why doesn't he stay down?" Jenks muttered, and Zack squeaked something derisive.

"Step *away* from the elevator," Pike said as he limped forward. "You two! Get out here and help me take her in!"

Heart sinking, I turned to the guys in the lift and winced. I was going to have to do something really ugly, or Zack was going to do something worse.

"Oh, no!" the larger one said suddenly, a hand going dramatically to his chest. "I can't move. She got me with a spell!"

I blinked, startled as he hit the back of the elevator and fell to the floor.

His buddy stared at him, shocked, and the "downed" vampire grimaced. "Dude . . ." he prompted, and the light of understanding blossomed.

"Me too!" the second officer said and, groaning, he fell down as well.

"Go, go, go!" Jenks shrilled, and I turned, lips parting. Pike was striding forward, murder in his eyes. Pulse pounding, I stepped into the lift and hammered at the "close door" button.

"Morgan!" Pike bellowed, eyes black as he lurched closer, one shoe missing. "You are mine," he panted as he caught the closing door and pushed it open.

"You should really stay down," I said, then leaned back and kicked his hand holding the door. Jenks frantically two-footed the "close door" button, and I spun for momentum, kicking Pike square in the chest to send him flying backward down the hall. He skidded to a tile-burned halt, shaking the pain from his hands and grimacing at me. I couldn't help it, and as the two vampires behind me went "ooooh" in sympathy, I gave Pike a bunny-eared kiss-kiss as the doors began to close.

"Witch!" he cried out as the doors slid shut, and I sighed in relief. Jenks was grinning at me from atop the elevator's speaker, but Zack looked positively whipped, and I took him in my hands before he fell off my shoulder.

My eyes went up to the numbers counting to ground level, then the vampires getting to their feet. "Hey, thanks, guys," I said as they congratulated each other with some complicated fist-bump thingy. "I really appreciate this. My spelling mouse here is getting tired."

My spine stiffened as the numbers clicked over to two, then one, and the rush of line energy filled me.

"Yeah, well, all of us in the tower got new undead," the one with the deep voice said. "Word is that you're here distracting Constance so Kalamack can get his goods on the street where they belong."

"We don't like you," the first added, grinning to show his small fangs. "But we like Constance less."

"Well, thanks," I said, then blanched as the elevator dinged and opened to utter chaos.

"Tink's a Disney whore," Jenks swore as he hovered by my shoulder, and Zack poked his head up through my fingers.

Uniformed officers were struggling to gain control of the first floor of the lobby, now full of people clamoring for attention. Office personnel on the second floor ringed the railing, pointing at what were probably onetime Pike and Trent look-alikes struggling to remain if not free, at least useful as a distraction. The noise was atrocious, and I watched as an old woman on the outskirts threw charms at the spell checker to keep it beeping. Armed personnel were turning people away at the door, and I winced when a blond in a suit and tie was shoved back onto the sidewalk where he flipped them off before running toward Fountain Square.

Sweet mother of Jesus, I think I started a revolution.

"Ma'am?" One of the vampires behind me gestured, and I stepped out into it, a pixy on my shoulder and my hands cupped around Zack. I grimaced when my hold on the ley line vanished the instant my foot hit the tile. Someone had invoked the lobby's no-magic-zone charm, and I looked up at the huge chandelier hanging over the space. It was pulsating a faint purple. If it went red, we were all in trouble.

"We have to get out of here," I whispered, seeing my car right outside where Pike had left it. Maybe if I kept to the edges I could get to the door.

"Ow! What the hell?" the larger vampire exclaimed as the doors began to close, and I turned to see that his buddy had hit him on the forehead with the butt of his weapon.

"No one will believe this if one of us isn't really hurt," the smaller guy said as the doors began to close. "You saw Constance's head of security. You think he bought that?"

"Yeah? I think you need some blood on you, too!"

"Hey!"

The doors shut, cutting them off as they began to hit each other in earnest. My eyes flicked to the elevator's display. The car was going all the way down.

Pike, I thought with a little shiver. He wouldn't quit. Constance would kill him if he did.

But that look that Joni had given to him—hunched and hurting—meant something.

"Your car is still at the curb," Jenks prompted, his gaze on the big plate windows.

Back to the wall and trying to stay unnoticed, I began edging to the door. I held Zack close, jerking when someone slid across the floor in front of me. They crashed into a bank of chairs only to be yanked up and propelled to a temporary holding area right in the I.S. lobby.

"Yeah," I said, again thinking it was odd that Pike had

left the keys in it. "Could you make sure no one tampered with it? If I reach the street, I'm going to leave fast."

Jenks dusted in indecision as he looked at the mess, then nodded, darting out the door as three Weres roared in, fists raised and howling until they were brought down.

"Just you and me, and sixty feet to cross," I said to Zack and, taking a deep breath, I began inching forward.

"Mo-o-o-organ!" Pike bellowed from the elevators, and my heart gave a thump. "That's Morgan!" he shouted, and everything seemed to stop as Pike staggered out of the elevator. My two escorts were still in the lift, truly down this time with blood leaking from their ears. "That," he panted, a shaky finger pointing at me, "is Morgan. Get her. And the mouse and pixy, too!"

I froze at the click of safeties going off. Guns would work where magic wouldn't. Grim expressions ringed me, some in hate, some in fear, some in hope. But no one moved.

"I said *get her!*" Pike shouted, and then I looked up, my gaze rising at a soft cry of dismay when the great chandelier began pulsating with an off-and-on red light.

"Run!" Jenks shrilled, suddenly with me again. "They're going to immobilize the floor!"

My eyes widened. "Make a hole!" I shouted, bolting for the door, awkward with Zack still in my hands. "Look out! Let me through!"

People scattered amid the shouts of fear and encouragement. I heard the pop of gunfire, and through the reflection off the big plate-glass windows, I saw a red and purple column of magic pulse down from the chandelier to hit the floor and rise up like an evil fog. People fled before it, but everyone it touched fell to the tile, pained expressions on their faces.

I threw myself into the revolving door as the evil red magic fastened about my foot like a steel trap. Agonizing sparkles rose up, cramping my chest and freezing my muscles. *So close,* I thought as I fell, taking it on the chin as I pushed my hands forward to try to free Zack.

I was too far away, and my hands opened to show Zack in a tight ball as the red haze stole over us. "Zack!" Jenks cried, and then he fell to the floor beside him, paralyzed.

But the revolving door was still moving, and with a little creak and whine, it shifted closed behind me . . . and the spell . . . broke.

I took a huge breath, my chest easing as I coughed and sat up in the tiny space. "Jenks?" Behind me, the red mist rolled up against the door. We'd made it. *Just* . . .

"I'm good," Jenks croaked out, and the rough rasp of his wings eased into a smooth hum.

"Zack?" I asked as I looked down.

He peered up at me in pain and bobbed his head, whiskers twitching.

My limbs tingled, and I got to my feet. Everyone on the lobby floor was paralyzed, most of them facing me as they lay on the tile and that red mist eddied. Watching. My eyes narrowed as I found Pike, the ugly expression on his face looking permanent as he stared at me. He was down like the rest, but his eyes tracked me as I stood with Zack in hand.

"Let's go." Head high, I pushed on the revolving door and stepped out onto the sidewalk. "We've got stuff to do."

The click of a safety spun me around, and I glared at the two guards who had been posted outside, now pale and unsure. "You want to mess with this?" I said, Zack cupped close as I gestured at myself. I was covered with floor dirt. My hair was a snarled mess, and Pike still had my phone and wallet. "You really want to mess with this!" I shouted again, pulling the nearest line into me until my tangled hair floated and my skin practically glowed. "I am having a *really bad day*, and I could use a little break," I added, sniffing as they reconsidered and shook their heads.

"Thank you." Chin lifted, I put Zack on my shoulder for everyone to see and I strode to my car. "Are we good?" I asked Jenks as I walked into the street. An oncoming car screeched to a halt, its driver wide-eyed.

"As sweet as newling piss," he said as I gave the startled driver a wave and got in.

The door slammed shut, and I sat there for a moment, shaking until I pulled the visor down and my keys dropped into my lap with a comforting sound of metal. The *brumm* of my engine was bliss, and, not believing I'd done it, I put my car in drive, checked to see that the way was open, and pulled out.

Pike had left the keys. Not given them to the front desk or security in case they had to move it. He'd left them here. *For me?* I wondered. Joni had told him something, something that had made her cry and Pike falter in his steadfast determination to bring me down.

He *had* tried to catch me. The anger in his eyes *had* been real. The effort to take me back to Constance at all costs *had* been real.

But so were Joni's unsaid words and my keys, and I looked at them swinging from the ignition, not sure anymore.

"You want to head out to Piscary's?" Jenks said as he messed about with the radio in search of the news of our escape. "Trent probably has this, but you never know."

The pull to rejoin Trent was real. I needed to hold him, to reassure myself that I was okay, and he was okay, and that apart from the coming lawsuits, life was going to go on. But as I looked at Zack shaking in the cup holder, I knew that would have to wait. "Church," I said as I took Zack into my hand, and the kid curled up and shook some more.

CHAPTER

24

"IS THAT MRS. SARONG'S SUV?" I SAID, ONE HAND ON THE wheel, one cupped about a very shaken mouse. We were almost at the church, and though no one had followed us from the I.S. tower, the likely consequences of what we'd done were beginning to filter into my uppermost thoughts. I may have slipped the I.S., but there would be repercussions.

Jenks rose up from beside Zack, hovering before the window as I drove slowly down our street. Actually, there were several cars I didn't recognize sandwiched between the food carts, but it was the two *extre-e-e-emely* good-looking Weres hanging about the deep red SUV with the VIP stadium stickers that had me worried. I didn't like Mrs. Sarong, and she didn't like me. But then again, I *had* magicked her arena to get her to cough up the money she owed me for finding the Howlers' mascot.

"Yep, that's her," Jenks said, hands on his hips in his best Peter Pan pose. "David's here, too." He flashed me a relieved grin. "Trent and Edden. I can hear Kaspar crabbing about something." He tilted his head and looked at the steeple. "Etude is on the roof. And . . ." He took a deep breath, his sparkles vanishing for an instant. "Vivian?"

Jenks turned to me in midair, and I almost stopped the car. "I smell Vivian," he repeated.

"Vivian?" I echoed. I liked the woman, especially after

he had vouched for me at Alcatraz, but what was she doing his side of the continent, much less in my church? It wasn't ny fault I'd landed in Alcatraz. But as I passed the expensive, unfamiliar cars lining the street, I decided it was probably something else that had drawn them all here. *Constance, maybe?*

Zack squeaked, his head cocked in clear disbelief, and Jenks frowned. "I can so smell her," Jenks grumped. "That woman is magic on steroids. No wonder they made her head of the witches' coven of moral and ethical standards."

Sighing, I looked down at myself. I was in jeans, and my green shirt was filthy from sliding around on the floor and spotted with chocolate. Vivian knew me well enough to not think twice, but this had all the earmarks of a city-powers meeting, and walking in with my hair snarled and smelling of angry vampire made me feel unprofessional.

"I should have asked Al to teach me that brush-and-wash curse," I muttered as I pulled into my carport. Someone had taped a RESERVED sign on the small shelter. I'd say it had been Ivy, except it was hand-lettered; she would have used a stencil. I could hear music—Ivy's piano.

Jenks's dust shifted to an irate orange as he eyed the noisy crows, unusual for my street. "You could ask Hodin. I think he's here, too."

Just shoot me now. . . . My eyes went from Jenks's annoyance to Zack's slumped weariness. "Zack, you mind if I talk to Hodin before we go in and get you changed? He's a demon, but he's shown no inclination toward anything but being helpful." *And yet, I keep driving him away,* I thought when Zack shrugged. The human gesture on the gray mouse made me smile.

"Thanks. Jenks, would you please tell Trent I'll be right there so he doesn't come out? I'm sure they know I'm here. Oh, and tell him we got Zack and he's safe."

"You got it, Rache." Jenks dropped to Zack, whispering something to make the kid sigh before he flew up and away. I watched his sparkles fall, then blew the car seat free of his dust.

"He's really one of the nicer demons," I said, then rolled the passenger-side window all the way down. "Ho-o-o-odi-i-i-in?" I shouted. "I know you're here!"

Zack's eyes widened when a soft bong came from the church's bell and a dark shadow dropped from the trees across the street. It was an enormous, bedraggled crow swooping in under the carport to alight in the open window. Ugly claws scraped the sill, and as his red, goat-slitted eyes focused on Zack, he cawed, wings opening to send a few ragged feathers spiraling down.

"Come here, Zack," I whispered, remembering what it was like to be that small, and the kid scrambled over the console. "Um, I talked to Al yesterday," I said as I held Zack close, and the crow made an odd, deep-throat rattle. "He tossed me to Alcatraz because you helped me bury Nash," I added, and Hodin's red, goat-slitted eyes narrowed.

"Look, it's devilishly hard to talk to you when you're a crow," I said. "You want to shift and tell me what you're mad about so I don't have to keep guessing?"

Zack squeaked as the crow dissolved into a silver mist, his tiny paws patting my palm as he tried to back deeper into my cupped hands. "It's okay," I whispered as the mist spilled into the car, thickening and taking form until a narrow-faced, angry-eyed, sullen demon sat beside me. He had chosen to show up in dark jeans and a leather jacket, his black hair long and shining like a raven's wing. *And really nice boots,* I noticed as I twisted to face him squarely.

"I did not help you bury an elf. I taught you an ancient elven funeral rite. And in return you put a bell on your grounds?" he said, low voice harsh.

"Oh." My gaze went to the belfry. "Yeah. Well, maybe it's not for you, huh? Ever think of that?"

Hodin sniffed, turning to look out the window at nothing.

"Al isn't talking to me," I said, but he didn't move, either to leave or to look at me. "He flung me to Alcatraz. I let him do it because at the time I thought I deserved it," I added, and his hand tightened into a fist. "He did it because I *reminded* him that I wasn't going to let them put you in a bottle because you mix demon and elf magic. He thinks you're to blame—"

"I know what he blames me for," Hodin interrupted, his gaze still turned from mine. "What do you want?"

I truly didn't know, but clearly something hung between us. "Demon and elf magic is water from the same stream," I said, feeling Zack's warmth in my palm. "You're the only one with the experience to maybe help me stitch them back together. The rest of the demons . . ." I hesitated. I was sure that Dali had sent me to Al in the expectation that Al would force me to cut off all communication with Hodin and stop using elf magic. Seeing as he hadn't, they might take things into their own hands.

"I'm following what I believe will heal us," I said, voice quavering. "Both the demons and the elves. Ignoring and denying doesn't heal. Inclusion and acceptance does. And if Al won't help me . . ." My words trailed off, and my eyes dropped to Zack. "I'll miss him," I whispered, feeling his loss to my core. But I couldn't look to him anymore if he refused to see past his pain.

I blinked back the hint of tears when Hodin turned to me, the ugly, harsh unforgiveness gone. "He dropped you into Alcatraz?"

I nodded. "His way of telling me I'm being uncommonly stupid."

"At least he put you somewhere you could get out," he muttered, looking almost jealous.

"What's going on in the church?" I asked, feeling as if the new understanding between us was paper-thin and gossamer—but it was there.

Hodin grimaced. "They're arguing over what to do about you and Constance," he said. "One wants to kill you to resume normal operations. The rest disagree."

"That's nice." *Normal operations?* There would be no normal under Constance, and my worry flooded back. I didn't have to guess as to who wanted to buy Constance's favor with my death. "You want to come in?" I asked suddenly. "I mean, since you're here."

Zack made a tight squeak. Hodin blinked, a soft smile easing the faint wrinkles about his brow and eyes. "Thank you, yes," he said, and I nodded, head down as I reached for the door.

Thank the Goddess I have Zack, I thought, then said aloud, "Zack, you mind if I carry you in? There's a lot of magic users in there, and not everyone might know you're a mouse."

He nodded, and I awkwardly got out, taking a moment to simply stand there and breathe in the late-afternoon air, relishing it. I'd almost forgotten it was spring. The robins were singing to the coming sunset, wanting rain for the mud to build their nests. The church looked beautiful all lit up, still and serene with the shadows hiding the construction-flat grass and new paint around the windows. Someone had cut the grass in the graveyard, and the scent was like heaven.

Calm, I butt-bumped my door shut, the thump loud in the shadow-drenched street. The graveyard was quiet and only a thin trail of smoke rose from the fire, unseen behind the six-foot wall.

"You're going to make a stir," I said as I turned to Hodin, but he was gone. "Ah, Hodin?" I called, then froze, stock-still at the flurry of black wings and trailing feathers coming at me. "Damn it, Hodin!" I hissed, flinching as he landed on my shoulder, head bobbing in amusement and his claws pinching right through my shirt. My heart pounded, and I hesitated, tasting how it felt to have him there, finally deciding it was okay. "Crap on toast, warn a person," I muttered, and he made a soft, amused throat rattle as I started up the walk. Trent might guess who was actually on my shoulder, and Jenks, of course. But to the rest it would look like crazy Rachel Morgan coming back to her church with a new stray.

"I've got salt to break the spell up in my belfry," I said to Zack, cupping him close when three scruffy Weres came out of the church, all of them cocky and smug with boxes of what looked like construction waste in their arms.

"Morgan," the first said as she passed me, her steps silent.

"Morgan." The second gave me a wink, and my nose wrinkled at the scent of Brimstone.

The third didn't say anything, flushed as he ducked his head and smiled shyly at me.

Chatting amicably between themselves, they loaded their boxes into a beater station wagon, voices rising as it started and they drove toward town in a puff of blue smoke.

"Brimstone," I whispered, and Hodin bobbed his head, content, apparently, to "be the bird." Weres and Brimstone didn't go together. Clearly Trent had been successful. My steps quickened, and a glow of pride gave my feet an extra boost as I took the steps two at a time. My boyfriend the drug lord, common thief, and distributor.

My smile deepened at the sight of the polished nameplate, and I ran my fingers across it as if it was a touchstone as I opened the door and went in. "Trent?"

"Where is he?" Kaspar bellowed, and I fell back, my shoulder thumping into the wall by the door as the tall, angry elf practically pinned me to it.

Hodin took to the air, his crow chortle sounding like laughter as he flew to the open rafters in the sanctuary. Cries of surprise rose and, ticked, I stared at Kaspar. The air crackled between us, and it was all I could do to not slam him across the dark foyer with a burst of line energy. "I got you your Brimstone, and you walked out of there without Zachariah," Kaspar bellowed. "Explain—"

"Cool your jets, Kaspar," I said, giving him a shove. The piano stopped, and Trent's silhouette loomed in the archway to the sanctuary. Relief filled me. He was okay. Someone would have called if he wasn't, but it was still . . . "Zack is fine," I added, eyes on Trent.

Hands fisted, Kaspar shook. "You saw him and did nothing! You left him!"

Gaze still on Trent, I used my foot to push the door shut, and the foyer went dark. The sanctuary was bright with light, and a small movement drew my attention to Mrs. Sa-rong at the piano. She'd been the one playing it. Her eye-brows high in question, the woman was ready to rip out my throat and smile while doing it. *Kill me to appease Constance? Sounds about right.*

David stood beside her with Edden, both men looking highly capable but in completely different ways, David with his duster and hat, and Edden with his holster and gruff confidence.

"Dude, he's right here," I said when Kaspar drew himself up, and the high priest's expression blanked when I lifted my cupped hand and Zack gave him a peace sign.

"Zack!" Kaspar stumbled back. Trent shifted to catch him, but the older elf rallied, staggering forward with his eyes wide and his shoulders hunched in placation. "Sa'han," the man whispered, holding out his hands as if Zack would jump to him. "Are you all right?" His eyes flicked to mine. "You left him as a *vermin* while you turned back?"

My angry words choked to nothing as I flushed. I'd swallowed our easy way out.

Kaspar reached for Zack, jerking at Jenks's wing clatter. "Hey, she got Zack free and no one died," Jenks said as he hovered between us. "So ground yourself before I clip your wings and pix you within an inch of your life!"

Trent sidled closer. "Someone had to drive the car," he said as his arm slipped behind me. "You did good," he added, his obvious worry and relief going right to my core.

My eyes closed as I wrapped my free arm around his neck and leaned in, pressing our bodies together until Zack made an uncomfortable squeak and I backed up, grinning. The vampire pheromones had made me randy, and Trent's hand lingered, pressing the small of my back with a hint of something more. "So did you, apparently," I said, eyeing him.

Trent was always graceful, but something had shifted when he had stolen his Brimstone. His mood was darker, more mysterious. His thoughts seemed preoccupied with possibilities. A heady, lingering magic tainted his aura, electrifying. Even with his arm around me, he held himself with a sly, domineeringly confident stance. I'd seen it before on the floor of the coven's meeting room when he showed me his daughter for the first time. Elves, apparently, were at their best when stealing stuff. *Figures.*

Again Kaspar reached for Zack, hesitating at Jenks's aggressive wing clatter. Zack, though, was tired, and I reluctantly pulled from Trent. "Jenks, would you show Kaspar my spelling salt for me? There should be some spring water up there, too. Use the blue ceramic bowl. I haven't had a chance to de-spell the crucible yet." I turned to Kaspar, Zack still in my free hand. "You *do* know how to break a common transformation curse?"

Clearly frazzled, Kaspar gazed at Zack, his cupped hands extended. "Yes."

It felt amazingly good to hold my hand to his for Zack to make the switch. The kid turned to me before Kaspar could cover him protectively, saluting me with his furry hand. He looked exhausted, ears and whiskers drooping.

"This way, your most arrogant pain in my ass." Jenks hovered before the door to the belfry stairs, a brilliant gold dust lighting the small space. For all his crass words, he was pleased. Me too. It wasn't over yet, but Zack was safe. Whatever was currently happening in the lower levels of the I.S., I was betting it wasn't pleasant.

My smile faded as I thought about the two living vampires who had helped me to the surface. They'd known there would be repercussions, and they'd accepted them with no thought other than the hope that Trent would be successful and they wouldn't be forced to choose between Constance and tricking humans into fulfilling their elders' needs.

Tired, I slumped into Trent as Kaspar followed Jenks up the cramped staircase. "I'm so glad to see you," I whispered in the dark foyer. "You look great. I want to hear all about it later."

He smiled, his hand pulling me closer into him with a confident tug. "Same here. Short story is we ran into five of Constance's men at Piscary's. They didn't even have it unloaded yet. It's going out as we speak. For free," he added, clearly pained.

"Ah, it's good for your karma." His lips were so close, and, giving in, I pulled him down for a quick kiss. He made a soft sound as his arm tugged me to him, and desire dove to my core, spurred by the sound of our lips parting. *How fast can I get rid of those people in my front room?*

"Thanks for the heads-up on the Brimstone," he whispered. "I saw Jenks, and I thought you were in trouble."

"I was." Giving his hand a squeeze, I stepped from the dark into the light. Edden and David looked up and I gave them a little wave, beamed at Vivian rising from the couch, and nodded warily at Mrs. Sarong. Hodin had perched himself on a dark rafter, ignored for the most part.

"Hodin?" Trent said as we crossed the sanctuary, his lips unmoving as the crow bobbed his head in greeting. "He helped you?"

"No. He was hanging around outside." I liked Trent's arm at my waist, and I sighed as it slowly slid across my back and vanished. "I invited him in," I said, hearing more in those four words than me asking Hodin if he wanted to listen. I had invited him in. He had somehow become a part of everything that made the church what it was.

Whatever that is, I mused as I looked at the snacks arranged neatly on Kisten's pool table. The makeshift kitchen was still in operation, too, and the two couches and chairs surrounding the slate coffee table practically beckoned to me. My live-in guests, though, were gone.

"Hey, could you do something for me?" I asked softly, wondering if Sarong had scared them off, or if they were merely giving me space to do my work. *I hate city-powers meetings. Someone always ends up dead.*

"Coffee?" he guessed, and I groaned.

"That would be fantastic," I said, trying to decide who I was going to say hi to first, Mrs. Sarong or Vivian. "But actually, could you call Triple S and see if their blue, size-four splat ball refills break down in the gut or pass through unbroken?"

"Security Spelling Supplies?" he said as he reached for his phone. Then he hesitated, eyes going to mine in worry. "That's why you didn't shift," he all but breathed.

Wincing, I nodded, the taste of that blood-laced chocolate rising in my memory. I might never eat chocolate again, and I'd hate Constance for that if nothing else.

He gave me a last, comforting touch on my shoulder as he leaned in to whisper, "I'll let you know." Nodding to everyone, he retreated to a quiet corner where he snuck glances at Hodin while searching for Triple S's website.

Mrs. Sarong rose from the piano bench in expectation, but it was Vivian I headed for, my hands outstretched. I was both happy and worried to see her.

"Vivian," I said, not caring that I'd insulted Mrs. Sarong in the delicate but telling niceties of polite circles. *Maybe you shouldn't be lobbying to kill me, my dear.* "It wasn't my fault," I said as I gave the smartly dressed woman a hug, eyes closing as I breathed in the scent of redwood, agreeing with Jenks's assessment. She could throw lethal, white spells better than anyone I knew, having been trained as a toddler. That she'd stood up for me when the coven had deported me to the ever-after for being a demon meant a lot. "I wasn't there trying to get anyone out. Though I should," I muttered as I saw her confusion and drew back. "They're still feeding them that magic inhibitor."

Her welcoming smile faltered. "Alcatraz? Oh, you're fine there," Vivian said, her Seattle accent pleasant even as she turned to Mrs. Sarong with a frown. "That's not why I'm here. We have an issue with how you're handling Constance. Or rather, how you aren't."

"Yeah . . . I had to get Zack first," I said, as Mrs. Sarong click-clacked across the room in her tiny white heels, attitude trailing behind her. At least she'd left her boy toys outside.

"Mrs. Sarong." I extended my hand, and she smiled as if I'd crawled out from under a rock. "Good to see you again."

"And you as well," the older, extre-e-e-emely sophisticated woman said as she took my hand, barely touching it before drawing back and wiping it on her white business suit. When it came to Weres, the higher up in the pack you were, the more polished you were, and Mrs. Sarong had a very large, very successful pack.

"I, ah, am sorry you're all here before the reno is finished," I said, gesturing to include everyone. Trent was still on the phone. David looked tired, and Edden uncomfortable, and Vivian . . . Vivian was decidedly worried. A sharp wing snap pulled my attention up to Hodin, who was studiously trying to ignore the three young pixy bucks facing him, wooden swords brandished. "Ah, would you like to sit down?"

Grimacing, the older woman sat dead center of the couch, her white leather bag beside her. Eyes on the floor, she brushed at the hint of sawdust. Vivian rolled her eyes and sat on the couch across from her where her coffee waited. I felt a tweak on my awareness as the witch warmed it up with a thought, then she sighed as she sipped it.

I looked longingly at the makeshift kitchen. "Edden, David. Do you want any coffee?" I turned to Mrs. Sarong. "Mrs. Sarong?" I asked, smiling. I'd give her the rainbow mug. But she shook her head as well, so I went to fill it with straight black for myself. Kaspar was thumping about upstairs as the dark brew chattered into the mug, and I hoped Jenks got back down here before the pixy bucks decided to attack Hodin. They knew who he was.

"So . . . what's up?" I said as I turned, warm cup in hand. "I've come home to demons, assassins, blood-hungry vamps, and fire trucks at my curb before, but never this."

Wincing, Edden shifted from foot to foot. "It's an inquiry of intentions."

Mrs. Sarong moved her purse to her lap and rubbed her fingers together in distaste. "It's a threat, Rachel," she said flatly.

And now we can begin. I leaned back against the makeshift kitchen table, ankles crossed as I glanced at Trent and sipped at my coffee. Warm and nutty, it slipped down to bring me back to life. *Thank you, Stef,* I thought, not sure if she'd made it or not. "Really." I strengthened my hold on the nearest line and, feeling it, Vivian frowned at the elegant Were across from her.

"It's not a threat," Vivian said darkly. "Trent has informed us that you intend to remove Constance as Cincy's master vampire, and we are all understandably concerned about the power vacuum that will create." She hesitated. "Not to mention the collateral damage you will engender in the attempt."

I helped myself to a chili cracker, biting through it with a loud, obnoxious crunch.

"Seems not everyone is sure you will be able to handle Cincinnati," David said from the snack-covered pool table, a bag of cheese curls in his hand.

Yeah, I had that same concern, but I brushed the crumbs from me and tried to look confident. "I've got this," I said as a faint whoop of success came from the belfry. *Zack is back.* . . . "I won't know about the collateral damage until it's done, but I'll be as careful as I can."

Vivian winced, and Mrs. Sarong's condescending gaze traveled up the dirt smear on my thigh. "As you were in San Francisco?" the alpha female said. "Stay clear of my arena."

"I'm glad you brought that up," I said. "I had the situation in San Francisco in hand until the coven butted in. The damage I did removing Ku'Sox was minuscule compared to the destruction he wrought while I was banished. The takeaway here is, back off and let me work."

"I agree," Vivian said firmly. "Let the woman work, Ellen," she added, hesitating when Etude sort of monkey-swung his way in through the front door, slamming it open with his feet to land with a window-shaking thump inside the sanctuary.

"The dewar leader will be down shortly," he said into the stunned silence, grinning to show his black teeth.

"Well, thank Cerberus for that," Mrs. Sarong muttered, clearly unnerved.

Trent pulled the phone from his ear, apparently on hold.

"Mrs. Sarong, could I ask you to wait on any more discussion? We have one more coming in," he said, and Mrs. Sarong turned, irritation creasing her brow.

"You heard the gargoyle. Zack will be down shortly."

"His name is Etude," I said, and the large gargoyle flicked an ear in appreciation.

"Zack speaks only for the dewar, not the enclave," Trent said. "But we can't hold a city-powers meeting without a vampire delegate. He's on his way."

My eyebrows rose. "He? He who?"

Vivian crossed her knees, foot bobbing. "It's the vampires who are the problem."

Trent made a thin smile, the phone still to his ear. "They're a major third of Inderland. They should be represented, *especially* if they're the problem."

"He who?" I said again, but Trent's attention had returned to his phone, his head down as he listened.

Etude's tail flicked, and at that same instant, the bell high overhead gave a single bong.

My eyes went to Hodin and he made a bird-shrug. I hadn't felt any magic, either, and a shout of complaint came from the belfry. Clearly it hadn't been Kaspar or Zack. Someone had actually rung the doorbell. *Trent's vampire representation, perhaps?*

"Don't everyone get up," I said as I set my coffee aside. Mrs. Sarong would have to wait to throw down her ultimatum, but she'd probably appreciate the bigger audience.

I managed a smile at Etude as I passed the gargoyle, even if the scent of iron and bird feathers reminded me of Bis. Mood faltering, I looked up at the rasp of pixy wings.

"Rache! It's Pike!" Jenks shrilled, and my reach for the door hesitated. "And Doyle. It's not a doppelganger. I'd swear to it."

I looked over my shoulder at Trent, my suspicion rising when he gave me a relieved nod and closed out his phone. *Vampire representation,* I thought sourly, glad I wasn't going to turn into a mouse in front of everyone. "How many people did he bring?" I asked softly, visions of an unexpected skirmish floating in my head, and the pixy shrugged in disbelief. I'd bested Pike in his own tower. If he tried anything here, he was demon chow.

"Just Doyle. Even his assassins have backed off."

Anger flooded me, and as I reached for the door, David settled protectively behind me. Seeing him nod, I opened it.

CHAPTER

25

IT *WAS* PIKE, HIS SKIN LOOKING RED AND SORE BEHIND THE gaps in his burned clothes. His scarred face was ugly in anger, and he held a wad of useless brown-paper bathroom towels to his side where his stitches had pulled. Doyle was just as angry, but at least his suit was intact.

I cocked my hip as Trent moved to my side and Vivian leaned against the archway to the sanctuary behind us, her coffee cup in hand and the tips of her hair floating, evidence of her pulling power from the nearby ley line. "Selling Bibles?" I said, and Pike's eyes narrowed.

"Kalamack called me," he said, his gaze flicking to Trent. "Something about a meeting."

My lips parted as Trent reached past me and shook Pike's hand. "You *called* him?"

"When I heard you got Zack. Yes," Trent said. "He's Constance's scion. He should see this," he added as he gave Pike a warning look and backed up. *See this,* he'd said, not *be here.* Clearly more was going on than a rival vampire being invited to a city-powers meeting, and I wrestled my anger down until I figured it out.

Doyle shifted his feet. "Ms. Rachel M. Morgan?" he said and my attention shot to him.

"Yes," I said, thinking he sounded like a demon when he said it all together like that.

"Just checking," the man said as he held out a trifolded piece of paper and I took it. "That's a warrant for your arrest."

"Oh, God," David muttered, and Vivian sighed heavily.

Jenks hovered over my shoulder as I opened it to see that, yep, that was exactly what it was, dated yesterday. "What for!" Jenks shrilled, but it wasn't Brimstone distribution, or even for busting out of the I.S.—which wouldn't stick because I'd never been charged with anything when they brought me in. It was for failure to halt when instructed, fleeing a crime scene, and malicious destruction of city property.

Twin Lakes Bridge, I mused, remembering. "Seriously?" I said as Jenks's dust made the ink glow. "I didn't kill anyone. It was Pike."

"That's not what you're wanted for," Doyle said smugly. "We got six I.S. agents who saw you maliciously destroy their cars and vanish into a ley line when you were instructed to stop for questioning." Smiling, he held out a pair of cuffs.

I refolded the paper and creased the line with a sharp fingernail. "Right."

"Pike, dar-r-r-ling," Mrs. Sarong drawled as she pushed her way forward, hand extended as if they were old friends. "So good to finally meet you in the flesh, so to speak. Come in. You can sit beside me." She hesitated, shocked when she noticed his burned clothes, reddened skin, and the blood-soaked brown paper held to his side. "Did Morgan do that?"

"This is a city-powers meeting," I said as I tapped Pike's chest with Doyle's warrant. "Here in Cincinnati, it has rules. No spell casting, vampiric bespelling, manhandling, killing, or abduction." I looked at Doyle. "Legal or otherwise. You try anything with Zack or anyone else, I will turn you into toast and feed you to the pixies. Think you can sit quietly and listen?"

"City-powers meeting?" Pike echoed, clearly surprised, and I stood beside Trent, smug even as I worried about that warrant. They had me dead to rights, but I was busy.

"Yes. At my church. 'Cause I'm a city power, and it's my turn to host it," I said flippantly to try to hide my unease. I'd been a part of a few of these impromptu meetings—even called one once—but coming home to one in my church made me feel as if it was more of an intervention than the usual fact-finding, alliance-building endeavor. *Yay me.*

Pike chuckled, wincing when something pulled. "Is any of that chili left?"

Arms crossed, I stared at him, blocking the door. All his weight was on one foot. It would be easy to knock him down. Somehow, I resisted the urge. Maybe it was the warrant in my hand.

"Oh, good Lord," Edden whispered, and I relented.

"Fine. You can come in," I said, sullen as I shifted aside. Trent wanted him here. I didn't know why, but I would trust that.

Mrs. Sarong eyed Pike. "You will not sit by me," she said, then turned away. "We're trying to decide who we are going to kill. Constance, or Rachel," she added over her shoulder. "The entire city is in disarray, and it has to stop."

"Oh." Pike smiled as he pushed past me stinking of dried blood and sweat. "I vote to kill Rachel."

I huffed my annoyance, but David touched my shoulder in encouragement before hustling after Pike. Doyle took a step forward to follow, and I put up a hand. "No," I said, and he reddened. "You delivered your warrant. You can wait in the car. I'll get back to you."

"Ah . . ." Doyle started, and I slammed the door in his face. "You can't do that! You have been served!" came faintly through the thick oak door, and I frowned, not liking how Pike was looking at me when I strode into the sanctuary.

"You're going to pretend that warrant doesn't exist, aren't you," Pike said as Trent passed us, his hand leaving tingles when it traced across my lower back. "Magic and money make right? You'll make a great city power."

I followed Trent, a guilty anger roiling my gut. "I see

you got your babysitters back," I snipped. "Safe again under Constance's protection. Congratulations."

Pike took an angry breath, hesitating when he saw Etude hunched by the window, his red eyes shining. "Don't judge me," he said softly, and the gargoyle's ears pinned. "You are exactly like her in putting yourself above the law. What's it going to be this time? Blackmail? Magic?" His eyes went to Trent. "Or money?"

"You should shut up until you know what you are talking about," I said, but guilt was an unexpected prick at my soul. Frustrated, I went to the slate coffee table and plunked myself down at one of the chairs. Mood bad, I slapped the warrant on the table. It sat there in front of everyone until Edden put a single finger on it and slid it across the table, retreating to a sunny window to look it over. From the rafters, a single black feather spiraled down as Hodin crow-hopped to a new rafter, interested as well.

"I'm sure you can get it sorted out," Vivian said comfortingly, but her brow was furrowed in worry.

"Jenks, will you warn Kaspar and Zack that Pike's here?" I asked suddenly, and the pixy's hover bobbled and his dust shifted to green.

"Yell if you need me," he said, then darted into the foyer and up the belfry stairs.

"Go-o-o-od chili." Pike eagerly helped himself to another bowl and sat beside Mrs. Sarong. Nose wrinkled, the woman shifted away with a little sniff. Edden sighed as he set the warrant down, and Trent stepped forward to take it. Head lowered, he took it to the piano and David, Hodin mirroring the move in the rafters.

"May we continue?" Mrs. Sarong said dryly, eyeing Pike's torn clothes and enthusiastic spoon-to-mouth. "I've already gone past my allotted time for this. As I see it, Rachel's continued claim to Cincinnati and her attempt to drive Constance out—the legal vampire representative, I may add—is making more unrest, not less."

"I'm working on it," I said as I watched Pike eat as if

he'd never seen food before. A good Brimstone cookie would do that to you, though.

"This is not a trial, Rachel," Vivian said encouragingly. "We simply want to know how you are going to get Constance to leave."

"And if we can help," David added, earning a derisive look from Mrs. Sarong.

I slumped where I sat, wanting my coffee but not enough to go get it. I hadn't really thought about the how, having been more concerned with Zack. "I can move now that Zack is safe," I said, not addressing Mrs. Sarong's exact concern.

Pike noisily scraped his bowl. "I thought you were here to force her compliance." He looked from Mrs. Sarong to Vivian in disbelief, then wiped a bit of chili from his lips. "You think Morgan can get Constance out of Cincinnati?"

I didn't like the silence, hearing an unspoken doubt in it as Hodin shifted his feathers.

"Rachel, it's *you* who are tearing the city apart," Mrs. Sarong said, clearly appreciating Pike's disbelief. "All you have done is send her a lily?"

"Hey!" I barked, and everyone but Trent and Etude jumped. "That *lily* drove her from her daylight quarters. A *master* vampire. No one died. No one got bitten. Do you have any idea what it would have cost to accomplish that with manpower?"

A flicker of understanding slowed Pike's spoon-to-mouth and, seeing it, I sat up. "Tell me, Mrs. Sarong," I said, rising to go get my coffee. "Have you given any thought to your new normal under Constance? Have you met her? Seen firsthand how she manipulates her camarilla? What she's *doing* to the vampires?" I stifled a grimace, remembering Kip helping Joni out of Constance's line of fire. "Her own people are scared to death of her, not because she might accidentally drain or kill them. No, they're afraid that she's going to push them past their limits, luring them into behavior they've worked all their lives to avoid. Constance is insane. Not just undead insane, but down-to-the-core nuts." Pulse fast, I glanced at Pike. "No offense."

"I'm the last person to argue with that assessment," he said as he set his empty bowl on the table, that same odd look lurking in the back of his eyes. He was thinking. *About what?*

"I got out of the I.S. because her *own people* helped me," I added, feeling uneasy. "Give me some time. I'm taking care of it."

"You don't have time," Mrs. Sarong said stiffly, dark eyes angry. "Kill her or kiss her ring. Not next week, not tomorrow. Today. Our first home game is in three days, and if I can't open my stadium because of city unrest, I will lose millions."

"You're worried about your bottom line?" I said, incredulous, and her chin lifted.

"Ah . . ." David raised a fast hand. "I'm not advocating murder."

"Me either," Edden piped up.

"You are unbelievable, Ellen," I said, and the Were flushed, probably because I used her first name. "I had to get Zack free before taking stronger action. I will *not* sacrifice the leader of one faction of Inderland to make another feel safer." Shaking inside, I leaned back against the cushions. "Or do I have your okay to do nothing if Constance picks up, say, your daughter, Mrs. Sarong, dresses her to look like me, and drains her over a long weekend?"

"I wouldn't put my daughter in that position," Mrs. Sarong said coldly.

"You think siding against me will make you safe?" I said in disbelief, then froze, turning to look to the front of the church at the small scuff of noise. Slumping, I exhaled to drive the anger from me. It was Kaspar and Zack. Kaspar's hands were wreathed in a purple-tinted aura of unfocused force, hatred showing in the clench of his jaw. Zack didn't look much better, but at least he wasn't dripping potential pain from his fingers as he stood beside him in my blue terry-cloth robe. Jenks was on his shoulder, whispering in his ear. They were looking at Pike.

"If Pike touches you, he dies," I said to Zack, and this time, Pike didn't laugh.

"What did I miss?" Zack said with an affected lightness, and Kaspar jumped to follow when the young elf paced forward, his bare feet silent on the newly sealed floor as he went to stand with Trent. Trent had been very quiet while I took a stand, not because he didn't agree with me, but because he was watching the room, seeing the unsaid alliances . . . weighing our options.

We make a good team, I thought as his worried eyes met mine.

Edden shifted to make room for Zack at the piano bench. "Mrs. Sarong is suggesting Rachel step up her game."

"I'm sure, as a demon, you have killed before," Mrs. Sarong prompted, and my jaw clenched. "Assassination is often the fastest, least damaging way to achieve change."

"I'm all for that," Zack said, looking not nearly nervous enough as he sat beside Edden. "You need some help, Rachel?"

"Count me in," Jenks added. "Give me five minutes. I need to pee first."

Vivian covered her eyes as if she had a headache, but David chuckled, helping himself to two more cookies before handing Zack the bag. Motions stiff, the kid dipped a hand in and began to eat them with a methodical swiftness. He was probably starving, if not from shape-shifting, then from avoiding eating while Constance's guest.

And yes, there were names and faces that haunted me, people who died because I hadn't been quick enough, or I'd made a poor decision, or simply because they had the bad luck to be at the wrong place at the right time. But never intentionally. My vision went distant as I thought of Peter, a living vampire in agony looking for passage to his second life. *That was a mercy killing.*

My focus sharpened on Pike. He was staring at me, thoughts unknown. "I'm not killing Constance," I said, and Trent seemed to relax even as Hodin made a bird-chortle. "I'm convincing her to cut her losses and leave. That's it." But how, I wasn't sure yet.

Mrs. Sarong frowned at her watch. "Cerberus's balls. I

have wasted too much time here to be delicate. Rachel. If you do not kill Constance and end this feud, we will band together to kill you to end it."

"Whoa, whoa, whoa," Edden said as my lips parted. "I didn't agree to that."

"I'd like to see you try." Jenks dropped down before her, brilliant sparkles falling from him.

"This is not why I'm here," Vivian said quickly. "Mrs. Sarong, you do not speak for anyone but yourself. Killing Rachel is not a solution. She said she's handling it. For God's sake, if you don't want another San Francisco, let her work."

Grinning, Pike settled deeper into the couch. "This just got interesting. I vote with Mrs. Sarong to kill Rachel."

"Hey!" I exclaimed, feeling attacked. "If you don't like how I'm handling Constance, handle her yourself."

"That is what I'm doing." Mrs. Sarong's eyes were brilliant. "Fix it, or I will by taking you out."

Pike snickered as he rose. "I think I'll have another bowl of that chili."

"One of you has to die," Mrs. Sarong said, "and frankly, Rachel, you are the easier target. Living in a church with no security the way you do."

Jenks's wings rasped. "Try our security. I haven't shaved a Were's tail in a while."

"Letting anyone in who shows up at your door. Trusting everyone," Mrs. Sarong continued, her expression twisted as she looked over the sanctuary cluttered with other people's lives and needs.

David smirked, leaning to whisper something to Zack that made Etude, way on the other side of the sanctuary, chuckle.

My coffee was cold, but I didn't dare warm it. I'd probably set it on fire. "You'd be surprised how few people I trust," I said, not happy that Hodin, much less Pike, was hearing this.

"You certainly don't show it," the stiff woman said, but I was watching Trent. He'd gone to get a second cup of coffee.

It put him right next to Pike, and that was where he stayed, a faint glimmer of magic playing about his fingertips. Kaspar, too, had shifted closer to Zack in protection. Jenks's dust was starting to look like migraine sparkles. Hodin was the only one seeming to be enjoying himself, the bird bobbing his head as if in laughter. Things were getting out of hand, and I wished Edden wasn't so vulnerable.

"That's because I don't have to," I said as I crossed the room to get beside the FIB captain. If spells started flying, I wanted him in a bubble. "Look," I said when I felt Vivian strengthen her grip on the nearest ley line. "And listen good. Some of you know me better than others, but for those of you who don't, I'm going to be really clear here. If you kill me to put Constance in charge, it won't only be Constance's unbalanced, ego-driven politics you will have to deal with." I turned to Kaspar. "The man over there who saved your species from extinction?" I turned to Vivian and Mrs. Sarong. "The one who keeps the Brimstone flowing so you don't become prey?" I turned to Pike. "Or you from having to take the unwilling and start an interspecies war? The only person besides myself and Etude who has ridden with demons in the Hunt and might have half an ounce of pull with them? If you kill me, that man is going to return to being a power-hungry, zero-empathy, backstabbing bastard set on world domination."

Across the room, Trent saluted everyone with his coffee. Vivian nodded as Mrs. Sarong made an ugly face. Pike looked confused, as if not knowing how big a power-hungry, zero-empathy, backstabbing bastard set on world domination Trent could be, but David? David's expression was deadly serious. He'd once told me I'd saved Trent's life by showing him he could be someone other than what his father had made him.

"And trust me," I added as Etude chuckled, the sound like rocks in a crusher. "He's a lot more dangerous now than he was three years ago when he had his fingers in everything east of the Mississippi."

"Not everything," Trent said modestly as he took a sip.

"How is he dangerous?" Mrs. Sarong said, a delicate hand placed on a knee. "I see a man losing things, not gaining power."

Jenks landed on my shoulder in a show of solidarity. "Things don't make you powerful."

"They help," Kaspar muttered, and Pike nodded.

"Perhaps. But I showed Trent that magic had no rules. You really want that plus his money combined in an elf set on revenge?" I hesitated. "Kill me to curry favor with Constance, and *that* is what you will get."

For a moment, there was only the sound of a passing car. Then it was gone, filling the church with silence.

Etude shifted his great feet, his claws leaving not a mark on the new floor. "I didn't come here to threaten Rachel Morgan."

"Neither did I," Edden said, and I gave him a thankful smile.

"Me either," David chimed in. "I came to see what I can do to help her. Mrs. Sarong, go chase a ball to hell."

Zack stood, his youthful face red in rebellion as Kaspar tried to get him to stay silent. "I'm not making one move against Rachel," he stated firmly.

"Sa'han," Kaspar protested, and the young elf rounded on him, looking powerful even in my blue terry-cloth robe.

"Are you serious?" the kid said, and Jenks chuckled. "She just got me away from the most depraved undead who has lived in the last three hundred years! Threatening to kill the one person who isn't afraid to stand up to Constance is not my idea of a good life choice."

A knot of worry slowly unraveled around my chest, and I took a breath, now understanding why Trent had invited Pike. He had arranged this, got Mrs. Sarong's opinion out in the open where it could be seen. And in the process, confirmed the support of those who were behind me. I wasn't sure how I'd get Constance to leave, but now I knew who I could depend on, and that was more than half the task. *Thank you, Trent.*

"Okay," I said, and all eyes came back to me. "I've heard

your complaint, Mrs. Sarong. Now you need to leave." I looked at Pike. "You too."

Mrs. Sarong stood. "I have stated my position, and I will hold to it."

"As have I," David almost growled as he settled in more firmly beside Ivy's baby grand. Seeing him there, a shiver coursed through me. He had the strength of a loner and the clout of an alpha, and his unsaid threat wasn't empty.

Vivian stood as well, clearly unhappy. "Rachel." She came to me and took my hands as Mrs. Sarong click-clacked to the door. "I'm leaving, too." Her eyes pinched in regret. "My official stance is that the witches are giving you time to settle this. Nothing more. Use it," she said. "Coven intel thinks that the DC vampires sent her here for you to kill or be killed. Either way, it's one less thing they have to worry about. They don't care who wins."

Ivy had said something similar, and I nodded, concerned. The church's door slammed shut, and Jenks's wings tickled my neck as he settled in. "Then they're going to be disappointed when I send her back to them, unscathed." I glanced at Trent, who was on the phone again, then at David and Edden, both clearly staying. "It was good seeing you," I added, giving her a quick hug to feel the ley line swirling in her, and I tightened my grip on my internal energy balance before they tried to equalize. "Are you staying in town? Maybe we can have lunch."

Pike snickered from the couch, clearly thinking I had no tomorrow.

Vivian frowned at him, then her features eased. "I'm at the Cincinnatian until this is settled. My treat, okay? Sorry about Ellen. She is a true alpha bitch. Let me know if you need a character witness."

My eyes slid to the warrant as she turned to leave, and my shoulders slumped. *Oh, yeah . . .*

"Sa'han, please," I heard Kaspar beg, and Zack stood, his expression sour as he tied my robe tighter about his waist.

"Fine, fine!" the kid grumped, but he looked ready to drop, and Kaspar probably wanted to get him back to his own security. "But can you give Rachel and me a moment first?" he added, and Kaspar made a respectful half bow and retreated.

Etude's low, rumbling snore echoed in the sanctuary, and I smiled as I went to give Zack a hug. But it faltered as I met his eyes and saw his grief for Nash, what they had done to him, to them both. Pike had moved to the make-shift kitchen, and the hair on the back of my neck pricked. I hesitated, not wanting the ugly man to see our pain lest he think we were weak, but heartache didn't make one weak. Heartache meant you had loved, and therein lay an immeasurable strength.

"Zack, did Kaspar tell you . . ."

Zack's fair hair fell to cover his eyes, but then he lifted his chin, bangs shifting. "He did."

Jenks rose from my shoulder as two cars started up. "Hey, uh, Rache? I'm going to do a search." The pixy gave Zack a nod good-bye. "Someone left a bug. I can hear it. Probably that moss wipe Kaspar," he muttered, then flew to where Trent, Edden, and David stood discussing Pike, the living vampire helping himself to another bowl of chili.

But I was grateful they were leaving us alone, and I took Zack in a long, encouraging hug, breathing in the scent of cookies and the zing of unspent ley line energy, feeling his youth, and under that, a core of strength that was thousands of years old.

"She needs to die," Zack said, his muffled voice cracking, and I let him go.

"Probably." I looked at him, seeing his old soul and his new body all mixed up. "But I'm not going to do it, and neither are you." I hesitated, needing to know. "I didn't have time to ask you before. When you were in the I.S. tower, did anyone . . ."

His jaw tightened, and he glared over my shoulder at Pike. "No," he said flatly. "No one even scratched my skin." His expression twisted, and he blinked fast, his eyes suddenly swimming. "Nash . . ." he choked out. "He took it all for me. I never asked him," he pleaded. "God, Rachel, what they did was beyond understanding. She *can't* be allowed to be Cincinnati's master vampire."

"I agree." A lump filled my throat, and I put my arm across his back to lead him to the door. "I can't—" My voice broke, and I took a slow breath. "He's been laid to rest," I said softly so the words wouldn't clog within me. "The mystics themselves led him to the Goddess."

He scuffed to a halt in the foyer. The dark seemed to make the truth easier to bear, and awareness slowly dawned on him as to what that meant. "Kaspar said . . ."

"The ritual is yours." His hands were in mine, and I felt the ley line prick against my palm. "I gave it to Trent, but I'm giving it to you as well. The mystics wouldn't have taken Nash to be a part of the Goddess if he hadn't been worthy of it."

Zack's head dropped, and again he was a kid who had lost someone, struggling to understand. "I never asked him to," he quavered, and I pulled him close and gave him a rocking hug.

"I know. So did he." I pushed back and tried to meet his eyes. "Go home. Do what makes you happy. Think of Nash and know he died for what was important to him. No one can ask for more than that."

Sniffing, Zack looked past me to find Kaspar. "Keep me in the loop," he said, voice hard. "I was serious about helping you."

The boy was gone, and the leader of the dewar was back, and I nodded. "Promise," I said, squinting when Kaspar opened the door and the light poured in. Arms about my middle, I watched Kaspar meet Zack's stride as they went down my steps and back into the world. Kaspar was already yammering about something, but Zack clearly wasn't listening, his thoughts somewhere more important.

The sound of a closing car door drew my attention to Doyle, and I frowned, reality crashing back. I gave him a wave before I went inside, leaning against the closed door as I collected my thoughts. The homeless vampires were gone and the church felt empty.

Mood uneasy, I scuffed to the couch. David and Edden were quietly going over a map at the piano, and I felt Trent's eyes heavy on me as I flopped down into the cushions. A hint of vampire incense rose, and I held my breath, waiting for it to dissipate.

Until I realized it wasn't coming from the couch, but Pike, a paper plate of chips in his hand. "The meeting is over," I said. "And the chili is gone. You need to leave. Spy."

Pike grinned to show his small fangs. "Rebel."

"I'm not a rebel. I'm a realist." I gazed at Hodin, then to Trent, still talking with Edden and David at the piano. My head snapped up when Pike shifted to sit beside me.

"I think you handled it pretty well," he said around a sigh. "For an amateur."

"Yeah? What would Constance have done?"

He thought for a moment and ate a chip. *He's eating crunchy things, and I asked him about his gnomon. Way to go, Rachel.* Uneasy, I looked across the room at Trent, flushing when I realized they were discussing that warrant, not the city map.

"Mmmm, probably gotten blood angsty," Pike said distantly. "Threaten to drain those who oppose her. Cause a bloodbath." He noisily ate another chip. "Pick out another doll. You saw her. That was her SOP. You did pretty good, if somewhat soft-gloved." His eyes came to mine. "No one died. Yet."

"Yay me," I muttered, foot bobbing. *Failure to halt and malicious destruction?*

My focus sharpened when Pike stood, that plate of chips still in his hand. "I'm not surprised the FIB and gargoyles stood by you," he said, looking at Edden. "Maybe most of the elves. A half-assed commitment by the witches balanced out by an unexpected small but militant faction of the Weres." His eyes went to the three men by the piano. "The way you got out of the I.S. surprised me. It never occurred to me that I.S. employees would help you."

"Yeah, well, we all make mistakes," I said.

"But the takeaway for me from this is that Mrs. Sarong felt the need to threaten you," he said, finger raised as if in lecture. "She could've simply sent someone to kill you. That tells me something."

Maybe he had a point, but I failed to see it.

"You still want to meet with Constance?"

My bobbing foot stilled. Across the sanctuary, the low murmur of David's and Trent's voices stopped. "You mean outside of the I.S.? Not through that warrant?"

He nodded, a faint smile quirking his lips. "The warrant was Doyle's idea. She'd rather take care of you herself. You really put a chip in her fang."

My head began to hurt. Yes, it was what I wanted, but any meeting was going to be her trying to kill me as I tried to convince her to cut her losses and go back to DC. *How am I going to do that?* And yet, it was my car keys left on my visor that my thoughts kept returning to, the look Joni had given Pike before she left the room. "Why are you helping me?"

"I'm not helping you. I'm giving Constance a chance to rethink her dispute with you."

I arched my eyebrows, and Pike shrugged. "Constance needs to know you have an in with the coven of moral and ethical standards, enough that you can drop in at Alcatraz and leave unscathed. That you make demands of demons, even if they do fling you across the continent. That you host city-powers meetings in your church with elves, gargoyles, Weres, and witches—all at the same time." He shook his head ruefully. "And that you are confident enough to kick them out and disregard their advice."

"Yeah, well, Mrs. Sarong's advice sucks."

Chuckling, Pike picked through his chips. "That you have the ear, the bed, and the heart of the man who farms her Brimstone. She needs to be reminded that though the I.S. has an official, long-running stance of antagonism toward you, you have enough pull to move seamlessly within both the I.S. and FIB to get what you want, when you need it, be it information or simply someone to look the other way. Why is that, I wonder. None of them like you much."

I squinted at him, wondering at his distant expression. *Does he think I could handle Cincinnati?*

"She needs to know that your church is being rebuilt by the people she displaced, that threatening Zack only pissed you off," he continued. "That she should avoid underestimating you and work something out that is beneficial to both of you and won't end up with her dead twice."

My eyebrows rose. "You think she might agree to run the vampire affairs under me?" I said, and Pike's focus sharpened.

"I doubt it, but she might allow you to function as an enforcer under her. You have clout, Ms. Morgan. And she needs to respect that. Understand that. Work within it, maybe, or risk being driven back to DC and that floor of rented rooms they gave her under the Smithsonian." He hesitated. "You say you want to live here. Be careful, she might let you." He ate a chip and looked at Etude sleeping by the door. "Does tonight work?"

Tonight? I glanced at Trent clustered with David and Edden. Jenks had returned and was watching me, clearly hearing everything we were saying though he was across the room. Yes, I wanted this, but I wanted to know something else first.

"You left the keys in my car for me," I said suddenly. "Why?"

Pike's head went down, his smoke-grimed hair hiding his eyes. "No, I didn't."

He had, and I leaned forward, my elbows on my knees. "You trying to catch me wasn't fake," I added, remembering the hatred in his eyes as he tried to down me in the tower. "What gives?"

His shoulders shifted as he set the empty plate on the table. "I gave you," he said, his eyes losing their rim of brown behind the rising black, "an eleven percent chance of making it out of the tower. But if you did?" His head tilted. "If you managed to evade Constance and me both, I figured you shouldn't have to take the bus home."

He believed in the eleven percent, and I eyed him specu-
latively. "I don't get you, Pike."

"That makes two of us," he muttered. "Do you want me
to arrange something with Constance tonight or not? Mrs.
Sarong is right. You need to castrate the calf, or let it grow
into a bull."

Tired, I sent my gaze across the church to see what everyone thought about it. Hodin chortled softly, which could
mean anything. Jenks rose up and down, his sparkles meaning a solid "yes." Edden, Trent, and David were silent, varying degrees of dismay and worry on their faces.

"Sure," I said slowly, and Trent's jaw tightened as he
reached for his phone. "Tonight. Midnight. The Turn memorial down by the waterfront." I stood fast, and Pike took
a step back, grimacing as if he hadn't meant to. "Tell her
she can bring one. Her best," I added. "I am."

CHAPTER

26

A LOUD THUMP JOLTED THROUGH ME, AND I JERKED. THE fast movement tore the splat ball I was filling, rendering it useless. "Damn it to the Turn and back," I muttered as I tossed the pellet into the trash and shook a new one from the box. Careful to keep the tip of the syringe from touching me and knocking me out, I filled it with sleepy-time potion. The thumping continued, getting louder when my door squeaked open. Surprised, I looked up, but it was only Rex, the orange cat appearing a mite peeved. "Come on in," I said as I went back to my work. "It's the only room with less than thirty people."

I was exaggerating, but the church *had* gotten noisy, driving me into the belfry to prep for my meeting with Constance. Pike was gone, but I could still smell vampire incense lingering on the fainting couch. David's car and Edden's cruiser hadn't moved from the curb, meaning they were still arguing over where to put everyone so they were both useful and not in the way. It was flattering that so many wanted to help, but I was beginning to worry about the fallout.

Rex rubbed against my leg on his way to the window, but his leap to the low sill halted comically fast as the bell overhead gave a soft bong and the screenless opening was suddenly full of a large crow, his feathers unusually shiny in the late sun.

"Hey, Hodin," I said as the cat made a back-arched hiss. "I'm glad you're still here."

"Caw!" he barked aggressively, wings extended, and Rex retreated to hide amid the boxes, watching with evil-cat eyes as Hodin hopped into the room, dissolved into a mist, and solidified into a peeved-looking, scholarly demon.

A flicker of guilt washed through his red, goat-slitted eyes as they came back from Bis, but it vanished when he saw my prepped splat balls, his eyebrows going high to make me feel as if I was finger-painting horsies in a 400-level sculpture class. "Come on in," I said, seeing as he was already here, and he took another step, making the bells on his black robe chime. I hadn't seen this particular spelling robe before, it being rather plain compared to his usual embroidered finery. His dark hair was bound up under a matching flat-topped hat, and pointy-toed shoes rather than his customary slippers poked from under his hem. Though more casual than his traditional spelling robes, it was still more formal than his leather and untamed hair, meaning he was either trying to impress me or he wanted to help. I was betting the latter.

"I'm here to offer assistance," he said, and I met his eyes through the dresser's mirror, exhaling in impatience.

"Hodin, I thought I was clear on this. You are not my teacher," I said, my gaze flicking to the stack of books that Al had given me—no, stolen for me.

"A friend can give advice," he offered, his lips pulled back in a weird sort of smile.

"You aren't my friend, either," I muttered, as I made a mental note to take the books to Junior's if I survived tonight. I could give Dali a piece of my mind, too, for sending me into the lion's den like that. *God save me from demons.*

Hodin shifted and the bells on his sash chimed. "Is that so?"

"That is so." He was behind me, and I didn't like it as I decanted a portion of the primed sleepy-time potion into the syringe. "I invited you to listen in on the city-powers meeting because it's always smart to have a demon other than me knowing what's going on. I'm trying hard not to be mad at you, because it's not your fault that the rest of the demons are acting like spoiled, entitled children who got their feelings hurt, but so help me, if you try to step into Al's shoes, you will find out the hard way how I bankrupted him in two years."

"Really."

His flat utterance turned me around. "Really," I said, looking him up and down. "I'll continue to stand beside you because I said I would and because I believe in what you're doing, but I won't take instruction from you. If you don't have any intel—which I will accept—then you need to leave before Al finds out you're here and throws me back into Alcatraz."

"Mmmm."

The single utterance hung in the bird-laced silence, and I went back to injecting the last splat ball. That made forty-nine. Maybe it was overkill, but they'd last for a year.

"You should make that witch Stephanie do that for you," he said as he leaned to look.

"She has work, and besides, she's not my familiar." I exhaled, jaw clenching. The pearls I'd taken from Nash hung from a corner of the mirror, faintly clicking as the old dresser shifted. I hadn't known what to do with them, but cleaning them had seemed appropriate, and the long strand circled Hodin's reflection. He was apparently in no hurry to leave, staring up at Bis as if in guilt.

"Hodin, I don't want your help. Not because Dali said so, but because Al is right. If I can't do this on my own, then I won't be able to handle what follows on my own, and I'm tired of needing help, okay?" Maybe I was being dramatic, but I didn't like the idea that he might be trying to take Al's place—even if Al might have left it for good.

Hodin seemed to hesitate, and then, as if having decided something, he drew a small but elaborate cricket cage from the ether. "Then perhaps you will accept something to practice your immobilization curse on," he said as he set it on the dresser and slid it to me with a loud, attention-getting scrape.

I drew back, even as my gaze lingered on it, captured by its singular beauty and function. "I know how to do an immobilization curse. I used it on Pike this afternoon."

He bobbed his head, his attention on the moving insects. "Then practicing it can't be construed as me teaching you anything. As it is, you're only proficient enough to down one at a time. A curse is faster than a vampire, but not two." He grinned, the unusual expression looking odd on his typically serious face. "Practice will amend that."

Practice will amend that, I mocked in my head, thinking he sounded like Al. "It's beautiful. Is it spelled to keep them in there?" I asked as I tapped the cage and a cricket began to sing, spurring the others to join him. There were high turrets and delicate scrolling, heavy on the Asian influence with the black gold wire twined about itself to make a snug, elaborate enclosure for a handful of black crickets crawling up the sides and top, all chirping merrily.

"Ah, yes, it is, actually." Suddenly unsure, he clasped his hands. "The two on the top, there. Try it. Unless you feel it is beyond you," he goaded, and I felt myself warm.

Technically he wasn't teaching me anything, so I focused on the two crickets and tightened my grip on the nearest ley line. *"Stabils,"* I said, feeling the energy ball up in my palms before I flicked it at them. My magic coated both crickets, but only one froze, dropping to the floor of the cage with a sad thump to leave the other calmly cleaning its antennae. "Huh," I muttered as I broke the curse and it shook itself upright, chirping like a startled bird.

Hodin gestured for me to try again, and I focused harder on two much closer crickets, narrowing my attention until they were my entire world. *"Stabils,"* I said again, sending the energy at them, but as before, only one went still and fell over. *Crap on toast, this is embarrassing.* "Are you sure multiple applications are possible with this curse?" I asked.

The bells on Hodin's sash rang as he shifted closer, and Rex's eyes widened to a predatory black. "You're like a child babbling sounds that will become words. Again," Hodin said, but if it was meant to be encouraging, it wasn't.

Maybe if I use two hands, I thought as I broke the curse and the cricket began to hop frantically as if trying to escape. *"Stabils,"* I whispered, gesturing with both hands, and nothing happened. It hadn't worked at all. *Not a two-fisted curse, then.*

Hodin took a breath and, frustrated, I looked up with an annoyed "Stop!"

Brow furrowed, he frowned. "How are you going to kill Constance tonight? Sleepy-time charm her to death?" he said as he reached to inspect my splat gun pellets.

Uncomfortable with him being so close, I moved to the fainting couch, sitting with my knees almost to my chin. "Weren't you listening this afternoon? I'm not killing her," I said, and he arched his eyebrows in a silent rebuke. "Pike is going to try to convince her to take me seriously," I added, and Hodin blinked as if I was a fool for trusting Pike. "Apparently I impressed him with my interspecies connections. He thinks I'm a real threat, and if she believes him, she might settle down. If she doesn't, I'll turn her into a mouse and send her back to DC in a box."

My eyes went to the cricket cage as an idea surfaced. "Hey, can I keep this?"

"No," he said flatly. "It would be easier to kill her and become the subrosa. Anything less, and it will be work, work, work to keep her suppressed."

"Killing her only looks easy. I'm not doing it," I muttered, remembering Al saying the same thing. Even if the DC vamps had sent her here for one of us to kill the other, I'd land in jail or be forced to flee to the ever-after. No, I had to send her back with her fangs filed down, proving I could handle the Cincinnati vamps on my own so they wouldn't just send another.

Hodin made a low growl, and my chin lifted. "This is what I'm doing, okay? I'll pin her down with an immobilization curse and turn her into a mouse."

Hodin grinned. "Can I have her?"

"No. She goes back to DC with the countercurse." Yes, the woman had to be stopped, and yes, transformation was better than killing her, but still . . . Turning her into a rodent to force her compliance was . . . demonic.

Uneasy, I focused on two crickets across the room, thinking, *Stabils.* But as before, only one went silent, the other continuing to chirp, filling my belfry with the sound of fall.

"Perhaps if you focus the curse by directing it to the auras in question?" Hodin suggested.

Peeved, I stood up from the couch. "All right. You need to leave. Now," I demanded, pointing at the window, and he grinned, red eyes glinting.

"I'll leave you to your practice, then." Hodin turned to the window.

"Hodin?" I called, and he hesitated with his back to me, clearly listening. "If I do crap out on this, will you tell Al—"

"No," he interrupted, and then he was gone, winking out with an enviable ease.

Someday I will be able to do that, I thought, my attention going to Bis before dropping to Rex as the cat came out from between the boxes. Immediately he jumped onto the top of the dresser to pat at the cricket cage, and I lurched forward before he knocked it off.

"Hold on there, Mr. Wild Kingdom," I said as I moved him to the floor. "If you want crickets, have your daddy Jenks find you one in the garden. These are for me to practice on," I added as I stood on a box and set the cage out of his reach beside Bis.

I had barely gotten down before a light knuckle-knock sounded at the door. Hand to my head, I sighed. *What part of "I'm in the belfry" don't you get?* "If someone isn't on fire, go away!" I shouted.

"It's me," Trent said, and my grimace shifted to a smile.

"*You* can come in," I said as I shuffled about for an empty splat ball hopper.

His smile was wide as he did just that, firmly shutting out the rising argument concerning popcorn salt. Looking over the small space, he exhaled in relief. "How's it going?"

"Okay. That's my last one." Turning, I dropped the filled hopper into my waiting bag.

His eyes traveled over my frizzy hair, down my black tee, jeans, and running shoes. "Is that what you're wearing?"

A faint warmth rose as I gathered my curling hair into a ponytail and let it go. "Yep." I wanted to be able to run, and Constance wouldn't be impressed with my best slacks and the pearls I had taken from Nash. *Or maybe she would,* I thought, eyes going to them.

His head bobbed. "Great. So you're ready?"

"As much as I ever am." Stiff, I stood and stretched. "I might get something to eat, though." I cringed as the loud, rhythmic thumping began to tremble the floorboards.

"Food. Yes." Trent held out a hand, the pearl on his ring glowing faintly. "I have an errand to run, and I want you to come with me. We can get something to eat on the way."

"Now?" There was a tingle as my hand fitted in his, and he pulled me into him with a little, welcome thump.

"Since you're done," he said, voice soft. "You need a break and something to eat besides chili and chips."

I chuckled, my front pressing into his. "It's good chili, though."

"If you like chocolate in it." He gave a tug, pulling me deeper against him, his gaze heavy on mine until the lingering vampire pheromones in the church seemed to hum against my skin. "Come with me? Burger and fries. Lots of ketchup."

"Well, if there's going to be ketchup," I said, and he chuckled, letting me go so I could shove everything I wanted with me tonight into my bag. The cage I'd rigged up for Pike was already in there, and I stifled a surge of anticipation. This would work. It had to.

"Where are we going?" I said as I carefully left the door cracked for Rex, but I don't think Trent even heard me as we hit the foyer and the noise became even louder.

Simply put, it was a mess. As quiet and empty of refugees as the church had been during my city-powers meeting, it was now that loud and noisy, full of displaced families with kids trying to cope, childless couples watching them in horror, and singles laughing at them both. David and Edden were at the baby grand with three capable-looking alphas and a fourth who was probably a witch, judging by the number of jewelry-disguised amulets. An overly bright, industrial work light made a hot spotlight on a map strewn with lines and notations, making it obvious they were talking proper deployment of people and spells.

David looked up at our dark shapes in the foyer, giving me a smile before going back to his discussion. Jenks was with them, and I winced when he rose up over it all and headed our way. Stef, who was busy applying a deep-tissue-pain charm on someone's hammer-smashed thumb, looked up at his wing clatter, following his path to me. I gave her a wave and ducked out after Trent before I was recognized by anyone else. We'd never get out of here.

"Hey, Rache!" the pixy said as he darted out the closing door, and I hesitated on the brightly lit stoop. "You think you can just check out of Hotel Morgan and Jenks?"

"Running an errand," I said as Trent and I took the stairs together and headed for his car, somewhere in the dark.

"That's why you got all them charms in your bag, eh?" he said. "I'll get my bandana."

Jenks zipped off, and the breath I took to protest sort of spilled away as his bright gold dust settled. "Okay . . ."

"And I thought Quen was overly protective." Trent's arm went around my waist, tugging me closer and starting more tingles. "But I've never said no to a third pair of eyes." A loud, whooping cheer rose up from the church, and Trent winced. "Wow. How can you work in that?"

"Well, I *was* in the belfry," I said sourly. I missed my quiet church, but really, I couldn't kick them out. Not when it might all be over in four hours.

Trent pointed his fob, and his car started with a satisfying *brumm* of Detroit muscle. Hand slipping from me, he rushed forward to get my door, and I felt special as I got in, and carefully settled my bag on my lap. I watched his slim, quickly moving shadow as he went around front. The dark seemed to bring out the elf in him, and I smiled, thinking I was lucky.

I rolled my window down for Jenks as Trent slipped in with the delicious scent of cinnamon and wine, new leaves . . . and long, breezy nights. "Jenks!" I shouted, and the pixy darted in with his red bandana shoved in a back pocket.

"Tink's tampons, there are people everywhere!" he said as he landed on the rearview mirror. "Rache, you should just snip the dead vamp so these people can go home."

"I'm beginning to see the appeal," I muttered as Trent put the car in drive and did a three-point turn in one tight move and headed to the waterfront. For one blessed moment silence filled the car—until Jenks dropped down to the console, his pixy curiosity getting the better of him.

"So, where are we going?" he asked as he checked out a sippy cup one of the girls had left. We were heading for the waterfront, and the options of where to eat were vast.

"Ah." Trent's lips quirked in the come-and-go street-lights. "I, ah, promised Ellasbeth that since I was in town I'd look in on her cat."

Jenks sniggered as he messed about with a tube of lip balm nearly as tall as his waist.

I sat up, never having seen her apartment before. "Doesn't she have a sitter?"

"She does," Trent said quickly. "But she thinks the cat would appreciate seeing someone she knows." Grimacing, he muttered, "That cat knows the UPS man better than me, but it's easier to accommodate her than try to convince her of that." His eyes went to the clock on the dash. "Perhaps it's her way of reminding me she exists. Twenty minutes on her couch, and then we can grab something to eat. I'm thinking soup and sandwich?"

I'd prefer steak and ice cream for my last meal, but soup and sandwich wouldn't weigh me down, and I nodded, wondering how I got here, in Trent's car, checking on his ex-fiancée's cat before going out to convince the city's master vampire to go back to DC. *At least the church is being fixed.*

My eyes flicked to Jenks, now fiddling with the vents. "Hey, Jenks? About the church . . ."

His wings shifted, lighting his space in a bright glow. "It's a mess, isn't it," he said, his dust shifting to an anxious orange. "Even so, I'm going to miss it when we move out."

Chin in my cupped hand, I stared out the side window. "Me too."

Trent made a tired sound, head shaking as he turned to go to the uptown waterfront. "You two are worse than a married couple. Each one so worried about what they think the other one wants that neither of them end up happy. Rachel, do you want to move?"

My lips parted, and I looked from Jenks to Trent. "There are too many bad memories there. It's not fair to Jenks."

"Okay." Trent checked behind us before making a quick left to cross the bridge into the Hollows. "Jenks, how about you? You want to live in an apartment with flower boxes?"

The pixy sat on the sippy cup, wings drooping. "I don't need more than that."

Trent sighed, his eyes flicking behind us again. "Let me try again. Do you both really want to move, or are you making your decision on what you think the other person wants?"

"Do you know how many places we've looked at?" I blurted.

Jenks's wings rasped. "We've been talking about it for months."

A fond smile quirked Trent's lips, clear now as we hit the main Hollows thoroughfare and the lights turned the street to noon. "Do you. Want. To move?" he said. "Honest now."

Jenks slumped, wings going still. "Not really."

I turned in the seat to face him. "But Matalina?" I fumbled. "The kids leaving. I thought . . . Sometimes it takes hours for your dust to brighten after you come in from the garden!"

A sad smile creased his young features. "If I leave, what will I have to remember her by?" he said. "But you need to be somewhere that hasn't been blown up, where you haven't had to fight for your life every three months. How do you sleep at night?"

Pulse fast, I flicked my gaze from Trent to Jenks. "I sleep because I know you're there watching my back."

A smile blossomed over Trent's face. "There," he said softly. "That's better."

"I don't want to move," Jenks said plaintively.

"Me either." I cupped my hand around him, and he rose up, sparkles a brilliant white. "I'm getting used to working in the belfry, and once the mob leaves, we can take a corner of the sanctuary and put in a kitchen." I smiled thinly. "If I'm not in jail in the morning, I want to talk to Finley."

Jenks grinned and lit on my hand. "Me too."

"Thank the Goddess," Trent muttered, clearly relieved as he flicked on his signal and turned into a gated lot. The arm rose immediately, and I looked up at the modern residential tower two blocks off the river. "You want to come in?" he said as he pulled into a visitor parking spot. "Or you could stay here and talk to Doyle," he added.

"Doyle?" I followed Trent's gaze to the street, immediately recognizing the I.S. investigator easing to a halt in a curbside parking spot. My thoughts went back to Trent's constant glances at the rearview mirror, and annoyance crossed me. The warrant. Was he serious? "Such a choice," I said sourly.

"I'm in," Jenks said, but I wasn't sure which would be worse, telling Doyle to chill out until I settled with Constance, or dealing with Ellasbeth when she discovered I'd been in her apartment. So I just sat there until Trent noticed and slumped into his seat.

"Are you sure Ellasbeth won't mind?" I said, and Jenks made a small burst of sparkles. "I'd be ticked if I found out you brought a nameless woman up to pet my cat while I was gone."

Trent put a hand on my knee, his smile encouraging.

"You're not a nameless woman, you're the person who keeps her daughter safe, and I'm sure she assumed you'd be with me."

"Yeah, all right." I wasn't convinced, but I grabbed my purse and got out. There was a real door attendant, and I touched my hair as it blew in the strong wind off the river. Turning to Doyle, I waved, only to get a frown in return. He stayed in the car, though, and I wondered if he was waiting to see if I survived Constance before hauling my ass in for destruction of property and fleeing the scene.

"Are you sure?" I said as the door attendant saw us.

"Positive."

His hand went to my back, propelling me forward. I would have given him a smack on his shoulder, except I kind of liked the mix of possessive demand making tingles down my spine. He was different since stealing his Brimstone back. It was more than the pride of having done it himself. He was . . . more dangerously elfish.

"Mr. Kalamack. Welcome back," the attendant said as she opened the door for us.

"Thank you, Theresa," Trent said familiarly. "Won't be but twenty, thirty minutes." Turning, he looked behind us at Doyle. "He's not with us."

"Yes, sir."

Jenks's wings rasped from my shoulder. "We're checking on Ellasbutt's cat."

"Ah, I'm Rachel Morgan," I said when Theresa's gaze shot to mine, drawn by Jenks's voice. "I keep Lucy and Ray safe when they're with Trent."

"Yes, ma'am. Enjoy your night." Theresa smiled, but I was increasingly uncomfortable.

The small lobby was empty, and an elevator was there waiting. Trent hit the button for the floor just below the penthouse and we started up. Fast. "Hey, can I use your phone?" I asked as Jenks swore at the sudden pressure shift, and Trent silently handed it over. "Pike still has mine."

"Who you calling?" Jenks asked as he made faces to

pop his ears, adding, "Oh, for mother pus bucket of a moss wipe," when I found Ellasbeth's number and hit connect.

She picked up almost immediately. "Trent?" Ellasbeth said, and Trent winced at her voice, loud in the small space. "What's happened? Is it Rachel?"

Jenks hovered close, a manic grin on him. "She's worried about you. That's so sweet."

I glared at Jenks to shut up. "Ah, sorry, Ellasbeth. It's me. Trent's fine, but I lost my phone and I wanted to talk to you."

The elevator dinged, and we got out. I could hear the girls in the background, and I was so glad they were nearly three thousand miles away. Ellasbeth was silent, and I felt myself warm. "Yes?" she finally said, and my breath came in a rush. It was nice up here, and I wondered how much this had set her back.

"Do you mind if I keep Trent company while he's checking on your cat?" I said, and Jenks snorted.

Ellasbeth sighed. "He's standing right there, isn't he," she said flatly.

"Yes, but I'm not setting foot inside your apartment unless you say it's okay. I can wait in the lobby with Jenks." I hesitated, then added, "I'm sorry in advance if Constance tries to kill me here. We've got a meeting tonight, but she might get impatient."

Trent's steps slowed in indecision, and then we went down the corridor toward the river.

"It's fine," she said, but I could hear in her voice she wasn't entirely pleased. "I know Trent won't remember, but my cat's name is Elouise. There's some wine in the fridge and a prepped cheese plate I left for the cat sitter. If it's still there, help yourself."

"Thanks." Okay. Now I could go in. I mean, really. "Do you want to talk to him?"

"Trent? No, but could you ask him to call me tonight after the girls go down?" she said, clearly distracted as Ray's piping voice rose close and insistent. "Good luck with Constance."

"Thanks," I said, but she had already hung up. "And thank you," I added to Trent as I handed him his phone.

His eyes showed his worry as he tucked it away. "She never would have known you were there."

"It wasn't that big of a deal to ask," I said, my confidence restored. "Now I can sit on her couch and not feel as if I'm invading her space."

Jenks landed on Trent's shoulder. "Must be a woman thing."

But Trent had stopped at a double-wide door. It was at the end of the hall, which meant it was a corner apartment. Lots of windows. Pricey. He punched in an eight-digit code at the door, and it unlocked with a muted beep.

"Ah, would you mind taking your shoes off?" Trent said as I went in, and I immediately slowed, appreciating the open floor plan and comparing it to the places Jenks and I had been looking at the last three months. Damn, the woman had money, because I'd never be able to afford so much view of the river and Cincinnati.

"Lights, on soft," Trent said, and the hidden bulbs glowed faintly to make a pleasant twilight on the soft grays, whites, and teals she'd decorated with. The living room looked out on a good-size balcony, the kitchen was to the left, and bedrooms presumably to the right. There was a large TV, and I smiled at the girls' toys carefully placed in all the lower art nooks.

The shelves above the toddler's-reach line held art, lots of it, each strikingly different from the last, and all of it looking as if it was original.

"Nice," Jenks said as he came back from his quick recon. "Nothing from Art Van here."

"Out of my tax bracket," I murmured as I put a hand to the wall, kicked off my shoes, and dropped my bag by the door.

"It was less than you might think." Trent carefully set his shoes by mine, laces even. "She got it cheap because there were plans for a twin building that would block her view, but then she convinced her dad to buy the project and the second tower was tabled. They're going to put in a private park instead. That was my idea, actually."

"Very nice." My sock-footed feet sank into the soft carpet off the small entry as I went to the shelves with their elaborately framed pictures of Lucy in the pool, Lucy and Ray on their ponies, all four of them on a blanket, eating ice cream in Eden Park, a birthday at Carew Tower. My focus blurred as I remembered my seventh birthday party at the hospital. I was probably the only one still alive apart from the nurses.

I moved to the window, guilt for interfering in Trent's life growing heavy. *Damn you, Ellasbeth.* I'd say she'd done this intentionally, but it had been Trent's idea.

Hands on my hips, I looked out at the giant Ferris wheel at the river's edge. It was supposed to have been temporary, but it was still here, the spinning colored lights making an obnoxious display. The Turn memorial was adjacent to it with an open-air café between them. There were a few people taking advantage of the late hours to grab a coffee and snack, and I wondered if David was already down there getting people to leave. Actually, since I'd brought everything I needed, Trent and I could sit up here and wait, eating cheese and crackers until it was time to go, keeping an eye on everything and making sure that no one was setting up an ambush.

"Here, kitty, kitty, kitty!" Jenks's voice came faintly, and then he hummed out of the back rooms. "I can't find the cat."

"It's white," Trent said from the kitchen, and I turned at the pop of a bottle being opened. "Try under the bed," he said as he set a green, foaming bottle on the counter to settle. "I'm not drinking that sweet syrup she likes when she's got this." Mood expansive, he turned to get a pair of glasses from a high shelf. "Apparently she's got twenty cases of it stashed somewhere." He grinned. "They wouldn't take them back when she left the altar."

Good Lord, it's their wedding champagne, I thought, arms over my middle as I sat at one of the two chairs facing the eat-at counter.

"You want some cheese?" Trent asked as he filled two glasses. "It's still here."

It sounded better than soup and sandwich, and I nodded, leaning forward to ogle Trent's backside when he turned and buried his head in the low fridge.

"Mmmm, nice presentation," he said as he turned and set the plate down, peeling the wrap off with an overdone flourish. "I'll have to ask where she got it. I know she didn't make it."

Compliment followed by a jab, I thought. *He's still mad at her.*

"I found the cat," Jenks said, suddenly hovering over the counter, sparkles spilling into my champagne until I waved them away. "It's under the bed and won't come out. Ohhh, goat cheese. I like goat cheese. Don't mind if I do," he added as he dropped down and took his chopsticks from his back pocket to help himself.

"Do you want to eat at the window?" I asked. Yep, I'm going to try to convince a crazy vampire to abandon control of her given city before the sun comes up, but no need to go down there unfortified.

Trent nodded, and glass in hand, I rose. The lights were low, but I nevertheless closed the sheers before I sank into the couch. The expensive fabric still smelled like the store, and I fingered the coordinated throw Ellasbeth had bought to help keep sticky fingers from staining it.

His sock-feet were silent as Trent followed me in, setting the plate of cheese on the low table in front of the window before easing himself down beside me. His arm comfortably stretched behind my shoulders, and we sighed at the same time. "This is nice," he said as he clinked his glass with mine, and we both took a sip and turned to the view.

"Sure . . ." Jenks alighted beside the goat cheese and took another wad. "But how long do you think you could sit here and do nothing before you got bored?"

My side was warm where Trent was touching me, and I smiled, relaxed with that calm-before-the-butt-kicking. "I could think of a few things to keep busy," I said, and Trent's eyes flicked to mine, hearing something not said.

"Me too," he whispered, and the scent of cinnamon deepened as he tugged me closer.

Jenks eyed us, wings stilling. Then his gaze shifted to the hall. "Cat is out."

I leaned forward out of Trent's reach to see. Sure enough, a big white cat was staring at us from the top of the hall, her tail twitching. "Hi, Elouise," I said, hand out to coax her closer, but she just stared at me with her blue eyes.

"Who names their cat Elouise?" Trent griped as he helped himself to more cheese. "I mean, really?"

I settled back into Trent's warmth. "Is she her familiar?"

Trent nodded, then washed the cheese down with a sip of champagne. "Yes. Apparently she's almost thirty years old."

"Ought to be out of her nine lives by now," Jenks muttered, clearly not liking the unfamiliar feline.

But I was feeling relaxed, whether it was the champagne or knowing Doyle was waiting in a cold car while I was eating cheese and looking out on the world. It would all be over by sunrise, and I wouldn't have to worry anymore. I was tired of worrying.

And as I set my drink aside and snuggled in deeper against Trent, I felt a faint stirring of pending desire. He was warm and smelled good, and those damn vampire pheromones I'd been breathing in all afternoon were getting hard to ignore. Smiling, I played with his fingers holding his glass until he set his champagne aside with a soft click. Taking his hand, I began to trace glyphs on his palm. A quiver shook both of us as I lowered my internal guard and our personal ley line balances shifted and flowed . . . equalizing in a tantalizing sparkle of magic.

"Ah, I'm going to go play with the cat," Jenks said as I found Trent's dark eyes. "Here, kitty, kitty, kitty."

"You are wicked, you know that, right?" Trent said as the cat's bell jingled when she ran after Jenks and into the back rooms.

"And crazy, according to some." I nestled in deeper, sending my hand across his chest, feeling him sigh in pleasure. "Thank you," I said as I idly fingered a button that, if I got my way, I was going to undo shortly. "For setting up the city-powers meeting and inviting Pike. I don't think he would have convinced Constance to meet with me if he hadn't seen how . . ."

Trent took my hand in his and kissed my fingers. "Involved you are in city matters?" He smiled and kissed them again. "I was going for threat, but it all works." His arm pulled me even closer, and a faint tingling ebbed and flowed between us. "David and Edden are ready to work around your plan," he whispered, his breath shifting my hair. "I know you're a less-is-more operator, but I'll feel better with them around."

"To keep my back door open, and her people off us." I looked out the window at Cincinnati, sparkling beautifully in the early night. "I don't want them involved any more than that." My thoughts went to the immobilization curse, and I winced. I had been confident about using it until Hodin had intervened.

Clearly concerned, Trent nodded as he leaned forward for more cheese.

Splat gun, pain amulets, magnetic chalk, I thought, knowing I'd need more if things didn't go to plan and I had to fight off Constance's people. Maybe with a mouse in a cage. "I've got a couple of fast ley line charms, and of course, a circle works against almost anything in defense. That's why I wanted to meet at the Turn memorial." I pulled out of his grip long enough to down my champagne. "There's circles engraved in the patio and the line is nearby," I added as I reached for it. A tingling rose in both of us, our bodies so close they were acting as one.

Trent's brow creased in worry even as he wrapped his arms around me in a sideways embrace. "Edden has agreed to stay at the outskirts to keep additional players from complicating the moment. David will have his people in the shadows if there's trouble. All that's left is the running and screaming." He hesitated. "And I'll be with you."

I twitched, not wanting to have this argument. "You're too important to risk like that."

His lips were set in a thin line. "This is my job as the elven Sa'han," he started.

"Then you can do it from the outskirts like David and Edden," I interrupted.

"But I will take my stand beside you because I love you," he finished, and I slumped. *Damn it. It's going to be twice as hard now.*

Uneasy, I rested my head against him, and finally he began to relax. "Ellasbeth has a nice place," I said, startled when my fingers began to tingle, the hint of unfocused ley line energy dancing about the tips as he held my hand.

"I think so, too," he said, his tone shifting. "If I was single . . ."

I turned to him, grinning. "You are single."

"You know what I mean," he said, then pulled me to him and kissed me.

My eyes closed, and I kissed him back, tasting champagne as the pent-up sexual need the vampires in the tower had instilled in me unfolded with a sharp snap. I shifted, my leg pinning him as my lips moved harder against his, feeling him respond. My arm wove under his, and I pulled him even closer as he pressed me into the couch. Desire flamed, and a soft noise of encouragement came from me as I drew away, breathless but wanting to see him, see his own desire for me in his eyes, letting it kindle mine to higher reaches.

The aroma of wine and cheese mixed with his scent of wild wind and open grasslands as he gazed at me, his breath slow and steady, promising more.

"I'm not doing this on Ellasbeth's brand-new couch," I said, pulse fast.

"Fair enough." His hand shifted, pinching the throw between him and my shoulder. Breath held, he shifted our weight and pulled us both laughing to the floor.

My hair went everywhere, and I loved him all the more as we tumbled together, finally ending with him on top, my shoulder against the side of the couch, the underside of the low table half over us. "Mmmm, interesting," I murmured as I reached to play with his hair. I liked his weight on me, pressing down, hinting at more as the lights from the city bathed us.

His smile was gentle, and he shifted the hair from my eyes. "I love you when you are kicking the bad guy's ass," he whispered, then gave me a gentle kiss. "I love you when you are working the problem to avoid it," he added, his lips touching me again. "I love you when you create a new spell with the lines making your hair all staticky and in disarray," he continued as he smoothed it from my forehead and kissed me there. "But I love you best when you are relaxed and in my arms. Like now."

Again, he leaned to find my lips with his. They tasted of magic, and I lost myself in him as my arms went around his neck. Breath fast, I traced my lips over his neck, nibbling harder and with more demand as he moved against me. My hands shifted, and I undid the top button of his shirt, then the next, and the third until I could touch his chest.

He sighed, his lips making hop-skips down my neck as his hands found my breasts, touching, pinching, bringing me alive with little jolts of sensation. Wanting my shirt off, I arched my back, and in a smooth motion, Trent pulled it up and over, tangling my arms and pinning me there.

My eyes flashed open, and then I gasped when he bent low, pushing my chemise up until his lips found me, warm as his hands clasped one of my wrists, the other at my waist, hinting at going lower. I was pleasantly trapped, and I could do nothing but arch into him as his motions grew rougher.

But my breath caught when the faintest jolt of line energy zinged across my synapses, racing through my body from his hand at my waist to his fingers holding my wrist beside my head. I knew he felt my surprise as his motions slowed and the tingling energy abated. Breath close, he shifted to lie beside me, letting my wrist go as he found my eyes. There was a hint of question there, of vulnerability he'd never opened himself to. We'd never used ley lines like this, though it was common enough. There was too much potential risk, and he was too careful, too closed.

But he'd started it, and a quiver rippled through me at what this might lead to.

I took a breath to ask him if he was sure. Seeing it in my eyes, he covered my mouth with his, and I relaxed into a slow, satisfying kiss, my entire body coming alive.

And then, slowly, carefully, as we kissed and our hands explored, I let the barest hint of ley line energy slip from me to him.

A low growl of sound came from him as he felt it, and his teeth fastened on my lip for a bare instant. His head dropped, and he nuzzled to find my breasts again. My back arched, breath escaping me in a soft sound. My fingers traced his back, going lower as magic trickled from them, making him shudder.

We are wearing too many clothes, I mused, and then a flash of thought about Jenks raced through me. But he'd left knowing what was going to happen. He'd keep the perimeter. Keep us safe.

My eyes opened and my tracing fingers slowed when Trent pulled back, worry coloring his usual hot demand. "I've never let myself use the lines before," he whispered. "Like that."

Because he was too afraid to trust, I thought as I smiled up at him and laced my hands behind his neck. "You started it," I said, smile dancing about my lips. I drew him to me, whispering, "We can go slow until you know if you like it. Not everyone does." But for those who could trust, it was . . . amazingly fulfilling.

He nodded, and as his hands found my breast again, I took a slow, intoxicating breath and touched the ley line to fill my chi. God help me. Constance could wait and Ellasbeth would get over it. I sent my hand across his back to spill magic into him, but then quivered when a heady

warmth spilled into me, alive and scintillating, tasting of
ash and cinnamon and wine and dangerous, dangerous elf.
A groan of pleasure slipped from me, and my hands flashed
from his back to find his zipper. His lips were on me, tugging, pulling, tingling with unfocused magic, and I could
hardly think.

My eyes flew open when the flow eased. Breathless, I
found him looking at me, blinking in surprise at my reac-
tion. "Oh, God. Don't stop now," I said as I finally got his
zipper down. "The more you give me, the more I can send
back into you."

"Mmmm." A hint of deviltry flickered in him, and he
bent low over me once more. My breath came in a fast pant
as his hands touched my bare skin, and it was as if the line
filled me, racing through me in scintillating waves in time
with his heartbeat, filling my chi until I was aching with it.

"S-slow . . ." I gasped, gripping him tighter as I clenched
into him. "God, slow down. I thought you said you'd never
done this with the lines."

His eyes were dark with a heady demand, his hands
never ceasing their steady motion, ever closer to my waistband. "I shall try to improve, nevertheless," he said. And
then he found my mouth with his.

My pulse hammered, and I let a trickle of the energy he
had given me back into him, my hands moving lower, finding him taut through his clothes. Finally I managed to get
his zipper down, and he sighed in relief at his new freedom
as I shoved his pants as low as I could before hooking my
foot in them and dragging them nearly off.

His lips against mine held a light magic, pulling me into
a delicious limbo as the masculine-tasting energy he had
filled me with slowly returned to him until our balances
equalized. He'd shown me he could give, and I opened my
eyes, my need for him growing stronger. He was beautiful
over me, with his shirt open and the light of Cincinnati
outlining him, making delicious shadows for my fingertips
to explore.

"We are both wearing too much," I said.

"That was my thought as well."

He reached for my waistband, and I ran my hands over his shoulders, gripping him tight as I pulled up so he could shimmy everything off. His own pants were kicked aside, and then he was back, easing down over me with a careful, demanding weight.

Delight filled me as I ran my nails down his back trailing ley line energy and he shivered, his lips on me hesitating a bare instant before bearing down harder. As his lips found mine again, I poured magic into him, feeling a sudden throbbing in my hands where I held him.

Oh, God, yes, I thought as his knee pushed my thighs open, and I slid my hands down even more, guiding him in. Warm and taut, smooth and exhilarating, he slipped into me in one easy move, his weight starting a rhythm that pulled me into motion. Every part of me seemed alight, and holding him to me as we moved, I let the barest hint of magic slip to him.

Trent shuddered. "No, don't stop," he almost grunted when I eased back, afraid it had been too much, and my hands spasmed as he pushed into me again in one glorious motion. Tingles raced through me from the inside, and I groaned as new paths burned through my synapses in a delicious sensation.

I reached up, my hands behind his neck, my breath fast as my lips found him. I wanted more, and as we moved with each other, he gave me everything, each rocking motion ending with a little jolt until I was gasping for air, wild with need.

"Oh, God. Now . . ." I moaned, fingers clamped tightly on his shoulders, straining for fulfillment, just out of reach.

"More?" he whispered, but he was slowing, and, with a panting gasp, I found I could bear one more instant of waiting. I could.

"Yes," I whimpered, almost dying from need. "Yes."

Again Trent pushed into me, his breath held as I shuddered, shaking under him as ley line energy overflowed and set me to a slow burn. "More?" he rasped, begging me to say yes.

"Yes . . ." I said, strained, and my hands fixed on him, groaning as he pulled back, tingles racing through me as energy flowed like fire between us, stretching to the breaking point.

"Again . . ." he choked, and then he pushed deep, tipping me into heaven.

I shook under him as I climaxed, my body claiming the energy flowing between us with the quickness of a whipcrack. Trent groaned as it left him, a massive shudder shaking him as he reached fulfillment as well. Atop me, he strained, our breath mingling as our souls chimed and the energy we had been playing with rocked back and forth, slowly equalizing in ever-lessening waves. I could feel him everywhere, suffusing me, making me feel loved and needed, our longing joined into one being. Belonging. Together.

And then he shifted, and it was over.

Pulse fast, I tried to catch my breath. I managed to get one eye open, and I looked at him above me, spent and wonderful. My hands eased from his shoulders, and his attention fell to me.

"Mmmm." His head tilted, and he kissed me lightly, tasting of salt. "Why did we never try that before?"

"You weren't ready," I said, and he grinned. But it was tempered with the knowledge that he hadn't been. It was more than trust, for he had trusted me for a long time. It was more than love, for we had shared that, too. It was the freedom, perhaps, to be vulnerable. For an elf, it might be the hardest thing of all.

Wincing, Trent carefully eased himself down beside me, shifting me sideways as we were still, ah, together. My hair was everywhere, and he pulled the afghan over us before arranging my curls so he could see me.

"Going to be a minute or two, huh?" he said, eyes flicking down, and I felt myself warm.

"After that? Yes," I said, still embarrassed that my witch anatomy didn't let go right away. Trent always seemed to take it as a compliment. All I knew was that it felt more than good as he held me on the floor of Ellasbeth's apartment overlooking the entirety of Cincinnati.

"I'm not going back to Seattle when this is done," Trent said.

"No?" I felt my muscles ease their grip as he brought reality back to my forethoughts.

"No." He took a slow breath, and I felt his heart beat. "I don't have to prove myself to them." His gaze returned to me. "I'm glad you and Jenks decided to stay at the church. You're right that my place is too far out to be of use for your job. But if you ever change your mind, there's an office and spelling lab waiting for you off the great room."

"Thank you," I whispered, shifting my head against his chest so I wouldn't have to look at his face. It wasn't that I didn't want to live with him, but the person I had become needed to be here. In the Hollows.

"My mother found it useful," he said, voice wistful as if he knew my thoughts. "I know you would, too. When you are ready." His fingers shifted my hair. "No rush. Anytime in the next fifty years or so is good."

I smiled at that, and the hidden thread of tension in him relaxed as my muscles fully let go and he pulled himself from me with a happy sigh. "Fifty years?" I said, and he nodded.

"I'm not going anywhere," he said.

"Me either," I whispered, but my eyes were on the dark sky past him. *Why,* I wondered, *do I keep risking my life when I have so much to live for?* "Let's just get to the sunrise intact, then see how it goes," I added, and his hold on me tightened as if he'd never let go.

CHAPTER

27

I HAD OFFERED TO DRIVE, WHICH MIGHT HAVE BEEN A MIS-
take. I was fidgety and nervous, and Jenks was eyeing me
from the rearview mirror as if I'd lost it as I worked us
through Cincy's late-night traffic. I didn't like going in with
Trent. Oh, he knew his stuff and there was no one I'd rather
have watching my back other than Jenks, but if I'd learned
anything in the last few months, it was that both he and I
would sacrifice anything to keep each other safe—and that
made for second-guessing.

"I don't see you," Trent said, talking to David on his
phone. "We're almost there."

I peered up at the arch of the wheel as I entered the park,
the gaudy lights of the slowly spinning spokes and gondolas
a stark contrast to the black sky.

Jenks clattered his wings. "There he is," he said, and I
followed his gaze to a dark storefront. "Next to the Skyline
Chili kiosk."

Trent leaned forward, his suit rasping. "Where . . . Oh.
Got you. The Goddess help me, that's good. I can hardly
see you."

My lips pressed, and I gripped the wheel tighter as I
went to the front of the empty lot. I appreciated that David's
pack had cleared the area, but now that we were here, I
wanted them gone. "David, stay out of it," I said loudly, and

Trent sighed and put his phone on speaker. "I mean it," I said. "If I need you, I'll send Jenks. Keep Edden out, too, until the first responders come in. Even the undead don't mess with paramedics."

"I'll try," David said, his voice small through Trent's phone. "But Edden says bullets are faster than vamps."

"Yeah?" I pulled into a parking spot right beside the brightly lit but empty ticket booth. "Remind him that undead vampires are faster than his finger. He stays out until the paramedics get here, or I'm not ever asking for his help again."

Trent chuckled as he scanned the wheel. "You didn't ask for his help this time."

"Hoy!" David suddenly exclaimed. "There he goes! Sorry, Rachel. Doyle got past us. We thought he was with Constance. She's a few blocks back."

My eyes flicked to the rearview mirror as I put the car in park. Bright lights bobbled and bounced as an I.S. cruiser raced in over the speed bumps—headed for us. "That's okay," I said grimly. "I wanted to talk to him anyway. See you when it's done."

"When it's done," David agreed, then softer, in threat, "Kalamack? Prove me wrong."

Trent frowned as he hit the end key with a decisive tap.

My eyes went from Doyle's car to him, and I set a hand on his knee. "He's only worried."

"So am I." Trent undid his seat belt and got out, pulling himself straight in determination as he went to head off Doyle, whose cruiser was now rocking to a halt two rows back. Jenks followed him out, but his attention was on the surrounding park, eerie with the wheel spinning and no one in sight. The gondolas were huge, glass encased and air-conditioned. One was even set up as a posh dining car for proposals and parties. Now, though, the SkyStar only looked creepy, silently turning with all the gondolas and waiting benches empty.

Nearby was the actual Turn memorial, which, in Cincinnati, was a heat-twisted boxcar with the names and ages of a handful of refugees scratched upon one interior wall. They represented the uncountable thousands who had fled the West Coast where the plague had begun, moving east with the produce farmed there. None of the people who had reached Cincinnati in the tarnished car had survived.

Jenks snapped his wing in warning before he landed on my shoulder, smelling of the wind off the nearby river. "David did good. The area is clear."

"Good. Thanks." I leaned against the car, arms going over my middle as Trent stood in front of Doyle, blocking him. The I.S. officer had a duplicate warrant in his hand. He shifted to get past Trent, becoming red-faced when he stopped him. *I can't risk Trent like this.*

"Hey, can I ask you a question?" I said suddenly, and Jenks's wing pitch shifted.

"Sure. As long as it doesn't involve leaving you."

A remembered fear bubbled up from nowhere, of when Landon smashed Jenks with a frying pan. Holding Jenks in my hand, not knowing if he was alive or dead, had been the most agonizing thing I'd ever endured. *Love is not a liability, but Trent is* not *coming with me.*

"Do you think Trent will hang back if I ask him?" I said as Trent and Doyle began to argue, their words faint over the wind off the river. "Constance can bespell the unwilling or she wouldn't have survived this long. I'm going to have a hard enough time besting it." My brow furrowed, and I gestured helplessly. "He doesn't have anything to cope with that."

"Then I suggest you do that," Trent said loudly, but it was his hand glowing with a faint magic that was keeping Doyle back, not his words.

"You sure? He's bigger than me. And he's got magic," Jenks said.

"True, but do you think he will?" My breath shook as I exhaled. *I'm sorry, Trent.*

Jenks hovered before me, his worry obvious. "He's going to be pissed."

I nodded. "He'll lose his Sa'han status if a vampire

binds him. If this was between him and Constance, I'd say risk it. But it isn't." I pushed off the car and started over. "He doesn't need to be there," I whispered.

Jenks's wings rasped as he followed. "Remind me to never fall in love with you, Rache."

He thinks I'm asking Trent to stay behind because I love him, I thought, knowing that Trent would see it the same way. Maybe I was.

Head high, I gathered my resolve as I strode forward as if I owned the parking lot. "Doyle!" I shouted, and both men turned, their argument falling short. "I need until sunup before I come in for that warrant."

Doyle squinted at me, clearly angry. "You expect me to believe that?"

I settled before them. The wind off the river was cool in my hair, and I remembered the stink of Alcatraz and the smell of old iron. "I expect you to stop chasing the glory of bringing Rachel Morgan in for a petty crime when I'm trying to save Cincinnati from a monster."

Doyle's eyes narrowed, shifting pupil black even in the dark. My attention went to the string of cars approaching, slow and threatening. "Sorry, Doyle. You're going to have to wait. A bigger lion just got to the water hole."

Jaw clenched, Doyle dropped back to stand with us and face the six black SUVs and the iridescent, cream-colored Jag now pulling into the accessible-parking spots. Behind them, eight more black vans parked at the outskirts, their engines running and lights aimed at us.

"The woman knows how to make an entrance," Jenks smart-mouthed, then flew up and away, wings rasping.

Trent inched closer. "Maybe we should have brought more people."

Worry about our coming argument kept me quiet as the doors opened and men and women in black got out. They didn't move any closer, staring at us as Pike bolted from the Jag to get Constance's door. "More people mean more problems," I whispered.

Doyle rubbed his stubble in indecision as Constance

emerged, looking small in her white, skintight dress, heels, and immaculately styled hair. Her jewelry caught the lights from the car, reminding me of Joni. Pike had dressed for the occasion as well, looking good in a dark suit and his hair now cropped close to help hide the burns. Clearly agitated, he waved for everyone to stay put when Constance started forward.

"Morgan? Who is that with you?" Constance said imperialistically. "Pike, who is that vampire beside her? You said she had no support among the undead. Is he a living vampire? He's wearing a badge. That's one of my people!"

"It's Doyle," Pike said, having regained her side, and the I.S. officer fidgeted. "I believe he's trying to serve her a warrant."

Constance's rapid pace faltered. "You work for me?" she said, her eyes narrowed as she closed the gap between us. "Go stand with the rest," she barked at the man.

Doyle inclined his head, motions stiff as he turned on a heel and walked to his car.

Constance was staring at me when my attention returned, her perfectly glossed lips and narrowly plucked eyebrows twisted into a mocking confidence as her fingers toyed with her jewelry as if the multitude of strands held a secret she was dying to share. The lights from the moving wheel played on her, turning her a surreal, ever-changing blue and gold. Pike was unusually quiet beside her, his expression unreadable. "You were serious about only one," she said flatly as she eyed Trent.

"I only need one," I said, quashing my guilt for having Trent at my side when I was talking about Jenks.

She sighed in annoyance, turning to wave her slowly encroaching entourage back. "How very old-school. Fine. We will do this with minimal staff. Pike?"

I jerked, catching myself when she turned with a vampire quickness and strode to the wheel. "Stop the wheel so we can get on," she demanded, and Pike gave me a silent look before jogging to the controls.

"On the wheel? Is she kidding?" Trent said as Constance

halted with her tiny toes edging the white line as if staying behind it was the most important rule in the world.

A small confined space going up and down and in circles with two vampires? What could go wrong? "Ah, I thought we could sit in the open beside the memorial?" I said, and Constance beamed a long-toothed smile at me. The pheromones would be overpowering in the tiny, glassed space—and she knew it.

"No. Pike insists that you have considerable back-alley support." Her eyes closed as she breathed in the night as if able to smell David at the outskirts. "I'm taking that away. Pike?" She turned back to him, smiling wide. "This next car is fine."

The gondola came to a hydraulic-hissing stop. Pike lurched forward, his burn-reddened hands fumbling at the door lock before he managed it and it swung open. The usual attendant was long gone. "Leave your bag," Constance directed as she strode into the car and sat down on the wide, long bench, patting it in invitation. "Trent, you'll be beside me. Pike and Morgan will be across from us. Boy, girl. Boy, girl."

I was not leaving my bag, and I took a breath, catching Trent's elbow when he shifted to step forward. "I want you to stay here. Jenks will spot me."

"Jenks . . ." Trent's voice trailed off, a myriad of emotions crossing him in the chancy light from the wheel.

I turned my back on Constance, my gut twisting. "It's not your skills, it's your status," I said softly, and frustration drew his features tight. "You are the enclave's Sa'han," I said urgently when he took a breath to protest. "If you get bitten, it's gone. Don't make me responsible for you losing it again. Not when you're finally regaining your birthright."

"You were not responsible for me losing it the first time," he said, and I grabbed the swinging door with one hand as Pike took one long step and got into the gondola.

"Yes, I was," I said sharply, and his next words caught. "Trent, the Sa'han must be more than capable, but also smart enough not to risk himself when it's not his fight."

"This is my fight."

"Only through ties of love, and that's not enough. Trent, *it's not enough*," I added forcefully when he began to protest. A lump was growing in my throat, and I forced it down. "If you want to prove to the enclave that you are the Sa'han, then prove it. Do your job. Stay here." I hesitated. "Protect me from outside treachery while I handle this. It's my battle, not yours."

He frowned, ducking his head and shifting his weight. "Is that really why you want me to stay? Because the Sa'han wouldn't get involved?"

I managed a smile. "No. I want you to stay because if you get bitten, you'll risk that treatment of yours, and the probability of you dying under it is greater than the probability of me dying in this gondola."

Pike chuckled from inside the car, and I felt myself warm.

Trent furrowed his brow, heartache a hint at the back of his eyes. "Maybe I don't want to be the Sa'han," he said, and my smile became pained.

"It's too late. You already are." I hesitated, my chest hurting. "Be right back," I added with a false lightness, and Jenks dropped down to hover between us.

"Keep her safe," Trent said to Jenks, and the pixy's dust warmed our fingers as Trent's hand slowly slipped away. Eyes never leaving mine, he took a step back.

Relief washed through me as I turned to the open door, but worry tightened me right back up again when I saw Constance's waiting smile. At least Trent would be okay.

The car rocked slightly as I got on, and I went to sit across from Constance, an unsettling five feet between us. Anything less than eight made fending her off chancy, and I began to appreciate her genius. Pike stood beside her, stoic and jaw set. Jenks had gone in ahead of me, and he circled the car once before landing on my shoulder.

"He took that pretty well," the pixy said, and my guilt thickened.

"He's used to Quen making him sit things out," I said,

but having him there to keep the square open and calm when I came back down with a contrite Constance would be a godsend.

"Kalamack!" Constance called, and Trent's jaw clenched. "Get the wheel going. Stop it at the top. Don't bring me down until I tell you."

His eyes flicked to mine, and when I nodded, he used a simple pin to lock the door from the outside before going to the controls. After a moment of study, he punched a button on the panel and the car lurched back and up.

"Marvelous." Constance played with her jewelry as Pike swayed to find his balance. "I haven't been on a Ferris wheel since I was a little girl. George's was larger, but this is pleasant."

The first Ferris wheel? I thought as the noise from the machinery vanished and I slid the tiny, mesh-covered window open. It was beginning to smell like vampire, and we hadn't even gone up three stories.

"Well?" Constance sat before me with her ankles crossed, her confidence absolute.

I set my bag beside me, pulse fast. "Thank you for your time. I'll try to make this quick," I said, thinking it wouldn't hurt to be polite. Behind Constance, the city began to spread out as we rose. It almost hurt, seeing it there, helpless before her. I tightened my hold on the ley line, my neck tingling from the heavy pheromones she was kicking out. *Thank God Trent isn't here,* I thought, stifling the urge to take out my splat gun.

Pike stood beside and a little in front of her, his hands hanging at his sides, waiting. His empty expression struck me as odd, but he twitched as I resettled myself on the hard bench, making him wire-tight and faster than a cracked whip.

"First, I want you to publicly apologize for Nash Lendorski's death," I said, and Constance blinked in true surprise.

"You want me to . . ." Her words trailed off as her eyes narrowed. *"You want?"* she added, her anger obvious.

"Holy sweet mother of Jesus," Pike whispered, a hint o
what might be fear in his eyes.

Jenks's wings rasped, and I twitched my head to get hin
to shift off my shoulder. The faint draft from his wings wa:
setting my scar off. She'd brought it alive without even trying. Chin rising, I took a steadying breath, my grip on the
ley line solid and sure. I could reach a ley line at the top o
Carew Tower. The top of the wheel was easy. "Second, you
will rein your people in. No more taking over bars or apartment houses. This shock-and-awe will stop."

Pike shifted his weight, running a hand over his stubble
in unease as Constance stiffened. Her eyes had become
pupil black, and I thought she'd quit breathing, focused on
me with an unnerving intensity. Her parted lips showing a
slip of fang was a clear message to back down, but I wasn'
done yet.

"Third, I will inform you of the local vampire territories
that have kept us frictionless for generations," I said. "You
will respect not only them, but the Weres' traditiona
grounds as well. Your people will be given Piscary's old
space, which is probably thirty-nine percent of Cincinnati's
total vampire carrying capacity. Plenty of clout if you uti-
lize it well. Waterfront, downtown, and a good section of
the rail. As far as the witches go, leave them alone, or you'll
find your age charms suddenly not working."

"*You* will give *me*?" she said, voice rising, and from over
my shoulder, I heard the small snick of Jenks loosening his
sword. Pike drew himself straighter, burn-reddened face
paling.

"Fourth, you will keep your fingers out of Kalamack's
distribution," I said, and she almost choked. "It's off-limits,
as is my church. Obviously."

"Obviously," she said, her multitudes of necklaces shaking as she trembled.

"And lastly, you will stop trying to control my city," I
finished, tensely ready for anything. We had reached the
top, and the gondola swayed slightly as it came to a halt.

"And if I don't?"

I glanced at Pike's loosely held hands. "Then I will make you." I hesitated. "Or you could return to DC. That might be easier for your ego. I'll tell everyone you hit me first, if it helps."

Her chin lifted, and a trickle of self-preservation struck me to the quick at the icy, choleric anger turning her eyes entirely black. The old undead were all crazy. Every last one of them.

"Leave?" she whispered as she played with her jewelry, and my expression blanked as a wave of angry vampire incense flooded the car.

"Oh, God," Pike whispered.

And then she lunged, a tiny ping of something hitting the floor.

"*Stabils!*" I shouted exuberantly, hand outstretched. *Got you, you overgrown mosquito,* I thought smugly as the line raced through me—and then . . . died.

What the hell? My head hit the back of the gondola as she landed on me, and I saw stars. Constance's weight pinned me to the bench, one hand gripping my throat, her knee on my gut. Her black eyes were inches from mine, her lips pulled back to show her teeth. I could hear Jenks's wings snapping in anger and Pike's muffled swearing as he fended him off.

"It didn't . . . work . . ." I rasped, lungs aching, and her savage smile widened as her necklaces rocked into me.

Bewildered, I scrabbled to find a line, sensing nothing. It was as if they weren't there. I'd been fine until I'd tried to use one, and then it was gone as if . . . Remembering the metallic ping, I looked at the multitude of her necklaces, finding in their midst a ley line charm pulsating with the same ugly hue I'd seen in the lobby of the I.S. She had her own personal no-magic zone. *Son of a bastard . . .*

"Surprise," Constance said smugly, and I shuddered at her low voice as my entire side flamed in an unwanted desire. "I didn't get to be this old by not knowing how to pin a witch."

"Constan-k-k-k," I choked out as her grip tightened. My one hand pried at hers, the other stretched for my bag and

my splat gun. A no-magic zone only blocked ley line magic
I wasn't helpless—yet.

"Do you know the grief I'd take from my kin for allow
ing anyone, even a witch-born demon, to rule me?" sh
said, and I shuddered at the warm spit that landed on m
neck. Images of Ivy flashed through me and were gone,
smoldering memory of passion left in their wake.

"I was given all, and I will *keep* all," she said, and, fin
gers scrabbling in my bag, I tried to look past her at the dr
scent of pixy dust. Pike had retreated to a corner, hi
scarred face red and bleeding as Jenks pinned him there
Panic flashed through me at the thought of those shelterin
at the church, trusting me to keep them safe. I was going t
fail because of a ley line charm? *No way in hell.*

"Y-y-ya think so?" I ground out. I held my breath, m
fingertip brushing the smooth finish of my splat gun. Eye
bulging, I inched my reach lower.

Constance's smile widened, clearly enjoying my denial
They all did. Fear and adrenaline made the blood sweeter
"You will leave this gondola mine, or you will leave i
dead. That scar of yours burned its way to your soul," sh
whispered as she pressed deeper into me, and I choked
"You know us," she breathed, eyes lidded as she soaked i
my anger. "You know the ecstasy we carry, sprinklin
about as if flowers. Why do you even protest? Do you thin
it makes you more desirable?" Her eyes opened, black t
show me reflected in them. "It does."

"Not . . . happening . . ." I clamped down on the wave
of promise flowing from my neck. And when her eye
closed again and she leaned in, my grip settled on my gun
Adrenaline surged. I kicked out, sending her pinwheelin
back. Gasping, I stood, weapon pulled.

"Constance!" Pike swung at Jenks as he darted madly t
keep him in the corner.

I fired three shots in panic.

Constance sprang away, dodging the balls with a weir
dexterity. I followed her motion, splat balls breakin
against the glass wall of the gondola. Her eyes wide an

black, the small woman pushed from the wall to dodge a fourth, rolling to come up right in front of me. She was too close. I couldn't even invoke a circle. I reached for the amulet around her neck. If I took it, I'd have my magic back.

"Rachel, no!" Jenks shrilled. And then I froze, my left wrist in Constance's grip, my fingertips brushing the glowing metal nestled amid the disguising strands of gold and gems. I hadn't even seen her move.

"No . . ." I whispered, then screamed in agony when she crushed my wrist as if it was a breadstick. It was on fire, and I dropped my gun to pry at her fingers squeezing as if to pinch my hand off.

"Rache!" Jenks shrilled, and there was a thump as Constance caught my falling gun.

My breath came in with a little pant as she let up. My throat was raw, and I thought I was going to be sick.

"Shouldn't play with weapons," Constance said, and then, still holding my pulped wrist, she shoved my splat gun right through the window mesh and dropped it. Tight-lipped, Pike pressed against the door, the welts from Jenks's dust lumpy on his face. Jenks froze in indecision. Leave me to tell Trent to bring the gondola down, or stay to keep Pike back. Dusting an unreal orange, he stayed.

My wrist felt as if it had exploded. "You're . . . making a mistake," I panted, hunched in pain as she held my wrist, arm stretched between us. "You should find an accord with me."

"That's what I'm doing." Constance's eyes were utterly black, and then I gasped, feet sliding as she yanked me into her.

"Get off!" I demanded, trying to get my knee between us, and then I screamed as she squeezed again.

Jaw clenched, I went limp, arm extended, almost kneeling before her. My eyes met hers, and I quailed. Pike was swearing between Jenks's aggressive wing snaps, but Constance's pupils were my world, and I could hardly breathe. There was no pleasure; it was all pain. Only the really old ones could do that. *Crap on toast, again?* I thought, remembering Piscary. He had pinned me, too, and I blinked the tears of failure away. If they couldn't lure you with guile, they beat you by force.

"You're making a mistake," I said again, black dots spotting my gaze until she eased up on my wrist and consciousness flooded back. She'd want me awake for this. I could smell hot pixy dust, but Pike had quit trying to reach us, standing in the corner with Jenks facing him. That amulet was so close, but I couldn't . . . reach it.

"I bind you, and you bring the city together under me," she whispered as she came close. She nuzzled my hair from my neck, and I shuddered. "They follow you. God knows why. And then I will kill you so slowly you will beg for it. Cincinnati is mine. The old undead *owe* me this. They made me what I am, and they owe me! All of it!" she exclaimed, and I pulled my pulped wrist close when she let go to gesture at the city. Her eyes fell to me. "I'll start with you."

She let go. . . . "You will not. Have. Me!" I shouted, teeth clenched as I shoved her away and surged upright.

The insane woman screamed in anger as she fell back. I caught my balance, dizzy and sick. Gasping, I backpedaled, dropping to the floor and rolling to keep her off me. She followed, slamming my head into the hard metal. Darkness threatened, and I kicked out, sending her sliding into the locked door.

She came at me again, lashing out wildly. I shifted out of her way when I could, took my hits when I couldn't. Like a ravenous dog, she tore at me. I slowly lost ground, only my practice with Ivy and Constance's utter lack of martial arts experience keeping me out of her reach.

Until her fingers clamped on my shoulder and wouldn't let go.

She yanked me to her, mouth wide.

Panic gave me strength, and I slammed my knee into her groin, shoving out and back. Fire clawed at my shoulder as her grip was torn free, and then she was standing beside Pike, her pristine white dress covered in dirt and my blood, panting in a black-eyed fury.

I was hardly aware that Jenks was with me, dusting the bloody gouges she'd left behind. His sword was sheened with red and his wings were heavy with fatigue, but he was okay. I held my wrist against my middle and retreated as far as I could, but that amulet's reach was longer, and I could do nothing.

"Good going, Rache," Jenks said, concern evident in his voice. "I knew you could throw the blood bag off. Keep her busy. *I'll* get that charm off her so you can bring that moss wipe down."

Keep her busy? Is he nuts? I thought, panic swamping me. If Landon could bring Jenks down, Constance could. "Jenks, wait," I whispered, voice raspy and throat sore. There was more than one way to get that amulet off her, and I turned sideways, hiding my fumbling search for the mouse potion in my pocket. I'd wanted to immobilize her first, but one way or the other, this magic was going down her throat.

Jenks's dust paled as he saw the tiny ampoule. There was only one way to get close enough. I had to let her grab me. Slowly he nodded, and I stifled a shudder. *Here we go. . . .*

Ampoule palmed, I wiped her spit off my neck, stiffening as the remaining tendrils of desire and passion winged through me to leave me shuddering with unresolved ecstasy. Thoughts of Ivy, longings for Kisten were twined into it all. There had been love there. Here there was nothing, and she was *not* going to break my skin.

"If you think you can take the city from me, do it," I said raggedly. "But keep your teeth *off* me." *Come a little closer, you whacked-out dead bag of skin. I dare you. . . .*

"You." Constance began an eerie weaving, side to side like a caged animal. "You will not break easy." An ugly smile blossomed. "The night holds promise, Pike."

But Pike didn't move, his expression twisted in distaste at what he thought was going to happen. "Blah, blah, blah," I taunted, then coughed to clear my throat, shocked at how broken my voice sounded. It was truly a contest of endurance now. Cincinnati lay in the balance. "You can't best me by bespelling me. And you will, by God, not best me by strength. I win, and I'm going to bring you down, you sorry sack of O-negative. Get your whacked ass *out* of my city."

Jenks's wings hit a higher pitch. I stood in apparent confidence, but inside, doubt trickled through me: thoughts of the sun and wind I might never see and feel again, of Trent, soft with sleep beside me, of Jenks, the big ideas that sustained him slowly dying as he faltered, alone in the church. For the first time, I wondered if I was going to survive this.

And Constance saw my doubt, tasted my fatigue on the air thick with pixy dust and vampire pheromones. "Hold her," Constance said with a curt gesture to Pike. "Hold her so I don't have to."

But Pike didn't move, his eyes narrowed as he looked from Jenks hovering at my shoulder to me. "No . . ." he said, his unexpected rebellion making his subtle anger look noble. "She's your prey. Not mine. And she's right. If you can't best her yourself, you don't deserve her blood. I'm not holding anyone down for you again."

For a moment, it was as if she hadn't heard, her eyes slowly widening. "You dare—you dare say no!" she screamed, the gondola swaying. "Hold her, or you will both die, and I will gorge on your blood for a thousand years!"

Pike casually shrugged, and Constance stood, trembling in a silent rage.

It was all I needed. Her eyes were off me, and I did the last thing anyone would expect.

I jumped at her.

CHAPTER

28

CONSTANCE SHRIEKED IN OUTRAGE AS I BODY-SLAMMED into her, my broken left wrist tucked as we both fell into the bench. Her hard angles cushioned me, and then the black pits of her eyes found mine, her mouth open wide in a snarling anger.

"Now!" Jenks shrilled, and I one-handedly popped the top from the potion vial.

"Try this on, blood bag," I rasped, and poured it down her throat.

"No—g-g-g-g," Constance gurgled, and then I lurched, catching myself against the bench when she suddenly wasn't there. Her clothes collapsed in a hush, and there was a soft thump as a shoe fell over.

"My God, where is she?" Pike exclaimed, and I grimaced, counting on Jenks to keep him back as I frantically patted Constance's clothes and jewelry for her small shape. My fingers tingled at the pulse of magic, and it was there that I found the small brown mouse she now was, nestled amid a mass of gold and gems. She was out cold from the pain of transforming, and I exhaled, shoulders slumping.

"She's still here. She's a mouse," I said as I wearily sent my gaze over the gondola, finally spotting my bag shoved in a corner. All I had to do was get her in the cage before she came to.

First things first. My wrist throbbed as I uncoiled the glowing amulet from around her, staggered to the busted window, and dropped it over. Power flooded back and I leaned heavily against the cool metal, eyes closed as I felt it vibrate. *I'm going to hurt so bad tomorrow.*

But I turned, eyes flashing open at the sudden snick of a knife being pulled. "Whoa, whoa, whoa!" I said, hand outstretched at Pike as Jenks rose up, sword bared. "What the Turn do you think you're doing?"

Pike's eyes narrowed on the mouse curled up in the jewelry, his hatred making the very air sour. "I thought you were going to kill her, not turn her into a mouse."

I shook my head. "I told you before—hey!" I shouted as he lunged at her, knife swinging. Balance shifting, I tucked my broken wrist close, grunting as I pivoted my foot up and slammed it into him.

Pike pinwheeled back, catching himself in an angry hunch.

"Knock it off, fang boy!" Jenks exclaimed, and Pike pulled himself upright, expression closed. He looked awful, his suit torn by Jenks's slashes, his already scarred face mottled and blotchy from pixy dust.

"She can't . . . That has to die twice," he said, pointing, and I wondered at the hint of fear. It wasn't for him. *Joni?* I mused, exchanging a knowing look with Jenks. "I thought you were going to kill her!" he repeated. "I never would've . . ." His expression hardened. "Kill her. Or I will."

My bag with the cage was on the other side of the gondola, totally out of my easy reach. Hand pushing the air for patience, I sank down on the bench between her and Pike, tired. If he jumped me again, I'd down him with a word. Constance, too. "What good would that do?" I said softly, still shocked at how rough my voice was. My shoulders slumped and I cradled my broken wrist, trying not to move it. "If she's dead, I'll end up in jail. DC will send a new master vampire. . . ." I looked up, understanding blossoming. "You think that by killing her you can ingratiate yourself with the incoming master vampire?" I asked, knowing

I was right by his sudden grimace. "Have a seat. We need to talk."

But he didn't, and I think it was only the memory of me downing him in the belfry that kept him unmoving, that knife in his hand as I sat and tried to keep from throwing up. I had survived—barely—and as I looked out over Cincinnati glinting in the new night, a feeling of helplessness crept into me. I was going to have to handle it all, but if the last ten minutes had taught me anything, it was that I couldn't do it alone. I *could not be* who I was without help. It had taken everything I had to bring down Constance, and I had almost failed.

Yet, as I looked at Jenks and remembered Trent, and David, and Etude, and even Vivian, I decided that wasn't a bad thing. *Maybe I can work with this,* I thought, eyeing Pike in interest.

"You thought I was going to do your dirty work for you, eh?" I said, finding a compliment in there somewhere, and Pike grimaced. "I said have a seat." He didn't, and I pulled on the ley line until my wrist was in agony and the tips of my hair began to float. "Sit! I have a better idea than trusting that some nameless master vampire will take you under his or her wing for freeing Cincinnati up for their rule."

Pike glanced at Constance, then Jenks. The pixy's wing pitch rose in threat and, flipping his suit coat out of the way, Pike gingerly sat down across from me.

I tried to straighten, but my ribs hurt too much. "I'll keep you safe from your brothers," I said, and Jenks's dust brightened in surprise. "You know I can do it. I already have. I keep you safe, and you run the affairs of the vampires under me."

"Under you," Pike said flatly, staring. "Why would I risk that when DC will send someone to replace her?"

My eyes went to a soft clink of jewelry, but it was just Jenks poking about. "Oh, let's not bring the DC undead into this, mmmm? No one needs to know she's a mouse, right? Who's to say where you're getting your orders from? You run into anything you need help with, I'm there." I hesitated. "Or do you like the people you care about being savaged by someone who doesn't give a flying flip if they wake up dead in the morning?"

It was as if the world held its breath as we swayed. Cincinnati and the Hollows spread around us, the night sounds faint from our height. The city would be safe if the next five minutes fell my way, even if flashing lights were beginning to flood to the waterfront.

I have to nail this down and nail it down fast. My eyes went to my purse and the mouse cage.

"You can't save us," he whispered, a hard-suppressed heartache in his eyes.

"I saved Ivy." I started to get up, wincing and easing back down when my ribs twinged. "I can save you. You save Joni. And anyone else you trust. The scion of Cincinnati's subrosa will need some muscle." I stifled a sigh at the rising sounds of sirens. "Jenks, do you think you can get the cage from my bag?" I asked, and the pixy nodded.

"I love it when a plan works," he said, silver sparkles falling thick as he darted to the dusty corner and flipped my bag over to get to the opening.

"*This* was your plan?" Pike said incredulously, and I pulled my attention from Jenks, now bumping about in my purse. "You would be drained, dead, or bound to Constance by now if not for me."

"I know that. Which is why we are going to have to work on our timing if we're going to continue working together." I shifted, ribs hurting. "Are you okay? Jenks got you good."

Pike stared at the tightly curled mouse nestled in Constance's jewelry. He took a slow, pained breath, touched his swollen face . . . and finally slid the knife back in his boot. "Why do I feel as if I just signed my own death warrant?" he muttered, elbows going to his knees, his head down and his shoulders slumped in fatigue.

I smiled, one ear listening to Jenks's muffled swearing. "No, you just freed yourself," I said as I tried to make a sling for my wrist out of my shirt, my vision threatening to go black until I gave up and stopped moving my arm. "And

oni, and anyone else you like working with, but the se-
crecy has to be absolute, because if anyone ever finds out
that Constance isn't the one calling the shots, we're both
going to be wishing Sharps had ground our bones for bread
at Twin Lakes Bridge."

Pike looked up, hope almost painful in the back of his
eyes. "You think you can . . ."

My head rose at the sound of pixy wings. "I know I can,"
I said as Jenks finally pulled the mouse cage free and laboriously lifted it into the air, his dust a heavy wash.

"Could you have put any more junk in that purse of
yours?" Jenks said as he set the small but foolproof cage on
the bench. "Good job, Rache." Immediately he flew back to
my bag, diving inside to bump about again.

Good job? It didn't feel like a good job. It felt like a
seat-of-the-pants job, but that was about par. Frowning, I
awkwardly picked Constance up by the tail and dropped
her into the cage. The movement jolted the vampire awake
and I immediately fastened the latch, shoulders slumping
in relief as Constance began making tiny, panicked sounds
as she sat on her haunches and rubbed at her arms as if trying to push the fur off. Damn it all to the Turn and back. I
was going to have to do her job, but with Pike, I just might
be able to.

Tired, I lifted the cage high to look at the very unhappy,
very odd-looking mouse with canines almost as long as her
whiskers. *Prehistoric Rodentia.* "Oh, Constance," I said,
voice mockingly high, and the mouse flung herself at me
and the bars with a sudden, shocking fury. "I'm so glad we
found an accord and you agreed to handle the vampires
under my authority."

Pike looked up from dabbing at one of his deeper
scratches, a faint smile easing his pinched features.

"What's that?" I lifted the cage, pretending to listen as
she screamed at me in tiny, high squeaks. "You want all but
a few handpicked favorites to leave so the people they
kicked out can go back to their homes? What a wonderful
goodwill gesture on your part."

Pike chuckled, his stance easing even more. Across the gondola, Jenks reemerged from my bag, one of my pair amulets as large as him rasping along behind him. *Thank you, Jenks.*

"And how nice you decided not to harass Kalamack's Brimstone interests anymore," I said to Constance as Jenks dragged the heavy amulet across the floor. "Or challenge the Weres' territories? That's a wonderful idea. Happy streets, happy bottom line, and isn't that what everyone wants? Especially the DC vamps?" Eyebrows high, I looked at Pike as I set the cage down, and Constance attacked the bars with a frightening vengeance. "Think you can manage most of that?" I asked him, relief filling me when I bent to take my amulet and the agony in my wrist retreated to something almost bearable.

"What about when someone wants to talk to her?" His brow furrowed. "Or two houses disagree about blood rights? Someone will notice she's not coming out of her rooms."

"That's where I come in," I said, able to look at my swelling wrist now that it wasn't exploding anymore. "I can imagine that no one really wants to see Constance. Would you go down to talk to her if you didn't have to?"

He shook his head, focus distant in thought. "You keep my brothers at bay and we run the city together."

"More or less, meaning I have more, you have less," I corrected him. "I stand between you and your brothers, and you run the vampire affairs under me how I want them to be run. At my direction. The same way you'd be doing under Constance only without the blood or sex. If you get yourself killed by carelessness, that's not my problem."

He grinned. "No blood or sex? I'm not sure the benefits are commensurate with the task."

But his good humor told me we almost had this settled, and I smiled, slumping deeper into the bench. Constance had shifted her efforts into knocking the cage over, and I was toying with the idea of letting her do it. She was close to the edge, and hitting the floor might calm her down a notch. Relenting, I used my foot to nudge the cage from the drop-off. Immediately she attacked my foot, but her teeth were ineffective on my boot, and I pushed her all the way to the back, where she squeaked at me until Jenks dusted her into a higher fury.

"One problem," Pike said as he used a handkerchief to clean Jenks's irritant-dust from his face. His scars stood out in sharp relief, Jenks's new scores almost unnoticeable amid the chaos of lines. "No one will believe any of this if they don't see Constance walk out of here."

Jenks looked up from his insulting hover over Constance. His expression was worried, but I wasn't. "Yep," I said as I leaned to the broken-mesh window. Peering down, I could see emergency lights flashing and the enormous lights from a news van shining on a veritable mob. Edden had moved forward, and between the Weres, vamps, and news crews, there was a growing air of a circus. But who I wanted wasn't down there, and taking a breath, I looked . . . up.

"Hodin!" I shouted toward the city-lit clouds. "You want to stay in the garden? Jenks needs a doppelganger charm!"

Pike's eyebrows were high when I pulled my attention back inside. He knew about doppelganger charms. Everyone did. They were only legal on Halloween because the expensive ones were so convincing that they couldn't be parsed out from reality. Demon doppelganger curses were even more convincing. And expensive. But seeing as nothing would mean much if I couldn't tie this up with a nice bow, it was worth finding out if Hodin would do it for a place he could call home. *Sorry, Al. He's here, you aren't.*

Jenks darted up, then down, and finally to me. "Rache, are you sure?" he said, and then a black shadow thumped against the glass. It was an enormous crow, bedraggled feathers falling as he eyed me with one red, goat-slitted eye and ugly claws holding him there.

"The crow . . ." Pike said as Hodin dissolved into a feather-laced mist that poured through the tiny window and into the gondola. "At the meeting?" Pike got to his feet with a vampiric quickness, his eyes fixed on the tall shape taking form even as he retreated. "*That* was a *demon*? I thought it was a prop. You know. The crazy demon living in a church."

Yeah, that was me, but I didn't need a prop to pull it off. Mood sour, I painfully got to my feet, one hand on the swaying wall as Hodin solidified in his leather jacket and black jeans, wavy hair loose, and an empty, waiting expression on his long face. He'd been there the entire time, watching to see if I survived. He probably wanted the church for himself.

"How about it?" Jenks hovered too close, making Hodin frown. "You want to rent space in the garden? We need a doppelganger charm and ten minutes of your time."

I cleared my throat to get Jenks to back up, but his pride that he was going to be what got my biscuits out of the fire kept him moving irritatingly back and forth between us. I managed a smile when Hodin arched his eyebrows. Technically he wasn't helping me, seeing as I'd already downed Constance. But I was sure Al wouldn't see it that way.

"It would be a curse, not a charm." Hodin looked at Pike disparagingly. "And for me to pretend to be an undead woman, even for ten minutes, would require space in the church, not the garden."

Damn it, he *had* been watching, and I winced, the pain in my wrist breaking through my amulet as I held it close. If Hodin lived in the church, Al would never believe I wasn't taking instruction from him.

"You convincingly pretend to be her until Pike gets you back to Piscary's and you get six months in the garden," I said, and Jenks landed on my shoulder, content to let me settle the deal.

Hodin sniffed. "A year. In the church. The room with the window looking south. And I want the demon bell removed."

Jenks's wings rattled, tickling my neck. "That's Ivy's old room."

Hodin's gaze dropped to the pixy. "I like the closet."

Pike shifted from foot to foot, and I nodded. "Ivy's room. Six months. Stay out of my belfry. And my books. And my spelling supplies."

Hodin grinned, looking like a different person. "Agreed," he said, and I shivered when I felt a pulse of intent spill from him, dimming the lights as it passed to race over Cincinnati like an ill wind or promise. *Great. . . .*

There was a second tweak on my awareness, and he vanished to reappear looking exactly like Constance, all the way to her hair in disarray, and dirt on her dress. He even had her eyes, the red, goat-slitted orbs glamoured to a vampire black. "Be careful what you wish for," he said as he draped her necklaces over himself, and Pike swore softly. *Voice, too.*

"Okay, Jenks. Bring us down," I said, and Jenks vaulted through the torn screen to leave a blanket of falling sparkles.

Hodin was frowning at Constance's shoe, and I wasn't surprised when he picked it up, studying the diamond-encrusted heel for a moment before it vanished to reappear on his foot. From the mouse cage came a squeak of outrage.

"Welcome to the dark side, Rachel Morgan," Pike said, and I looked up to see him holding out his hand. Head tilted, I fitted my fingers into his. His grip was warm and solid, and unwelcome, pheromone-based tingles raced through me when he let go and his fingers iced from mine.

"Welcome to the light, Pike Welroe," I said to hide my unstoppable shudder. "Behave yourself, or I will throw you to the wolves. Literally." The gondola gave a lurch, and I lost my balance. Pike caught my elbow to send another tingle of vampire pheromones through me, settling at my core before melting away.

"Don't threaten me with empty words," Pike whispered, and I tugged free of him.

"They aren't empty, and you know it," I said, uncomfortable with Hodin standing there, even if he did seem engrossed in the long-toothed mouse screaming at him.

Pike chuckled, his gaze going to my wrist and back again. "Deadly skills mean nothing when you bind yourself with words like *honor* and *fairness*," he said. "All your knowledge is as useful as a twig if you're afraid of the consequences of using it."

"I'm not afraid. I just see more options than you," I said as I watched the encroaching roofs. We were almost to the bottom, and Jenks was again at the broken mesh, hands on his hips.

"Rache, stow the vamp's clothes," Jenks said, but my reach faltered when Hodin muttered a word and they vanished. "You ready for the press?" the pixy asked as we neared the ground and the morass of noise focused into clear shouts and demands. "I think Trent called them in to keep a lid on the vampire/Were aggression. Edden wouldn't stay back, either. Apparently he saw your gun go out the window, and that was it."

"I'm good," I said as I stood, feeling every coming bruise as I went to get my bag to stash Constance. "Hodin, keep your mouth shut. It will be more convincing if I do all the talking. Pike, you and Hodin go first."

Jenks darted away as Pike and Hodin moved forward to the door and I retreated to the back, carefully stuffing an infuriated mouse into my bag. The gondola rocked to a halt, and I winced as the noise redoubled. Angry, frightened faces ringed us, coming and going in the moving light. Tattooed Weres and private security vamps in suits pushed them back until the landing ramp was clear apart from Doyle at the controls, locking the wheel down. Trent shouldered his way through, recognized by everyone. Jenks was with him, and two more pain amulets dangled from his grip. He found my eyes, his relief almost overwhelming.

My God, I think we did it, I thought, and Pike's head snapped to me, clearly sensing the sudden wash of love coursing through me. My smile faded at the unexpected hint of vulnerability in the back of his eyes, and he nodded, knowing I saw it. The only thing more unpredictable and dangerous than an undead vampire was a living one who had given up on love—and then had the chance for it thrust upon them again in a bittersweet threat. *Joni . . .*

"You will see it through," Pike said, and I nodded, eyes flicking nervously to Hodin/Constance when he delicately snorted.

Doyle barked at everyone to stay back as he opened the door. But his surly mood became uncertain as he looked in at Pike's scratched everything, my weary slumped form holding my bag like a fig leaf, and Hodin/Constance's haughty stance between us.

"Bring the car!" Pike exclaimed, and I breathed the fresh air as Jenks's spent dust swirled in the corners and evaporated. "Then jump the curb!" he demanded at the sudden crush at the door. "I'll make a statement before we leave, but I want some space!"

The news crews surged forward and, just as predictably, both David's and Constance's people forced them back. The noise swelled when Hodin/Constance stepped out, chin high as she hesitated before the door so Trent could slip in.

"Congratulations?" Trent said as he dropped the additional pain amulets over me, and I slumped in relief. "Jenks told me what happened," he added, his eyes dropping to my tightly held bag. "I have your splat gun. David's got that amulet you threw out. Damn it to the Turn and back, Rachel," he said, frowning at Jenks's merry grin before the pixy darted out to occupy the press. "We have to come up with something better than this."

"Watch the wrist!" I almost hissed as he tried to pull me into a relieved hug, and he jerked to a halt, his indecision creasing his brow. "It's okay," I added softly as a sudden fatigue swam up, almost downing me now that the adrenaline was spent. All that was left was the news conference.

Piece of cake, I thought, looking for the sparkle of pixy dust, finally spotting it sifting over Pike and Hodin/Constance's diminutive form still on the landing. They were almost silhouettes in the bright lights from the news crews as Pike ignored the media's shouted questions, more concerned with talking to his security. Mics were extended over the shoulders of the living wall, and the demands for information were getting louder.

"What are you going to do with her?" Trent said, his lips not moving as he slipped one careful arm around my waist to help me shuffle to the door. "Can I give her to Jon?"

I shot him a sharp look, but he was smiling. What to do with Constance *was* a problem. I would have let Pike keep her, seeing as she needed a source of blood and somewhere six feet down to survive the day, but I wasn't confident he wouldn't kill her when I wasn't looking.

"Morgan! Rachel Morgan!" a small woman in a power dress shouted as I came blinking into the mobile news lights, and the Were standing in front of her suddenly howled, dropping back to hop on one foot. Not moving, the reporter beamed a dangerous, toothy grin at the encroaching security. "Is it true that you and Constance are fighting for control of the city, and if so, was there some consensus reached tonight?" she asked, then extended the mic.

"You are beautiful," Trent whispered, and I shivered as his hand slipped from me and he took a step back.

I didn't feel beautiful. My breath came in shakily, pulse fast as a wave of shushing and demands for silence filtered out. But my words faltered when Hodin delicately cleared his throat, catching Constance's haughty demand perfectly.

"There's no argument between Morgan and myself," Hodin said, and my head snapped around. A startled yelp escaped Pike and he let go of Hodin's elbow as the demon slowly winked at me. I quailed, imagining the damage he could do in ten minutes. *I worked too hard for Hodin to screw this up.*

"Morgan and I are not friends," Hodin said, and Pike's brow furrowed in worry even as Constance's ill will flowed from Hodin as if it was real. "But there's no reason to swat the fly if it doesn't land on your beloved," he added, and the news crews pushed forward. "I *am* Cincinnati's master vampire," he said, louder. "The demon whore looks to me!"

Damn it all to hell, he was talking. My anger did not go unnoticed, and at Trent's subtle push, I stepped forward to stand even with Hodin. "This is what you wanted?" Pike whispered, his hand hiding his words, and I felt myself warm.

"I do not look to Constance," I said loudly, and the mics turned to me. "But we have come to an agreement. She will handle vampire affairs within the traditional borders of Cincinnati and the Hollows—"

"As is my God-given right!" Hodin said, drowning me out as he shot me a look. "However"—his expression softened to a wicked evil—"as a goodwill gesture, I have agreed to take Piscary's orphaned children as my own and will shortly withdraw my people from the traditional Were territories."

My held breath eased out, and a faint shout rose as Hodin's statement was carried to the back of the crowd.

"Was this at Rachel Morgan's request?" the reporter asked, mic extended.

Hodin widened Constance's smile, almost baring her teeth. "What do you think?"

Jenks snickered from Trent's shoulder. "You forgot about apologizing for killing Nash."

Hodin spun, and both Trent and Jenks darted backward. "Bring the car! Now!" Pike shouted, and the reporters surged forward. "The interview is over!"

Hodin's eyes narrowed, and my lips parted when I saw a hint of demon red in them. "No one tells me what to do!" he shouted, Constance's high voice ringing out. "I was given all, and I will hold all! I am Cincinnati's master vampire. I will always be Cincinnati's master vampire!"

The crowd moved, and there was a sudden surge of fear as the lights from the news van unexpectedly went out. *Thank you, Jenks,* I thought as I saw the telltale shimmer of pixy dust, then gasped when Constance, or Hodin, rather, was gripping my elbow, yanking me down so my ear was near his mouth.

"The subrosa is a hidden position," he said, eyes flashing pure demon red. "You can't publicly claim anything. Those who need to know, will. You are, after all, standing beside Constance unharmed and with a new . . . familiar in your spell bag." He smiled at me with Constance's fangs, sending a shiver through me. "Your city's unrest is settled. Well done, madam subrosa."

Unharmed? I thought as he let go and allowed himself

to be hustled to the black SUV that had jumped the curb, scattering the crowd. More lights were bursting in showers of sparks, and the news crews were freaking.

"Morgan!" Pike shouted as Hodin tucked himself inside the car, looking small against the black interior. "Constance requires you to accompany us back to Piscary's."

His scarred features were tight at the thought of riding back to Piscary's with a demon who could . . . do anything. High over the noisy crowd was the faint glow of pixy dust. Flashing lights were filling the parking lot, but far more at the outskirts were vanishing into the night. They would talk, meeting in bars and living rooms all over the city, and already I could feel a new peace taking hold. *Now it is done,* I thought, grateful for Jenks still out there busting lights like piñatas.

"I'm sorry, but I can't," I said, and the living vampire frowned. Left wrist cradled close, I awkwardly lifted my bag over my shoulder and handed it to Trent. "Will you call Ivy's sister and ask her to mouse-sit?" I said, and Trent's eyes widened. "She's going to need blood, and I don't have anywhere six feet down for her. Oh, and the gondola wall needs to be hosed down with salt water," I added, and he nodded, holding the bag closed with a tight grip.

"You can't, huh?" Pike said darkly. More people were scattering, and I could hear the I.S. yelling at people to stop. No one did.

"I have plans tonight," I said, then gave Trent a half squeeze and stepped closer to the car, voice soft as I added, "You have six to eight weeks to show me that you can handle the vampires without my constant help, or I'll find someone who can."

His eyebrows rose. "Six to eight weeks?" Pike questioned, and I wobbled deeper into the chaos, Trent suddenly at my elbow.

"Rule one about the good guys, Pike, is that we always pay our dues." Pulling myself tall, I scanned over the dispersing crowd. "Doyle!" I shouted. "Where are you? I'm ready for my warrant to be served!"

CHAPTER

29

THE HARSH BUZZ OF THE FLOOR'S DOOR UNLOCKING pulled my head up, and I turned as I finished tucking my wonderful, scrumptious, totally-not-jail-approved green shirt into my jeans. I didn't know who I had to thank for the civvies. Trent, maybe. Or Edden. It would be more than nice walking out of here not wearing jail-orange.

"Rachel Morgan!" the floor guard exclaimed as if I didn't know he was coming for me. "Get your stuff. Someone came to claim you."

Claim me, I thought, smirking as I fluffed my out-of-control hair and listened to the click of dress shoes coming down the tiled hall. As if I was a dog or cat picked up by the pound.

But it wasn't Trent. It was Pike.

"Pike," I said, my welcoming smile fading as the guard squinted at the door lock, clearly unfamiliar with the code to open my door and my door alone. "Surprise, surprise."

"Morgan," he said evenly, adding an impressed, "Wow," as he stared at the frizzy chaos of my hair.

"Not a word," I said, flushing. Charms weren't allowed, and the conditioner that Jenks had snuck in to me had vanished before I'd had a chance to use it. "You look better," I said, and he inclined his head, still sneaking glances at my veritable 'fro of red. Even after six weeks, his hair still had that burned-off shortness, and his face was clean-shaven. He looked tired as he waited for the guard to figure the door out, standing with a red, oversize envelope with my name on it in his hand. His suit was black and his tie was gray. Wrinkles edged his eyes, and he seemed thinner. Not a good look when he'd been trim to begin with.

Why is he here? I thought, wondering if it was something to do with that red folder.

"I thought Trent was picking me up," I said as the guard finally got my individual door to unlock, and it slid to the side.

"He's in the lobby." Pike's grip on the large envelope tightened. "You would have been out sooner if you hadn't smart-mouthed the judge."

I grinned, remembering how I'd turned my time served into three days, into a week, then six. Jenks had thought I was crazy, Trent had, too. David, though, had known. He was a smart man. "I wanted some time to, *a*, let my wrist heal, and two, remind you that you need me." I eyed him. My door was open but I didn't come out. "How's it going?"

Pike frowned, his gaze going to the envelope. *Yep, it's work.*

Pulse fast, I stepped into the hall, immediately feeling out of place beside Pike's professional polish. At least I wasn't in jail-orange.

"Got what you want?" the guard said, and I turned to look into my private cell. "Once you leave, it hits the incinerator."

I fingered the rim of my wrist cast decorated with the names of half the inmates on the floor and a good portion of the guards. I couldn't wait to get it off. Jail medical care didn't cover a charm to mend my wrist, and neither Hodin nor Al had shown up to fix it. I slumped, looking at my orange jumpsuit wadded up on the thin pillow. "I got what I want. Thanks."

Pike tapped the envelope on the palm of his hand, and we started down the hall. Eyes were watching, most of them uneasy at who I was walking out with, and I nodded and smiled, trying to reassure them that I wasn't Constance's plaything—that this was all to plan. They were all good people caught doing questionable things for reasons that had seemed important at the time. The story of my life.

"You look pale," Pike said, and I glanced up from studying the sound of his steps. He had a faint limp.

"And you smell funny under that five-hundred-dollar cologne you're wearing," I said. The guard behind us chuckled, and I added, "So, how's the city?" to try to smooth Pike's grimace. "Word is vamp-on-vamp crime is down."

His focus was somewhere down the long hall and into the past, or maybe the future. "It's still settling. Calm before the storm." Pike took a slow breath and leaned closer, his exhale sending a delicious tingle through me as he whispered, "You really thought I wouldn't find Constance hiding in a college dorm?"

Erica, I thought in a pulse of worry. My eyes narrowed. "My options for a light-tight area and a source of blood are limited. If you so much as—"

"Relax." Pike sniffed in amusement as he pulled back. "Ivy's little sister is fine. They're both fine. I stop in a couple of times a week to give the girl a break, but honestly, how much blood does a mouse need?" He glanced at his finger and chuckled. "The entire dorm is taking care of her, but if I heard of a vampiric mouse, someone else might and put two and two together. Get her back."

"Soon as I have a place for her," I promised, and he nodded, handing me the envelope. I automatically took it. The thought to ask about Joni rose and fell. If she wasn't okay, he wouldn't appreciate me bringing her up. Besides, he looked too content for her not to be, and a flicker of satisfaction made me feel good. *Small wins, big dividends.*

"That's your stuff. You can skip the exit interview," Pike said, eyeing my new smile.

"Thanks," I said, honestly pleased as I felt the bumps of whatever was inside. I broke the seal and looked in to see Trent's ring. My phone and wallet were in there, too, both of which had been in Constance's possession when I'd put myself in Doyle's custody. "Thanks again," I added, and Pike nodded once.

The stiff paper rasped as I put my black-pearl ring on. My phone was dead, and it felt odd when I tucked it in a back pocket. My wallet went on the other side. That was when I noticed the USB drive.

"Oh," I said as I shook it out and it fell into my hand. "I don't think this belongs to me."

Pike slowed as we reached the end of the hall and the guard hastened forward to the door. "It's your to-do list."

"Mmmm." I dropped it back in the big envelope as the door beeped and opened. "I'm not that good with lists. Maybe we should have coffee and talk tomorrow." I smacked the envelope into his chest, and he reached for it, almost in self-defense.

"You want to meet openly?" he questioned, a worried slant making the scars on his face stand out.

"Why not?" But my pace slowed as I went through the doors and into a lower-security area. "Is it your brothers?" I said softly as the guard pointed at an X on the floor and went to the desk to get my paperwork.

Pike rocked to a halt beside me, his gaze going to an elaborate ring on his index finger. It was glowing, and I figured it was canceling out any listening charms, making me wonder if the no-magic-zone amulet had been Constance's idea, or his. "No. I haven't seen any evidence of them since Constance laid down the law." His gaze sharpened on mine. "Or maybe it's just you."

I lifted a shoulder and let it fall to try to hide my unease. I wasn't used to plans hiding within plans. Up front and in your face was more my speed. "I'd think that since you work for Constance, and she and I have an understanding, frequent communication between us would be expected." I hesitated, grimacing at my institutional white sneakers. *Edden,* I decided. Trent would have included a sassy pair of size nines in my exit attire. The man did love shoes. "How is that going, by the way?"

Pike glanced at the guard looking over my paperwork.

"I've run into a snag," he said softly, lips hardly moving. "No one wants to see her, that part is fine. I've downsized her staff to a bare minimum. About two-thirds of her heavies have gone back to their original masters, and all but the most insistent of her hangers-on. The remaining are at Piscary's where I've set up residence." He paused. "I can still smell lily."

"It's your imagination," I said, a memory of Nash on the table rising and falling.

The guard tapped my paperwork even and gestured to the next double door. This one didn't need a card to unlock it, and I felt better.

"And Stef's apartment building?" I prompted.

"Was never really needed," Pike said as he rocked into motion beside me. "So yes, the original tenants are back in their old leases. Stephanie is apparently still at your church." He turned to me. "God knows why. I wouldn't feel safe sleeping with a demon across the hall."

I smiled as we followed the guard, pleased. I'd never really gotten to know Stef before being incarcerated, but what I'd seen proved she was well worth knowing.

"That's good," I said when I realized Pike was waiting for a response. "Not bad for six weeks. See if you can get the rest of her heavies to leave."

Pike shook the USB into his hand and threw the envelope away in a passing bin. "Those who are left are mine. I'm keeping them," he said as he fingered the small flash drive. "Which brings up my next question. What did you want with fifty-six acres of unusable, toxic land outside of Cincinnati?"

Fifty-six acres? I thought, then blinked, figuring it out. The abandoned property at the edge of Cincinnati. "Fifty-six acres?" I said slyly. "I thought it was more."

"It is." Pike's frown was far more angry than I would have expected. "But it's the fifty-six lots that have to be dug out and the soil removed and disposed of that are costing me hundreds of thousands. Maybe millions."

I grinned. "She *bought* them?" I said, delighted at Pike's fist-clenched annoyance. "Capital." I grinned.

"You did that intentionally," he muttered, and my smile widened.

"Me? Naw," I lied. "I was looking into all my options as I apartment searched. I had no idea that Constance would buy it out from under me. I mean, who does that? Out of spite? Just to be mean?"

Pike reached to open the door for me, and I froze as the delicious scent of frustrated vampire washed over me. "Well played, Ms. Morgan," he whispered in my ear, and I stifled a shudder as feeling went straight to my groin. "Be careful. The game isn't over yet."

My chin lifted, and I shoved the sensation deeper until it vanished. Breath held, I pushed past him, slowing when I found myself an office away from the lobby of Cincy's local jail. There was one more desk to get by, but I could see past the big one-way glass to the lobby and, beyond that, the sun-drenched parking lot. Late March had shifted to early May, and I slumped at a sudden wash of regret. I'd lost six weeks of sun, six weeks of wet knees in the dirt, six weeks of rain, and fog, and moon, and stars . . . meaningless conversations over breakfast with Jenks and dinner with Trent. Little things, but the stuff life was made of.

I frowned at Pike's soft, knowing sound and, blinking fast, I scanned the oblivious people waiting in chairs to visit their loved ones. "I'm sure Constance can put a spin on her generous purchase to make her look less the fool and more the city benefactor," I said as I followed the guard to the exit desk. "Make it into a park or something."

"I suppose," he grumbled, making that same odd sound when I spotted Trent and Jenks in the waiting room—and I smiled.

"Hey, thanks for the escort," I said as the guard flipped through my paperwork before signing it and spinning it to me. "My ride is here." I smiled at the guard. "Sign here?" I asked as I took a pen from the cup and reached for the cover-our-ass paperwork. A quick scrawl of my name, and I straightened, so ready to feel Trent's arms around me that it hurt.

Jenks must have heard me through the one-way glass because he had come to hover before it, hands cupped around his face as he tried to look in. He'd been popping in and out of my cell for the last six weeks with renovation reports, and I could hardly wait to see the back end of the church with its new kitchen and the three-sided back porch where the living room had once been. Trent, too, had risen, standing at his chair as he clearly tried to end his phone conversation.

Trent . . . Flushing, I tried to smooth my hair, sensation spilling through me as I headed for the door. "Well, I'd like to say it's been a pleasure," I said, jerking to a halt when Pike pinched my elbow. My suspicion narrowed as I looked at him. His eyes had a nice rim of brown, but I didn't like that the guard who had accompanied us had turned, intentionally not watching.

"What," I said flatly, and at the window, Jenks began spilling a threatening orange dust. Trent ended his call, and the no-magic disk hanging in the lobby began to glow a sickly purple in warning.

Grimacing, Pike pulled me a few steps from the desk. I went because it was easier than hitting him. "As I was saying . . ." Pike pulled me closer until my entire side tingled. Oh, there was air between us, but that didn't seem to matter. "We might have a problem your smart-ass attitude can't handle."

I looked at his hand still holding my elbow, then him. "Let me guess." I arched my eyebrows and gave a little tug to no avail. "Constance might be biting you, but you're not sipping the dust anymore, and it's beginning to show. Losing some speed? Not able to hear Takata's hidden track?" His grip eased in surprise, and I pulled away.

My elbow felt cold, but I didn't touch it. "A week or so of her denying you might be expected as punishment, but you're right. It could be a problem, one I might have a cure for." I gave Jenks the "few seconds" gesture, and he buzzed back to Trent. "I need to bring someone else in on this."

Pike predictably frowned, but he hadn't said no. "Magic?"

he scoffed, and I shook my head. Magic could come close, but he needed the real thing.

"I know an old undead who might be willing," I said, and his expression became doubtful. Peter's master, or, far safer, Ivy's mom. She hadn't been in line to be the city's master vampire, but she'd probably want to have a card or two in the game for when Ivy crossed over. My smile faded. I would have asked Nina, but she hadn't been dead long enough to instill him with the proper strength.

"Good," Pike said, his relieved exhale surprising me. "I'll give you time to work, but sooner is better."

Feeling a little anxious, are we? I thought sourly. "It shouldn't take long. Oh, and I'll make up a list of in-the-know contacts for you tomorrow. I'd appreciate the same from you."

Pike's hands went to his narrow hips, that USB still in his grip. "Okay," he said slowly, gaze going to Jenks, again hovering impatiently at the window. "But the fewer who know she's a church mouse, the better. My brothers . . ."

"Won't be a problem even if they do find out," I said, eager to end the conversation. "Trust me, I don't want this getting out any more than you do."

Nodding, he dropped back, clearly not going to accompany me into the lobby. Trent was inching his way closer and I wanted a shower using my own soap in the worst way.

"Relax, Pike. I'm surprisingly good at keeping secrets," I said, my smile widening as Trent moved gracefully among the chairs. "Let me see my to-do list." I held out my hand, and its smooth shape filled my grip, still warm from his body. "I still want coffee when we talk this over. Say . . . Junior's tomorrow? Noon."

"Good God, I'm taking meetings with a demon," he muttered, but he seemed grateful as I tucked the USB in my pocket and headed for the door. A flash of worry went through me at what I had gotten myself into—and then it was gone as I left the room and returned to my life.

"Trent," I whispered as Jenks dropped down, a hand to his nose as he got a whiff of me. "I am so glad to see you."

Beaming, Trent stared at my wild hair as he took me in his arms, pulling me almost crushingly close. "My God. I missed you," he said softly. "Do you want to get something to eat, or just go home?"

Home. It had a whole new meaning now. I wouldn't let go of him. Tears pricked, and I sniffed them back, saving them for when I was alone in my new tower room that looked out on the city that was mine to protect.

"Rachel?" Trent tightened his grip, and we rocked apart, both of us smiling through the tears. I knew he wouldn't kiss me here where everyone was watching, but then he pulled me close, and my breath came fast when his lips found mine and I lost myself, pulse racing as my fingers spasmed and he broke from me.

"Good God, find a hole in the ground, will you?" Jenks muttered, but his dust was a clear silver, tingling of magic as it spilled between us.

"Do you have everything? Can we leave?" Trent asked. "I've never picked anyone up from jail before. Wow, your hair is . . . amazing," he added, and Jenks muttered, "Good save, Cookie Man."

I glanced at the one-way glass, the faint tingling at my neck telling me that Pike was still there. *He will always be there,* I thought as I turned my back on him and slipped my arm around Trent's waist. "We can leave," I said softly. "I have everything I need."

Jenks's wings rasped as he darted to the door to run vanguard. I exhaled a breath I felt I'd been holding for six weeks. From beside me, Trent did the same, our fingers tightening on each other.

Sure, Ivy and Nina were still VIP hostages in DC, hopefully oblivious that Constance was a mouse and that Pike and I were playing a careful game. But that was something I was going to change before the sun went down. Secrets were lies, and lies killed friendships. I wasn't alone. I'd never been alone, and as I walked beside Trent with my head high, I vowed that I wouldn't let a secret make me alone.

Al, I thought as Trent opened the door for me. I stepped out, shivering despite the sun as Al's remembered rage slipped through my mind. Alcatraz had been a warning, but it was a warning I wasn't going to heed, and I wouldn't apologize for it. Hodin had been there when I needed help, and Al hadn't. Sometimes it was that simple.

My frown eased as I looked up at the distant buildings, hearing the traffic and breathing the good Cincy air tainted with commerce and the clean smell of the river. It was more than Trent and Jenks coming to pick me up. I could feel the entire city waiting to see what I did next—if I was truly Constance's plaything, or if perhaps, she was mine. Enough people trusted me, were willing to stand with me, had stood with me. That was more than enough for me to find my courage.

Because this, I decided as Trent held my hand and Jenks flew at my shoulder, this was *my* home, and from here . . . I could do anything.

Rachel Morgan must keep her friends close—and her enemies closer—in the next Hollows novel from #1 *New York Times* bestselling author Kim Harrison.

TROUBLE WITH THE CURSED

Rachel Morgan, witch-born demon, has one unspoken rule: take chances, but pay for them yourself. With it, she has turned enemies into allies, found her place with her demon kin, and stepped up as the subrosa of Cincinnati—responsible for keeping the paranormal community at peace and in line.

Life is . . . good? Even better, her best friend, Ivy Tamwood, is returning home. Nothing's simple, though, and Ivy's not coming alone. The vampires' ruling council insists she escort one of the long undead, hell-bent on proving that Rachel killed Cincy's master vampire to take over the city. Which, of course, Rachel totally did not do. She only *transformed* her a little.

With Rachel's friends distracted by their own lives and problems, she reaches out to a new ally for help—the demon Hodin. But this trickster has his own agenda. In the end, the only way for Rachel to save herself and the city may be to forge a new understanding with her estranged demon teacher, Al. There's just one problem: Al would sell his own soul to be rid of her. . . .

Coming June 2022 from Ace

Ready to find
your next great read?

Let us help.

Visit prh.com/nextread

Penguin
Random
House